CW00968151

Special thanks to the following people for helping breathe life into the Godsverse:

Adam Goldstein, Alejandro Lee, Anna Carlson, Azia MacManus, Becky Fuller, Ben Coleman, Beth C, Brian Pickering, Bugz, Caledonia, Carl Bradley, Chad Bowden, Chris B, Chris Call, Daniel Groves, Dave Baxter, Deaven Shade, Dustin Cissell, Ed Vreeburg, Edward Nycz Jr., Emerson Kasak, Eva M., Gary Phillips, Harry Van den Brink, Hollie Buchanan II, Jake Schroeder, Janice Jurgens, Jason Crase, Jeff Lewis, Jennifer & Charlie Geer, Johnny Britt, Jonathan, Joshua Bowers, Journee Gautz, Jude M, Kenny Endlich, Logan Waterman, Louise Mc, Luis Bermudez, Matt Selter, Matthew Johnson, Michael Bishop, Moana McAdams, Nari Muhammad, Nick Smith, Celeste, Brian, and Niobe Cornish, Paul Nygard, Rhel ná DecVandé, Richard A Williams, Rick Parker, Rob MacAndrew, Robert Williams, Ronald, Rosalie Louey, Ruth, Stacy Shuda, Talinda Willard, Tamara Slaten, Tony Carson, tvest, Viannah E. Duncan, Victoria Nohelty, Walter Weiss, and Zachary.

GODSVERSE PLANETS

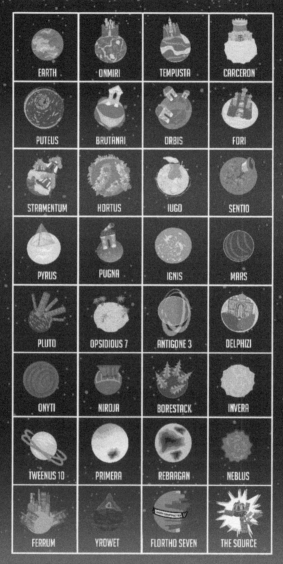

EARTH	ONMIRI	TEMPUSTA	CARCERON
PUTEUS	BRUTANAI	ORBIS	FORI
STRAMENTUM	HORTUS	IUGO	SENTIO
PYRUS	PUGNA	IGNIS	MARS
PLUTO	OPSIDIOUS 7	ANTIGONE 3	DELPHIZI
ONYTI	NIROJA	BORESTACK	INVERA
TWEENUS 10	PRIMERA	REBARGAN	NEBLUS
FERRUM	YROWET	FLORTHO SEVEN	THE SOURCE

1000 BC – BETRAYED [HELL PT 1]
/PIXIE DUST

500 BC – FALLEN [HELL PT 2]

200 BC – HELLFIRE [HELL PT 3]

1974 AD – MYSTERY SPOT [RUIN PT 1]

1976 AD – INTO HELL [RUIN PT 2]

1984 AD – LAST STAND [RUIN PT 3]

1985 AD – CHANGE

1985 AD – MAGIC/BLACK MARKET HEROINE

1985 AD – EVIL

1989 AD – DEATH'S KISS
[DARKNESS PT 1]

2000 AD – TIME

2015 AD – HEAVEN

2018 AD – DEATH'S RETURN [DARKNESS PT 2]

2020 AD – KATRINA HATES THE DEAD
[DEATH PT 1]

2176 AD – CONQUEST

2177 AD – DEATH'S KISS
[DARKNESS PT 3]

12,018 AD – KATRINA HATES THE GODS
[DEATH PT 2]

12,028 AD – KATRINA HATES THE UNIVERSE
[DEATH PT 3]

12,046 AD – EVERY PLANET HAS A GODSCHURCH
[DOOM PT 1]

12,047 AD – THERE'S EVERY REASON TO FEAR
[DOOM PT. 2]

12,049 AD – THE END TASTES LIKE PANCAKES
[DOOM PT 3]

12,176 AD – CHAOS

ALSO BY RUSSELL NOHELTY

NOVELS
My Father Didn't Kill Himself
Sorry for Existing
Gumshoes: The Case of Madison's Father
Invasion
The Vessel
The Void Calls Us Home
Worst Thing in the Universe
Anna and the Dark Place
The Marked Ones
The Dragon Scourge
The Dragon Champion
The Dragon Goddess
The Obsidian Spindle Saga

COMICS and OTHER ILLUSTRATED WORK
The Little Bird and the Little Worm
Ichabod Jones: Monster Hunter
Gherkin Boy
How NOT to Invade Earth

www.russellnohelty.com

CONQUEST

Book 9 of The Godsverse Chronicles

By:
Russell Nohelty

Edited by:
Leah Lederman

Proofread by:
Katrina Roets & Toni Cox

Cover by:
Psycat Covers

Planet chart and timeline design by:
Andrea Rosales

BOOK 1

CHAPTER 1

Kimberly

Location: Earth

I dropped a pinch of pixie dust in the tunnels under Trafalgar Square in London and vanished. One of the great benefits of being a pixie was the ability to travel around the world in an instant. We were hunted to the point of extinction and had to keep our heads on a swivel, but as long as you had a pouch of pixie dust, you could stay one step ahead of the monsters and demons who hunted you.

And on a good night, you could hunt them.

That was my job. Specifically, I hunted the ones that preyed on my kind. I was very good at it—some said I was the best, and those people had both good taste and a keen eye. Truly, I was exceptional.

In my two hundred years of life, I had captured and banished over a thousand demons and, by extension, saved hundreds of pixies from being sacrificed for any number of dark plans. Pixie blood was good for that sort of thing. Of course, for every fairy I saved, another one fell. I tried to focus on the ones I saved, not the ones I'd failed to protect. If I let that burden weigh on me, I would never get out of bed in the morning.

When I reappeared, I was in Seattle, the home of the most amazing coffee in the world and current location of the demon Thriaska. He'd built a lair somewhere in the city, and it was my responsibility to find it. He was the latest in a long line of demons hunting my people, and I was looking forward to sending him back to Hell. You couldn't kill a demon, but you could banish them. Inevitably, some human would use the wrong summoning spell so that, once again, that demon was free to terrorize Earth.

"Where are you, Thriaska?" I muttered under my breath. "Enjoy your freedom because tonight you're going back to Hell."

It wasn't wise to use pixie dust in the open, so I chose to use my legs and hoof it to the coffee shop where I was meeting my informant. I enjoyed walking. It allowed me to think, and the chill reminded me that I was alive. I smelled the crisp cold in the fall air that whipped past my face. There had been a storm recently, and the ground was still wet with rain.

Two miles down the cold, damp street, I turned into a little coffee shop. One thing that survived was coffee, even during the Apocalypse, and afterward, it became one of the most precious goods on Earth, transforming Seattle into one of the most important cities on the planet.

Honestly, I preferred Seattle at the end of the twentieth century when it was known for grunge music and gloomy days more than for coffee and tech billionaires. I'd gone to college in Seattle, back when things like education mattered to me. That was another life, over two centuries ago. Before the Apocalypse.

It was just like it sounds: all the pious men and women were raptured to Heaven while everybody and everything else was stuck on Earth to deal with the consequences. And there were extreme consequences. The dead rose from their graves. Demons invaded our planet. Nations collapsed. There was nothing we could do except learn to survive in the new normal.

I was there, and I remembered everything. I had only been immortal for a decade at that point and was sure I would not survive the horrors, but I got strong quick. I had forgotten much about my ancient life, but the Apocalypse was still raw in me.

"Good evening!" a squat girl with a nose ring said from behind the counter. "What can I get you?"

"Hi," I replied. "Large coffee, extra shot."

She nodded and went about pouring the coffee. When she was done, I brought it to a table in the corner and waited. My contact was late. She was always late. She had been around since the beginning, so little things like time didn't matter much to her.

I had an infinity to fill, so I didn't usually begrudge anyone a few minutes. Heck, hours or weeks. But tonight, time mattered a lot to me; in fact, it was everything. Thriaska had kidnapped a pixie girl earlier that morning, and it was only a matter of time before he killed her like he'd killed the others.

Pixie blood was quite possibly the most valuable resource on earth, save for unicorn horns or dragon scales. Both of those monster species became extinct long ago, while pixies molded into society quite well. We were really, really good at blending in. We looked like humans—save for our pointy ears—we smelled like humans, walked and talked like humans.

Some of us even took human mates, like my mother did. Others just kept their heads down and used their magic carefully. In any case, it was my job to keep pixies safe, even if it meant hunting demons and monsters ?? to the ends of the Earth, one at a time until they learned that we were off-limits. Monsters had thick skulls, and it often took caving them in before they got the message.

The bell over the shop door rang, and a cloaked woman walked into the shop. I eyed her as she walked across the room and muttered something to the waitress. After a moment, the barista poured a drink, and the woman brought it to her mouth.

"This is divine," she said with a sweet smile, belying that she was anything but what she appeared. "Is there anything better than good coffee?"

"Good, right?" I asked as she came toward me.

Lilith had been around since the beginning of everything. She was Adam's first wife but refused to lay with him unless they were equals and was thus banished from the Garden of Eden, which forced her to make a deal with a demon.

She pulled off her hood and let down her long, dark hair. Her thin lips creaked up, accentuating the wrinkles under her soft, brown eyes. "Best in Seattle. So much better than that Starbucks monstrosity they used to make here. Remember that? What was that thing called, a Frappuccino?"

"I think so."

"Yuck. Sugar water, if you ask me. This though, just the perfect amount of bitterness, like you, my dear."

"I'll take that as a compliment, Lilith," I said. "After all, I run on spite and bitterness."

"And coffee, darling," she replied. "Of course, perhaps I shouldn't complain about them too much. Back in my day, I would have killed for sugar water. All we had were figs and apples."

I nodded. Starbucks was the reason Seattle was a bastion for coffee, but they couldn't survive the Apocalypse. Almost nobody did. Some days, in my shame,

I wished for it to come again, if only so humanity would remember what it was like to cower in true fear and the feeling of relief that came over us when the demons vanished.

Life was different after the Apocalypse, for a while at least. People were nicer. Food tasted sweeter. The world looked brighter. I thought maybe humanity's better nature would take hold of them.

But it didn't last.

Eventually, the stories turned into legends. Those who had seen the horror with their own eyes died off, leaving the next generation, who birthed the next generation…the truth vanished to memory, just a footnote in a textbook. The world rebuilt itself in hope and prosperity and then fell to war, only to be rebuilt again. The cycle continued until little remained of the world I remembered.

I took a long sip of coffee. "This is better than Starbucks ever was."

She nodded. "Much better, darling. Much, much better."

Enough coffee talk. "Did you find him?" I asked.

Lilith sighed. "You are probably the rudest girl I have ever met. Did you know that?" She relished being a demon. She didn't see them as evil, just misguided and misunderstood, the same way humans and fairies were. Some of them were downright polite. She didn't think that a few bad apples should spoil the bunch.

"Yes, but I don't care. He's going to kill again, and soon. If he kills one of my people while I'm sipping coffee with you, I'll never forgive myself."

Lilith took a long sip of her coffee. "Why not? It's not like they'll go to Hell. Not really, at least."

She wasn't wrong, technically speaking. While dead pixies were sent to Hell, they weren't punished like humans. Being monsters, they got off on a technicality and were able to work the land, in the auspices of Hell, at the Devil's behest.

"They're still slaves."

"Potato, potahto," Lilith said. "I'm just saying, if another pixie died, it wouldn't be so bad. They'd get out of here, at least." She swirled her hand in a circle, looking at the shop around her.

I chuckled and took my own sip of coffee. "If you hate it so much, why don't you go back? Or to Mars, or Venus? Or Europa?"

I didn't understand much about the inner workings of Hell, but I knew enough demons to know that in the last two hundred years, the Devil had made deals to annex land for Hell on multiple planets in the solar system, easing the tension that led to the Apocalypse in the first place.

"I know you're joking," Lilith said. "But please don't be so cavalier. First off, those satellite Hells are much too cold and remote for me, and second…Hell doesn't have coffee. I desperately need coffee in my life."

"I understand that." I took another sip of coffee. "So… Thriaska? Where is he?"

Lilith's eyes flashed. "Fine. I'll take you to him so that you can have your revenge, okay? You know, you used to come to me for advice and counsel, instead of just information. I miss the days when we would just…talk."

My eyes dropped to my hands in my lap. "I'm sorry. It's just—" But I didn't feel like finishing my sentence. I had a job to do, and I hated apologizing for it. "Can we go?"

"Yes," Lilith said. "After I finish my coffee."

I grumbled. "Fine, but if she dies before we get to her, or Thriaska escapes, I'm sending you back to Hell tonight."

Lilith smiled. "You can surely try."

CHAPTER 2

Akta

Location: Pluto

Pluto was my least favorite planet among those that the devil, Katrina, had annexed for her interplanetary vision of the underworld. It was dead, cold, and nearly empty. Unfortunately, that made it a perfect hiding place for escaped souls. Pluto was an inauspicious swamp of villainy.

It only took me a few moments to travel from Earth to Pluto, though the distance was over three billion miles. Traveling between planets was difficult, even for a pixie like me who had learned to move between places without the use of the pixie dust as a crutch. I trained for years, learning to jump between worlds without being stuck in the empty vacuum of space. Every jump was fraught with danger. Miscalculating by mere meters could mean missing the planet entirely. Countless pixies drifted through space, frozen and alone because they forgot to carry the one or made some other logistical mistake when planning their route.

From the planet's surface, the sun looked like a distant star. Earth wasn't even a hint of a glimmer on the horizon. There were no settlements on Pluto, only pits of Hell confined to caves and a skeleton crew to man them. Pluto wouldn't be ready for inhabitation for another thirty years, during phase four of the Devil Katrina's plan to modernize Hell. She had a thriving underworld on Mars and a growing one on Europa. Deep in the core of Venus, she developed a third, but Pluto was barely a distant point on her roadmap.

With a snap of my fingers, I transported myself from where I'd been standing at the edge of an ancient lake to the entrance of a large cave halfway across the planet. Blue flames lit either side of the entrance, and directly inside was a small reception desk where a goblin, warty-nosed and tinged a mossy green, sat typing on a computer.

There was little technology on Pluto yet, and no infrastructure, save for the data banks in its core storing huge caches of data on every person in Hell, their level of suffering, their penance, and their expected time until they were rehabilitated.

Rehabilitated.

Lucifer and Velaska, the previous Devils, would laugh hysterically at the thought that a soul could be rehabilitated, but Katrina had a plan—a rudimentary one, but a plan nonetheless—to move souls out of Hell once their penance was up.

It was bold, ambitious, and destined to fail unless Katrina could convince the demon lords of Hell to accept her plan. Even then, I doubted God would approve the measure. I had met him before, and he had no interest in letting sinners into Heaven. Unless the god of wine had changed his tune sometime in the past 3,000 years, Katrina was just spinning her wheels.

Still, it was nice to see a Devil trying to do something; anything. The others I've met had no interest in helping anybody. They aimed at keeping the status quo, and some of them didn't even care that much. Lucifer was fine with blowing the whole place up. That's what caused an Apocalypse on Earth.

"How may I help you?" the goblin at the desk asked in a froggy voice.

"There's a soul jumper on Pluto," I said. "I need to turn on a tracer."

All souls now had tracers, which made things a lot easier for me, but it made the hunt far less fun.

"ID number?"

I pulled a piece of parchment out of the purse on my belt. Even though the underworld has gone modern, some things didn't need changing. I still wore the same belt I had when I came to Earth 3,000 years ago, filled with leather pockets, pouches, and scabbards to hold my knives.

"327491A362J."

The goblin typed into her computer. After a few seconds, the printer kicked out the location, and she handed it to me. "There you go."

"Thanks," I said. "Can you circle their location on a map?"

"No," the goblin replied, frowning. "I can ping it to your tablet."

I shook my head. "I don't do that."

"Oh," the goblin sighed. "One of those."

She pulled out a map from her desk and circled the location she had pulled up for me. It wasn't that I hated technology, but there was something to be said for taking your time. Not every moment of a day needed to be productive, and using a pen and paper forced me to ground my mind to the moment.

"Here you go," she replied. "Now go away."

***

I had been in the employ of the Devil for over 3,000 years and could recall a time when Hell was little more than a feudal village. Being able to visit distant planets was a novel way to spend my time. I had trekked through every inch of Hell, looking for demons and monsters who had deserted their posts and souls that escaped the pits. I hated being stuck in the oppressive heat of that place.

Now I had many other planets to explore. It was a fine change of pace. It was nearly impossible to beat the tracer, which made hunting less fun, but at least it got me out to see the universe every once in a while, and sometimes…just sometimes, things got interesting, and I was genuinely surprised by what I found when I reached a tracer location.

After traveling to the site the goblin had given me for soul 327491A362J, for instance, I was amazed to see a glowing blue ball on the ground instead of a ragged soul. When I picked it up, it throbbed with heat. I twisted it around, admiring how the hazy cloud inside seemed to dance with my fingers. I had never seen anything like it before.

"It's my soul," a voice behind me said. "Or at least the part of me with the tracer on it." A man stepped out of the darkness. I recognized him from my case file. "You can keep that. I won't be needing it anymore."

He wasn't much of a threat, compared to the rest of the souls of Hell. He had been assigned a level four gluttony pit, and his stomach paunched over his ratty clothes, accentuating his food vice. He was supposed to have his face stuffed with beetles for eternity, but due to his proclivity with magic, he had been given a work release. The magic he learned made his skin glow blue, and his eyes shimmered a haunting white.

"You're not a ghost," I said.

"Not anymore," the ghost said. "I have morphed into something grander. I have graduated beyond your pits. Now, I am a wraith. I am a monster, the same as you, and thus untouchable."

"That's not what my file says. You aren't sanctioned for this level of magic. I'm afraid I have to take you in for flushing."

The wraith shook his head. "I'm not going back to the pit."

"They all say that."

He looked like he had seen the edge of the abyss, and likely he had. The pits ranged on a scale from 1-10, and a four tended to be on the mild side of vice: they had an addiction, for sure, and a warped soul. Usually, it wasn't until you got to level eight and up that you started to see the really awful humans, and those were the ones who had the balls to escape the pits. Their punishments were harsh enough, and their temperaments volatile enough that escape made sense to them. Most fours never even thought of escape because they colored within the lines.

"Convenient you stayed here," I said. "You should have run."

"Then, I would always be running," he said. "I am too powerful to run."

"Even the powerful can die."

"Funny, I was just thinking the same thing—about you."

I kept a dagger on each hip, four throwing daggers on each arm, four more on each leg, and then the special weapon in the back of my belt. It was The Dagger of Obsolescence, entrusted to me by Katrina after the Apocalypse, and one of five weapons that could kill her. I was charged with protecting it. If it fell into the wrong hands, our Devil would be at risk; the whole universe would be at risk.

"This is your last chance," I growled. "Come with me peacefully."

The man chuckled. "Oh, you are very cute, pixie. You have no idea."

"No idea of what?" I grabbed my daggers, ready to unsheathe them.

The man lifted a burlap sack. He reached inside and pulled out five orbs, just like the one in my hand, and threw the balls across the ground. As they rolled to a stop underneath me, I noticed that the ground had been streaked with blood. The marks had been hidden by the darkness until the blue glow highlighted them.

I was standing on a pentagram, surrounded by a circle. "Oh no," I muttered.

"*Adiuro vos ad locum istum*!" The orbs exploded around me, including the one in my hand, and the pentagram glowed blue. "*Adiuro vos ad locum istum*!"

Pain surged through my body as I fell to the ground. Ropes materialized and wrapped my legs together. "You will pay for this!"

"I don't think so," he said, moving towards me. "Your devil will pay. And the gods will quake with fear."

I grabbed the dagger from my side and swung it at him, but he easily dodged it.

"You are strong," he muttered appreciatively. "*Adiuro vos ad locum istum*!" More ropes dug into my wrists, where they were now tied together.

"I don't know what you're planning, but you won't get away with it." I kicked against my restraints, but my legs were bound too tightly together.

He knelt behind me and pressed his hand on my back. His fingers scalded me, burning deep into my skin. I tried to force him off me, but it was no use. His hand traced down my back. "I'm doing all right so far."

He pulled the Dagger of Obsolescence from my belt, the runes that lined the jagged blade sliding across my back. I kicked his hand, but the binding spell pulled me back to the ground. I was helpless.

The wraith pulled himself back to standing and stood before me. "That was easier than I thought. Legends of your glory have been exaggerated."

I fought against the charm he was using to hold me, twisting to look over my shoulder at him. "I will find you, and I will make you pay for this."

"Yes," he said, reaching into his bag and pulling out another blue orb. He sounded bored. "You've said that before."

He crushed another blue ball in his hand, snapped his fingers, and vanished. When he was gone, the blue light faded. The circle released me.

It took me a moment for the fire in my belly to quell and leave me alone with my shame. I had failed in my charge, and now the Devil's life was in danger. I needed to warn her.

CHAPTER 3

Julia

Location: Hell

Dark. Nothing but darkness.

Where was I?

My hands jerked, but they were not free. I tried to straighten my back, but I was bound with chains.

Maybe I could teleport? I closed my eyes and imagined my apartment in my mind. I pictured every inch of it until it was as real for me as if I were there myself.

"Go," I whispered.

Teleporting only worked if you envisioned your destination perfectly. It wasn't supposed to work in Hell, but Katrina had found a way for us to use our powers and made pixie dust for us just like the kind we'd used back on Earth. Akta had learned how to teleport without pixie dust, but it was a skill I never mastered, no matter how many times she tried to teach it to me.

Go.

Nothing. Katrina didn't care how we teleported, just that we did so at her beck and call. We were very helpful scouts. After she'd annexed half the solar system for her underworld expansion, she needed people who could travel quickly between worlds, and pixies fit the bill. We became errand boys and girls, trackers, and invaluable members of her team.

Maybe that's why I was bound here.

The demons of Hell had plotted against Katrina from the beginning of her rule, after all. They didn't like modernization. They didn't like change. They didn't like being ruled by a woman…and a mortal woman at that. At least she used to be before she absorbed Lucifer's power.

I needed to stop letting my mind wander. Concentrate on your home, Julia. Envision it in your mind's eye. Let it engulf you. Then, be there.

"Go," I whispered once again, but nothing happened. There was nothing I could do. I was stuck.

"Are you awake in there?" a gruff voice spoke. "It sounds like it."

"Let me out of here!" I cried.

"Finally." A door swung open, and light filled the room. I craned my neck around and noticed the stone cell around me. My chains hung from the wall, and I saw the light reflected on runes carved into them. Magic bracers, of course. They were meant to stop all magic production, including teleportation. There was no chance for me to escape.

"I thought you would never wake up." Into the room ambled a tall hobgoblin, bald, with sharp teeth poking out the bottom of his mouth. He lumbered forward and grabbed me by the head, pulling me to my feet.

"Don't fight," the hobgoblin said. "I don't want to hurt you."

"You have a funny way of showing it," I grunted.

He laughed. "I'm not the one who brought you here. I'm the one keeping you safe."

"I sure don't feel safe."

The hobgoblin knelt and unlocked the bracers on my legs. He pulled the chains through the bracers, and though the shackles still bound me, I could move my legs freely. "This is the safest place in Hell. I guarantee you that. More secure than the Devil's castle."

"Doubtful." The Devil's castle sat at the furthest edge of Hell, surrounded by a moat of lava and protected by a thousand-foot magical fence. I heard it once held back thirty legions of angelic guard without letting a single one through, but Hell was filled with old wives' tales.

The hobgoblin shrugged. "Believe what you want, but I would rather be here than there. Especially with what's coming."

"What's coming?"

The hobgoblin grabbed the chain around my neck and pushed me forward. "Move."

***

I had lived in Hell for over two hundred years, and in that time, I'd learned not to give anything away unless I absolutely had to. Show no fear and let no weaknesses bubble up into your exterior. If your enemies knew your weaknesses, they would exploit them, and since the enemies of Hell were demons and other monsters, they would be excessively aggressive in their ability to destroy you.

The castle that the hobgoblin led me through was a relic from a bygone era, a time before Katrina, my first days in Hell. When I fell into Hell at the end of the twentieth century, the monsters that dwelled in Dis were just starting to understand the conveniences of Earth. However, they mostly lived like the middle ages, in thatch huts, pulling themselves with horses.

Hell had modernized drastically since then. There were skyscrapers, fast food restaurants, and every manner of convenience, all due to the work by Katrina. A child of Earth and blood, she wasn't content to live in a dirt hovel, so she innovated. The demons hated the modernization. They were set in their ways and had been doing things the same way since the beginning of the universe.

"It's nice," I said, examining the medieval tapestries hanging from the walls. They depicted demons bargaining with and then killing humans. "Homey."

"Our lord believes in tradition," the hobgoblin said.

All demons believed in tradition. None took kindly to Katrina bulldozing their perfect plots of Hell to build a highway system, but she was more powerful than all of them combined. They acquiesced to her big personality because they had no other choice. There were plenty of ways for Katrina to vaporize them.

The hobgoblin pushed me into a throne room, austere and ornate, with gold molding and plush purple carpet. In the center of the room stood a throne, gilded from top to bottom. A broad, red demon with a wide face and burning yellow eyes was seated there.

"Lord Asmodeus," the hobgoblin said. "The pixie, as you requested."

"Excellent," Asmodeus said, leaning forward. "Bring her."

The hobgoblin prodded me until I stood at the foot of the throne. Asmodeus stank of sulfur and his toothy grin brought a chill to my spine.

"You are bigger than I imagined. Pixies are depicted as small things, barely the size of a human hand." He held out his fingers in front of him. "I thought you would be no more than three apples high."

His eyes sunk into his face, and when I stared into them, a tremor shot through my body. I could not show my fear. Demons fed on it. "That's a common misconception," I said. "We come in all sizes."

"Yes. This is very good to know." Asmodeus leaned back once he had fully studied me. "I thought we might need a dozen of you or more for the ritual, but now that I see you, I think just one will do fine."

"Fine for what?" I asked.

"For what is next."

I sighed. "I don't like riddles. You're going to kill me, obviously, or try, and I'm going to try not to get killed. At some point, I'll escape. It's not my first time, so the least you could do is tell me what you're planning. It's the courteous thing to do."

Asmodeus lurched forward, laughing. "When has a demon ever been courteous?"

"Lucifer was courteous to me," I said, staring into his dead eyes.

"Yes, an ANGEL!" Asmodeus laughed even harder. "He was always weak, proven by the fact that he was killed by a mortal."

I raised my eyebrows. "And you're led by one now, so what does that say about you?"

The smile left his face. "That will be rectified soon."

I placed my hands on my hips. "So, your plan is to kill Katrina, then?"

He shook his head. "That is much too small for my ambitions. I aim to make her and the universe suffer. Forever."

"Interesting thesis," I said. "May I offer a suggestion?"

"Sure," Asmodeus laughed.

"How about you…not do that, let me go, and stop being a little bitch about this place moving into the 23rd century? Katrina is the Devil now. Deal with it. Quit being such a baby."

Asmodeus grinned. "And if I said you were to die, and your loved ones have their blood spilled across a great sacrificial tablet, and you should just deal with it…would you?"

"Hell, no," I replied, indignant. "I would fight and rage against you until my last."

Asmodeus peered into my face. "Then perhaps we do understand each other. I will never accept a human on the throne of Hell. She has made a mockery of my beloved home, and I will fight against her until my last breath."

I sighed. "Fair enough."

"Then, we understand each other?"

I shook my head. "No, because if you knew me at all, you would know I won't stop until you're dead."

"Many better than you have tried."

"Many better than you have tried to kill the Devil, and yet she still stands."

"It only takes once for the Devil to die," Asmodeus grumbled." Everybody who has ever lived has a 100 percent survival rate until one day when they don't. Katrina's death is inevitable."

"Perhaps," I replied. "But not by you."

Asmodeus gripped the edges of his throne. "That is where our opinions differ. I believe we will bring about a new world order, and you believe you will stop me. Only one of us will be correct, and you are in a vastly disadvantageous position."

I chuckled. "I've had worse."

Asmodeus rose. "You should know, when I win, I will wipe out all of this so-called progress that Katrina has brought. Monsters will be back to their rightful position, under the boot of demons, instead of equal to them. So, really, I'm doing you a favor. Monsters are not meant to think, and once this is all over, you will never have to think again. Isn't that magnanimous of me?"

"Not at all," I said. "I don't need your favor."

"A pity you do not see it my way." He stepped down the stairs. "At least you have made this day interesting. Now, go back to your cell and spin tales of your escape. Soon enough, you will fulfill your great purpose."

"I'll be gone by then," I said, brimming with unwarranted confidence.

"We shall see."

CHAPTER 4

Katrina

Location: Devil's Castle, Hell

"Isn't it beautiful, Carl?" I took a deep, satisfied breath, staring out from my balcony at the great expanse of Hell.

"It's quite majestic, my lady," my imp assistant, Carl, said. That wasn't his real name, but all the demons had names too complicated to pronounce. I had tried for the first hundred years of my reign to learn the guttural grunts of the demon language, but those glottal stops burned the back of my throat. Finally, my servants told me that calling them by the closest name I could pronounce was less offensive to their ears.

"You're goddamn right it is," I said with another deep sigh. I had spent every day of my reign trying to pull the denizens of Hell out of the late 1400s and into the twentieth century, at least to start. Everything was coming together for me. Hell had finally started to look like the Earth I remembered, with superhighways cutting across the barren wastelands and towns springing up to satisfy the travel habits of traveling monsters.

No longer were there souls stacked ass to ankles and piled high at every turn. Addressing the overcrowding problem was my first act when I came to power. Annexing Mars, Europa, and Venus, first, and the rest of the solar system next, I spread the souls of Hell across the solar system into the kind of ordered system that would make the most cynical data scientist smile. Humanity grew at an exponential rate with each passing day, and by the turn of the next millennium, I would have to expand out to Alpha Centauri, but that was a long way away.

Of course, excavating new planets was a logistical nightmare. It takes tremendous effort to excavate the gooey center of a planet, and I had to do it basically alone. God was no help, and the demon lords showed little affection for my plans to modernize their world. Hades and Anubis originally crafted Hell together with the other gods, which meant they had all the power of the Heavens at their disposal, while I only had independent contractors pulled from the pits of Hell and demons I had to pay double overtime.

God could have finished the work with the snap of his fingers, but he wouldn't help me do anything, even after I saved his life during the Apocalypse. Of course, he didn't stop me either. I thought he would throw a hissy fit when I started to gut Mars with a proverbial melon baller, but he was as absent as an alcoholic father. Every time I'd met with God, he had done nothing but made things worse for me.

"How is the construction on Venus coming?" I asked, turning around to Carl.

Carl looked down at his tablet and flipped through his report. "The surface of Venus looks like it will be perfect for level seven, eight, nine, and ten pits. However, we are having problems with the demons. They don't like the smell."

"The smell, Carl?" I chuckled. "This whole place smells like sulfur and rancid sweat."

"Yes, your worship, but that smell is pleasant to a demon. Venus is hazy, and…well, it's not very pleasant smelling. The union—"

"No, Carl," I said, squeezing the bridge of my nose. "I can't deal with the union today."

Unionized demons were the worst. One of the downsides of modernizing was spreading the idea that every worker had autonomy, and they could band together in collective bargaining. I should have punted Karl Marx into the sun so quick when he started proselytizing for the democratization of all the inhabitants of Hell, but it was more than a decade before I sent him to his own little rock in the bowels of Venus. By then, his ideas had taken hold, and now there were unions breathing down my neck every time I had a good idea.

"I know you're not happy about it," Carl said. "But they have filed a grievance."

"Put it on my calendar for next week," I replied. "I want those pits built, Carl. There's war brewing on Earth, and we're running out of space on Mars."

Carl flipped through his tablet. "According to my numbers, we're at 87 percent capacity on Mars."

"That's a few decades at most. It's not long enough." I sighed. "Where are we going to go once we fill up this solar system? The Alpha Centaurians have yet to answer my calls."

"Maybe humanity will die out before then."

I smiled. "That's a nice thought, Carl. Thank you for that."

Carl gulped. "You're…welcome, your majesty."

"Do I have time for a nap?" I asked.

Carl shook his head. "No. Unfortunately, not. You have a pressing matter that just showed up out of nowhere."

"I don't do pressing matters, Carl," I grumbled. "You should know that by now."

"It's the pixie. She demands an audience with you."

"What?" I said, rage glowing in my eyes. "Who is Akta to demand anything of me? I'm the Devil!"

"That's what I told her, but she insisted, and she insisted I tell you she demanded a meeting and that you won't like what she has to say."

"I never like any meeting, Carl. But especially not with her." I paused for a moment. "I find her lack of emotion...unsettling."

"Should I tell her to 'pound sand,' as you so eloquently put it?"

"No." My heart was pounding. Akta never showed up with good news. I hadn't seen her in decades, but the last time she showed up at my doorstep, I had to battle two lords of Hell for control of the pits. It nearly killed me. If she was coming again, then there was a heap of trouble coming for me. "Show her in."

***

A scowl clouded my face listening to Akta tell me all about how she'd lost my precious dagger. The worst part was that even though she'd screwed up, she didn't seem very upset about it. She spoke every word with an even cadence like she was reading a book report to a group of her classmates.

"So what you're saying," I said when she finally finished, my fingers lightly strumming the arm of my throne, "is that you've lost one of only five objects in the solar system that can kill me, and you have no idea what the people who stole it aim to do with it."

"Well," Akta replied. "I assume they mean to kill you with it."

There was not a hint of sarcasm in her voice. Akta did not do sarcasm. "I think that's a good assumption. I'm very disappointed in you. You know why I gave you that dagger, right?"

"Because I am the best." Again, not a hint of irony or sarcasm, just dry certainty hanging on every word she spoke.

"That's right," I said with a low growl. "Because Lucifer told me you were the best he ever had. Of course, I also killed him with that dagger, so perhaps I should have known you were not the best after all, even back then."

"In fairness, just because I am the best does not mean I'm infallible. What it means is that I always clean up my mistakes. Always. I will find this dagger and bring it back to you."

"And what am I supposed to do until then?" I asked.

"Watch your back." Akta shrugged. "Hire more guards."

I frowned. "And what if they are the ones trying to kill me?"

Akta thought for a moment. "Vet them better, I guess. Or stay alone in this castle, without seeing anyone. Of course, that makes you look like a coward." Akta's eyes lifted to the ceiling. "Come to think of it, I don't remember the last time you left this castle, so perhaps they already think you a coward."

I took a long breath. "You are the only person in all of Hell who would dare call me a coward."

Akta shook her head. "That's not true. I'm just the only one that would say it to your face. However, I did not call you a coward. I simply said locking yourself inside your castle would be cowardly. Brave men can be cowardly. I have been cowardly once or twice, though I cannot think of an instance off the top of my head."

"Talking to you gives me a headache," I grumbled.

"Yes, ma'am. I am sorry. I'm not much of a talker. I'm more a doer."

I stood. "Then go find my dagger, and don't come back here again until you have it."

Akta dropped her head. "I'm afraid I can't promise that, ma'am. There may be occasion for me to come back here and get further instructions from you, or perhaps my investigation leads me to your castle for some other reason. However, I will promise not to bother you with trivialities unless you should request it."

"I will not request it," I said. "I can guarantee you that."

Akta nodded. "Then I will not bother you with them. Only with extremely important matters that require your immediate attention."

"If you must." I waved her off. "Just go."

Akta nodded, then vanished in a puff of purple smoke. Pixies were more trouble than they were worth. I wondered whether the other weapon I had secured was safe in the armory. I needed to check. If it had been taken as well, then I would be in big trouble.

CHAPTER 5

Kimberly

Location: Seattle, Washington

Lilith kept track of all demons in the Pacific Northwest. She was sort of their den mother, having been on Earth longer than any of them. Some even called her the mother of demons, though it was little more than an honorary title. She had birthed a handful of them, but all of them looked up to her. Nothing happened in her territory without Lilith knowing about it.

At any one time, roughly a hundred angels and a hundred demons lived on Earth, carrying out their lord's work. While demons invaded en masse two hundred years ago during the Apocalypse, they had been coming to Earth since the beginning. They lived in the shadows and worked under the table. After the Apocalypse, they slithered back into the dark once again. Very few demons had a free pass out of Hell, but that didn't stop them from coming when people summoned them, when the Devil sent them on an errand, or when they found a crack in the veil between the living and the dead.

And they weren't all bad, honestly. Most of them were innocuous enough. They liked causing havoc, but usually in harmless ways, like a little kid who loved firecrackers. Mostly, demons tried to tip the scales of a mortal's soul. That was like…an ice cream cone for the demons. They would tempt and twist humans, extracting every ounce of good from them. It was better than sex for a demon to watch a pious person become cruel and a pure person fall to depravity.

Every once in a while, they crossed a line and broke one of their lord's rules. When they did, the Devil washed her hands of them, and they became pariahs. That's when I could hunt them down and send them back to Hell. There weren't many rules that angered the Devil, but they had to live by a code while they were on Earth. They weren't allowed to murder humans, or monsters, for one—though they could convince them to kill themselves.

Thriaska was one of those outside of Katrina's protection because he had committed atrocious crimes. I had tracked him across the continent on his spree of murdering pixies. He started in Ontario, Canada, moved down to Detroit, and then across the Great Plains to Seattle. I picked up his trail near my long-deserted hometown in Colorado Springs.

Thriaska was not the easiest demon to track. Usually, when a demon went on a rampage, they reveled in creating viscera and overly graphic crime scenes, but Thriaska was different. His scenes were clean. In every location, he ground the bones into dust and used it to create a sigil. It was his calling card. He also carefully selected his victims, gathering only those people who had no families, so there was nobody to miss them. This was the first time he'd slipped up in all my time hunting him. His victim was an orphan, but her foster family loved her and called in her disappearance. It was a big mistake on his part, and I would make him pay for it.

"Remember," Lilith said, pulling her car up to an old warehouse. "If anybody asks, I didn't tell you anything. I can't be seen cavorting with the enemy."

I smiled at her. "We're not enemies. We're just on different sides."

"Yes, dear, that's an enemy."

"Not necessarily," I said, opening the door of her Bentley. "Two football teams can be rivals without being enemies."

Lilith smiled. "The fate of the world never rested on the outcome of a football match."

I stepped out of the car. "There are about three billion people in this world that would disagree with you."

"Yes, well, that is just one of the things I hate about humans. So concerned with trivialities, and you know what I think of trivialities. And humans."

I did. She was not a fan of either. God took Adam's side in their great dispute. She only wanted equality and to lie beside Adam instead of under him. A reasonable request by any standard, but God did not see it that way. Instead, he cast her out of the Garden of Eden and pulled a rib from Adam to make Eve; she was made of him and thus below him. It turned Lilith's stomach to watch them romp around in the Garden, Eve looking to Adam for instruction like a doe-eyed child. Lilith saw Adam's betrayal on the face of every human she passed, and it ate at her.

"Don't wait up," I said. I turned to the run-down building in front of me.

Thriaska prized utility above luxury. He wasn't the kind of demon with an exquisitely-furnished penthouse for headquarters, drenched in champagne and orchids. He was down and dirty. An old warehouse or a dock was his base of operations.

I unfurled my wings and flew to the top of the warehouse. I peered down through a skylight in the center of the roof. Thriaska paced in a makeshift laboratory, his green eyes glowing. Huge horns rose from each side of his head, which was streaked down the center with a mohawk. A dozen jars of white powder filled the tables on either side of him—pixie bones. I'd found a bottle in Boise, and it twisted my stomach into knots. Seeing a dozen jars made me violently nauseous.

"This won't hurt much," Thriaska said, his voice raspy. He walked across the laboratory and picked up a scalpel from a metal table. "You shouldn't be so scared. You have a great purpose."

"Please!" a woman screamed. "Let me go!"

He was ready to kill the woman he'd captured. Lilith had taken too long with her coffee, and I was nearly too late. I would have to work fast. I spun around the skylight for a better look and saw the young woman tied to an operating table. Her hair was wet from sweat and matted to her face, which glistened with her tears. She couldn't have been older than seventeen. Her eyes bulged with every piercing cry that left her mouth.

"I do so enjoy your screams," Thriaska said, walking toward her. "They are like music to my ears."

"Please," she screamed. "I—"

"No more talking. I simply can't take any more right now. Too much…ecstasy." Thriaska stopped in the middle of the room. "It's a pity. You don't even know why you are important, do you?"

"I—I just want to go home."

Thriaska chuckled. "Well, that won't happen, my love. However, I can tell you that your death will bring about the most noble pursuit in all the universe."

I wanted to let him monologue more to see what I might learn, but I couldn't risk him hurting the girl. I grabbed the daggers from either side of my belt, enchanted to kill a demon. Daggers once held by my mentor, Julia, and her ancestor, Akta, the two greatest monster hunters of the past three thousand years, until me. I threw down a pinch of pixie dust and vanished, popping back up directly between Thriaska and the girl.

"Ah!" Thriaska said. He stepped back for a moment, but he wasn't startled. He simply smiled at me as he held his scalpel out toward me. "I was waiting for you to show up, pixie. I thought my clues were too hard for you to track."

"Stay back," I said. "You're not going to hurt another one of my people."

Thriaska shook his head. "You know I can't do that. I'm so close to making it all come true, and then we'll have a grand old time."

"Making what come true?" I asked.

Thriaska waggled the razor in his hand. "That's the question, now isn't it? What could possibly make me disobey the will of Hell, come to Earth, piss off the queen of demons, and send you after me across a whole continent? Must be a pretty big reward for me to do all that."

I considered his words for a moment. "I don't really care. I just need you to stop and go back to Hell where you belong."

He planted his feet firmly on the floor and held his chin high. "We don't belong in Hell. We belong here, just like you. We were here once, do you remember?"

I nodded.

"It was so much fun." Thriaska smiled, though he clearly didn't know how. His lips just opened widely, exposing his black teeth. "We didn't have any rules then. It was bedlam: Hell on Earth, and there was nothing humans could do to stop it."

"We did stop you. Katrina stopped you."

The demon sighed. "Please don't say that name. It is so foul against my ears. Katrina. Devil. She will be dealt with in time, but that is not my charge."

"Charge?"

"Mission, I suppose you would say."

"What mission?"

He took a step forward. "Now you're asking the right question. What mission would drive me here, away from my own people, and make me risk everything, just to kill a few pixies?"

"A dozen pixies, by my count."

"Three dozen, actually. I started on the Eastern tip of China and worked my way around until I made it here, nearly around the world from where I started."

I pointed my dagger at him. "And you're going to end right here."

The demon laughed. "Of course I will, darling. That's the plan, isn't it? I murder my way across Asia, then Europe, spilling pixie blood at every stop, and here, at the end, you kill me, spilling my blood and completing the circle."

"What are you talking about? You're not making sense."

Thriaska sighed. "There is one thing, though, that you should know."

"And what's that?"

"I'm afraid it involves your old mentor, Julia Freeman."

My jaw clenched. "What about her?"

"Well, I have done my part here, of course," Thriaska said, cocking his head. "But I'm afraid to complete the ritual, they'll need to sacrifice a pixie on the other side of the void. They have their sights set on your old mentor...In fact, if I'm correct, she's already deep in the clutches of the Demon Lord as we speak."

"Do you think telling me this is going to make me not kill you?"

"No." Thriaska held up his hand. "I'm telling you this because you can't stop it, and I want the guilt to gnaw at you for the rest of your life. In three days' time, Katrina will be dead, the Demon Lord will be in control, and we will once again be allowed our rampage on Earth."

"That's what this is all about?" I narrowed my eyes. "Bringing about the Apocalypse?"

"Oh no, that's much too small. We're bringing about something so much more immense."

"And what's that?" I asked.

"Oh, you'll see," Thriaska said with a malicious smile. "Now, let's begin." He lunged for me.

I held up my daggers to block the thrust of his razor. "You will not kill this girl!"

Thriaska pulled back and smacked me with his free hand. The force of the blow sent me flying. I hovered in the air for a moment, catching my breath before I flew back toward him. I kicked him away from the operating table as he went to slice open the girl.

"Stay away from her!"

Thriaska growled and rushed me like a bull. I rolled away to avoid him, and he went skidding across the warehouse. I turned and cut the ropes off the girl on the table, just as Thriaska charged again.

"Run!" I screamed.

I zipped upward into the air and kicked Thriaska in the face, sending him sprawling against a shelf filled with plastic containers. The girl, in a panic, tried to run past him. As she did, Thriaska caught her by the ankle. I rushed to get between them, but Thriaska smacked me away. When I rose to my feet, I knew it was too late. The girl dangled from his hand like a stuffed pig ready for the slaughter.

"Foolish," he said before diving the knife deep into her throat and tossing her to the ground like a discarded shoe.

"No!" I disappeared and reappeared next to her. "Stay with me."

The girl's legs thrashed until the life drained from her eyes, and then she was silent. Her blood pooled around her, and that's when I noticed the pentagram, painted in white, on the floor beneath her. The paint extended to the edges of the room, and as the blood dripped upon it, the sigil began to glow blue.

"*Ianua aperta. Tu solus est pulsate,*" Thriaska shouted. An energy pulsated through the sigil. Around the room, every jar burst, and the pixie dust clouded the air. "*Ianua aperta. Tu solus est pulsate!*"

I surveyed the dust, disgusted and saddened, then turned and rushed toward him. "Die!"

"YES!" He shouted, opening his arms. He let out a deep guttural moan when I plunged both my daggers into his heart. As the life left his eyes, he smiled at me. "It is done."

A great shockwave shot through the room, and Thriaska burst into a million pieces. The pixie dust evaporated into the air and left me with nothing except a bloody mess to clean up. I had failed to save the girl, but I did save the world from Thriaska.

It was a little too easy, though. And if he was right, Julia was in danger, and the whole world was on the brink of invasion from the demons of Hell.

I couldn't let that happen.

CHAPTER 6

Akta

Location: Dis, Hell

There was going to be an attempt on Katrina's life, and it would come soon. I could not allow such a plan to succeed. Katrina was not perfect, but she was the best Devil I had ever worked for. The demon lords would have a claim to the throne, but that did not necessarily mean they were behind this. I needed more information.

The city of Dis was filled with thousands of monsters trafficking information—for the right price, of course. Having lived in the bowels of Hell for three thousand years, I knew them all. Many I had tracked across the plains of Oblivion, back before it was a ten-lane super-highway.

By definition, informants were unsavory characters. They weren't all criminals, but they were plugged into the seedy underground. For that reason, there were only a select few I trusted. One of them was a friend I had known since my time on Earth, back when I took my revenge on King Odgeir. He worked for Asmodeus, a powerful demon who fell out of favor with the rise of Katrina.

Asmodeus was one of the lords of Hell who helped the Devil rule the underworld. In return for their service, they were free to accrue power and influence. Naturally, they built fiefdoms and battled each other for perfunctory power of one area or another. It entertained them.

But with Katrina, all of that changed. She no longer needed the lords of Hell to create a false sense of order. Instead, she created a bureaucracy to oversee all of Hell, and so the Demon Lords were cut out and cast off as if they never mattered in the first place. They still held their rank, but they were feckless. That made them angry. Anger could make the best person do horrible things if it festered for long enough, and the demon lords of Hell were made of anger and built of rage.

I stepped into the Old Hat, a seedy bar in downtown Dis that had somehow survived the gentrification around it. There was a fight at least once a day, and on a rough night, there was a fight every hour. My troll friend, Sven, just as lumbering and blue as when I met him three thousand years ago, was sitting at a table in the back, alone.

He had chosen the name Sven for himself, and I thought it suited his tall, strapping stature, even though he often slouched when he was uncomfortable. He didn't have a name back on Earth, but in Hell, he was more than just a being trying to survive. He was building a life for himself, and that life deserved a name.

Sven had few friends in Dis, which made him susceptible to Asmodeus's influence. The demon lord offered him things I could not: a family and a place to belong. I loved Sven, but I was often gone on trips to far-off planets, and he was not built for travel.

"Akta!" Sven cried out when he saw me, knocking over the table as he stood and wrapped me in a hug. "Hello, pretty." He was the only one I let compliment me in all the realm. He gave me another tight squeeze.

"How are you, buddy?" I asked with a smile, sitting down at his table.

"Good. Work, drink, sleep. You know." A bartender brought over another drink, and Sven took it from him with a smile before turning back to me. "How are you?"

I waved the bartender away. "Bad, Sven."

"Why bad?" Sven asked, scratching his head.

"Work stuff," I replied.

"Tell me, pretty," Sven said.

I lowered my voice. "If I tell you, you can't tell anybody, okay?"

He glanced around the room, then back at me. "Okay."

I leaned across the table. "Somebody stole the Dagger of Obsolescence from me."

"Oh my," Sven said, trying to feign surprise, but then his face dropped to one of confusion. "Why is that bad?"

I sighed. I had explained it to him a hundred times, but things took a while to sink into his thick skull. "Because it's one of only five objects in the solar system that can destroy the Devil."

Sven perked up. "Oh…so maybe Katrina will die?"

I shook my head. "No, she won't. I'm going to get it back."

"Oh," Sven said, sad. "Too bad."

My eyes narrowed. "Why would you say that?"

"Katrina is a bad one." Sven swigged his beer. "Everybody thinks so."

"Hey!" I said. "Don't talk like that. She is the Devil and my boss."

"Bad Devil," Sven said, sucking his teeth.

"Who is filling your head with those lies?" I asked. I knew it wasn't something he would come up with on his own. "Tell me now."

There was a long pause. Sven's eyes wandered before they caught mine again. "…Friends."

"That's disappointing." I took a long breath, pausing for effect and tension. "Might they know what happened to the dagger?"

Sven shook his head. "No."

"But they don't like Katrina, right?"

"No," Sven turned away. "They don't, but—"

"But what?"

"They are my friends."

I pressed my hand into his, and it sunk into the fat surrounding his knuckles. "I am your friend. Remember that. Haven't I always looked out for you?"

He sighed and looked down at his lap. "Yes. Akta good friend."

"Then tell me where you learned these lies."

He caught my eyes. "They took me to a church…"

"What church?"

"The True Path."

***

The True Path was a church dedicated to keeping reverence to the Old Gods that came before the God that ruled us now, the gods that roamed the Earth for thousands of years before they left to build a new civilization beyond the cosmos. That's how they operated: they'd start up a planet, leave one god in charge of a planet while the rest of them continued molding the universe in their image.

Earth got stuck with Bacchus, a vain, incompetent drunk. Too greedy and arrogant to keep reverence to the Old Gods, he ordered the temples—once devoted to his kin—to be destroyed and replaced by churches of worship to him. He made claims that he was all-knowing, all-powerful, and all good, though none of those were true, as evidenced by his sloppy hand in the Apocalypse.

The True Path formed as a devotion to the Old Gods, the only ones who could end the idiotic reign of Bacchus and return the demons to Earth. They had been a niche, fringe organization for decades, but in the past few years, they received an enormous infusion of money and grew a network all around Hell, complete with a cathedral in the middle of Dis.

They were annoying and preachy, but I had never considered them hostile to the reign of Katrina. After talking with Sven, I decided to investigate. Every ward of Dis had at least one church now, and I passed one every day on my way home. That seemed like the easiest place to start looking for a clue as to whether the church had a hand in the theft of the dagger.

From the outside, the church didn't look like much. Its symbol was a golden circle, symbolizing the sun and fire, with an upside-down cross inside it and horns protruding from either side. The True Path was obsessed with the cleansing power of fire. They believed that demons were the manifestation of that power, and it was their duty to cleanse the world in the name of the Devil and the old gods.

The wooden door to the old church was open, and I walked inside. Aside from pews lining either side of the small room and a small altar in the center, the room was sparsely adorned. There were several paintings of Lucifer on the wall, and Velaska, along with Hades, Zeus, Osiris, Ra, and Hera. Each pew held hymnals and tracts inside a shelf built into it. I picked up a hymnal and paged through it on my way to the altar.

"Can I help you?"

I looked up to see a rail-thin demon wearing a black robe. Small horns bulged from her forehead, and her eyes shone a deep, rich yellow.

"Maybe," I replied, setting down the book. "My friend told me about this place. He said you helped him understand his place in the world."

The demon pastor bowed her head. "We try to be a beacon of light in these dark times."

"Aren't they all dark times, here in Hell?"

"Not necessarily. Hell was once a haven for demons and monsters for thousands of years. We could work, live, and be free…"

"That's not true," I said, frowning. "You might have thought you were free, but you were slaves."

"Only in name. In practice, there were none who dared challenge us. The demon lords left us alone to roam and pillage, as long as we finished our great work."

I scrunched up my nose. "And that's not the case anymore?"

"What do you think?" The pastor peered at me for a moment. "You have an old soul, older than most. Do you think we are better off now than before?"

I shrugged. "I mean, it's better than before the Apocalypse when souls were packed so tight we could barely move."

"Yes, admittedly, that was not ideal. But look what we have given up, getting there. Our history, our culture. Highways run across our sacred land. Skyscrapers hide the heights of Hell from us. Do you not feel it is an abomination?"

I lifted my eyebrows. "I don't think about it much."

"Perhaps you should." She reached down and grabbed a tract, placing it in my hand. "Take this. Read it, and then come back and see me. I think it will be…illuminating."

"Thank you," I said. I hoped to glean the information I needed without cracking open a piece of demon propaganda. I turned toward the door, then stopped. "Can I ask you one thing?"

"Certainly. That is why I'm here."

"My friend…he said…you hate the Devil. Is that true?"

The demon pastor stared back at me, stone-faced. "We do not approve of what Hell has become and work toward bringing it back into harmony with the vision the old gods left us with before…"

"Before they abandoned us, you mean?"

The pastor shook her head. "Not abandoned. Left, like a mother leaves a child to fend for ourselves. We only seek to restore that balance."

"How will you do that?" I asked.

"With faith and prayer. Of course."

"Nothing more…physical?"

The pastor cocked her head, looking confused. "I'm not sure what you're talking about."

"Nothing," I said with a smile, holding up the tract. "Thanks for this."

CHAPTER 7

Kimberly

Location: Swiss Alps

Aziolith had been dead for a long time, but I still used his cave as my home base. It was the one place that Julia, he, and I shared, even if only for a little while, so it had sentimental value. Plus, the fact that it was high in the Swiss Alps meant that I didn't have to worry about intruders.

In the two hundred years since Julia's death, I'd learned a thing or two on my own, but my life was never the same without her, and as a tribute to her, I kept her pixie dust pouch tied to my belt, a relic of a bygone age. Julia Freeman taught me that our peoples' numbers were dwindling and needed to be cherished and protected. She taught me how to hold a dagger and fight a demon, and then, when the Hell rifts broke open, she died in the most horrible way possible. I looked for her ashes but never found anything in the demon rubble.

I carried on her quest hunting monsters and those who would do fairies harm. Admittedly, some of my methods were brutal, but it sometimes took a monster to catch a monster. I often found myself wondering if Julia would be proud of me. If she would even recognize me. Or would she just see a monster?

"Where is that book?" I muttered to myself as I passed the stacks of gold and treasure that lined the walls of the cave. Aziolith was a bit of a hoarder, and his collection kept me with all the money I would ever need, leaving me free to pursue the important work of protecting fairy kind.

At the far end of the cave, I'd made a bed for myself and constructed a library out of the first edition books strewn about the place, along with ones I acquired in my travels. Some nights I simply read them there by the fire, content and warm. I enjoyed traveling, and I loved my work, but if home truly was where the heart was, then my home was Aziolith's cave. It was the only place I have ever been truly happy.

I sat down on my bed and rummaged through the library full of accounts of fairies, demonology, and magic. I had read every book at least a dozen times. Thriaska had warned me in cryptic detail of an impending Apocalypse, and every time I encountered such an omen, I would dive back into my research. His warning sounded familiar to me, but I couldn't place it.

"Here we go," I said, finding *On the Topic of Apocalyptic Scenarios*, a 13th-century text that was the basis of demonic research on the topic for over a hundred years after it was written. What Thriaska had said reminded me of a prophecy I'd read. I flipped through the ancient text until I located the passage written by an old man named Mathias:

Shall the blood of the fae be spilled across the world, their bones ground, the line salted with their deaths, and the blood of the demon bound in the pentagram, then the blood of a pixie, spilled in the depths of Hell, will rip a hole in the fabric of life, and the dead will walk once again with the living, with the help of four siblings, riding in harmony, and the titan, who will retake its place among the stars.

Mathias was an ancient soothsayer, but he was never wrong. I had used his predictions to stop three other

Apocalypse scenarios. Funny that every demon thought they were the first to bring about the Apocalypse. It was a stale goal as goals went. I had thwarted dozens of attempts.

Demons were bent on returning to the luxuries of Earth and living their savagery out in the open. It was not enough for them to rule Hell; they desired to rule Earth as well. Trouble was, demons weren't allowed on Earth. If they were caught, they'd be sent back to Hell. They were too proud for subterfuge and transfiguration charms. They hated having to live under any kinds of constraints.

Back in the 70s, Julia was part of a mini-Apocalypse, even if it was contained to one town and one night. A cult used her blood to open a portal to Hell, releasing several hundred demons and the dragon Aziolith. In true Julia fashion, she managed to close the portal and befriend the dragon Aziolith. It was one of several portals she closed during her life, and I have closed many more since. The veil was thin all over the world, and demons tried to poke through it into our world.

So Thriaska was looking for the blood of a pixie spilled in Hell. It had to be Julia's blood. I needed to save her for the good of all humanity, which meant that I had to do something that frightened me more than anything else and that I'd been avoiding for the last two hundred years: Travel to Hell.

Luckily—or not—I knew somebody that could help me enter the city of the dead.

***

On an unassuming street in Scotland sat an unassuming house erected hundreds of years ago, which was not uncommon for that part of Scotland. The novel thing about the house rested within its walls.

The house contained a bar that acted as a safe zone between angels and demons. Legend had it that the owner accidentally summoned a demon with a stick of butter, and instead of the demon flaying him alive, they got to chatting.

Word got around that the owner of the house was a decent fellow, and that led to more demons visiting. When angels came to investigate this strange new congregation of demons, they were served beer and peanuts. Just like that, friendships formed across the divide of Heaven and Hell. While they worked for their own means outside of the bar, inside, there were no enemies, only friends. Every demon and angel passed through at one point or another. It was the favorite watering hole for my least favorite demon, Charlie.

The house was protected by an ancient barrier that made it invisible unless you knew exactly where to look and vaporized anyone who meant to cause harm. I passed through with ease; all I needed was information. The bar was, as usual, pretty rowdy. A dozen angels and two dozen demons were screaming Journey's "Don't Stop Believing" at the top of their lungs. It was amazing how much music from the 20th century survived through the ages. Probably because so many musicians made deals with demons in those days.

My eyes scanned the bar until I spotted Charlie sitting in the corner, nursing a beer three sizes too big for him. Charlie was an imp and a trickster. He also happened to have dirt on everybody in the underworld and knew everything about how the place operated. If I needed to get into Hell, he was the ticket. He'd even offered to get me in, multiple times, but I'd always managed to avoid it. I had already been to Hell once, as a child. The smell of sulfur and agonized screams of the damned never left me.

"Charlie!" I shouted, walking over to him.

"What's it to y—" Charlie rolled his eyes at the sight of me. "Not you again. You are nothing but trouble, and I know all about trouble."

I slid down next to him. "I need your help."

"Of course you do," Charlie said, swigging his beer. "Too bad I'm not for sale."

"That's absolutely not true," I replied.

"You're right. I misspoke," he said. "What I meant was, I don't want your money because it always gets me into trouble."

I smiled. "I think you'll like this favor, though. Remember when you told me to go to Hell?"

Charlie snorted. "Which time?"

"All of them. What if I was seriously considering it?"

"You want to go to Hell?" Charlie laughed and slapped the bar. "Didn't you learn from your friend Julia? Hell ain't a vacation spot."

"I'm not there to vacation. I'm there to stop an Apocalypse."

"Another one?" Charlie said. "Man, people just need to chill out down there with that. I mean, I know those guys hate Katrina, but—"

"They hate Katrina?"

"Oh yeah. Big time."

"Why?"

Charlie took another swig of beer. "I mean, she's a woman, number one. She's a human, number two, and she's a complete jerk, number three. Still, it's not worth it to kill her. We got a good thing up here. I say we just deal with it. She'll be dead soon enough."

"You think?"

"If the chatter in Hell is to be believed." Charlie nodded.

"You think they're trying to start an Apocalypse to kill her?"

"I mean, I don't know about any Apocalypse, but somebody's trying to arrange the pieces to kill her and take control. Way too much work if you ask me."

"Who?"

Charlie screwed up his face, thinking. "Asmodeus, probably. Katrina's basically pissed off every demon in Hell during her reign, but he's pretty sore about being ruled by a woman."

"Okay." I nodded, taking in all this information. "I need to get to Hell, and I need you to help me."

"I could kill you," Charlie said with a lopsided smile.

"No, that won't work. I need to come in past the gates. Otherwise, I'll be waiting for judgment for a hundred years, and this needs to happen now."

"I know a ghost who can get you past the gates, but it'll cost you."

"I have money," I replied. "More money than I could use in ten lifetimes."

"Rub it in, why don't you?" Charlie muttered. "Unfortunately, none of your money will be any good to him. You need a special coin. Rare on Earth, minted in the eighth century by Satanic monks. I only know three people that traffic in them."

"Give me a name."

"Sure, if it'll get you out of my face. But I'm gonna need something from you."

"What?" I said. "And before you answer, I am not giving you my soul or the location to Aziolith's cave."

"Fine," Charlie rolled his eyes. "I need something else. I need you to get something from my house and deliver it. I can't go back to Hell yet, for…reasons, and this guy's been waiting on this package for a long time. He's really chapping my ass about it."

"Fine," I replied. "I'll do it."

Charlie cocked his head. "Don't you want to know what's in it?"

"No. I don't care."

"Fair," Charlie said, writing an address on a bar napkin. "This is my address. Package is under the bed unless one of my brat kids stole it. You can't miss it. Oh, and it makes your hands go numb if you touch it for long enough." He flipped it over and wrote another address. "And this is the address in Rome where you have to drop it off. Got it?"

I nodded. "Got it."

Charlie smiled at me and leaned back from the bar. "I'd say 'godspeed,' but I think you'll need demon speed instead."

"I'm sure I'll be fine."

Charlie chuckled and reached into his pocket. "That's what your friend said, too." He pulled out an amulet on a string which glinted red like a ruby. "Wear this, or the heat of Hell will destroy you, got it?"

I snatched the amulet from Charlie's hand.

"And remember, if you die in Hell, it'll be a real mess for me, so do me a favor and don't die."

My eyes narrowed. "Yes, I will make sure not to die...so you don't have to do paperwork."

Charlie turned back to his beer. "Whatever gets you there, sweetheart."

CHAPTER 8

Katrina

Location: Devil's Castle, Hell

Even after two hundred years, I could barely make my way through the sinewy hallways of Lucifer's old castle without getting lost. The walls seemed to shift positions every time I walked through the warped corridors. The gothic black, twisted design didn't inspire much confidence, and every pillar screamed, "abandon all hope."

The one positive about this place was that if someone tried to assassinate me, they would have to navigate the ridiculous architecture. They'd be spinning around in circles to find the right room, and there were hundreds of rooms. I hung on to that positive thought.

"Hey, kiddo!" My dad's face brightened when he saw me walking into the throne room. "Fancy seeing you here!"

I had saved Dad from the pits right after I came to Hell and moved him here. That was the first time I'd broken the rules of Hell. But I was the first human to rule there and the first Devil with a family. I was insistent that something be done about eternal torture because everybody I loved faced it when they died. Heck, even people I hated didn't deserve torture for eternity.

I searched for my mother for a long time, but she was gone, and her records lost. That was what prompted me to modernize Hell. No soul deserved to be lost. The thought of what the demons were doing here, what they were carrying out in my name, made my stomach churn and kept me diligently working to fix the broken system every day.

Honestly, I was quite proud of my work in Dis. We leveled half the city to rebuild skyscrapers, allowing thousands more demons and monsters to walk its streets. For generations, the demons had been stuck in the pits of Hell, working at the behest of the Devil. I allowed them to leave the pits and build a life, get married, even form unions to hound me about working conditions.

There was no hope left in Hell, and I refused to abandon what little of it was left inside of me. It was one of the few things that separated me from the demons. Demons could not hope, or wish, or dream for a better world. If I abandoned the small part of me that could, then I would be no better than them…and I had to be better than them.

Besides all that, it was a lot less boring now.

"Hi, Dad," I said.

"Why the long face?" he asked.

"Somebody's trying to kill me."

There had been assassination attempts since the day I took office, as one faction or another found one of the five weapons that could murder me. Eventually, we acquired all of those weapons—except for the Sword of Damocles, which was at least accounted for in Heaven—and the assassination attempts stopped…until now.

Dad sighed. "Again?"

I nodded, and he joined me on my walk. I was heading toward the garden in the middle of the castle, the only place I actually enjoyed. Well, besides my dad's room. I slept on the couch there when I felt like a total failure, which was often.

I sighed. "Yes, again. I think it's just going to be a constant thing now. Or at least…it's never going to go away completely since everybody hates me now. I really messed it up this time."

He shook his head. "I don't believe that. Look at the royal family. There are like zero attempts on their life. Everybody loves them."

"Everybody doesn't love them," I replied, descending the spiral stairs that led to the dungeon, with the garden on the other side of it. "They just have good security. I'll bet they get constant death threats."

Dad scratched his bare chin. "You know, I never thought about it like that. Maybe they do."

"I don't know what I'm doing here, Dad. I feel like I'm out of my element, even after two hundred years." I hadn't admitted that to anybody. If these demons found out I was weak of mind, they would ratchet up their attacks.

"Well, you are, kiddo."

"Thanks," I said.

"What I mean is you're a human trying to do the job of a god. Even Lucifer wasn't good at it, right?"

"No, he was horrible."

"And he's an angel, or at least he was, I think. It's really confusing, actually. Anyway, he had two thousand years to get good at ruling Hell, and he never did! Remind me, how many of these demons have jobs now, with insurance? Could Lucifer or Velaska say they'd provided that?"

"No, neither of them could say that." I gave him a sheepish smile. "I wanted…I wanted these guys to rise above their station and attain something better."

"And all they want is to subsist and maybe have a warm drink now and then. They just want things to be like they used to be." Dad put his arm around my shoulder. "Katrina, you were given a horrible situation, and you're making the best of it. I think that's admirable."

"Thanks, Dad. Yeah, if these monsters don't like it, they can suck noodles." I turned to him. "I just feel like the worst."

He smiled at me. "Well, you're definitely not the worst. Thomas was the worst. He took control of being Devil, immediately invaded Heaven, and was killed in like a day. So, that one is the worst there ever was, bar none."

I laughed. "Yes, fair enough. Thomas was the worst."

Dad elbowed me in the ribs. "And how many of these Devils can say that they've killed not one but *two* of their predecessors?"

I grinned in spite of myself. Dad could always cheer me up. I was just a regular girl, a bike messenger, from Oregon. Not even Portland, Oregon, or somewhere exciting like Bend or Eugene. All I wanted to do was get stoned and avoid responsibility. Then the Apocalypse came, and all I wanted to do was survive. I fought hard and eventually traveled to Reno to pimp slap Lucifer. That led me to Hell, to intervene in the battle between Heaven and Hell. That led me to kill not one but two devils: Lucifer and Thomas.

"And you're young, still."

"I'm over 200 years old." I became the Devil after I killed Lucifer and Thomas. Since then, I'd been doing my best, but even at my best, I was scrambling to keep my head above water. Somebody always wanted to kill me, and it never stopped. It was exhausting.

"Yeah, 200 is old for a human, but compared to the gods, that's really young. They probably sucked at this when they were two hundred."

I scratched my head. "They still kind of suck at it now."
I suppose it was naïve to think that it would continue to be peaceful for me, that demons would welcome the new world order I laid out for them. It was, after all, very different from the thousands of years of rule they were used to from the previous Devils. Velaska kept the way of the old gods, and Lucifer was too incompetent at ruling to change anything.

Dad smiled. "There you go. So how can you expect yourself to be perfect if the gods aren't even perfect at it, and they literally made this place?"

"Fair enough," I replied. "Good point."

We walked through a door, and the dungeon broke into a garden, brimming with light, birds, and flowers. I walked there often. It led to the armory, which meant that I could kill two birds with one stone. It was the only place I had found in Hell that didn't smell like sulfur and brimstone, a refreshing change from the dank, harsh black walls of the rest of the castle. It was my quiet sanctuary. I enjoyed falling backward onto the grass and listening to the birds chirping.

Or, I usually enjoyed it…when there wasn't an intruder waiting there for me. Across the square, a blue demon dressed in black held a bow in his hand.

"Hey!" I yelled out.

The demon shot up and smiled at me. He pulled two arrows out of a quiver on his back and shot at me in rapid succession. One flew past me, but the other ripped through my left shoulder.

I looked at my shoulder, and blood oozed from it. "OW!"

"Katrina!" Dad shouted.

"Stay here!" I screamed.

The demon flung two more arrows before running back into the castle. I flung open the door and chased after him, but when I entered the building, I couldn't see anything. A stifling darkness collapsed upon me.

I fell to my knees and pressed my hand to the ground. Blood ran down my arm and pooled beneath me. As it did, whispers rose in the darkness, and a cold chill ran down my spine.

Die. Fall. Weak.

The world became hazy, and then my arm gave out. I fell to the ground and blacked out.

CHAPTER 9

Kimberly

Location: Rome, Italy

I rematerialized inside the back of a Harry Potter store in the "Roman Ghetto" on the south side of Rome. The store was run by a dryad who loved all things magica and was the perfect place to teleport into the city. I didn't mind materializing in front of a random monument if I didn't have any other choice, but I preferred to transition where people wouldn't ask questions, and Rome was a city where people asked a lot of questions.

Rome had a deeper history of magic than most, being home to many gods before they left Earth, and the seat of the Roman Empire, whose emperors were often magical creatures. I brushed myself off in the back room and then stepped into the front of the store.

The dryad who ran the store had undergone extensive plastic surgery to make him look like a human, including a complete facial reconstruction and bright, white veneers that shone across the room whenever he smiled, which he did when he saw me approach. His name was Vincenzo, but I called him Vince. He hated it.

"I thought I heard something back there," Vince said in a thick Italian accent. "I hoped it was a rat."

I smiled. "I didn't destroy anything this time, Vince."

"Praise be," the dryad said. "Are you here long?"

"Not sure. I hope not." I waved to him on my way out the front door. "I have to go, though."

"Have a great day," the dryad said. That's what I loved about him, though. In a world that questioned everything, he never asked questions.

I stepped onto the cobblestone street and turned toward the Parthenon; an old temple converted to an old church converted to a tourist destination. What I loved about Rome most was that every two feet, you ran into something that was older than the United States. The people who lived there treated the ancient monuments like they were not important and simultaneously revered them in equal measure. I watched tour groups marvel at ancient columns, and then drunks peed on them moments later.

I followed several narrow, winding streets toward the address Charlie gave me until I came upon a thin brownstone. I slammed the iron, lion head door knocker and heard the creak of footsteps. There were also whimpering sounds coming from the other side of the door, and when it opened, I saw a hook-nosed woman with pale skin and bloodshot eyes blowing her nose into a tissue.

"What do you want?" she asked.

"Charlie sent me," I replied. "I need help getting into the underworld. Are you Edna?" She was the one who could get me the coin I needed.

"Yes, but…this is not a good time," the woman sniffed. "I have—issues—"

"I'm afraid this can't wait," I said, placing my hand in the door as she tried to slam it on me. "You have to pull yourself together. This concerns the fate of the world."

"Doesn't it always. I just don't—I'm distraught!" She started bawling in the doorway. "Can't you see that?"

She fell to the floor and curled up in a ball, rocking back and forth. I knelt to her level. I didn't like being a therapist, but sometimes it was necessary to move the plot along. "What's wrong?"

She blew her nose on the wad of tissues in her hand. "My familiar, Gustavo…he's gone!"

"Familiar?"

Big sloppy tears fell out of her eyes. "My…cat!"

"He ran away?"

Edna kept sniffling. "No. He just left. I know exactly where he is, but he won't come home. He says we've grown a-a-apart, and he needs his space."

"This is a cat, right?" I asked, confused.

"He's the love of my life."

"Whatever," I sighed. I never understood people's connection to their pets. "Okay, so what if I get the cat back. Would you help me then?"

She nodded. "Of course. If my snooker-whiskers was home, then I could think straight."

"Fine," I replied. "Give me an address. When I get back, I need a coin that will take me to the underworld."

"D-d-eal!"

***

At the site where Caesar, the last great magical emperor, was stabbed so many centuries ago, laid the ruins of an old forum that had been converted to a cat sanctuary. Hundreds of cats lived there, coming and going as they pleased, happily pissing and shitting on the spot where Caesar bled out. It was a fitting tribute, probably. Certainly, Brutus and his conspirators would have approved.

It was midnight when the last of a million tours passed through the square, and the city was dead, or as dead as a major international city could be, and before I hopped the railing to the cat sanctuary. Two cats stared at me for a moment when I landed before deciding I was wholly uninteresting and going back to licking their butts.

"Gustavo?" I called, walking through the mossy ruins of the forum. Caesar apparently died at the spot where a large oak tree rose from the ground and hung over the street above. I made my way toward it slowly, zigging and zagging through the broken ruins. "Gustavo?" It seemed idiotic that the fate of the world depended on me finding a cat, but I had done weirder things while saving the world. "Gustavo!"

"What?" I heard a cat meow from the tree above me. "Keep it down. You'll wake the dead."

I looked up to see the glowing green eyes of a cat in the tree above me. "Gustavo?"

"How many cats do you think can talk?" he replied in a huff. "Yes, I'm Gustavo, idiot."

"It's nice to meet you," I said to him. "Can you come down here so we can talk?"

He scoffed. "Why would I want to talk to you?"

"I just came from seeing Edna. She wants you to come home. She really misses you."

"Of course she does. I'm the best thing that ever happened to her. The reverse, however, is less true. She's all right, I suppose," he added with a sigh. "A bit needy, though."

"Really? I mean, isn't there anything you like about Edna?"

The cat shook his head. "Not that I can think of."

I pressed my hand against the tree, trying to think of a new approach. "Doesn't she feed you?"

"Not as often as I'd like, but...yes, I suppose she does."

I studied the cat. Appealing to his stomach seemed to be working. "It must be a far cry better than the food here, though."

"True." Gustavo sighed. "It's mostly just dry pebbles and what I catch myself."

"I'll bet there's wet food at home."

"Well, yes, and yummy sardines, much better than mice, but I felt...stifled there. Edna is holding back my creative expression."

"And you get that here?" I gestured vaguely at the ruins.

Gustavo shook his head. "Honestly, not really. The cats here are plebian at best. I have been thinking of heading to Paris. The cats there know how to live."

I pushed back from the tree. "Listen, Gustavo. I've been to every corner of this planet, and I can tell you it's no better anywhere. Every city is pretty much the same, plus or minus ten percent."

Gustavo stuck his nose up in the air. "I don't believe you."

"Let me show you." I held out my arms. "Come down here, and I will take you to Paris right now."

Gustavo's eyes lit up. "Really?"

I nodded. "Really. And if you love it there, I won't bring you back, okay?"

"That is a deal." The branch rustled as Gustavo walked along it on his way to me.

"May I pick you up?" I asked when he was within reach.

"You may, and thank you for asking." He sniffed. "Edna never asks."

I gathered him up and thought of the Eiffel Tower. In a flash of purple light, we were standing in front of it. In the dead of night, I didn't mind traveling in the middle of everything. Besides, right now, time was of the essence.

"Here you go," I said, putting Gustavo down.

"It's beautiful," he said, turning in slow circles and gazing at all of the city lights. "So many lights everywhere. This truly is the city of my dreams."

"It is pretty, but look out there," I said, pointing to the skyline. "It's still buildings and cars and people, just like Rome." I paused and took a deep breath in. "And smell that in the air?"

Gustavo's lip curled. "It smells…like Rome."

"I know. There's different food here and different people and customs." I knelt beside him. "But in the end, it's still going to feel the same. After a time, you'll get bored." I stood up and walked a few paces away before turning back. "You have to ask yourself, Gustavo, why do you really want to leave Edna?"

"She's holding me back," the cat responded. But I could tell he wasn't so sure.

"Gustavo…" I said. My voice was nearly a whisper. "Do you love her?"

The cat sighed. "I do, but…"

I pet him along his back, and his butt arched into the air. "Let me tell you, cat, I haven't loved anything in two hundred years. If you love something, you should fight to make it work. Nobody else is going to love you like Edna does. You'll have to learn how to deal with her quirks, or you'll die alone."

Gustavo rubbed his cheek on my leg. "That doesn't sound so bad."

"I'm going to die alone," I replied. "Trust me; it's that bad."

"You're a real bummer, did you know that?" Gustavo said. "But I think you're right. Let's go home."

***

"Gustavo!" Edna shrieked when she opened the door, and I held the cat toward her. "My baby!"

She reached for him, but I pulled him back. "You're suffocating him."

"Excuse me?" Edna said. "How do you—"

"It's true!" Gustavo shouted.

I stepped into the door jamb so she couldn't close the door on me. "And he doesn't like that you just pick him up and don't ask him whether it's okay."

"I—I'm sorry," Edna said, dropping her hands.

"He loves you, and you love him," I said, petting his head. "You can figure it out. Just talk to each other, okay?"

She nodded. "Thank you."

I placed the cat in her hands. "You're welcome. Now, about that coin..."

"Of course," she said. "Anything you need for bringing back my schnooky-booky." She moved aside so I could enter, then closed the door behind me. Gustavo was rolling his eyes at her nickname, and I ignored him.

"I need to get to the underworld. Charlie said you have the type of coin I'll need to get there."

Edna had moved into the kitchen and was opening a can of sardines while Gustavo ran in figure-eights around her legs. "It's very dangerous for a human down in Hell."

I smiled. "Then it's a good thing I'm not a human. Or, at least all human."

"I have a coin that should work to bribe the gatekeeper, assuming the big jerk hasn't raised his prices in the last decade. Wait here." She reappeared from her bedroom after a few moments, holding a gold coin the size of her palm. "I hope you don't mind tunnels."

I frowned. "I never think about them, really."

"Well, I hope for your sake you don't get claustrophobic. Where you're going, you'll need to be very comfortable in tunnels." Edna put the coin in my hand. "Don't worry, though. I'll give you detailed instructions."

***

I blinked my eyes and reappeared in the middle of the Roman Forum, the largest marketplace in ancient Rome. It was little more than ruins, now. The place didn't look like much more than a partially paved-over hole, but underneath lay an entrance to the heart of the underworld.

I walked past temples converted to churches converted to rubble as I snaked my way through the structure to its base, where I would find The Lacus Curtius. People once believed it to be a Gateway to Hell until they realized their superstition was dumb. As usual, the superstition had more than a grain of truth to it. In this case, it had a whole load of truth to it.

"Mettius Curtius, I seek you," I said as I walked up to the hole, just as Edna had instructed me.

"Who are you?" a voice grumbled. As I stood there, a ghost materialized, dressed in the armor of the Roman legion.

"Do you guard this entrance to Hell?" I asked.

"I do," he replied. "To be specific, I protect those that try to enter Hell more than I guard Hell. The demons there can handle that very well themselves."

I pulled the coin from my pocket, minted in the eighth century BCE and forged with magic, with a bust of Caesar on one side and a butterfly on the other. "With this coin, I request passage into the underworld."

The ghost floated forward. "Do you know what you ask? No mortal may enter Hell and hope to survive."

"I have been there and survived already."

"Lies!" The guard drew his sword. "How dare you—"

"It's not a lie!" I shouted. "And even if it wasn't, why do you care? I have your toll. Grant me passage willingly, or I will return when I have figured out how to kill a ghost."

Mettius grumbled, sliding his sword away. Then, he held out his hand. "If your request be true, place the coin in my hand. Should it stay in my palm without falling through, you will be granted passage."

I took a deep breath and placed the coin in his hand. It shook for a moment but then stabilized, and Mettius's hand clasped around it. "May the gods have mercy on your soul."

I nodded to him and ducked into the opening. As I bent to a crawl, the foul stench of sulfur invaded my nostrils.

CHAPTER 10

Julia

Location: Asmodeus's Castle, Hell

The door to the cell creaked open, and I watched a familiar face enter, his body silhouetted by light from beyond the door. I squinted as the light streamed in.

"Hi, Julia."

I recognized him. He was a friend of Akta's and had become a friend of mine in the hundreds of years since I came to the underworld. "Hi, Sven."

Sven was a troll, which meant he was big, lumbering, and plodding. While most trolls stuck out their chests, broad and proud, Sven always tried to shrink into his gigantic frame and moved with smaller, more delicate movements than the average troll.

"I'm sorry," he said, holding his head low. He was cowardly and, though he sometimes came to the aid of others, was frightened of most things, especially being alone.

"You work for Asmodeus now?" I asked.

"I do," he replied. His voice sounded sad.

It wasn't surprising. The demon lords talked about unity and camaraderie. They gave monsters a sense of purpose and a common enemy to rally behind. Katrina. It was easy to convince monsters—or anyone, really—that their lives sucked because of somebody else, even though it was usually because of their own actions. Looking inward is a painful exercise. Instead, the monsters looked at

Katrina and her modernization efforts as the villain of their afterlives.

"Well, that's okay, I guess," I said. "Since you're here to rescue me now."

I knew the odds were low, but trolls were notoriously stupid, and Sven was particularly stupid among trolls. I had a chance to twist his mind and possibly set myself free.

Sven looked away. "Actually…"

"You are here to rescue me, aren't you?" I asked, trying to hammer his guilt.

He sighed. "I'm sorry that it had to be you. It couldn't be Akta. They promised. They said…it had to be you."

I chuckled at him, trying to keep the mood light. "Sven, don't be an idiot. Let me out of here, buddy. We're friends."

Sven shook his head. "Asmodeus is my friend."

"Please," I said. "He does not care about you. You have to want a—"

"I want Earth!" Sven said. His volume and abruptness startled both of us. "I want Asmodeus as Devil. I want things go back to how they were…" His lip curled. "…before Katrina."

My face dropped, and I shook my head, sick of acting like everything was okay. "Things can't go back, Sven. Don't you understand? No matter who's in charge of Hell, things are going to change."

"Lucifer didn't change."

"That's because he sucked," I said. "Don't make a huge mistake." I held up my shackles. "You can still be a hero."

"I'm sorry," he said, turning to the door. "Just wanted to say…I'm sorry. It will be over soon."

"What are you trying to do?" I asked. "If you're going to kill me, the least you can do is tell me the truth."

He turned back to me. "Ragnarok."

"What is that?"

"Apocalypse." The troll took a deep breath. "Biggest Apocalypse ever."

CHAPTER 11

Katrina

Location: Devil's Castle, Earth

My father found me in the darkness and pulled me back into the castle. Half dead, he dragged me through the dungeon and back to my bed-chamber. Healers worked on me through the night, working to mend the gash that ripped through my shoulder from the bow. Had it penetrated six inches to the right, I would have died.

Me. Dead.

I had not felt pain since I became the Devil, but as they worked to close the hole in my body, the pain coursed through my body, jolting every inch of me with a blistering pain. Even once they finished closing me up, the jagged scar ached when I moved it. They assured me the pain would subside in time, but they should have known better to lie to me, the queen of all lies.

While I yearned to rest, the kingdom of Hell moved on, and I needed to know exactly why I almost died. I rubbed the sore spot on my shoulder as General K'bab'nik walked me through the armory. He might have been a caveman once. His brow protruded from his face, and his eyes were narrow and beady.

Walking through this place reminded me of walking through a museum full of ancient artifacts. I had tried, on more than one occasion, to replace the army's swords and medieval weaponry with upgraded guns and laser rifles, but the generals refused. As a result, the armory was filled with the last artifacts of a bygone age.

"The good news is that the thief didn't steal much, just one object."

I looked over at him. "Why do I have a feeling there's bad news, General Kebab?"

He flinched. He accepted that I would never call him by his real name, but it clearly stung him every time. That tickled me.

"It's not good news. Unfortunately," the general said, choking down his irritation, "what they took was the Bow of Misery."

"And that's one of the five objects in the solar system that can kill me, right?"

He nodded. "That is correct."

"That doesn't make me happy." I poked my finger into the general's chiseled chest. "You had one job, general. Protect me."

General Kebab glowered. "Actually, I have many jobs, ma'am, including overseeing protection on your construction projects, this castle, and every other whim you might have for me." Resentment oozed from his voice.

"You're free to leave any time you want, general."

"I don't believe I am, ma'am." He straightened his shoulders and lifted his chin. "If I left, it would be bedlam."

"Worse than this?" I asked.

"Much worse," he said. "I know you only care about the weapons that can kill you, but many weapons can kill a demon. I've sworn to protect all of Hell, not just you, ma'am."

"Fair enough," I said with a sigh. "Where are the other objects that can kill me? I know we tracked them down a while ago."

He cocked his head, trying to remember. "The Lance of Conquest is on Mars, with the Queen. The Hammer of War is lost to the ages."

"What do you mean, *lost*? We were supposed to have all five. Why don't we have all five? Why would you lie to me about that?"

"My apologies," General Kebab said. "I suppose 'lost' is not the right word. It's more that it has never been found. We've searched for it, and we know it is somewhere in Hell, but we have no idea where. By Yilir's hand, it is hidden still, and in that way, you are safe from it."

"For all you know," I replied. "But it could have been found and sitting in somebody's dining room for all we know, right?"

The general cleared his throat and shot me a nervous glance. "We believe it still to be lost."

"Great. Well, that's something, I guess." I threw my hands in the air and began pacing. "If it's hidden, then it can't be used to kill me, but never lie to me again."

"Yes, ma'am," General Kebab replied, bowing his head. "As for the final weapon, the Sword of Damocles, you know where it is, ma'am. I believe you've held it before."

"I used it to kill Thomas," I remarked absently. "It's bound in Heaven. I think that one's as safe from any demon as anything can be."

"Still, you should warn Lucifer and the angels of what's happening down here."

"That's funny." I stopped pacing and caught his eye. "Do you think they will actually care about somebody trying to kill me?"

The general looked away. "No, but you should still do it, on the off chance that they do."

"They are so pompous, but fine," I grumbled. "What about the intruder? Do you know anything about how they got into the castle?"

The general shook his head. "No, but I've heard legends about a second door that can enter the castle. In all our searches, we never found it. I only know one person who ever used it."

"Who?" I asked.

"Akta."

"She's not a person," I spat. "She's a pixie and an annoying one at that."

"That's true, ma'am," the general replied. "But she's the only one I know of who's been through the gate."

"Let's just get this straight." I counted on my fingers as I spoke. "Right now, whoever is trying to kill me has the Dagger of Obsolescence and the Bow of Misery. The Lance of Conquest is on Mars, the Sword of Damocles is in Heaven, and the Hammer of War is missing somewhere in Hell, we think."

"That's…correct," General Kebab replied.

"Fabulous," I replied. "Carry on, general. Try not to get me killed, okay?"

"Will do, ma'am."

***

"So, not only did you fail to protect a second of my weapons from being stolen," I said to Akta. I had summoned her to the throne room. "But you also failed to mention there was an underground way into this castle which somebody could use to make their way to the armory, or me."

Akta shrugged. She was one of the only non-demons in Hell who showed no fear around me. "I thought you knew. I mean, everybody knew, didn't they? It was guarded by the Brambles of Agony, and Velaska invited suitors to use the door during her reign. It was…kind of a terribly-kept secret."

I scratched my head. "So, how long has this entrance existed?"

Akta held her hands out, palms up. "As long as I've been in Hell, my Devil."

She was so smug. I wanted to rip her head off and stuff it down her neck, but I took a deep breath. She was also my best soldier, and I knew she could be trusted. Even if she was infuriating.

I slumped down in the seat of my throne. I was beginning to feel defeated. "Is there anything else you aren't telling me?"

"No offense," Akta replied blankly. "But I don't know what you don't know."

I sat up and crossed my arms. "Nothing else about my castle or the attempts on my life?"

She shook her head. "Nothing like that. I'm following up on a lead, but right now, I'm working on nothing more than a hunch."

"What's your hunch?" I asked.

"I believe that The True Path church has something to do with this," Akta said. "Have you heard of it?"

"Those religious nutjobs?" I frowned, thinking of everything I knew about The True Path. "They've been trying to get an audience with me for months. They are not fans of mine."

"No, they are not," Akta added emphatically. "I have a friend…he told me some horrible things about you. He said he learned about them from the church."

"Even your friends are against me?"

Akta raised her eyebrows. "Ma'am, you are trying to modernize Hell. It's not going over well. Who do you know who would want you dead?"

I sighed. "Everyone, it would seem."

"I'm sorry, ma'am." She seemed genuinely sympathetic. "Heavy is the head, they say."

"If you find anything else, let me know." I leaned forward so I could hold my face in my hands. This was bad.

"I will, ma'am." Akta nodded. "I've read some of their literature front to back, and it's a bunch of nonsense, honestly. One thing's for sure, they don't like you. It's like an entire religion built simply to reminisce about the past and air their grievances about you."

"Great," I replied, wincing. "So they're a well-funded 4Chan group."

"I…don't understand that reference."

"Never mind." I shook my head. "Hey, before you go, show my generals where the second entrance to the castle is. The one by the garden."

Akta laughed. "No offense, ma'am, but those same generals have guarded this castle since the time of Velaska. They know about every entrance into and out of the castle, and probably ones I don't know about. There is no doubt in my mind about it."

I stopped rubbing my face and looked at her. "So they're trying to kill me, too?"

"I don't know," Akta replied with an arched eyebrow. "But they are certainly lying to you about not knowing about the door."

"It wouldn't be the first time today they lied to me." I threw my arms in the air. "Is anyone not trying to kill me?"

"I am not, ma'am."

"For now." I sighed. "Leave me. I have to make an uncomfortable call."

***

Since the time of Lucifer, there had always been a direct communication line between Heaven and Hell for emergencies. I hated using it, but when the stakes were high, it was necessary to get chastised by the pompous windbags in Elysia. I placed my hand on the wall behind my throne. A hologram of the archangel Michael appeared.

"What is the meaning of this, Katrina?" Michael hissed, his floppy hair cascading down his long robe. "Hell doesn't—"

I sighed loudly, interrupting him. Michael stopped speaking, mouth still open, glowering. "I know, I know. 'Hell doesn't just get to talk to Heaven without a reason.'" I mimicked his tone when I said it. "I know that, and I have a reason. Trust me, I would never, ever contact you unless it was important. Is Lucifer there?"

Michael looked around for a moment, suddenly sheepish. "He's here, but he's indisposed."

"Somebody has stolen two of the weapons that can kill me."

Michael didn't react. "That sounds like a you problem."

I paused, collecting myself. I wanted to punch his stupid angel face. "Not if they reach Heaven. We think they're after the swor—"

"Enough!" Michael scoffed. He waved dismissively. "In ten thousand years, there has never been an incursion from Hell onto Heaven."

"What are you talking about?" I threw my hands in the air. "There was just one two hundred years ago. It's literally the reason why I'm here in Hell."

Michael itched his chin, looking bored. "Yes, well, there hasn't been an incursion not led by the Devil, and you are not about to lead an incursion on Heaven, are you?"

I shook my head. "I would rather vaporize into a million pieces."

"Please do."

"Listen, I'm just trying to be a good Devil and a team player by warning you about this. I don't know what's happening down here, but we're struggling to figure it out as quickly as possible."

"Figure it out more quickly, and don't bother us with trivialities again," Michael growled. "Go back to your sulfur."

The communication cut out, and for a split moment, I thought about ripping open the gates of Hell and marching into Heaven myself. They could titter at me all they wanted, but the truth was I drove fear into their hearts. I saw it on their faces the last time I was there. They treated me like an uncontrollable monster they hoped would stay in its place. For now, I would, but I was getting very sick of them talking down to me.

CHAPTER 12

Kimberly

Location: Hell

I crawled for miles. I lost all concept of time and space.
Finally, I noticed the sting of sulfur in my nostrils getting
stronger. Eventually, I saw the light at the end of the long,
hot tunnel. Charlie had given me a medallion to alleviate
the incredible heat, and I found myself grateful and a bit
surprised. I worried that with the number of times Charlie
had screwed me throughout our time together, the trinket
would have been useless.

When I finally reached the end of the tunnel and stood
up, shaking out my cramped limbs, I stood in the middle of
a large barren field filled with broken clay. In front of me
ran a highway five lanes wide, with cars and trucks zipping
in either direction.

I certainly did not expect this level of modernity in
Hell, especially nothing that so closely resembled the
infrastructure on Earth. The Apocalypse had set humanity
back a good hundred years when it came to advancements,
and we were just starting to return to the status quo. The
first flying cars were set to hit the market in a couple of
years. I was already seeing billboards and commercials.

I walked toward the highway to get a closer look. A
large green sign stood at the side of the road.

BOD'UN: 3 miles

GR'ASD'N: 50 miles

DIS: 100 miles

Squinting, I could make out a little town down a sharp hill. Perhaps there would be a bus north to the Gates of Abnegation. I needed to get to Dis, but not without a guide to help me navigate the city. I knew where to find one, assuming he still lived inside the Dragon Caves.

After an hour's hike down the busy road, I arrived at a small town not unlike the place on Earth where I was born. It was little more than a stop on a freeway, with a few houses behind the prominent gas station immediately off the exit.

A sign for fuel towered high above the road, and I headed for it. If there was anyone that could help me get to Dis, the gas station attendant would be the most likely. I crossed the asphalt pavement of the street to get there. Two cars sat filling their tanks with petrol; the first a female orc in a red sedan scolding her kid as it tried to lock the car doors, and the second an older demon with white hair leaning against a motorcycle.

"Hey, baby," the white-haired demon grunted. "Want a ride?"

"Pass," I replied, walking into the station.

Inside the filling station, a tiny, green creature sat next to a large register flipping through a *Playdemon* magazine that he'd propped up on the "take a coin" jar. A fat, red demon stretched seductively across a bed on the cover, wearing nothing but a feather boa.

"Oh, yeah, baby," the creature said, drool building on his lip.

"Excuse me?" I said, jarring him from his concentration. The creature slid the magazine off the counter and flew into the air. "I need some help."

"Welcome to the Sip and Go." His green skin was now tinged with red. "I'm Yr'lut'ol. How can I help you?"

"Yes," I said, trying to remain as courteous as possible. "I'm a little lost. Can you tell me where I am?"

"Satan's asscrack," Yr'lut'ol said without missing a beat. "Right between nowhere and the gods' forsaken abyss."

That wasn't the answer I was looking for. "Do you have a map, maybe?"

He pointed to the counter between us. "Bottom shelf on your side."

I bent down and scanned the shelves. When I found the map, I opened it and spread it out over the counter.

"So, you're here." Yr'lut'ol hovered into the air and pointed to the northeast corner of the map. "About a hundred miles south of Dis and two hundred south of the Gates of Abnegation." Then he added, "That's where humans enter Hell."

"Is there a bus or something that will take me to the Gates?"

"Sure, toots." He grinned. "There are all sorts of buses between Dis and the Gates. Great tourist money in them hills, you know?"

"No, I don't know," I replied.

Yr'lut'ol shrugged. "Most demons ain't never seen the Gates. It's a damn shame. They take the kids on field trips all the time. It's nice."

"Where can I catch this bus?"

"One will be along soon enough, but I gotta say, you don't look like the kind of person that's got any money. Do you got any money?"

I worked on folding the map then set it down again on the counter. "I mean, I have a purse full of coins, but I don't know if they work here. I'm from out of town."

"Yeah, that's what I thought. Well, buses need money. Everything needs money."

"I have gold." I patted my belt, then froze. My purse wasn't there. I must have lost it in the tunnels. "Or I did. It looks like I lost it."

"That's a common story, sweetheart. Everybody's just lost their money and singing a sob story." He turned back to the register. "But Yr'lut'ol don't care. Broke is broke. You can put the map back if you're not gonna buy it. This ain't a library."

I took one last look at the page still open. "Do those buses take you to the Dragon Caves?"

Yr'lut'ol shook his head. "You definitely don't want to go there without money. The dragons will eat you up without a worthy sacrifice."

"I'll keep that in mind."

"Or don't. It's your funeral. Dragon Caves are northeast about seventy-five miles. Buses don't run out there, though. You'll have to walk or find a ride."

I looked out the window. The biker had just finished filling up. I sighed, knowing what I had to do.

"Hey," I said, walking toward the biker with a smile. "You still up for giving me a ride?"

***

The demon biker was surprisingly friendly. He had just retired from his job as an accountant and was bumming around Hell for a year before starting his new career as a torturer in a Hell pit on Mars. Apparently, retirement didn't mean much to immortal beings. They took one after every thirty years of work and then changed jobs. It sounded kind of nice.

There had not been any roads for the last twenty miles. The biker told me that the dragons had eaten any construction workers that came too close, so eventually, they gave up on the road-building project. It made for a bumpy ride. When we arrived at the Dragon Caves, he slowed to a stop and idled his engine. After studying the terrain for a few moments, he said, "You sure you want to go alone?"

I nodded. "I know my friend. He's very private."

The white-haired demon was still frowning. "It's not safe here, you know? These dragons are dangerous."

I chuckled. "I know, but this is Hell. It's not safe anywhere."

"Fair enough," he said before waving goodbye. He gunned his engine and drove away.

While he was on Earth, Aziolith had told me about his home in the Dragon Caves. Even the most brutal monsters of Hell feared to travel there. For that reason, it was peaceful—nice, even—every now and again, there was a blood feud to deal with when dragons got territorial. Otherwise, there was mostly silence throughout the cave system, except for the occasional dragon snoring. Aziolith encouraged me to visit him there when my time came.

My wings glowed blue against the orange fields of Hell. I flew across the barren wastelands, past the glowing eyes of the dragons watching me from their dark caves. They did not engage with me. Aziolith told me I'd know his cave because its entrance was lined with bones, and there were two orc heads on spikes on either side. More bones spelled out the words "Go away" in big letters across the top.

I found his inhospitality amusing. He had always been so kind to me. He took me on adventures and shared his secrets with me. He had never treated me like anything less than a dragon, even though pompous arrogance was a staple of dragon kind.

Eventually, I saw a cave that matched his description and landed in front of it. I had no idea if Aziolith would be happy to see me or not, but he was my only contact in Hell. He also knew Julia, so I hoped I could get him to help me.

"Aziolith?" I asked, walking toward the cave. "Is this your cave?"

"Can't you read?" a deep voice grumbled from inside. "Go away!"

"I'm afraid I can't do that, buddy," I replied. "I came a long way to see you."

"Hrm." The voice let out a low, thoughtful growl. "That voice sounds…familiar."

"It should. We hung out together for over a century. It's me. Kimberly."

There was a long silence, and then Aziolith's red head and shiny yellow eyes poked out of the cave and looked around until he saw me. He studied me closely, his scaly head cocking from one side to the other in disbelief. A smile crept across his face as recognition sunk in, a smile that was just as quickly replaced by a frown.

"Kimberly," he said. His words were choked. "I thought it would be much longer before you ended up here."

"Me too," I said. "Honestly, I didn't know if I would ever get here, but here I am."

Aziolith smiled a sweet smile at me, shaking his great head. "Don't get me wrong, it's good to see an old friend, but I am sad to see you all the same. How did you die?"

I paused. "I…didn't."

"What?"

I rubbed the back of my neck. "Yeah, I uh, kind of came here voluntarily."

"You came. To Hell. Voluntarily?" Aziolith rolled the words over on his forked tongue. "Why on Earth would you do that?"

"There was a demon."

He scoffed, rolling his eyes. "Of course, there was a demon. There's always a demon. What does that have to do with you being in Hell?"

"This one said that he was going to use Julia's blood to open a portal between Hell and Earth. One that can never be sealed again."

"Julia!" Aziolith said, shocked. "I wondered why she had not visited this month. I thought perhaps she was upset that my next move was checkmate."

"Good, you still hang out with her. I really need your help. I don't know this place or its customs, but you do…right?"

"I do."

I started walking back and forth in front of the great dragon, counting off my tasks on my fingers. "I need to get to Dis, and find out what happened to Julia, and save her before whoever has her finishes the job."

"Then we have no time to lose," Aziolith lowered one of his wings to the ground. "Hop on."

I hadn't ridden with Aziolith in a lifetime, and it brought a big smile to my face to grab onto his wing again. "Thank you."

"Of course." Aziolith looked back at me. "It is very good to see you."

"Same."

CHAPTER 13

Akta

Location: Dis, Hell

"Hey, you!" a kid shouted out as I walked down the streets of Dis. "Buy some shoes!"

There were two people with their ears to the street of Dis more than anybody else I had ever met there. They worked as unassuming cobblers, but they had more intel than any of my other informants combined.

Beatrice hadn't changed much in her millennia in Hell. She was loud, boisterous, and annoying, but now she had technology. Instead of hollering on the streets to anybody that passed, demanding they enter her store, she used walls of televisions.

Beatrice's digital eyes followed me inside. "That's what I thought."

They'd certainly moved beyond their small stand on the corner of the cobblestone street. Here was an entire warehouse of demons, elves, orcs, trolls, and changelings trying on shoes of all types, from running shoes to loafers. An assorted number of other Hell monsters bustled around, working. In the back of the store, a young girl watched everything from her perch on a lifeguard stand.

"Customer needs help on aisle three!" Beatrice shouted. Her voice was still as high pitched and creaky as when I met her, but she was as fierce as anybody I ever met in all my time in Hell.

"Your new signage is…very forceful," I said as I approached.

"It works!" Beatrice said. She didn't take her watchful eyes from the showroom floor. "Look at this place; it's popping."

I looked at the shoe sales going on all around me and nodded. "Yes, you are quite the businesswoman."

"That was never in question." She smiled and finally looked at me. "So, what can I do for you?"

"You know what I need."

"Yeah." She eyed my ratty boots. I hadn't replaced them in half a century. "But I'm guessing what you want is information."

"Please."

Beatrice climbed down from the lifeguard stand, hopping the last step and landing on the ground with a thud. "Follow me." She led me through the back room, where a dozen elves and leprechauns in full beards and green suits cobbled shoes. They pounded the shoes in rhythm, their movements so fast that I could barely follow their hands.

"Complete customization. It was a revolution when Dad and I came up with it. Everybody's catching up now, so we're working on the next innovation. We've seen some very interesting developments in elven shoe technology, and we've started employing them along with the leprechauns." She stopped to point something out on a shoe. The leprechaun seated there nodded. "Business moves quickly, and if you're not keeping up, you're dead."

"I wouldn't know," I replied. "My business hasn't really changed much in over three thousand years."

"Right. They run, and you catch them. 'Course, those new trackers must make things easier."

I shook my head. "I hate them. It ruins the fun."

"That's the price of progress, I guess."

I followed her down a small hallway stacked high on either side with fabric. "Do you ever miss sitting on the street corner, yelling at people for your dinner?"

"I complain about it all the time," Beatrice replied, pushing through a loose hanging sheet of fabric. "Of course, I complained about how it was back then as well. Things moved too slow then and too fast now. Feels like there was a time when it was just right, but damned if I can remember it."

Beatrice knocked on a plain white door in the back of the factory. "Dad. Akta's here."

"Well, bless me," I heard from the other side of the door. "Let her in."

She opened the door and held it for me. "I gotta get back to the floor."

"You're quite the slave driver, Beatrice." A thin man with pointy eyes and small round glasses sat behind a black wood desk cluttered with paper and fabric swatches. His eyes twinkled, looking at his daughter.

"Somebody has to be," Beatrice replied. "Otherwise, they'll take advantage of you."

"Thanks, Bea." I stepped inside the room. "Good to see you, Clovis."

"And wonderful to see you, too." Clovis came around the desk and wrapped me in a hug. I grimaced, but I tolerated it. "How is everything?"

"I long for the days that it was the same thing every day," I replied.

He gestured around the office. "I know that feeling."

"I'm afraid I'm not here for a social visit."

"Are you ever?" Clovis asked with a thin smile. "What do you need?"

"Two of the five weapons which can kill the devil have been stolen, and I need to find them."

Clovis touched his hand to his chest. "My word…weren't you charged with caring for one of them?"

I nodded. "The Dagger of Obsolescence. It was stolen from me."

"Tsk, tsk, tsk. What else was taken?"

"The Bow of Misery."

Clovis bit his lip, considering this information. "Well, at least it's not the hammer or the lance, I guess. Those are considerably more powerful than the bow."

"No, but it can still do the job. Somebody fired it at her and left Katrina with a wound in her shoulder that will take years to heal if it ever does."

The old man's eyebrows shot halfway up his forehead at this news. Finally, he shook his head and said, "I have not heard of anything, but I will keep my ear to the ground. There have been rumblings of something big happening in the coming days. Nothing substantial, just a rumor on the wind."

I stared daggers at him. "I don't need to tell you how important it is that we find these weapons before they are used, do I?"

He shook his head. "Of course not."

I sighed. There was a tricky bit of business I had no desire to bring up. "Clovis…what are your feelings about the Devil?"

Clovis rubbed his hands together and bit his lip, trying desperately to find some way to speak the truth without betraying the Devil. "She has changed much in her short time here."

I narrowed my eyes. "That's not an answer. Do you wish her harm?"

Clovis shrugged. "Beatrice and I have done very well in the new order, but many haven't. I never heard this level of animosity directed toward Lucifer or Velaska, and they were awful, as you know."

"Yes, but they didn't interfere with the way Hell operated."

Clovis nodded. "Things didn't change much for thousands of years, and now they have changed very quickly in very little time."

"Yes, and people are upset." I took a step closer, watching the old man for any unspoken clue. "Have you ever heard of The True Path?"

"The Church?" Clovis chuckled. "Yes. I always found them silly. I mean, a church built for demons in Hell? What's the point of all that, really?"

"What of their plans for Hell?"

Clovis cocked his head, thinking. "I have heard nothing, but I have not looked, either. Honestly, they are more a novelty than a concern for Katrina."

"Perhaps."

For a few moments, the room was silent. Finally, Clovis broke in. "There is a source I use often named Thriaska. He's just come back from a trip to Earth if memory serves, and if so, he'll be at The Old Hat, drinking and cavorting into the wee hours."

"Thank you, old friend," I stopped before I reached the door and turned to him. "You didn't answer my question, though. What do you think of Katrina?"

The old man shrugged and started sifting through papers on his desk. "I like her as well as I like any politician."

CHAPTER 14

Kimberly

Location: Dis, Hell

Aziolith flew us up to the edge of Dis, where he let me down. I slid off his wing and onto the ground. I had missed traveling on the wings of a dragon. One single flap of his wings moved us miles. For my wings to move me the same distance? It would take three times as long and ten times the energy. I'd be sweaty and exhausted.

"I can't maneuver inside the city limits in this form." Aziolith pulled a vial from around his neck and drank it. When he did, his body began to pulsate and throb, and then his mass was sucked in like a vacuum until all that remained was a lizard-skinned man a head higher than me, dressed in a blue suit and necktie. "Ah, that's better." He ran his hands along his slender figure, turning this way and that to look at himself. "I look pretty good, if I do say so. What do you think?"

I smiled, watching him. Dragons really were vain. "Very dashing."

"Then let us away."

"Where are we going?" I asked.

"We start at the seediest bar in all of Dis." He walked to the side of the road and waved his hand. "Taxi!"

"I have to admit, this is nothing like I expected." I walked over as a yellow cab pulled up. "It's like a modern city, the rival of anything on Earth. It was nothing like this the last time I was here."

He ducked into the cab. "That was hundreds of years ago."

"True." When I was a child, a banshee stole me from my mother and brought me to Lucifer's Castle. Back then, Hell was a barren wasteland. Dis was barely a city, and everything looked like it was from the middle ages, down to the unicorns that pulled carts across the city. Looking around now, I could have been in Chicago, or maybe Los Angeles, minus a bit of fire and brimstone.

"I'm sure Earth has changed in the century since I have been gone," Aziolith said, ducking into the cab.

I stared up at the skyscrapers. "Not...this much."

The cabbie was purple-skinned with a thick neck. "Where to?"

"The Old Hat," Aziolith said. "And don't dawdle."

"When was the last time you were in Dis?" I asked.

"It hasn't been long enough," he replied. "I dislike the noise and the crowds. This place was so much better in the old days. Before computers, and highways, and...all of this."

Aziolith didn't like modernization back on Earth, either. It was why he rarely left his cave, especially toward the end. Even a pleasant flight over the mountains was marred by "eyesores" like roads and towns and constantly interrupted by planes in his airspace.

"You know, I thought that humans were the problem back on Earth," he said. "I thought monsters would be more civilized. Clearly, the urge to modernize rests in the bones of all creatures, except me."

"It's not all bad. I mean, it would have taken us all day to get across town on foot, and now we'll be there in a couple of minutes. This is a nice cab, too." I said the last a little bit louder. The thick-necked purple thing nodded appreciatively.

"And that's a good thing?" Aziolith leaned forward in his seat, pointing into his palm to emphasize every point he made. "When everything took time, you had to be judicious. You couldn't just wander. You needed strict directions and a destination in mind. Your choice of quests took deep thought and planning. Now, everything can happen on a whim. It's disgusting."

I laughed. "You should take it up with the Devil."

"Ugh, Devil," Aziolith rolled his eyes. "Not my Devil."

"Preach it, buddy!" the driver said from the front seat. "She can sit on a nail and spin."

"Harsh." Aziolith raised an eyebrow. "I like it."

"Of course you would," I said. "If you hate it so much, why are you helping me?"

Aziolith turned to the window, watching the stores pass him by. "Because I love Julia more than I hate this place, and I don't want to see harm come to her."

The car stopped in front of a dingy bar. Everything around it was modern and fresh-looking, obviously built in the last decade, but the bar itself looked like it hadn't been renovated in a thousand years. It probably hadn't.

"Thank you, sir," Aziolith said, placing some coins in the driver's hands and sliding out of the seat with me behind him. "Now, don't make a scene here, okay?"

I scoffed. "When have I ever made a scene?"

"Always," Aziolith grumbled. "You always make a scene."

I didn't have a chance to defend myself before Aziolith pushed open the door and walked inside. The bar was small and cramped but fit a surprising number of monsters of all sorts...including one I recognized. In the far corner, I saw the huge horns rising toward the ceiling. Thriaska was seated there talking to a blue troll.

"That's the demon I killed," I said, pointing at Thriaska. "The one who told me that Julia was in danger."

"I told you we would find a lead here," Aziolith muttered. "Let's go, and remember, low profile."

"You don't have to tell me twice."

"No," Aziolith said. "I fear I should have told you many more times."

Then, I saw somebody else I recognized, though only through etchings and renderings. A pixie walked across the room with three beers and sat them down at the table. Akta. Here she was, cavorting with a demon; worse yet, it was Thriaska who was trying to end the world.

The blood rose in my veins as I stomped over. "Thriaska!"

"Oh, brother," I heard Aziolith whisper under his breath. "See? This is what I'm talking about."

Thriaska turned, and the smile dropped from his face. "Pixie? What are you doing here?"

Akta looked from me to him. "You know this person?"

Thriaska snarled. "Of course, she's the one that killed me!"

"Hold on, friend. Stay back," Akta said, stepping between Thriaska and me. "We want no quarrel."

I sighed. "Akta, trust me, you don't know what you're saying."

"How…" She narrowed her eyes. "Do you know my name?"

"I believe these are yours." I pulled the daggers out of my belt and showed her.

She looked at them in stunned awe. "How did you get these?"

"They were my mentor's," I replied. "You know her, probably. Julia Freeman."

"Julia?" Akta said. "My descendant?"

I nodded. "That's right. She trained me."

"She will be so sad that you died," Akta said with a sad timbre in her throat. "But I'm sure she will be happy to see you again."

"I'm not dead!" The music skipped, and everyone looked at me. They snarled and growled as their breath bore down on me.

"She's kidding!" Aziolith said, walking over to me. "It's loud in here. She thought Akta said 'head,' but clearly, she's not a head. She's a whole person…err…pixie. Go about your business." The bar's patrons squinted and mostly looked confused. Aziolith leaned in. "We need to go."

"I'm not going anywhere," I said, brushing him off. "Not until this demon tells me where Julia is."

Akta poked me in the shoulder and hissed, "He is here to help me find the masterminds trying to kill the Devil. I need him alive—and unharmed."

"So back off." Thriaska chuckled. "You don't call the shots down here, pixie."

I squeezed the daggers tightly. "I will cut your tongue out, demon!"

His tongue flicked the air. "I'd like to see you try."

"Calm down!" Akta shouted. By now, the rest of the bar had lost interest. Our interaction was not an abnormal one in a place like that. "What do you mean, where is Julia? I just—I supposed I just haven't seen her for a while."

I pointed my dagger at Thriaska. "That's because this asshole did something with her."

Akta spun around. "Is this true?"

Thriaska held up his hands. "Personally, I didn't do anything. But I played my part beautifully."

"Where is she?" Akta asked, taking a menacing step toward him.

"Clovis told me you would be formidable, and I should not cross you." Thriaska leaned forward. "And I have heard legend of your glorious victories in combat. But I'm starting to think that without your magic dagger, you aren't much of a threat."

Akta said. "How did you know I had the Dagger of Obsolescence?"

Thriaska leaned back and shrugged, speaking into his mug of beer. "I mean—I—just heard stories."

"Who cares!?" I slammed my hands on the table. "Tell me where Julia is now and who is behind the plot to kill the Devil."

Thriaska turned to me. "Pixie, there is not enough money in the world to make me turn on my boss." I noticed him going for his weapon too late. His hand had inched to the hilt of a sword laying between his knees. "You're welcome to die, tho—"

He went to draw his sword, but with one move, Akta swiped her dagger out of its sheath on her belt, through

Thriaska's neck, and out the top of his head. After a deep breath, she looked at the blue troll. "Come, Sven, help me with him."

The blue troll shook his head. "I…can't…."

"What do you mean?"

"He is friend."

Akta shook her head. "No, he is not. I am your friend."

"Both are friends."

The green ooze of the demon dripped down from the table to the floor. It smelled like rancid bile.

"Did he work for Asmodeus, too?"

"Yes."

"And that's why he knew what happened to Julia? Because she's being held by Asmodeus?"

Sven looked away. "I—can't—"

"Answer her or so help me—" I growled at him until Akta lifted her hand to stop me.

Akta hovered into the air and caught Sven's eyes. "Sven, she's my kin. If you know something, please tell me."

"I know." Sven dropped his eyes. "I know where she is."

"Can you take us to her?" I asked anxiously.

"No," Sven said. "I won't betray friend."

"Then you're betraying me." Akta pulled the dagger out of Thriaska's head and pointed it at him. "No, you'll show me…or I'll kill you."

"You wouldn't. Akta is my friend."

"No," Akta replied. "Not anymore." She stepped closer to him. "Now, you will help us, understood?"

The troll's face dropped to his chest. He looked as if his heart had been broken in half. "Okay."

CHAPTER 15

Akta

Location: Asmodeus's Castle, Hell

Sven's betrayal was like a serrated knife digging through my stomach. I held my dagger to his back as Aziolith flew us across the desert toward Asmodeus's castle. The demon lair had been erected in the furthest western edge of Hell, looking out over all of the realm from the top of a high cliff.

Aziolith looked back at me while we flew. "I hope you do not believe this means I like you, pixie."

"I do not believe that, and never have," I replied.

"Good, because that dagger you lost was my right before it was stolen by you and Lucifer in a petty betrayal of our deal."

I rolled my eyes. "That was three thousand years ago."

"Dragons have long memories," Aziolith said. "To me, it was yesterday."

"Wow," Kimberly said to me. "He does not like you."

"It wasn't my fault." I shook my head. "It wasn't me who refused to give the dagger back to him. It was Lucifer."

"Says you," Aziolith grumbled. "My hatred for the old Devil subsided slightly with his death, but it pains me to know that you were such a poor steward of my treasure."

"I would not want a dragon mad at me, that's for sure," Kimberly said.

"I've had worse." I sighed loudly. "But if it means that much to you, when we get it back—well, if we get it back—I will do everything in my power to make sure that it ends up in your hands."

"Your word means little to me, pixie, and whatever power you have is laughable. I could eat you with a single gulp."

"Yet, even being so insignificant, I have lasted here— and thrived—for as long as you have. And I've saved Hell more times than I can remember. Perhaps I am simply more cunning than you, or less lazy."

"Watch it, pixie," the dragon warned. "I can drop you."

"You're forgetting that I can fly." I laughed and spread my wings. "Please stop trying to intimidate me; it won't work. Don't forget who killed you the first time."

Aziolith grumbled and turned back to the sky. He was clearly finished speaking with me. I turned my attention to Sven. My dagger rippled through the muscles on his back as his breath rose and fell.

"I am sorry," he said.

"I don't care," I snapped. "Everybody else I ever trusted betrayed me; why would you be any different?"

When I came to Hell, I had reacquainted with Ylfingur, an old cyclops friend from Earth, and his son, Bjarngimur. They were true friends, and I trusted them until they betrayed me by trying to kill Lucifer. And now Sven, my only remaining friend in Hell, had betrayed me with the new Devil at the expense of my most beloved kin.

"Why do you hate her so?" Kimberly asked. "The Devil, I mean."

"Not like change," Sven replied.

"Who does?" Kimberly asked. "But isn't living in a house with air conditioning better than living in a hovel on the side of a dirt road?"

"No," he said, shaking his head. "Not to me."

"Amen, brother," Aziolith said without turning back to us. "The future is just dreadful."

"It's not because she's a human?" I asked.

"She doesn't belong here, ruling Hell," Sven said. "She should be punished like humans. Humans not lead us."

"So it's because she's a human," I said flatly. I was familiar with the logic: Devils were supposed to be gods and, barring that, angels. Katrina was neither.

Sven slowly shook his head. "She should not be the Devil."

"God appointed her," I growled.

"He was wrong."

"You're racist," Kimberly scoffed.

"I don't like her," he said after a long pause. "I like Asmodeus."

"Of course, you do. He's big, and brash, and ugly, and male."

"He's a demon!" Sven yelled forcefully. "He deserves Devil."

"Then he should have killed the last one," I growled.

"He will kill this one."

I shook my head. "Not if I have anything to say about it."

Sven looked back at me, sadness in his eyes. "You don't."

I pressed my knife deeper on Sven's back until it punctured the skin. Kimberly's hand pressed against mine. "Not yet. We need him to get inside the castle."

"I can get in without him," I grumbled.

She squeezed my hand harder. "Then don't do it… because he's your friend."

"He's a traitor."

Her voice fell to a whisper. "You'll regret it."

I pulled the knife back. Though every instinct in my body said to push it forward, deeper until my dagger ripped my friend in half, I wasn't a monster. I didn't kill indiscriminately. He would have his justice in front of Katrina, and she would not take pity on him.

***

Aziolith dropped us on the edge of the castle's cliff, and we stood for a moment appraising the black, gnarled spires of the castle.

"That's a big climb," Kimberly said, glancing at Aziolith.

"I've done worse," I replied, poking Sven's back with my dagger. "Move."

Aziolith frowned. "Can't we just fly to the top?" he asked.

"No," Sven said. "Dungeon in basement. Julia in dungeon. Door up ahead."

"Ah," Aziolith said. "Then I guess we're walking."

Asmodeus's land had been untouched in the modernization of the rest of Hell, but from the spires of his castle, the upgrades and renovations were all that we could see, stretching into the distance. Cities rising from the desert, roads bisecting it, and the world of Hell moving on without him. We reached the edge of the cliffside, and Sven walked forward with a key he pulled from his pocket.

"Hurry up," I growled at him.

"So, what's the plan?" Kimberly asked.

"You wait here with the troll," I said to her. "I go up and find Julia."

Kimberly shook her head. "No way I am staying out here. I'm the one who told you Julia was here."

"And I thank you for that," I replied. "But I can't carry any more dead weight."

She grabbed my arm and spoke through gritted teeth. "I am not dead weight. I can do anything you can do, except better."

"I highly doubt tha—"

"Oh, my god. Stop your bickering. I'll stay here with the troll," Aziolith said. "Not like I can fit through the door anyway, and I'm not drinking anymore of that foul potion."

I nodded.

Aziolith looked at Kimberly. "If you need me, whistle, and I will be there."

"Thank you."

I pointed down to Kimberly's daggers. "Are you sure you know how to use those things?"

She lowered them down to her side in ready position. "I'm sure. They have spilled much demon blood before."

"I hope you're right."

Sven unlatched the door and turned to us. "Cell seven, fifth level. This key open door." He put the key in my hand. "Be careful, pretty."

"Don't call me that." He had called me that when I met him, thousands of years ago. He was the only person I allowed to compliment me. "You never get to call me that again."

CHAPTER 16

Kimberly

Location: Asmodeus's Castle, Hell

The door swung closed once Akta and I were inside Asmodeus's castle. Alone, without a guide to help us. Who knew how many monsters lurked in the darkness, waiting for us? The troll, Sven, did, but we had left him behind at Akta's behest.

"Maybe we should have let him come with us," I said to Akta, who crouched into the shadows in front of me.

"He would have just slowed us down," Akta said. There was a dark edge to her voice.

"Maybe," I replied. "But he knew these dungeons."

She pressed her forehead against her palms as if in pain. "If I spent one more second with him, I would have killed him, Kimberly. All right? I would have slit his throat where he stood, and then I would have regretted it the rest of my life. So, no, I don't think he should have come with us."

"Fair enough. Then we do it on our own."

Akta gave me a curt nod, then moved forward through the halls, daggers in hands. I'd never seen somebody move so lightly on their feet in all my years. I was competent in the shadows, but really, I excelled out in the open, fighting multiple people. My feet were flat, and my steps were hard, so I picked myself up on my toes as I moved to mimic Akta's light, graceful movements.

The cobblestone under me was coarse and uneven, a relic of a bygone age, and slick from whatever was dripping from the ceiling. It smelled of mold and a soggy sweatshirt, wet from a workout.

"Hold," Akta whispered forcefully, and I stopped on my toes.

"I'm going to get some grub," a gruff voice growled from down the hall.

I pinned myself against the wall, holding my breath, and watched an orc with green skin and spiked pauldrons lumber past us. Akta peered after the orc for a few moments, then nodded before continuing across the hall. I followed her.

When we reached a spiral staircase, Akta lifted herself with her wings and floated into the air. I unfurled my wings and followed behind her. Akta stopped before reaching the top of the stairs and held up two fingers to me, then pointed forward.

Two ogres stood guard at the archway, facing away from us. Akta pointed left and then nodded to me to take the one on the right. I pulled out my daggers and inched forward until we were in place. When she nodded again, I stuck my daggers into my ogre's throat, and she did the same to hers. They dropped to the ground without a whimper.

Akta looked around then said, "Drag them into that alcove." She pointed to a darkened corner across from the stairwell.

I latched onto the arms of the guard and used every ounce of my energy to drag his body across the hallway. When I emerged, panting, I saw a streak of blood running across the hallway.

"Well, that's going to be a dead giveaway," I said.

"Indeed."

"What do we do now?"

Down the hall, a voice boomed, "Hey!" I turned to see a small imp pointing at us. "Intruders!"

"I guess it doesn't matter anyway," I said, throwing a pinch of pixie dust and disappearing down the hallway. When I reappeared, I sliced the imp across the throat. Being exposed played into my strengths. I preferred a fight out in the open. Still, I had little interest in fighting an entire castle of guards, even if that was clearly what I was about to do. The second the imp dropped to the ground, four other guards appeared. They stared at his body, then looked up at me, enraged. They drew their weapons and charged, snarling obscenities.

"Help!" I shouted to Akta. She disappeared into a puff of purple smoke and reappeared in front of me. She sliced a goblin across the throat and stabbed a horned demon through the stomach. I threw some pixie dust, disappeared, and reappeared behind the other guards, stabbing them in the backs just as Akta stabbed them through the chest. The cadre fell to the ground. Akta pulled her knife from one of the bodies and examined the carnage she'd caused.

"There's no hiding this," I said.

"No."

"They will be on us soon enough."

"I think we should run."

"Agreed."

We sprinted along the hallways and took another flight of stairs to the next level, killing two more guards along the way. Stealth was no longer the impetus. If we could not hide, then we had to leave the dungeon before they could capture us. Time—speed—was of the essence.

I teleported to the end of the hallway again and saw another cadre of guards. There was no time to fight. I teleported right past them and continued running. Their metal bracers clanked behind us, but we were faster than they were and quickly gained a lead on them.

Akta followed me, pulling a set of throwing knives from her pant leg and flinging it at the guards. We repeated the process on the next floor. By the time we were at the end of the fourth floor, twenty guards were chasing us, and that was after the several that Akta had taken out along the way.

I stopped at the end of the hall. "We have to get some more distance between them, or we'll never be able to save Julia."

"Then we make a stand here," Akta said, pulling another set of daggers from a band on her arm. She whipped them behind her, hitting two orcs in the head simultaneously.

I pulled out a silver dagger from my shoe and flung it at a hobgoblin chasing after me. I usually only used the knife to fight werewolves and other silver-sensitive creatures, but it was good in a pinch. I could replace it. I vanished and reappeared in the middle of the troop of soldiers. I liked fighting in close quarters, especially because my enemies couldn't attack without hitting one of their own. I stabbed an ogre in the eye and a troll through the throat.

As they dropped, I vanished and reappeared further down the hall to impale a goblin through the throat. I ducked the blow of a changeling with an ax, and the resulting blow embedded the ax in an imp's forehead. I spun and took down the changeling and then kicked the imp into another ogre before stealing the sword from a dead orc and impaling the ogre with it through his chest.

When I looked back at the hallway, Akta had just finished killing the final orc on the battlefield and was covered in the blood of her victory. I was doused with a hefty dose of blood, too. I pulled my silver dagger out of the hobgoblin's eye and wiped off the blade before sticking it back in my shoe.

"Is it weird that that was kind of fun?" I asked.

Akta shook her head. "The thrill of battle is intoxicating to many. I have long since grown past its allure." It was a dig, but she managed to say it without sounding judgmental.

"Maybe when I'm three thousand, I'll get over it, too."

She wiped the blood off her dagger. "It didn't take me that long. Come."

There were no guards on the next level, which I found strangely unsettling. We walked into the darkened hallway without the aid of the torches that had lit the hallways in the corridors below us. Also unsettling was the complete, absolute silence in this hallway.

"Look for her," Akta said. "I'll go left."

I turned to the right and peered through the wrought-iron bars that formed the window on the wooden door of each cell. They were all empty. At the end of the hall was an imposing, solid wooden door, no window.

"Julia?" I asked, whispering through the door.

After a long silence, a weak voice called out. "Who's there?"

"Julia!" I turned down the hall. "Akta!"

Akta came flying toward me. She pulled the key out of her satchel and stuck it into the keyhole. The lock clicked, and the door swung open. I rushed inside the room and saw her, beaten and bruised, lying shackled on the floor. Her thick hair was matted with sweat and blood, her brown eyes swollen.

"Kimberly?" Julia asked. Her voice was thin. "What are you doing here?"

I wrapped my arms around Julia's neck. "They said they were going to kill you to open a portal back to Earth and bring around a second Apocalypse."

"No, no, no, no, no," Julia said. "You're so stupid. You're so so so stupid for coming here."

I pushed back from her, frowning and studying her face. "I'm not stupid. I'm trying to save your life. They were going to kill you."

"No…Kimberly. You have doomed us all." Julia shook her head fervently. "It wasn't me they're after…it's you."

The door slammed closed, and we were stuck in darkness. I tried to jump away. I tried to vanish.

"It's no use," Julia said. "This is a dead room. Magic doesn't work here."

"There has to be a way."

"There's not," Julia said. "They planned this all, and you fell right into their trap."

CHAPTER 17

Julia

Location: Asmodeus's Castle, Hell

"Did I teach you nothing?" I asked, staring daggers at Kimberly. Nobody had come to get us since my ancestor and prodigy had idiotically come to save me.

Kimberly shook her head. "No, you taught me a lot. It's been two hundred years, and I've learned some stuff on my own, too."

"Don't be too hard on the girl," Akta said. "I am as complicit as she is."

"I'm sorry," I said with a deep sigh. I pressed my hand into my forehead. "It's not your fault, not either of you. I should have never been captured. I was stupid, and slow, and careless."

"It could happen to any of us." Akta shrugged and sat down beside me. "Why don't you tell us what they are planning?"

"I only know bits and pieces. They call it...Ragnarok."

Akta's eyes glittered in the dark, and she squinted as if trying to remember something. "I know of it. From legends from Hell, but they are old wives' tales, remnants of stories from when the old gods roamed this land."

"They didn't seem like legends to me. Your friend seemed very, very certain it was going to happen."

"My friend?" Akta frowned.

"The blue troll."

"Sven." The word was like a hiss when Akta spoke.

Kimberly looked at Akta, and her jaw clenched. "He was here?"

I nodded. "He's the one that told me what they wanted and what Kimberly's blood was going to be used for. What is Ragnarok?"

Akta bit her lip. "According to legend, thousands of years ago, the gods did battle with the Titans across the universe. One of the most powerful, Surt, was bound to the core of this planet. Should he ever escape, he would wreak havoc on the universe, destroy the gods, and bring fire and brimstone upon the whole universe."

"That sounds…bad," I said.

"If that's true, it will be so much worse than an Apocalypse," Kimberly said. "They're talking about destroying everything. The whole universe!"

Akta balled up her fists. "If that is what they are planning, then we must stop them."

The door to the cell creaked open. My hobgoblin jailer stepped inside and tossed two shackles inside at his new prisoners. "Put these on, both of you. Asmodeus will see you now."

"Piss off!" Kimberly said, rushing the jailer. He lifted a club in his hand faster than she could move and decked her across the room with it.

"Put them on, now."

Akta took the shackles and looked over at Kimberly. "Just do it. If we can get to Asmodeus, we can find a way out of this."

"There is no way out," the jailer said, chuckling. "But I appreciate your spirit."

Akta shackled herself and then helped Kimberly do the same. There was a burning fire in her eyes, and I knew she was planning something. She had once told me that sometimes you had to walk deeper inside the lion's den to find a way to save yourself. It was a skill I still hadn't mastered.

Once Kimberly and Akta were chained, the hobgoblin walked behind me and untethered me from the wall. "Don't try using magic," he said. "Those shackles deaden your aura and prevent it."

"I wouldn't dream of it," I said.

"I know you are all very capable warriors," the hobgoblin said, standing me up. "But I assure you that you only made it this far because Asmodeus allowed it. Now move."

The hobgoblin walked us outside, where a squad of orcs waited to escort us into the castle. We went up ten flights of stairs before leaving the dungeon behind and entering the opulence of a castle. The walls were hand-painted in a pattern of twisted black thorns and lined with paintings of demonic figures smiling in pompous uniforms.

Our shoes clacked on the black marble as we walked, though Akta's silent footsteps made it seem like she was gliding across the ground. At the end of the hallway, the walls opened into a huge room with high ceilings. Great spires on all four sides led up to a point at the top, which was decorated with a twisted portrait of the Creation of Man—instead of God pointing at Adam, though, there was a snake-like demon pointing at Eve.

"Ah," Asmodeus's voice crackled through the room. "You have finally arrived." He was seated on a throne made of black steel and purple velvet, smiling as we approached. "I didn't know if Thriaska would be able to convince you to come, pixie."

"Well, he was very convincing," Kimberly growled. "Right before he died."

"It would seem so. I had my doubts. But he assured me that you would make your way here if we kidnapped your precious mentor." Asmodeus grinned. "It seems that she still holds a special place in your heart, even after two hundred years."

"What do you want from me?" Kimberly asked.

"Your blood, of course. Pixie blood is the most powerful and rarest of any creature, and we needed some from a living, breathing fairy, not one who shed their mortal coil."

I lurched forward. "You will not touch one hair on her head."

"I'm afraid it's not her hair we're after, but yes, we will. It is the only way to bring an end to the rule of Katrina so that I can take my rightful place on the throne."

Akta laughed. "You really think by starting Ragnarok that you'll fix anything? You'll be dooming the universe to chaos."

"The universe could use a little chaos!" Asmodeus shouted. "If God wanted us docile, he never would have sent a human, mortal woman to lead us! It is an insult of the highest order."

"I tire of this," Akta said. "You are no different than any other power-hungry despot. You think you are aggrieved, but you are clinging to power you do not deserve."

Asmodeus stood. "Well, the good news is we are close to fulfilling the prophecy."

He pulled a dagger out of a sheath around his belt. I recognized it immediately as the one Akta kept on her; the Dagger of Obsolescence. One of the few objects in existence that could kill the Devil.

"Wait," I said. "I thought you had the dagger, Akta?"

"It was stolen from me!" Akta shouted. "I should have known you would have it."

"Of course, I have the dagger, and the bow is safely in my possession as well. Once we have retrieved all five weapons and the key to break the binding that holds Surt in his cage, none of you will have to worry about this anymore." Asmodeus licked the dagger. "Now, all I need is the hammer and the lance."

"And the sword," Akta said.

Asmodeus snickered. "Yes, and the sword. That will be last. Once we have the keys."

"Why do you need the weapons?" I asked.

"The Four Horsemen guard four seals. Once they are reunited with their weapons, they will break the seals, and the great monster Surt will use the flaming sword of Damocles to quake the Heavens. He will reward me by making me ruler of Hell."

"That is just…a terrible plan," I said, shaking my head. "I'm sorry, but I just can't get over how stupid you are."

"Smart enough to capture you," Asmodeus said, turning to me.

"Yes," Kimberly said. "But not smart enough to know that we have a secret weapon."

Asmodeus laughed. "And what might that be?"

Kimberly looked right into his flaming eyes. "A dragon." She let out a sharp whistle, and the entirety of the castle shook and quaked. A shadow moved across windows, and a shriek echoed through the great throne room.

"Guard!" Asmodeus shouted, but it was too late. The ceiling above us shattered, and the great dragon Aziolith swooped in and landed in front of us.

The hobgoblin jailer rushed the dragon, but with one swipe of his tail, Aziolith sent him across the room, crashing through the stained glass on the other side.

"Aziolith!" I cried at the sight of my old friend. "So good to see you."

"And you, Julia. We have little time, so please all of you, get on."

Aziolith shot fire at Asmodeus, who held up his hands to block the attack. Fire didn't hurt a demon, but the pressure of the blast still drove him backward. The dagger flew from his hands. I rushed to grab it, but the guards closed in on me from the edges of the throne room.

"Hurry up!" Akta said.

I hobbled forward and picked up the dagger as the guards descended upon me. I felt an arm grab me from either side and pull me to my feet. Kimberly and Akta flanked me.

"We have to go, now," Kimberly said as the guards closed in on us.

While Aziolith breathed fire, the three of us ran toward him. He lowered his wing to the ground so we could climb aboard his back. Once we were secure upon the scales and horns that riveted his back, the dragon spread his wings and lifted into the air. With a great flap of his wings, he shot upward out of the spire and broke into the air. He spun toward the horizon, and we headed toward freedom.

I bent down low and hugged the dragon. "Thank you for the rescue, buddy."

"It's the least I could do. We still are in the middle of a chess match, and I would hate for you to die before I could defeat you."

"This is a touching moment," Akta said. "But can we finish our escape before we devolve into sentimentalities?"

"I'm sorry to say that in the mayhem, I lost track of your troll friend," Aziolith said.

"If he's smart, he'll stay lost," Akta said.

"What do we do now?" Kimberly asked, looking back at the shattered spires of Asmodeus's castle.

I looked toward the Devil's castle looming on the horizon. "We tell Katrina all we know and hope we can stop Ragnarok before it comes to devour the whole of the universe."

BOOK 2

CHAPTER 18

Katrina

Location: Devil's Castle, Hell

I squeezed the bridge of my nose. I didn't think it was possible for an immortal being to get a migraine, but after listening to Akta, Julia, and Kimberly explain that Asmodeus was trying to bring forth Ragnarok, a splitting headache developed behind my eyes and shot through the base of my skull.

"So, let me get this straight," I said with another deep sigh. "Asmodeus is trying to collect the weapons to summon the Four Horsemen, so they can break the four seals and bring about Ragnarok. Carl, can you read that back?"

Carl looked down at his tablet. "That's what I have written down."

"I can confirm that, ma'am," Akta said. "Carl is a very good stenographer."

I rolled my temples with my fingers. "And a key, which will unlock the shackles to the Titan Surt and allow him to take his revenge on the gods."

Julia nodded. "Yes."

"And they need the Sword of Damocles because it was Surt's weapon before his imprisonment, and if he reclaims his weapon, then he can lay siege on Heaven, and the universe, once again."

Carl slid his finger along the tablet. "Again, that's correct, according to my notes."

I sighed loudly again. "And we have no idea where Surt is being held."

"No," Kimberly said. "But we can assume it's probably somewhere in Hell since he's, you know, huge and not very easy to hide. Maybe contained in Earth's core? That's just a guess."

Carl held his hand up politely before he spoke up. "I've searched through all our records, and there is nothing about the location of Surt. There's nothing about him even existing, let alone locked in the Earth's core."

"Ah," I replied. "Well, let's assume for the sake of argument—since that seems to be all we have to go on right now—that he is locked in the core of the planet."

"I would prefer not to enter conjecture into the record, mistress," Carl said.

"Then don't enter it!" I barked. "But we have to go somewhere with this line of horseshit, so it might as well be in the realm of wild ass speculation."

"Noted," Carl said. "I will strike all this from the record, then."

"Be my guest," I growled before turning to the pixies at my feet. "So, assuming that Surt is locked in the Earth's core, that means if they do unlock the prison of Surt, it will crack the world open like an egg."

"That's right," Julia said. "Like we told you, it's a really bad plan Asmodeus has, and he appears to be carrying through with it confidently."

"It probably would not crack the Earth open," Carl said.

"Excuse me?" I said to Carl.

"Well, if we are dealing in 'wild ass speculation,' as you put it, you might as well have accurate information." Carl typed into his tablet. "According to my calculations, Surt would be roughly the height of Hell, so while he would cause quite a bit of damage, he wouldn't destroy Earth, just cause flooding and volcanic eruptions the likes of which they have not seen on Earth since the formation of the planet."

"Well...I suppose that's good news. Is there anything else to announce before we shovel more shit on this shit sandwich?" I asked.

Akta held up the Dagger of Obsolescence. "Only that we recovered one of the weapons, which means that we're only missing one."

I nodded and managed a small smile. "Oh, that's nice."

"Technically, we are missing two weapons," Carl said, holding up his hand. "We now have the dagger and the lance, but Asmodeus has the bow, and the hammer has been...well, lost."

"Thank you, Carl," I grumbled. "I so value your addition to these proceedings."

"I know you're using sarcasm by the tone of your voice, but I am taking the compliment, just so you are aware."

Kimberly butted in before I could respond to Carl. "We can't leave the dagger here because your generals might be plotting against you."

"Right," I said with a nod. "I had forgotten that part. So, where do we put it?"

Akta turned to Kimberly. "I think we should give it to Kimberly and have her return to Earth with it."

"Because you're from Earth?" I asked, furrowing my brow.

"I am," Kimberly said.

"And you crawled here through the Gateway to Hell in Rome, against all logic and reason, to save your mentor, even though Asmodeus was sending you into a trap. It was your blood they were after."

"Something like that."

"Exactly like that," Carl corrected. "According to my notes."

I sighed. "I would be angry if I wasn't so impressed with your thick-headedness, pixie."

"Thank…you?" Kimberly said. "I think."

"That's as close to a compliment that you'll get from her," Carl said with a wry smile. "I suggest you treasure it."

"Thank you, Carl!" I yelled. "Do any of you have a plan that doesn't include returning to Earth or hiding like a frightened child?"

Julia nodded. "I do. We have to find the other four weapons before the demons do and make sure they can't use them to unleash Ragnarok."

"Well, that makes sense," I said. "Can we get a recap of where the weapons are?"

Kimberly pointed to Akta. "Well, the dagger is right there."

Carl looked down at his tablet. "And the lance is on Mars with the Martian queen, given to her by none other than Akta herself, who led the negotiations to annex her planet for your expansion plans."

"And the hammer…has never been found," Julia said. "But we think it's somewhere in Hell."

"So, Asmodeus's men could have already found that one."

Akta nodded. "Possible, but unlikely. They are powerful, but they are dumb. I doubt they could have done what nobody else has in the history of Hell."

"And you think we can?" I replied.

"Unclear," Julia replied. "But we are much smarter than they are, for sure."

"State your evidence," I said.

Akta thought for a second. "No."

"You are insufferable." I rubbed my temples again. "So, they have the bow. We have the dagger. The Martian Queen has the lance, and we have no idea where the hammer is, but it might possibly be somewhere in Hell."

"Correct."

"And what about the key?" I asked. "I've never heard about any key before."

"Right, the key that binds Surt to his cell." Kimberly stepped forward. "I have an idea about that."

"Oh, goodie." I let out a groan. "I can't wait to hear this one."

"Since they were placed by the old gods," she continued. "I think we can invoke the old gods and ask for their help to locate the key."

"I have tried to call them before," I said, shaking my head. "Nobody up there listens to my calls."

Kimberly shook her head. "Not you, me. I go back to Earth, track down a god somehow, and find the key. I'm half-human, so maybe they'll listen to me."

"The gods abandoned Earth centuries ago," Carl said.

"Then I'll fail, but it's worth a try, isn't it?" Kimberly said. "Who knows? They might even know where this hammer is."

"It's not the worst plan I've ever heard," I said after a long pause.

"There are no good plans in this situation," Akta said. "But if Kimberly takes the dagger back to Earth, she'll be protected from demons while she searches for the key."

"Fine," I replied. "Meanwhile, go to Mars and find the lance. Bring it back here."

"Queen Nebet will not like your request," Akta replied. "That lance was a gift, and her people feel very strongly about gifting."

"No, she won't," I replied. "They are a proud people, but I can't risk that lance falling into the wrong hands."

"It will destabilize our alliance," Akta said.

"So will the release of Surt on the universe."

"I—"

"It's not a discussion," I cut Akta off. "This is an order."

Akta nodded. "Yes, ma'am. Meanwhile, Julia should stay here to find the hammer."

"Great," I said, throwing up my hands. "And I'll just hang out here?"

Akta shook her head. "No, you'll do what you do best."

"And what's that?" I asked.

Akta smiled. "Reign hellfire on the dukes of Hell until they abandon their plans so we can all go home."

I smiled. "Okay, I like that part of your plan. I've been cooped up in this castle for too long. I'd love to cause a little chaos."

Akta stepped forward. "And now you have a chance to show these demons why you are the Devil, earn their respect, or their fear."

"Or both."

"Both is good," Julia said.

I pushed up from my throne. "Well, this is as good a plan as any other we have right about now. Godspeed, ladies."

A fire grew in my belly. I was ready to wreck the demons of Hell and show them why I was gifted with the power of the Devil. By the time I was done, the lords of Hell would bow before me or die in agony.

When Akta and Julia had exited the throne room, Kimberly approached me. "Excuse me, your majesty."

I sighed. "What can I do for you?"

"Can you, like, snap your fingers and send me back to Earth?"

I grimaced. I knew I couldn't help her. "I'm sorry, but I can't. I can only control your soul, not your body. I can teleport you around Hell, but I can't send you between realms."

Kimberly nodded. "That would save me several hours travel, so I'll take it."

"Don't die," I said, snapping my fingers, and in a flash, she vanished. "That goes for all of us."

CHAPTER 19

Kimberly

Location: Roman Forum, Rome

Katrina couldn't use her powers to return me to Earth, so I was stuck crawling through the same hole I used to enter Hell in the first place. It was just as cramped as when I took it down, but the struggle to crawl upward to Earth was a hundred times more difficult than getting into Hell. I nearly slipped a dozen times. The narrowness of the tunnel was suffocating, but at least it stopped me from falling backward.

Eventually, with aching bones and burning muscles, I reemerged beneath the Roman Forum and spilled onto the ground, gasping for breath. The bright sun of the midday sun shone on me, but I didn't care. Compared to the heat of Hell, the summer sun was a cool and welcome relief.

I pushed myself to my shaking feet and became aware that hundreds of people lining the streets were looking at me. I smiled and waved as several onlookers pulled out their phones and took pictures.

"Hi," I said, muttering.

"Hey!" a burly guard shouted and began running in my direction. Two other officers converged on me from different directions. I hated using my powers in the presence of normals, especially a horde of them, but unless I wanted to be arrested, I had no choice. I closed my eyes and imagined the Harry Potter store in the Jewish quarter, then threw a pinch of pixie dust. I disappeared in a haze of purple smoke, leaving the muggles with a story that nobody would believe.

***

I rematerialized in the back room of the Harry Potter store in the Roman Ghetto just as my friend Vincent was running inventory. I crashed through a pile of wands and landed on the floor, a few dozen boxes dropping down all around me.

"Ciao, Kimberly," he said with a fake smile. "Thank you for destroying my inventory. Do you know how long it took me to organize those?"

I didn't have the strength to stand, with every ounce of my body crying out in pain. "I don't, Vince. I'm sorry, though."

"I've come to expect it from you," he said, shaking his head. "I suppose you are in some sort of trouble, yes?"

"Always." I slid across the floor and pulled a crooked wand out of my back. "Whose wand is this?"

"Do you care?" he asked in a huff.

"Not really," I said, tossing the wand onto the pile of broken boxes. "I never read the books or watched the movies. Frankly, I don't know how you could care about this stuff when you know that magic is real."

Vince smiled, his fake teeth glimmering at me. Whatever he'd spent on those cosmetic surgeries to look human was worth it. There was no way to tell he was really a magical creature unless you looked very, very closely.

"I've spent my whole life in hiding, Kimmy. Every day of it, all I've ever wanted to do was tell the world that magic was real. But I knew that if I did, I would be hunted down and killed for revealing my true nature." He picked up a wand, straight and rather plain, made of brown wood. "Then, Harry Potter came, and every muggle kid in the world wanted to be a wizard. They believed in magic and believed they were wizards. Finally, it was a way I could talk about magic with every person I met, even if they didn't know it was actually real. Just being able to talk about it openly was freeing in a way I never thought I would be free."

"When you put it like that," I said, rising from the mess of boxes. "I suppose I see the appeal, in a way."

"So, what is this problem that you have?" Vince asked.

I shook my head. "I don't think it's something that you can help me with."

Vince was putting the boxes back together and raised his eyebrows. "Don't insult me, Miss Kimberly. I have been alive too long to allow anybody to insult me, especially you. Now tell me."

"Fine," I said, throwing up my hands. "I need to contact a god."

Vince chuckled. "Good luck. There hasn't been a god on Earth in centuries."

"I don't believe that," I replied. "There has to be one, hiding out somewhere on this stupid rock. Even if they're just on vacation."

Vince shook his head. "That's not how it works. The best you can get is a muse or a demigod. If they like a planet, they'll sometimes stick around. Once the other gods leave, they're the most powerful thing left." He paused to examine a label on one of the wand boxes. "Come to think of it, I heard a couple of muses stayed around after the others abandoned Earth. Apparently, the humans on this planet proved very attentive to the muse's suggestions."

"Any chance you know how to contact one?"

"I've never tried," Vince replied. "But there's a temple at the end of the block. Used to belong to Hera back in the day—Juno, as they call her here—before it was converted to a church. After Hera left, a couple of the muses that consorted with Zeus stayed behind to get away from her, and that temple was kind of their base of operations. I guess I would start there."

I rubbed my aching shoulders, readying myself for the next task. "Thanks."

Vince pointed a wand at me. "And don't forget to bring an offering."

"An offering?"

"The muses value beauty above everything else," Vince said. "They inspired some of the greatest works of art of all time. If you want to speak with them, you need to bring a gift."

"Any suggestions?"

Vince smiled. "I just happen to have a signed, first-edition Italian translation of *Harry Potter and the Philosopher's Stone*. Just came in a couple of days ago. I suppose I could let it go, for an old friend."

"I don't think a muse would appreciate a kid's book, do you?"

"If you don't think the muses inspired Harry Potter or that their magic wasn't involved in making it a global phenomenon, you are crazy."

"Fine," I said. "How much?"

"They go for $25,000, but since I know you have more money than a god, $50,000."

"That's highway robbery."

"I could just sell it to my collector friend, I guess." Vince shrugged. "But you pay for convenience and for wrecking my store."

I sighed. I could have just gone back to Aziolith's lair and picked out any one of the priceless books or artworks from my collection, but that would take time I didn't have. Besides, I did feel bad about destroying Vince's store.

"Fine." Luckily, on my way back to Earth, I had crawled across my coin purse in the tunnel. I reached into it and pulled out a handful of gold coins. "This should cover it."

I tossed them at Vince, who picked them up and counted them. "There's like thirty gold coins in here. Do you even know how much gold is worth?"

I shook my head. "Is that not enough? I can give you more."

"No," he said, pocketing the coins. "It's plenty."

"Then it doesn't matter," I said. "Can you just give me the book?"

He studied one of the coins. "It's a pleasure doing business with you."

***

Gods were fickle, capricious, and mercurial, from Zeus and Osiris down to the local patrons of small towns or forests. Even the least powerful god was more powerful than the most powerful human or monster. The Devil herself would barely stand a chance against one in a fight.

I walked out of the Harry Potter store and down the block into the square of the Roman Ghetto. Once a miserable place where Mussolini forced all Jews to live after kicking them out of their homes in WWII, the neighborhood had become a culinary powerhouse in the last days before the Apocalypse. The people there worked fervently to regain that label once Katrina ended it and sent demons back to Hell where they belonged…or, at least, most of the demons.

For my money, it rivaled New York or Paris for culinary delights. I tried to eat in the main square as often as possible on my way through Rome, even though it was in an inconvenient location near the water, away from any of the main attractions that usually highlighted my trips.

Past the main square rested a ruin of an old temple of Juno. It had been excavated in the 1900s, and a set of white columns stood at its entrance. Across a brick bridge, a small door led into the church. All the temples in Rome had been transformed into churches, a slap in the face for all the old gods that built Earth from clay.

I entered the church, where a tall, plump man with a tonsured head performed mass in the original Latin. The intimate congregation stood and swayed together, slowly and solemnly, singing the hymns.

The service lasted for thirty minutes, and then the attendees cleared the pulpits and followed the priest outside into the square. He shook hands with each of them, smiling all the while. I waited until the church was clear and then walked up to the altar.

"*Mi scusi,*" I heard from behind me. I turned around to see the priest staring at me. "*Desidera?*"

"Ummm…" I replied. "English?"

He nodded. "A little."

"I'm looking for the temple of Juno and Jupiter?"

"Ah, Juno?" he said. "Outside. The Ruins."

I smiled. "Thank you."

I walked outside and saw a portico that I had overlooked on my initial entrance into the church. The ruins looked like the burnt remains of a building, with a rotting archway held up by two columns. The grass underneath had risen to overtake the bottom of the brick walls.

I followed the railing around to the front of the ruins. A fence prevented me from walking on the grass, so I knelt on the near side of it, clutching the first edition *Harry Potter* in my hands. I knew a great deal about summoning rituals from my time as a demon hunter, though I had never used one to conjure something so mighty as a god. I placed the Harry Potter book at the entrance to the temple ruins. "*Diva potens tibi munus offero.*"

I sat down to wait. If the muse was happy with my offering, she would appear soon and accept the gift. Otherwise, I would have to find something else to entice her. I watched the entrance as the sun set behind the building, and the lights rose to illuminate the structure. People dressed in suits and dresses walked through the Ghetto, and the quiet restaurants bloomed into bustling eateries and hopping nightlife spots as diners funneled in. The chatter overtook the street, and minstrels wandered through, singing and playing their instruments.

"Did you really think that a single Harry Potter was enough of an offering to draw a goddess?" a sweet voice came from behind me. I turned to see a beautiful woman with blonde hair pulled taut into a ponytail. She wore a floral print dress and red shoes, and her skin radiated in a way I had only seen a few times in my long life.

"It's probably the most important work of the last century."

"A sad commentary on your history, then."

"My friend thought it would work," I said. "Did it?"

"Perhaps." Her bright red lipstick parted to reveal her teeth when she smiled. She bent down to pick up the book. "We inspired this, did you know?"

"Yeah?" I said. "My friend said you did. He'll be very excited to know he was right."

"We have inspired all the great works of this world, but this one was special to us. It allowed the world to talk about magic and gave comfort to millions of creatures around the world who had, until its publication, lived in the darkness. Do you know the entirety of Harry Potter Land in Hollywood is staffed by monsters and wizards now?"

I shook my head. "I did not."

"I'm very proud of that, despite some of its more problematic elements." The blonde woman stopped herself and cleared her throat. "But you are not here to talk about Harry Potter."

I shook my head. "I've never even read it."

"A pity." The woman gave a soft sigh. "It's quite good."

"I'm sure it is, but I'm here for something else."

"Of course. Everybody evokes the gods for their own ends and never ours. Did you ever think that is why we dislike humanity so much?"

"No, I didn't ever think about it." I shrugged. "I never thought about any of it, though, honestly."

"If you were only summoned to do favors, you would have a poor opinion of those that summoned you, wouldn't you?"

"I guess so."

Her nose wrinkled. "Well, get on with it."

"I'm looking for something. It's really important. A key to—"

"Unlock the beast in the center of the Earth?"

"Yes!" I shouted. "Have you seen it?"

"No," she shook her head. "I know of it, though. You are not the first who has come for it. Not even the first this week. I'm sorry, I cannot help you."

"But you have to help me," I said, stepping toward her. "I come on orders from Katrina, the Devil. If that key falls into the wrong hands, it could unleash Ragnarok."

"I know of such a key." She chuckled. "I can assure you it is very well protected."

"That's not good enough. Even now, there is a plot to summon the Four Horsemen and unleash Ragnarok. They already have one of the horsemen's weapons."

"Horse people. One is a woman," the muse said without malice. "Which one have they obtained?"

"The Bow of Misery." I pulled the dagger out of my belt. "And I have another."

She took several steps backward. "Why are you showing it to me?"

I peered at her, adjusting my grip on the dagger. "Because if you don't help me, I'm going to be forced to use it."

She wagged her finger at me. "It is not polite to threaten a god. It rarely works out well."

"I do not want to threaten you, but I am desperate." I pulled the dagger up to my chest. "Tell me what you know, so I can protect the world."

The muse arched her eyebrows. "Are you sure that's what you're doing?"

"Yes."

"Very well, if that is the story you are telling yourself.' She sighed. "My sister has taken up residence in the Uffizi, surrounded by the art she inspired in her life. If you can find her, perhaps she will tell you where she hid the key. I washed my hands of it ages ago."

"Thank you," I said, sheathing the dagger and placing it back in my belt.

"And thank you for the gift." She held the book close to her chest. "I truly do hope you know what you are doing."

"Me too."

CHAPTER 20

Akta

Location: Mars

I blinked and appeared on the surface of Mars, a hundred yards in front of a massive canyon. The red sand on Mars was stagnant due to the lack of atmosphere, which was part of why we initially thought that the planet had been abandoned like Europa and Venus. We were wrong. The people of Mars dug into the planet and lived in its belly. That's why, when Katrina proposed using the Martian core to annex Hell, they were reluctant to agree.

Martians led unnaturally long lives but had a sparse population. When Katrina pointed out that a single Hell pit only took up the room it would take to house their entire race quite comfortably, they began to see the upside— besides, she would pay them handsomely for the space. The Queen of Mars, Nebet, made a deal with Katrina allowing her to build an annex of Hell deep in the bowels of the Martian core.

My neck craned upward to view the highest structure on the planet, Olympus Mons, seven and a half times higher than the old home of the gods on Earth, Mount Olympus and containing the power of twelve Mount Etnas. It was the seat of power for the Martian government and my destination.

I blinked again and reappeared in front of the huge structure. When I placed my hand on it, the heat vibrated off my hand and through my body. Old magic concealed the entrance of the queen's castle.

"*Malkaŝu vin al mi*," I said, pressing my hand onto its surface again. A pulse vibrated through my fingers and echoed across the side of the mountain. I stepped back as the mountain itself began to rumble. The rock parted, revealing a silver door behind it. I walked forward and placed my palm on the pad that slid out from the side of the door.

The pad lit green, and the doors slid open, revealing a golden light. I stepped inside and the door shut behind me, as it had a hundred times before. A tall, thin, blue-skinned alien with black eyes and sunken cheeks slinked toward me. The Martians walked with small, deliberate steps, making it look like they were gliding more than walking, and their spine hunched, so it always looked like they were bowing.

The alien spoke softly, raising his thin arm from behind an enormous red coat covering his whole body. "Great Akta, it is an honor to welcome you back to our home."

"Thank you, Ikura," I replied, dipping my head to match his bow. "It is always a pleasure to be in your presence."

"And I yours." Ikura turned and gestured for me to join him on his walk back down the sleek metal corridors of their castle. "What brings you to our home today?"

"You have been keeping an object for Katrina that is of the utmost import to us."

"We keep many objects from many civilizations," he replied. As we walked, I noticed the tubes of lava that rose from the ground and made their way through the castle.

"This one is a lance, ancient, and very powerful," I replied. "I gave it to you as a gift upon the completion of our agreement to annex the core of your planet."

"Ah, yes," Ikura said. "I know of it. Quite beautiful and brimming with magical energy. We keep it safely stored in a vault far under this planet."

"I'm…afraid I need it back," I said, knowing that my words had the ability to offend the Martian vizier.

Ikura turned to me. "Why? I assure you that our armory is impregnable."

I stepped toward him, keeping my movements small and controlled. "That's what we thought about the one in Hell, too, but somebody stole another weapon from the Devil's armory. There are many agents out to do harm to Katrina. We can't risk any possible failure points. We can't be too careful."

Ikura stopped. "Are you insinuating that we are failure points?"

I shook my head. "It's not that, Ikura. Please, we mean no offense, but if these weapons fall into the wrong hands, the entire universe will be in jeopardy."

Ikura sighed and, after a long, disappointed silence, kept walking. "I thought you had more faith in us than that. You will have to make your case to the queen. She will be most unhappy to hear you have lost faith in us after we have done so much for you."

"That is not my intention, but I have my orders."

"I understand. We are all foot soldiers to another's whims, are we not?"

"We are, Ikura," I replied. "That is something that transcends borders and planets."

***

Ikura led me through the castle until we reached a high metal door to the throne room. It was adorned with Martian runes for intelligence, trust, courage, and balance—the pillars of the Martian code and the four principles that governed their society. They valued these qualities and had a reverence for words. Speaking the wrong ones had the distinct potential to excommunicate you from the Martian people and have ceaseless war declared on your people.

I remembered the day we brought the Lance of Conquest to the Martian queen. It was at the end of our negotiations to create a Hell on Mars. The queen was uneasy with our alliance, and the weapon was a way to ease her concerns that Katrina would destroy her planet. She was, after all, the Devil, and even on Mars, they knew the risks of bargaining with the queen of all lies.

The lance was a gift that showed trust, trust in the queen because the gift could kill Katrina, and trust that we believed Queen Nebet could protect it with her life if necessary. Now, I was saying that even her life was not enough.

"Follow me," Ikura said in a low voice.

The doors parted open for him, and we walked inside the futuristic throne room. The room featured a hundred metal pillars that rose into the ceiling. A dozen tanks of cool blue liquid lined the room. The liquid was a coolant pumped through the castle and mixed with the lava from the volcano, working to balance the temperature of the castle and keep the volcano beneath them from erupting.

In the perfect center of the room, equidistant in every direction, rested a metal throne. On it sat a tall, thin, Martian woman, dressed in a silver cloak and wearing a silver headdress that extended a full foot above her head. While the rest of the Martians hunched and bowed, their queen was bred to stand straight, and with an enormous amount of effort, she did so. The Martian body was thin and not fortified with enough back muscle to stand straight, so it was a constant balancing act to maintain this posture. However, it was what identified her position as above the rest of the Martians. She never bowed to anyone.

"Great Nebet," Ikura said, gliding toward the throne. "I present to you, Akta of the Forest, returned from Earth, and Hell, with a message to deliver from the Devil."

Nebet nodded gracefully. "Akta of the Forest. Long has it been since you have roamed our halls."

I smiled and bowed my head. "A hundred years, give or take, my queen. I know my arrival comes with no notice, so I thank you. I appreciate you seeing me. What I have to ask is of the gravest concern."

"Please, ask."

I swallowed, taking a moment to collect my thoughts. I had tried to think of the right way to ask for the lance but had realized quickly enough that an ask like this could cause an interplanetary incident. Hell would not recover for another hundred years.

"I'm afraid I must request that you return the lance we gave you. There are forces beyond our control working in Hell. They seek to steal the lance and every important weapon of Hell to summon the Four Horsemen and unleash Ragnarok on the universe."

Nebet thought for a moment, her face impassive. "Then it should remain here, where it is safe. There is no safer place in the solar system than in the vault beneath the surface here. It is impenetrable to all but my closest advisors."

"I understand, your majesty, but I have my orders."

"No, I don't think you do understand," Nebet said, every word pointed and deliberate. "That lance was given as a gift, and a gift is a sacred bond among my people. It was given as a sign of trust. If you break that trust, then I'm afraid we will have a problem."

I dropped my head. "It is not my wish to cause a problem with you. You are a trusted ally and friend. However, I have my orders."

Nebet let out a deep bellow. "Then it is time to renegotiate the terms of your occupation of our planet. That, too, was also given in trust."

I held out my hands. "Please know that I would never ask for this unless it was vitally important."

"And trust is vitally important to my people. I ask that you reconsider your request. Once a bond of trust is broken, it is not easily mended."

I had to think quickly. If I took the lance, I risked losing our pact with Mars and possibly creating an interplanetary incident. Still, I could not simply take the word of the monarch that the weapon was safe. "Perhaps," I said, finally, "if I could see the security system for the lance and confirm its safety, it might be enough to allay Katrina's fears."

Nebet sighed. "It brings no joy to me that you would ask such a thing, but given the unique circumstances by which you come here, I suppose I can make a concession. I will have my men bring you to our vault, and when you have seen the level of care we have taken to safeguard the weapon, you will be satisfied."

"I hope so, your majesty."

"So do I, for your sake."

CHAPTER 21

Julia

Location: Dis, Hell

"Hey!" a video monitor shouted as I walked toward the store. Beatrice's nasal voice screamed at me from inside a glass display on either side of the entrance. "Buy some shoes!"

Beatrice had always been direct, but while there was something endearing about her hollering when she did it in person, coming from a video monitor, it was ominous, off-putting. I opened the door to the store and saw her sitting on the top of a lifeguard tower in the back of the store. She pointed with a long metal rod. "Swamp monster needs help on aisle three, Stanley!"

A dozen monsters tried on shoes while elven retail associates helped them get the right fit. Only elves and leprechauns had the skills to mold custom shoes fast enough for all of the Hell monsters who needed them. Beatrice employed every decent cobbler in Hell to grow her empire.

"Julia!" Beatrice shouted, her voice filled with exuberant enthusiasm. "You're back!"

I walked toward her, a bit confused. Beatrice was never happy to see anybody except for her father. She dropped her metal rod, leaped down from her chair, and wrapped me in a hug.

"I thought I would never see you again. We heard Thriaska gave Akta bad information, and—and we feared the worst."

"That's not exactly what happened, but all is well," I said with a smile. "They found me, and I am free. It's nice to see you again."

"We couldn't have lived with ourselves if you died because of our intel."

I rubbed her head. "Well, technically, I am dead."

She looked up at me. "I meant dead-dead."

"Ah," I chuckled. "No, I'm not dead-dead."

"Tell Akta we're so sorry we believed that demon Thriaska. We'll never trust him again."

"I don't think you'll have that problem. Last time I saw him, he was very dead."

"Good!" Beatrice wiped her eyes. "He deserved to die for making us look bad. You know what happens if that kind of thing gets out? It could ruin our business. Gut our quarterly earnings!"

Beatrice and her father had been in Hell as long as anybody I knew and had a knack for picking up pertinent information from monsters passing through their store. They were innocuously pleasant in a way that put people at ease, and in over three thousand years, very few were wise to the fact that their information could be bought for the right price.

"It happens," I replied with a smile. "We all know what it's like to trust the wrong demon, but I'll let Akta know you were worried."

"It was worst than that." Beatrice blotted her eyes with her shirt. "We were beside ourselves with worry. We didn't know what to do."

"Well, maybe I can use that guilt to ask a favor."

Beatrice chuckled. "I would expect no less. What do you need?"

"I kind of need to know what you know about a certain…hammer."

"You could only be talking about one thing, then." Beatrice's eyes scanned the store. "Let's not talk out here. Come with me." She led me through the back room where leprechauns and elves cobbled together shoes at lightning-fast speed and knocked on a door in the back. "Hey, old man. Somebody's here to see you."

Clovis's haggard voice spoke from the other side. "I'm busy today. Tell them t—"

"It's Julia." Beatrice smiled at me.

"Julia!" There was the sound of a chair scraping along the floor, then footsteps. Clovis's voice turned from exasperation to enthusiasm. "Why didn't you say so? Let her in!"

Beatrice pushed open the door, and Clovis was already standing there, waiting to greet me. "Good to see you, Julia. We thought you were done for."

"Not done for." I shook my head. "Not yet, at least. I'm very much alive, but I don't know how long any of us will be if you can't help me."

"Oh, my, grave concerns all around. You and your kin never have it easy, do you?"

I shook my head. "Unfortunately, that's always the way."

Clovis walked back around his messy desk and sat down. "Please, please, sit down, just move the papers."

I picked up a set of papers and laid them on the floor, then sat down across from him. "What do you know about the Hammer of War?"

Clovis and Beatrice both laughed. "I know people have been chasing it for as long as there's been a Hell. Old wives' tale if you ask me."

"Why do you say that?"

Beatrice leaned onto the desk. "People have scoured every inch of Hell, and there's never been any sign of it. You know about the Bow of Misery. That was found rather quickly. And the Dagger of Obsolescence?"

"That one we know."

"It was forged out of Death's scythe, eons ago."

"The Lance of Conquest," Beatrice continued, "was found on a dig site during Lucifer's reign. But the Hammer of War? Nobody has been able to even sniff it in all the eons I've been here."

I leaned forward. "It has to exist somewhere, Clovis. Tell me everything you know."

"You know how much that information is worth on the open market?" Beatrice asked.

"Is it worth my life?" I replied. "Remember, your intel almost killed me."

"Touché," Beatrice said. "All right, but this is your one favor."

Clovis took off his glasses and cleaned them on his shirt. "I'm afraid there's just not much to say. There's a lot of hearsay and conjecture that…"

"Not good enough," I said. "I need you to synthesize all the information you know and give me a real, tangible lead. Of all of the things you've heard, what's the absolute best lead? We don't have a lot of time, and so I need to chase the best possible thing."

"Very well," Clovis nodded. "A couple of months ago, they were excavating for a new skyscraper on the outskirts of Dis, and there was a rumor that they found a scroll. It was very intriguing to The True Path. They bought it for an exorbitant sum and brought it to their church, where they keep it under lock and key."

"And you think that what they found was a clue to the location of the hammer?"

Clovis put his glasses back on his head and wrapped the frames around his ears. "I don't know, but if you're saying that somebody is trying to find the Four Horsemen's weapons, then it makes sense that they found something, doesn't it?"

I stood up. "And that's the best lead you have?"

"It's little more than conjecture, but it's something. I'm using Akta's assumption that the church is involved in this somehow. They would not have started this quest to find the horsemen's weapons without a credible clue as to where they could all be found." Clovis narrowed his eyes. "They wouldn't attack Akta unless they were desperate or confident. It's not much, but everything else I know is simply not very credible or from a long time ago. Even this is a whisper on a prayer off the lips of a criminal, passed down from monster to monster. I can say that the greatest minds in Hell have looked for the hammer for generations, and every one of them has come up empty."

"I think this time they might be close to recovering it," I replied. "Asmodeus was so confident that he would start Ragnarok. So confident that he captured me to lure Kimberly down here. Do you know the risks associated with that kind of deception? I just can't believe that they would risk it if they weren't 100 percent sure they would find all four weapons."

"I agree with you there."

"Which means they know something we don't know, and if that's the case, then maybe this scroll is the answer. I have to get it and hope you're right."

"Then I wish you the gods' speed."

"I need their luck more than their speed."

"Then I wish you that as well."

***

The True Path's main church was in the center of Dis's newly renovated downtown, resting between two fifty-story skyscrapers. The church itself was old, or at least it looked old. I had visited the greatest cathedrals on Earth, and it was every bit their rival, with intricate detail on every column and exquisite monsters carved into the façade.

However, like most things about the church, the architecture rang hollow. It was beautiful, but it reeked of imitation, desperation, and the need to be taken seriously. The church spent years trying to justify its existence with little to show for it. Recently, when the fervor for Hell to return to its traditional roots grew into a frenzy, the church was able to focus the hatred of monsters toward Katrina. It gave them something to believe in.

I crossed the busy intersection and walked up the marble stairs into the church. Underneath the church rested a reference library open to any monster with curiosity and an afternoon to kill, including me. The church had been actively recruiting monsters for years, but their message finally caught on with certain sects over the past year, as Katrina's modernization was felt more acutely by the monsters it displaced.

Monsters used to be their own bosses, or at least that's how it felt to them. Technically, they were slaves, but in reality, they were able to roam the countryside with little interference. Now, those monsters who once worked with little oversight were forced to clock in and clock out with complicated computers and report any accidents that happened on site, instead of just sweeping murders under the rug, and excessive torture was now punished instead of encouraged.

No, the monsters of Hell did not like the changes to the old-world order, and the church promised a return to "normalcy," when monsters were monsters and humans were subservient instead of being in charge.

Inside the church, the ceiling vaulted high into the air, and the walls were painted with horrific depictions of demons slaughtering and ruling over humans. The church was relatively empty, except for a small assortment of monsters lighting candles and praying in the vestibules around the church. Each one honored a different god of old and the dukes of Hell: Lucifer, Mammon, Asmodeus, Beelzebub, Azazel, and Mephistopheles.

Lucifer had been killed by Katrina during the Apocalypse. Beelzebub and Azazel had crossed Katrina in the decades after the Apocalypse ended, and their heads now rested on pikes in front of her castle, but the others still very much resided in Hell and exerted their influence over its operation. Rumor was that the remaining dukes funded the church, part for publicity and part for recruiting. Nobody had ever confirmed who ran the church, but it was well known that a large endowment allowed it to run without question.

One thing was sure, The True Path church was influenced greatly by the Catholic Church, and everything down to the black robes of the clergy was meant as a twisted take on it. An impish deacon with a white collar and black robe strolled up to me, wringing his hands in front of him.

"Can I help you, sister?" the demon asked, cocking his head.

I nodded. "Yes, I'm looking for the reference library."

"Down the stairs at the front. Do you have a library card?"

"I'm afraid not."

"No bother. No bother. Our library is open to all curious parties who seek knowledge. I assume you are an active member of the church, then?"

"I am."

"Oh, that is very, very good. We are so glad you have joined our noble mission."

"Me, too. It is the most important mission in the world."

"We very much agree. To return to the world as it once was is the noble pursuit of all monsters. The only noble pursuit."

"I agree. Long live the gods of old."

"Long may they reign in the heavens, and long may a demon reign in Hell."

"Yes…" I stopped for a moment. "I heard your library has a very important scroll you bought from the construction site recently. Is that true?"

The deacon smiled. "That is a rumor, my dear."

"Ah," I replied. "I am a bit of a scholar myself. I would very much have liked to see it if the rumor were true, that is."

"I see, and what is your noble pursuit when you are not aiding us in ours?"

"Magical weapons and armor," I replied. "I heard your scroll might hold a secret to finding a very important weapon."

"Oh, it does so much more than that," the imp said with a smile. "It is the answer to everything."

"Then you do have it?"

"Bother. I suppose my lips are too loose for my own good. But yes. Yes, we do."

"Fabulous," I replied. "May I see it? Just for a moment?"

"Of course," the deacon replied. "I am also a seeker of knowledge. Follow me."

CHAPTER 22

Katrina

Location: Devil's Castle, Hell

Heaven.

I hated the pompous angel jerks that ran Heaven and their sanctimonious boss. I heard it in their voices every time I talked to them: They looked down on me and disagreed with how I ran things in Hell. They didn't think we should modernize. They didn't think we should make things different or better. They just wanted to keep the status quo, and I challenged that stagnant way of thinking.

But they had no idea what was even going on in Hell. Lucifer ran the place for thousands of years, and he didn't know what was going on there. He was clueless before his death, which he welcomed as an escape from the heat, and he was willfully ignorant even after his death now that he resided in Heaven.

But I could take it.

I was forged in it through two years of Hell on Earth. I saw every little deficiency of Hell, and I wasn't about to just let them go when I actually had the power to fix it. I placed my hand on the blue stone behind my throne, and a blue light shone in the middle of the room.

"Michael!" I shouted as the light materialized and morphed into the silhouette of an angel. "I can see you, idiot."

The angel was crouched down behind a chair, trying to avoid me. He looked at me, feigning surprise. "Oh, Katrina. I didn't see you there."

I sighed. "Yes, you did. You just didn't want to talk to me."

He pushed himself to his feet. "You aren't wrong there. You never have good news, do you?"

"You aren't wrong, either," I replied. "This is Hell. There's never any good news. Heck, if there were, I certainly wouldn't share it with you since I hate you and all."

"Well, the hatred is mutual," Michael said with a smile. "I suppose you have more bad news, then?"

"Not quite bad news. Just annoying news." I stepped down from the throne. "I need to talk to you about the Sword of Damocles. It h—"

Michael held up his hand to silence me. "We have that handled, thank you very much, is that all?"

I moved closer to the blue vision. "You don't understand. The Lords of Hell are trying to start Ragna—"

"Don't finish that sentence," Michael said forcefully. "We are aware of what they are trying to do, and we have calculated for every eventuality."

"You have?" I blinked. "Then what are you doing about it?"

"I'm not going to explain myself to the Devil. How dumb do you think I am?"

"Very."

"You are both a demon and a human. Two things that don't keep secrets well." Michael crossed his arms. "As

I've already said, the sword is safe in Heaven, and demons cannot enter Heaven, so…"

I frowned. "And what if they have a sleeper agent in Heaven?"

Michael scoffed. "Impossible."

"Is it?" I asked. "Aren't demons just fallen angels?"

He nodded.

I cocked my head to the side, absolutely gob smacked by the brazen idiocy Michael showed to me. "And you don't think that even one angel up there could be sympathetic to the demons down here? There's not one friend, family, brother, sister, aunt, cousin, uncle—"

"Don't be silly." Michael chuckled. "Heaven is a paradise."

I shook my head in doubt. "I've been there. It's not so great."

"Well, you actually like Hell, so what do you know about great things?"

I balled up my fists. Nothing made me angrier than talking to stubborn jerks, and Michael was the stubbornest I knew and the most condescending. "I'm trying to make the best of a horrible situation. A horrible situation I'm in because of you, by the way."

"It's not so horrible, Katrina. It could be much worse."

"How?"

"You're not being tortured, at least," Michael said. "If you weren't the Devil, you would be eternally tortured for your sins."

I growled deeply. "Are you kidding me? Every single second of this afterlife is torture to me."

"You know what I mean."

Behind Michael, I saw Lucifer's horns bobbing up and down. "Lou! Lou!" I called.

Lucifer turned to me, his yellow eyes shining even through the blue screen of Heaven. "Is that Katrina? How are you?"

I sighed. "Horrible. Can you please tell Michael here that there could be a sleeper agent in Heaven?"

Michael waved me away with both hands, dismissively, and walked out of the light.

Lucifer laughed. "Honestly, I think that's a little ridiculous, though I love a good conspiracy theory. Heck, I created a bunch of them myself."

"It's not a conspiracy theory, asshole! It's an actual conspiracy!" I shouted. "The dukes of Hell are trying to unleash Ragnarok down here. That is a fact! And they seem to have a plan to make it work, which means they have a plan to get the Sword of Damocles. Do you understand that?"

Lucifer reached into a bowl he was holding and popped a handful of popcorn into his mouth. "I do, but I don't think there's a sleeper agent up here."

I sighed. "Can you just look around for me?"

"Katrina," Lucifer said. "If there's a sleeper agent here…if I even bring it up…you know…"

It hit me then. "They're going to think it's you."

He nodded. "They're going to think it's me. So, I can't help you. I'm sorry."

"Can I ask you something, Lou?"

"Make it quick. I want to watch *Mork and Mindy*."

"How big a threat is Surt?"

Lucifer's hand, full of popcorn, stopped abruptly on the way to his mouth. "Really big. The universe barely survived his rampage last time. In the whole galaxy, he is one of the greatest threats to our safety."

"So…he's a big ole threat, right?"

"Yes, that would be fair to say."

"Then how about you act like it!" I threw my hands in the air. "You have no idea how these demons work. They are so much worse than when you led them. They hate me, and they already almost killed me once. Those crafty bastards have been plotting something. They have the Bow of Misery. If they get the other weapons and the key, they'll unlock Ragnarok, and Surt will rampage the universe once more."

"You sound grumpy like you aren't getting enough sleep." Lucifer sighed. "How are you holding up?"

"Poorly." I glared. "You remember what it's like to be Devil, right?"

Lucifer chewed thoughtfully. "Yes, it was hard for me, and I didn't actually…do anything. You're actually doing something."

I crossed my arms. "Nobody likes me. But what else is new."

He popped another handful of popcorn. "I like you."

"You don't count."

"Why?"

I smiled. "Because I killed you."

He shrugged, popping another handful of popcorn into his mouth. "And yet, I still like you. That's got to count for something."

"Thank you."

He swallowed. "I'll look into it, Katrina, but don't expect much."

"It's Heaven. I literally never expect anything from you."

"That's a good policy."

CHAPTER 23

Akta

Location: Queen's Castle, Mars

Ikura led me past the throne room through a long, pristine hallway toward an elevator at the other end of it. He placed his long slender fingers on the computer pad next to the door, and after a moment, the screen turned green.

The doors slid open. "After you," he said.

I stepped into the glass elevator, and my eyes went wide as I looked out upon the center of the volcano, bubbling and brewing beneath me. Large ramps led around the volcano, and hundreds of Ikura's people walked across them. Blue cooling liquid flowed into the volcano, while red lava flowed through tubes away from it. "Wow."

"Yes," he said. "We do not often allow outsiders into the bowels of our operation. You should feel very honored."

I turned around to face him. "I am, truly. Our relationship is very valuable. I treasure it and hate doing anything to damage it."

Ikura pressed the button for the bottom floor, and the elevator started to descend. "The queen is a proud woman, and you have offended her. Still, she will mend. The fact that she has allowed you into the depths of our castle tells you everything you need to know about her trust in you."

I nodded solemnly. "I appreciate it. I still don't know how I will convince Katrina that you should be trusted with the weapon, but that is my burden, not yours."

"Once you have seen the precautions we use to protect the lance, I don't think you will have any problem convincing your Devil to entrust us with it. Then we can put this unpleasantness behind us."

The elevator stopped, and the door slid open to reveal a dark hallway. While the throne room was sleek and clean, the metal in this hallway was clunky and bulky. Ominous red lights overhead lit the hallway, casting harsh shadows on the walls.

Seeing me eye the hallway, Ikura spoke. "These beams have a hundred levels of metal on top of them, as well as the heat from the volcano beating against them. To keep the structure above it mechanically sound, they need a special construction."

I felt the struggle of those beams intimately. Often it felt like the weight of Hell weighed on my shoulders. "Makes sense."

"Follow me."

Ikura walked down the hallway, and I followed behind. The fortifications made the hallway much smaller and more cramped than the levels above, as well as considerably uglier, but they had nobody to impress in the bowels of the castle.

As we walked, I thought about how often the ugliest parts of us are the ones that are the most important, the ones that do the heavy lifting of our personality, while the pretty parts are the ones we show to people. *How many of my own hideous beams protected me from the pressure placed upon me and the heat working against me?*

When we reached the end of the hallway, we stood in front of a thick black metal door covered in runes that I did not recognize.

"What do they say?" I asked.

"They are magical protections to keep any unwanted elements from entering into our armory. We have collected them from races all over the galaxy. The weapons inside could destroy civilizations, so we used all the help we could get."

"I see," I replied as I watched Ikura plug a code into a computer panel.

His long fingers created rapid combinations that I couldn't fathom, not even if I had three hands. Once he was done, a speaker overhead let out a chime while a door rose from the ground, letting out a plume of cold steam as it opened. When the steam cleared, I looked upon a room lined with more thick, heavy rods.

Other Martians flowed back and forth between the rods, taking measurements and typing on their pads fervently. These Martians did not float elegantly like Ikura but loped around with long strides, their long bodies barely able to keep upright as they moved.

"Pay no mind to them," he said.

"Who are they?" I asked, my back burning as we moved through the facility.

"Disposables. Those who were not bred correctly. We use them for our least glamourous work."

"That's horrible."

Ikura cocked his head, watching them work. "They are fed and cared for. We treat them with the utmost respect, given their deformities. We used to just kill them, so this is a major improvement."

I bit my tongue as we walked through the corridors. Eventually, we stopped before a black column, triple the thickness of the rest.

"Disposable!" Ikura shouted. The word sent a shiver down my spine. "Open this lock now."

One of the Disposables shuffled over and looked down at his pad. "Authorization."

Ikura seemed visibly disgusted that the Martian would speak to him but swallowed his anger and swiped the pad from the alien's hand. He entered a code, and the metal column began to rotate. As it did, the heavy black metal column rotated and slid apart, revealing a blue cylinder underneath filled with bubbling liquid. In the center was the Lance. I recognized it immediately. White staff with a long, curved metal tip at the top, covered in runes known only to the gods themselves. It was the Lance of Conquest.

"There we are," Ikura said with a smile. "As you can see, your lance is protected more here than it could ever be in Hell. There is no way anybody could get to this weapon unless they were personally brought here by one of those with access, of which there are only five in all our colony, and they are only the most trustworthy of us. In fact, I dare say you should allow us to protect the other weapons since you seem to be having trouble keeping them safe yourself."

"I'll take it under advise—" A screech filled my ears, and I fell to the ground. My hands shook violently, and it felt as though my skin was being ripped from my bones. The fire in my back consumed me. I screamed again, and when I looked down, I saw a black mass rise from my body and coagulate into a massive wolf with glowing eyes and a hulking jaw.

"What is the meaning of this?" Ikura shouted. The wolf grabbed Ikura by the side of the head and smashed him into the glass again and again until the glass cracked and Ikura's skull was crushed. Red lights screeched and blared above me, and the Disposables rushed toward the walls, where they pulled laser guns from cases.

Three disposables came running, holding shock canes that glowed with lightning. The monster slashed through them with ease, sending their blue blood flying all over the walls. Then, the monster turned its attention to the glass, smashing it with its huge claws until the glass shattered and the blue ooze splashed across the floor.

The wolf reached into the cage and grabbed the lance just as the remaining squadron of Disposables pulled out laser guns and fired. They hit the wolf directly, but instead of falling backward in pain, the monster grew in size and stood up on two legs. It swung the lance and attacked the Disposables with it expertly, dusting them with several well-timed strikes. When it had finished, it rushed off down the hall.

I pushed myself to stand, my head reeling from the sounds of the alarm and flashing red and blue lights. The door to the armory began to close, and I rushed under it, tumbling forward at the last second to avoid being trapped inside. "Stop!" I shouted to the wolf as it ran into the elevator. I slid inside just as the doors closed. Now I was trapped in the elevator with the monster.

The wolf swiped at me with the lance, and I disappeared to avoid it, reappearing on the ceiling. Again, the monster slashed the lance, and I jumped to avoid it. I disappeared again and rematerialized in front of the monster, stabbing it in the jaw with one of my daggers. There was no effect. The monster swiped at me, and I disappeared again, this time appearing outside the elevator.

I unfurled my wings and rose into the air, chasing the elevator until it came to a stop. I waited in the hallway for the doors to open. Twelve soldiers in silver suits stood with me; laser guns pointed at the doors.

I ducked to avoid their blasts when the door opened, and the wolf-creature leaped out. The soldiers fired, but they were no match against the power of the monster, who slashed through them with the lance like they were nothing, then hurried into the throne room.

"What's the meaning of this?" Nebet screeched. When she saw the wolf, she screamed and covered her face.

It rushed for the queen, and I leapt forward, smashing against it with my legs and kicking it into the opposite wall. The monster snarled at me but, perhaps realizing the queen was not its main target and it had gotten what it came for, disappeared through the doorway, down the hall, and out of sight.

An uneasy silence filled the space, interrupted only by the buzzing of damaged lighting. "What just happened?" the queen said finally.

"I'm not sure," I replied. "But if I had to guess…I was possessed by a demon, which was just activated to steal the lance."

"So, this is your doing then?" Nebet said.

I turned around, my head bowed. "Not intentionally, but yes. Don't worry. I will make it right."

"I am worried." Nebet sneered at me. "And I don't think it's possible to rectify this."

Honestly, I didn't either. "Then I will try for the rest of my days. That is all I am capable of doing."

"I want it noted that my armory was perfectly protected until you showed up," the Queen said.

"I do recognize that, queen."

"Good," she snarled. "Now go find that demon."

I nodded and made my way toward the door. "With pleasure."

CHAPTER 24

Kimberly

Location: Uffizi Gallery, Florence, Italy

The Uffizi Gallery in Florence was nearly demolished during the time of the Apocalypse, along with most of the important museums around the world, including the Louvre and the Prado. Demons enjoyed nothing more than destroying human culture. They smashed through statues, ripped tapestries, and burned paintings. Some they covered in feces.

Luckily, museum curators were crazy and cared about art more than their own lives. They saved as many pieces as they could and either hid or traveled with them for the two years of the Apocalypse. Since that time, museums have rebuilt as best they could, and the Uffizi was no exception. Priceless pieces from smaller collections were consolidated into a few galleries in every country where the surviving masterworks lived.

The most important piece in the Uffizi Gallery was The Birth of Venus, painted by Botticelli at a time when few artists understood the human form. A museum employee, Gabriella Rossi, stole it in the first days of the Apocalypse and nurtured it like a baby until she was able to return it to the gallery a half-decade later, to the utter gratitude of a nation. Had she not acted with such bravery, the Birth of Venus surely would have been destroyed.

A statue to Gabriella Rossi stood in the front of the gallery, holding the rolled-up painting under her arm, which was not easy since the painting was almost six feet high and nine feet long. How she survived with it was still a mystery to many non-magical people, but the magical community knew she was able to enchant the poster tube to fit in her hands and then concealed herself from monsters at every turn.

I passed the smiling sculpture of Gabriella, raising the painting in victory, on my way into the horseshoe-shaped gallery and purchased a ticket from the booth in the front. I didn't know what I was looking for exactly, but I hoped I would know it when I saw it. There were several thousand images in the gallery, and any of them could draw the attraction of a god. I joined a tour to get my bearings, hoping to spark something inside of me. If nothing else, perhaps I would learn something from the bubbly tour guide who was smiling at me in her oversized red blazer.

"Welcome," the spritely guide said as she stood at the front of a long hallway. "This building dates back to 1560. Built by Giorgio Vasari for Cosimo I de' Medici, it was meant to house the administrative and legal offices of Florence. 'Uffizi' means legal offices in ancient Italian. However, over the years, it morphed more and more from offices into a gallery, until 1769 when the gallery was opened to the public for good and stayed that way ever since."

I sighed to myself. I hated tours. As she led us down the hallway, I was already tuning her out, instead focusing on the impressive paintings that stood thirty feet tall and lined the gallery. Seeing these works in person always put me in awe.

"We're going to go upstairs and start from the beginning of this wonderful gallery."

The group followed the guide to a room numbered seven. "This room is dedicated to important works from the early Renaissance." She gestured toward a painting of a green woman holding a green baby, with a cracked-out shepherd on one side standing next to a friar, and on the other side a cardinal in a silly hat, and a bored woman next to him. "This piece is called Santa Lucia de' Magnoli, drawn by Domenico Veneziano between 1445-1447 for the Santa Lucia de' Magnoli Church in via de' Bardi. This is one of the few masterpieces from that era. If you look at the brushwork…" She continued, but I couldn't bear to listen to her presentation. All I could see was how misshapen all the characters were and how I could have been a master painter if I'd lived in the thirteenth century.

The tour guide continued around the gallery, stopping every once in a while to regale us with new information about the paintings. Sometimes it was hard to believe anybody could have considered some of these masterpieces, even during their time. Then, she turned a corner as I came face to face with Botticelli's Birth of Venus. It was perfection. It was like the painting leaped forward one hundred years in a single image.

"Painted by Sandro Botticelli between 1482 and 1485, the Birth of Venus defined this era of Renaissance painting." The tour guide had so much enthusiasm for the piece that it was hard not to get attached to its wonder and the way the light hit the goddess as she emerged from her clamshell, suspended forever with a slight, coy smile. "Venus is portrayed naked and vulnerable, emerging onto the seashore, as the wind blows gently and melodically, caressing her hair. Her handmaid, Ora, waits for the goddess to dress her. It is my favorite piece in the whole gallery, and that's saying something because I love every single piece in here."

After the tour guide admired the painting for a long moment, she continued with the group, but I couldn't leave the painting. If there was a work of art that deserved the respect of a goddess, the Birth of Venus was it. I scanned the room, looking for anything out of the ordinary, but the gallery was filled with tourists, all staring slack-jawed at the painting that took up an entire wall of the gallery.

"Are you coming?" I heard the tour guide say to me. Her smile was so pleasant and warm that I couldn't tell her no.

"Oh, yes," I replied. "I'm sorry."

"Please hurry," she said. "There's a lot to see, and it's easy to get lost."

I nodded and followed behind her as she led the group around the horseshoe. She spoke about the beauty of all the pieces, but never with such exuberance as she did with The Birth of Venus. Eventually, she wound around the other side of the gallery, where she reached a gallery labeled 42.

"This gallery is very special," the tour guide said. "It houses many of the great sculptures from in and around Tuscany. Many of the sculptures were destroyed during the great Apocalypse of 2020, but we have been able to preserve some and replace others. It is a favorite place for children and adults to take pictures, as the statues within are quite…lively…I think is the right word."

She walked inside, and the group followed behind. Immediately, I understood what she meant. In much of the Uffizi, the statues were plain and boring, standing straight up or with their hands on their lap as they sat. However, in this gallery, the sculptures danced and laughed and ran. There was life to them in a way that there wasn't in any of the other rooms.

I stepped forward and noticed the intricate marble work that crafted a woman's arm as she lifted it into the air. I moved around to another one, who had raised her arms high into the air, her legs extended like she was going to push off the ground.

I crouched down to get a better look at a third, a woman bending down to pick up a flower on the ground. She smiled a slight smile, and the longer I stared, the more the mouth seemed to turn up upwards. I swore I saw goosebumps rise on her arm, and then I saw that her chest fell and rose ever so slightly.

"Go away," a small voice whispered. It had to have come from the statue. "Are you daft?"

"What?" I looked back at the group of tourists behind me. "Who said that?"

"I did," I heard again from the statue. "Go away."

"Oh my god," I said, leaning in. "You can talk."

"Of course," it hissed. "I know that. I'm the one talking."

"You have to help me," I said, thinking myself slightly crazy for talking to a statue. "I need—"

"Not now. Come back later."

"And then you'll help me?"

"Only if you go away. Right now."

I stood up and turned away without a second thought. I needed to come back when the gallery was empty, which meant I would have to wait until after closing. Luckily, that would be easy for me as a pixie. All I had to do was remember the room down to the last detail and then drop a pinch of pixie dust when I wanted to come back. I studied the room until it was perfectly clear in my mind, and then I walked out with the group, a small smile on my face.

CHAPTER 25

Julia

Location: The True Path Cathedral, Dis, Hell

The imp deacon led me down several staircases, past the golden-framed pictures of demons and Devils that came before, from Lucifer, to Velaska, to Hades, and all the way back to Anubis, and the dukes of Hell, who governed Hell from the time of the Fall.

The deacon clasped his hands together at his chest. "We have the greatest collection of literature on demonology and the history of Hell in all the underworld, did you know that?"

I shook my head. "I did not. How is that possible since your institution is still quite young?"

The imp smiled at me, his pointed, yellow teeth shining. "We have very generous benefactors and many who believe in our mission."

"What is that mission?" I asked, keeping lockstep with him.

"Don't you know?" he asked. "You are a member, after all."

I swallowed, then dipped my head, trying to come up with a workable lie. "I am, but I am quite new. I'm sorry. I didn't want to seem like I was green, but I've only just joined in the past month. That's one reason I'm so interested in your library."

"That's okay, child," the imp said. "Our membership grows every day. We want to restore order to Hell. We were meant to be ruled by a god, an angel, or a fallen angel in the form of a demon, not a human. We aim to remind the underworld of The True Path, which lies not in modernization, but the remembrance of our past."

"I see," I replied. "Who do you worship at the end of the day? That's the part that has always confused me. Who do we pray to?"

"Excuse me?" the imp asked, confused.

"Well, every church worships something, right? God, Yahweh, Allah, the Way, Buddha, Vishnu, Ra, something. So what does the church worship?"

The imp spread his arms wide. "We worship the holiness of Hell itself, of course. We worship those that came before and the purity of our task."

"And what is your task?"

"To save humanity."

I laughed. "Excuse me, but that is expressly *not* what demons do here. Their job is to torture humans, isn't it?"

The imp shook his head. "Absolutely not."

I stopped in my tracks. "I've been in those pits. I was tortured in those pits until Lucifer saved me. There is no salvation going on there."

The imp turned to me. "Just because you don't see it doesn't mean it isn't there. Our job is to punish the sins out of humanity so that they might attain purity and return to the Source."

My brow crinkled. "The Source?"

"The source of all things, and the seed of all creation."

My jaw worked silently while I worked to find words. Finally, I managed to say, "I have never heard any of this."

The imp continued down the stairs. "Of course you haven't. You have bought into the notion that Hell is some sort of punishment, but it is so much more than that." We reached the bottom of the stairs. "Ah, here we are."

The deacon picked up a small torch on the wall and proceeded down the dark hallway. When we reached the end of it, he opened a creaky wooden door riveted with thick iron and walked inside. Following him, I entered a small library filled with first edition books.

The priest placed the torch on a clasp jutting out of the wall. "We cannot use traditional lighting in this room for fear of damaging the books. In fact, if you would please put on a pair of gloves." He pointed to a pair of white gloves, and I placed them on my hands. They were small at first, but once I tried them on, they expanded to fit my fingers.

"Very good," the imp said. "Just a bit further." He led me deeper into the library, past the stack of books, into another small hallway between two bookshelves. "After you."

"Where are we going?" I asked.

He smiled at me. "Our most precious books rest in a special vault, carefully hidden from prying eyes. The scroll you seek is there as well." He led me to a much smaller door, which he opened and gestured for me to enter. When I did, he nodded to me slowly and then closed the door behind me. A latch slammed down on the door, and I was locked inside. I instantly felt like an idiot for being captured yet again.

"What's the meaning of this!" I shouted. "Let me out!"

"I'm sorry, my dear Julia, but I recognized you immediately. Asmodeus has been looking for you. You are essential to our plan."

"No, I'm not," I said matter-of-factly. "I don't even have the blood you need!"

He sighed. "This is true, but I am confident that your protégé will return to save you again, as she did before, and then we will have her for a second time."

"Do you really think so little of us?"

"Yes, we do," the priest said with a laugh. "We're counting on it, in fact."

I spun from the door and looked around at the priceless books scattered around the room. "This is getting old. Can you at least tell me which of these books you got from the dig site? Then, maybe this won't be a waste of time."

"I suppose it wouldn't hurt. It's not really a book, though, is it? It's the map on the desk, not that it is much use to you. We have already deciphered it and are close to finding the resting place of the hammer."

"Wonderful," I said.

I walked over to the large map on the table, barely held together by magic and cloth and yellowed by the decay of time. I bent down and recognized the writing style immediately. If I remembered correctly, there was a book in Aziolith's library just like it. A quick look at the creasing on the map showed that it had come from a book, folded for gods knew how long.

If I could get out of the room with the map, I could bring it to Aziolith. Dragons had long memories, and if he could give me some information, then I might be able to figure out where to look for the hammer.

"Don't bother trying your magic," the imp said. "It won't work in here." The deacon sounded smug, but I doubted that he knew that I had learned new tricks since I came to Hell. I rolled up the map and clasped it tightly in my hands, then stomped over to the door.

"Do you know what pixie dust is, really?" I asked.

"I truly don't care," the deacon replied. "Sounds like pathetic fairy magic."

"You should care," I said, dipping my hand into a small cache of dust I kept in a purse on my belt. I pulled out a pinch of it and rubbed it in a circle on the door. I took the rest and rubbed it on my gums. "It's a focusing agent. Yes, it can make us disappear at will, but it can also focus our magic to do all sorts of things…like this."

I closed my eyes and pictured the door exploding in front of me. When I opened my eyes, I slammed my hand against the door. A quake blasted the wood into the deacon, sending him falling backward. I stuck my hand through the new opening and picked up the latch. The door swung open, and I stepped over the unconscious deacon, out the door to freedom.

***

In an instant, I was in front of Aziolith's cave. I had been there hundreds of times before and knew it well. It was my haven in the brutality of Hell, the one place I knew I could be at peace and was truly safe. Not even the Devil would dare confront a dragon and upset the balance of power in Hell.

"Aziolith!" I shouted. "Are you here?"

"Hrm," Aziolith replied. "What if I said no?"

"Please don't say no." I tried to keep the desperation out of my voice. "I need your help."

Aziolith poked his head out of the entrance to his home. "This is becoming an annoying trait of yours to need help."

I nodded. "I know, and I'm sorry, but neither of us wants Ragnarok, right?"

"I'm unclear on that point, honestly," Aziolith replied. "Returning to Earth could be quite pleasurable."

I scoffed at him. "Not during the Apocalypse, it wouldn't be."

"Hrm, true," Aziolith groaned. "I did not have a very good time last time, honestly."

"Yeah, I was there. I remember. So how about we stop it, huh?"

Aziolith moved closer until his long neck extended out of the cave and curled around me. "Very well, you make a compelling case."

I pulled out the map and spread it onto the ground. "Do you recognize this map? The script looks familiar, but I can't place it. I thought—"

"Well, I'll be," Aziolith said with wonder in his voice. "This map came from one of my favorite books on Earth. I noticed a tear from a ripped page eons ago. I never found it in my travels...now it looks like you have."

"What was the book? I can't remember."

"It was a book written by one of the original architects of Hell." He thought for a moment. "This is a copy of the original blueprint to Hell itself."

I stared down at the map, speckled by waypoints and drawings indicating the original location of Dis, the dragon caves, the Gates of Abnegation, the Devil's Castle, and many other landmark places. It was written in an ancient language I didn't recognize.

"So, one of these might be the location of the hammer?" I asked.

Aziolith nodded. "However, it will also likely show the final resting place of Surt, along with many other secrets. This map is very powerful, in the right hands."

"In our hands."

Aziolith raised his eyebrows. "Perhaps. Trouble is, I don't recognize any of these symbols. I speak a hundred languages, and this does not look familiar to me. Perhaps an older demon than I could help you. More helpful still would be to find the original author."

"Do you know who that is?"

Aziolith looked up into space. "Her name was Yilir, consort of Charon before he passed away."

"Where is she now?" I asked.

Aziolith slowly shook his head. "I don't know, but Charon was a great friend of Akta's, so you might ask her."

"Thank you," I said. "I will do just that."

"Do you have time to finish our game?" Aziolith asked.

I shook my head. "Not now, old friend, but soon."

"I understand," Aziolith said sadly. "When you come back, Julia."

"Aren't you sick of me beating you?" I asked with a chuckle.

"Honestly, no. It is always quite enjoyable. And this time I am very sure I will win. I am so close to checkmate."

"Keep dreaming, old friend. Next time, I promise we'll play."

Aziolith smiled. "I will hold you to that."

"I hope you do."

I hoped there would be a next time. As I turned away from him, I got the sinking sensation that we were going to fail and that there was no stopping the inevitability of Surt returning to Earth.

CHAPTER 26

Katrina

Location: Asmodeus's Castle, Hell

I wasn't one for subterfuge or shrinking in the face of insurmountable odds. I fought demons when I was just a human and beat them back even then, without any powers. If they thought I feared them now that I had the powers of the Devil coursing through my veins, they had better think again. I would burn every castle in Hell down to find the conspirators and take my revenge.

Asmodeus's castle was one of the oldest and nicest in Hell. I had interacted with him several times over the centuries. He always came across unpleasant and petulant, but even he shut his mouth when I killed Beelzebub and Azazel after their attempted coup.

After I ripped them in half and disintegrated their flesh in the moat of lava surrounding my castle, I thought he understood my raw power. It seemed that in the ensuing centuries, the demon lords forgot my raw power. It was time to show them what happened when they pissed me off.

"Asmodeus!" I shouted, pushing open the doors to the castle and entering its foyer. A squad of demon soldiers rushed toward me. I slammed my fists together to form a shockwave which sent them all flying backward. I had no desire to kill the demon soldiers, even if they had betrayed me, but I certainly could not let them interrupt me.

"Listen to me!" I screamed. "I am your Devil. I have no quarrel with you, though you work for a traitor. Let me talk to your boss, and I will let you live. Stop me, and I will burn you from the inside and leave you nothing but dust." The demons stood straight at attention. "That's what I thought."

Beelzebub and Azazel had tried to usurp me a hundred years ago, and legend of my cruelty to them still lived on to this day. Nobody bothered to mention how I had tried to reason with them or how I had wanted nothing more than to live peacefully with the demons I ruled, but those two were impolite. No, they were downright treasonous.

The demon lords did not believe me powerful when I first came to Hell, but the decimation of the armies of two great demon lords and sacking of their lands to build the first of my superhighways showed the rest of Hell that I meant business. None had dared cross me since then. Until now.

I stomped through the castle into the throne room. Debris and rubble littered the ground, and a group of imps worked to clean it up. Looking up at the giant hole in the ceiling, I realized that must have been Aziolith's escape route when he rescued Julia, Akta, and Kimberly.

Asmodeus sat on his black stone throne, grinning at me. "I wondered how long it would take you to come for me."

"I do not wish to fight with you," I said, lowering my hands.

"Of course you do," he snarled. "That is exactly what you are here for. Devils are nothing if not hotheaded. It's one of your few redeeming qualities."

"I just want to know why you would come for me after all this time."

"Because you work to destroy the very fabric of Hell." Asmodeus pushed off his throne and walked toward me. "And I am not alone. Thousands stand with me. I am just their figurehead."

"Who else leads this army against me, then?"

Asmodeus laughed. "It is not an army with a leader. It is a hydra. When you cut off a head, two come to take its place."

I planted my feet on the floor and crossed my arms over my chest. "I have killed hydra before. I will kill this one too, including you if I must."

Asmodeus shrugged. "It doesn't matter. If I am dead, the cause still lives on."

I stomped forward angrily. "Then I will kill each member until this attack against me stops."

Asmodeus smirked. "You can try, but our victory is inevitable. You are as good as dead."

"If that's true, then tell me who works with you. Is it the church?" I asked.

Asmodeus laughed. "If you burn down the church, that will only infuriate its parishioners more, but I will tell you true. While some members of the church work with us, many don't. This is more than any one clan or organization. It is a movement that snakes through all of Hell. It has been coming a long time, Katrina, and now you shall reap what you sow."

I stomped up the steps to his throne. "Do not make me kill you."

"I cannot make you do anything," Asmodeus replied. "At least, not yet."

The smirk on Asmodeus's face grew until it turned into maniacal laughter. I grabbed his face and lifted him into the air. "Tell me what I want to know!"

"Never!"

I took hold of his legs and pulled them until they were no longer attached to his torso, and he screamed all the while. Finally, I had a use for my dungeon and its instruments of torture.

"Stop her!" Asmodeus shouted as I dragged his torso behind me, leaving a trail of blue ooze on our way out of the castle. None of the guards dared to help him. They knew what I would do to them if they did.

CHAPTER 27

Akta

Location: Mars

The smell of sulfur followed the demon's path through the Martian castle, only dissipating as I neared the front entrance. I pressed my hand on the pad in front of the door, and it slid open for me. Outside, on the surface of the planet, everything smelled faintly of rotten eggs, which meant the demon wolf's scent blended in with the other pungent stenches. Luckily, the same could not be said for its footprints, which were perfectly preserved in the clay.

The demon wolf didn't plant its feet like a normal wolf. Every twenty yards or so, it landed on the ground and left a solid footprint in the soil from one of its massive front paws. One of them was easily the same size as the three-headed dogs that Cerberus birthed so many eons. Her bloodline ended when Katrina killed her during the Apocalypse. A pity. Katrina would have liked to have a guardian as loyal as Cerberus now that her life was in danger.

The wolf's tracks ran several hundred yards in a straight line and then turned around the edge of a crater. I followed them to a cave on the edge of the cliffside, where they seemed to disappear. I followed it inside.

"Good dog. Good dog," I heard from inside the cave. Inside, there was a blue light and low hum from what I recognized as the same wraith I had chased through the caves of Pluto.

"You!" I shouted when I saw him. The demon dog snapped to attention and leaped between the ghost and me.

"You truly are the best tracker I have ever seen," the wraith said. The Lance of Conquest rested in the middle of a summoning circle in front of him. "Unfortunately, you are too late once again."

He held three blue orbs in the air and smashed them onto the ground. The blue light swirled into the air. *"Dominus meus misit me ad te. Dominus meus misit me ad te. Dominus meus misit me ad te!"*

The blue light collapsed around the lance, creating a blinding light that forced me to turn my head. When it softened, and I could see again, the lance was gone.

"What have you done?" I asked, furious.

"What I must do, for the good of Hell," the wraith replied. "I'm sorry, in a way, for involving you in this. But in another, more prescient way, I am glad to be the one to watch you suffer for the glory of my master."

"Asmodeus," I said.

The wraith laughed. "You truly have a myopic view of the world. This is bigger than Asmodeus. It's bigger than any one being."

"Then who?" I shouted. "Who do you work for?"

"The chain breaker himself," the wraith said with a smile. "He who will destroy your world, and every world, when he ascends."

"Surt."

Anger flashed across the wraith's face. "Do not speak his name! You are not worthy. When he returns, he will free me from my cursed life."

"That's stupid." I scoffed. "He's going to devour you."

The wraith laughed. "It is no more stupid than your loyalty to the human atrocity, pixie."

I took a step toward him, but the wolf growled at me more fiercely. "At least she works toward a noble good."

The wraith shrugged. "In your eyes. We all do a very good job of justifying our own actions and making them seem righteous."

"Tell me, how is destroying the universe righteous?"

"This universe is an abomination, created by petulant children." The wraith gestured around him. "My master will cleanse it with fire and remake it in the image of the Titans, the true rulers of this galaxy."

"And you'll be there to watch the universe burn, then?"

"Of course not. I will be released from my bond and returned to the Source, like all of us should be. This miserable excuse for existence will be vaporized."

"I won't let that happen." The wraith laughed again, and fire boiled in my eyes. "What is so funny?"

"Tell yourself whatever you need to keep going. You should know that you've done more than anyone to ensure that Ragnarok comes to pass. I know how important it is that you have a mission in life, futile as it might be."

The wraith pulled two more orbs out of his pocket and smashed them on the ground. Before I could fly toward him, both he and the demon wolf vanished into the ether, and I was alone in the cave.

Now, not only was I responsible for the death of several Martians but for the loss of another weapon that could summon the Four Horsemen.

It was not a banner day.

***

By the time I returned to the Devil's Castle in Hell, Julia was already standing in front of the throne, deep in conversation with Katrina. The Devil never looked happy, but she looked even more perturbed than usual.

"Akta!" Julia exclaimed excitedly. "Good to see you're still alive."

"Ah," Katrina said, turning to me. "There you are. Please tell me you have some good news from me."

"I'm afraid not," I replied. "While the lance was safe for a time, it has fallen into the hands of the dukes of Hell and Surt."

"That's not good," Julia said.

Katrina digested this for a moment. Finally, she said, "No, that is not good news." She pushed her hair away from her face. "Luckily, I have captured Asmodeus and brought him to my dungeon."

Julia shook her head. "I fear this is bigger than just Asmodeus."

"I agree," I replied.

Katrina nodded. "That's what Asmodeus said, too, but he's the best lead we have right now."

I threw my hands in the air. "Do you think he will ever tell you the truth?"

Katrina paced slowly before the throne. "I don't know, but if he doesn't tell us what we need to do, I will find every duke and noble in Hell and bring them to me."

"I fear it might come to that," I said, nodding. "I have hit a dead-end in my search."

"Funny you should say that," Katrina grumbled. "I'm actually glad you're back. Julia needs your help before you go to Asmodeus."

I turned to her. "What is it?"

"You were friends with Charon, yes?"

"I was." Until Katrina killed him, he was one of my best friends. It broke my heart when I found out he was dead, and it took me decades to forgive Katrina for her impulsiveness. I bit my lip to avoid speaking any of my pain in losing him.

Julia nodded. "Did you know his paramour, Yilir?"

"Of course. She was one of the original architects of Hell." I gestured around me. "She built this castle, actually."

"Then I have many, many words for her," Katrina grumbled. "This place is the worst."

"What happened to her?" Julia asked.

"She was bound in a mirror. We freed her for a time, but when the mirror broke, she wound up stuck inside it for all time."

"Do you know where the mirror is now?"

I thought for a few moments. "Unfortunately not, but I think I know who does."

"Great!" Katrina shouted, clasping her hands together. "Then you have a lead. Work together to find the mirror. We've already lost two of the weapons, and we need Yilir if we're going to find the hammer. Meanwhile, I'm going to shake the tree and get the other two weapons to fall out."

"What about the sword?" I asked.

"It's in Heaven, and hopefully safe, for now. That's more than I can say about any of the other weapons. None of this is over until they get all the weapons, the key, and unlock the tomb of Surt. Let's make sure that doesn't happen, okay?"

"We'll do our best," I said.

"So far, your best hasn't been good enough," Katrina snapped. "You'll need to do better than that."

CHAPTER 28

Julia

Location: Dis, Hell

"I'm not even quite sure if he still works in this part of town," Akta said as we stalked through the alleys of Dis. It wasn't a particularly nice area. A thick film of dirt coated the ground, and dumpsters overflowed with rotten meat and spoiled food, spilling onto the street around them. The whole place stunk.

While Katrina focused her attention on the center of Dis, building it into a sleek, sexy city center, the outskirts of the city didn't have the same air of respectability. Many of the buildings in the lower west side of town were built from a combination of the old thatched roofs and the newer concrete ones.

Outcasts and degenerates lived in the lower west side. Ones who were either unwilling or unable to adjust to life in the big city but refused to leave Dis outright for one of the smaller hamlets outside its border. Dis was their home, after all, and had been for generations. Just because the world moved on without them didn't mean they wouldn't cling to the past for dear life.

I thought back to The True Path church as we walked through the derelict streets. Every single house seemed to have a sticker on it with their logo, an upside-down cross with long horns protruding from either side, all contained inside a bright, yellow circle. Even if just half of the monsters living on the lower west side were devoted to The True Path, it would make for a formidable force in Hell, perhaps even one that could rival Katrina's army.

Akta reached the end of the street, and we stopped in front of a red metal door. She knocked three times. "B'rahg! Are you in there?"

"Go away!" an unpleasant voice hollered from inside. "I'm not accepting visitors today."

"No!" Akta replied. "We're not going anywhere until you open this door."

"Christ almighty," the voice behind the door growled. The door opened, and a fat orc stood glaring at us. The rolls of his stomach rippled under his tight shirt as he took a deep breath. "I thought it might be you."

"It's been a long time," Akta said.

"Not long enough, pixie," B'rahg replied. "What can I do for you?"

"I'm looking for something, and I'm hoping you can help me find it."

"Cryptic, but it's a good bet you're right. If there's a magical object in Dis, odds are that it's passed through my hands at some point."

"The mirror of Yilir. Do you remember it?"

"Sure," B'rahg said, disgusted. "Stupid thing was busted across its face when I got ahold of it. I sold it off to a sucker a couple years ago."

"Do you know where it went?" I said. "Who you sold it to?"

B'rahg turned to me. "Who said you could speak?"

"Watch it, B'rahg," Akta growled. "That's my great-great-great-great grand-niece."

"I can tell you're related." B'rahg sniffed the air. "She has your impetuousness and reeks of fairy."

I smiled. "Thank you."

B'rahg growled. "That wasn't a compliment."

"Says you," I said. "Now, do you remember where you sold it, or don't you?"

"It was a long time ago," He rubbed his fingers together, raising an eyebrow as he did so. "I don't know how I could possibly remember."

Akta was smart and knew how to play the game. "I am here by order of the Devil. Name your price."

"Oh, the Devil, huh?" B'rahg crossed his arms and turned away. "I have no sympathy for Katrina or any desire to help her."

I looked down at the corner of a window next to the door. The True Path emblem was proudly displayed there. We'd have to try a new tack. "Then don't help her for desire," I said. "Clean her out. She's rich and powerful. Even if you hate her, don't be an idiot and miss this opportunity."

B'rahg thumbed in my direction when he spoke to Akta. "She's definitely your kin." He chuckled. "All right. I think a thousand should do it."

"That better be good information," Akta said. "But fine."

"Wonderful. Then I can tell you I sold it to a pawnshop in G'ru'l. They seemed to be very interested in it despite the fact that it was very, very broken. Paid top dollar even though it wasn't worth a pittance."

"Thank you," I said. "We'll have Katrina send the money right over."

"See that you do, or my men will hunt you down."

I chuckled. "There was a time that would have scared me, but those days are long gone. You'll get your money. You have my word."

B'rahg smiled. "Since you're related to Akta, I believe you. She always had a stupid sense of honor that I'll never understand."

"You should go now, Julia," Akta said. "B'rahg and I have more to discuss."

"We do?" B'rahg said, confused.

Akta sat down at a rickety chair in the kitchen and nodded. "We do."

***

When I had the information I needed, I took my leave of B'rahg and Akta. She had her own magical object to track down, and frankly, I didn't want to know how she was going to get B'ragh to open up more. I didn't mind her company, but I was used to working alone, hunting for clues in the shadows.

G'ru'l was twenty miles south of Dis. I found a picture of the city online and studied the main street until it felt real in my mind. Then, I threw a pinch of pixie dust and teleported myself there.

The city was small but clean. There was little of note there. It was just another non-descript city in Hell that you passed on the interstate while traveling between more important ones. There were thousands like it on Earth, most of them derelict and run-down, or simply abandoned. The monsters in G'ru'l treated their city with respect. It was well-built and clean. The lack of cars zipping down the street was a welcome respite from the hustle and bustle of Dis.

Most of the shops in G'ru'l were on a single road. Of course, most of G'ru'l was a single road that ran through the middle of town. The pawnshop was located on the main strip, a quarter-mile off the interstate. I could still hear the cars on the freeway as I crossed the street to the pawnshop, and exhaust fumes wafted into my nose.

The shop was small and cramped, and the banshee behind the cash register eyed me as I moseyed through the aisles, looking for the broken mirror. There was all manner of tchotchkes piled up through the cramped store, from watches to cameras to golf clubs. In Hell, even the most mundane object could hold great power, like the mirror did.

"Can I help you?" the banshee said. A shriek on the edge of her voice reverberated her question a second time in my ear.

"I don't know," I said. "A fence named B'rahg said he sold you something a couple years ago, but I don't see it here."

The banshee floated closer. "It's very possible we have it lying around somewhere or in the back. Fences are some of my best customers. They rarely remember the things they pawned, and by the time they come back, I've usually already sold it."

"Well, I'm hoping you didn't sell this object. It's a mirror, broken and cracked along its face."

"Doesn't sound like much to go on. I usually don't traffic in junk."

I stepped closer to the glass case filled with used cameras and weaponry. "It would have been filled with magical energy, so it might have had some value."

"Yes," she said, wrinkling her nose. "I do remember something like that. I had a request for a silver mirror a couple of years ago. It was a special order. It took me a while to track it down, but I finally did because I am the best."

"I don't deny it," I said with a playful smile. "So, what happened to it?"

The banshee scratched her chin. "As I recall, it was a pretty standard transaction. The buyer asked me to fetch it and paid me handsomely for my troubles. Once I secured it, he paid and left. Honestly, I didn't know what the fuss was about, but he was very excited. It seemed like a normal mirror to me. Less than normal because it was cracked. I couldn't even see my reflection in it. Not much of a mirror at all."

I narrowed my eyes. "Could you describe this guy to me?"

She shook her head. "No need. I recognized him immediately. He's both a deposed duke of Hell and our mayor."

"One of the dukes of Hell bought the mirror?"

"That's right. Mammon the Gluttonous," the banshee replied. "And now he's the friggin' mayor. Imagine leaving your castle as a duke of Hell and winding up the mayor of our little town."

"Thank you," I said, turning to the door. "You've been very helpful."

"Any time," the banshee said. "I won't even charge you this time, but if you don't buy something next time, there is a steep price."

"For not buying?"

"For walking through the door."

***

You would never have found a mayor's office in the old Hell, but now it was a staple of every small town. Of course, there didn't use to be small towns in Hell, except for tiny communes dotting the landscape where a dozen demons created a community with each other or single houses built in the great expanse to escape the drudgery of Dis or a bounty on your head.

Now, there were more monsters than ever, and it was hard to go more than a couple of miles without finding a new town popping up. G'ru'l was no different. It wouldn't have existed in the old world, but it did in the new one. I could see why the demons missed the old way of doing things, but it wasn't feasible to hold back progress just because monsters felt weird about Hell moving into the future. I applauded Katrina for even trying. She was fearless, taking on the Dukes of Hell right to their faces and never backing down for even an instant. Not even Lucifer had those balls.

The mayor's office rested in a steepled building a mile walk from the pawnshop. Over the doorway was a sign that read, "Abandon all hope." It was a popular expression in Hell, but all most of us had was the hope that things would get better. Hope built Hell. Hope powered Katrina's modernization effort. If anything was precious in Hell, it was hope, and I had no desire to abandon it. Perhaps my life would be easier if I had. But I couldn't give up and settle for a quiet life in the suburbs. Hope fueled me to change things. Without it, I was nothing but an empty husk.

I stepped into the building. In front of me stood a life-sized image of a smiling Mammon, the largest and fattest Duke of Hell and also the least powerful, even before he became a mayor. His fiefdom was small, and as such, he was the first duke to sell out to Katrina, pocketing a large chunk of change and abandoning his castle to create the first length of her superhighway.

Mammon's kingdom was located between Azazel and Beelzebub, so it was essential for Katrina to take it after she confiscated the land of the two traitors. She offered a generous payout to both dukes before they rose against her, but they chose instead to attack and died for it. Mammon was much more calculated and rational. He took the payout, and he kept his head, literally.

A Gorgon with her snakes circling her head in a beehive sat behind a long, tall, wooden reception desk that blocked me from moving past. "Can I help you?" she said in a nasal voice.

Behind her, a group of halflings worked on old computers. There was also a big door, cracked half-open, with loud snores coming from it.

"Yes, I'm here to see Mammon," I said.

"Are you a citizen of G'ru'l?"

I shook my head. "Just passing through, but I'm hoping to move here soon, and I'd love to ask the mayor some questions about the town."

The Gorgon turned to the door behind her, which was swinging gently open and closed with each snore. I peered through and saw a pair of stubby legs propped up on a desk.

"He's indisposed," she said, spinning back to me.

"He's sleeping," I replied. "I can hear him."

"You're right." The Gorgon smiled a vacant smile. "That is why he's indisposed."

I leaned down to her level. "Does he sleep in there a lot?"

She nodded. "That's pretty much all he does, but when he's in there, at least he's not destroying the town."

"Is he not a good mayor?"

She shrugged. "He's fine, I guess, but he's a duke of Hell, or he was, and that means the answer to every problem is violence. It's exhausting. Do you know how many towns I had to convince him not to burn down last year?"

"How many?"

The Gorgon scrunched up her face and leaned in as if she was about to tell me a secret. "Eight. He loved razing and pillaging, but mayorship is mostly about listening to monsters complain about their problems and then working to fix them."

"That doesn't sound like something a duke of Hell would be good at."

"No, but he has name recognition, and he destroys anyone who runs against him."

"That's not very fair."

"It's not—" She stopped and looked at me for a long moment. "You know what? I like you. Go right in."

"Really? Thanks!"

"Don't thank me," she said with a chuckle. "He'll probably rip you in half for disturbing him, but at least it will be interesting."

CHAPTER 29

Kimberly

Location: Uffizi, Florence, Italy

I waited until the museum was closed, and only the graveyard shift of guards remained around the gallery. Then, I closed my eyes and imagined the room where the statue had spoken to me. I dropped a pinch of pixie dust, and with a flash, I was there, in the middle of the gallery, as the statues cracked their backs and began to move from their sculpted positions.

"That feels good," one of them said, stretching her arms into the air.

"I don't think I could have stood there for another second," said another.

One by one, they all caught sight of me, and their movement stopped. Horror came across their faces.

"It's okay," a woman's voice called from the corner. "I told her to come back." The woman stepped over to me. "I'm sorry for being so rude earlier, but I couldn't have you blowing my cover with the normals."

"It's okay," I said. "But how did you know I was not normal?"

"The smell," she said, sniffing the air. "You smell like magic. Delicious magic."

"And what does magic smell like?"

"Like you. When you have been around as long as we have, you start to smell the subtle hints of pixie dust or the sweat of a magical creature."

"And how long have you been around?" I asked.

She turned to a nude male statue, stretching his arms high into the air. "When were you chiseled, Frank?"

The statue bent to the right. "1457, I think."

She turned back to me. "So, it would have had to be about 1463 for me. I look good for going on 800 years old, ay?"

"Definitely. That's amazing," I said. "How did you all survive the Apocalypse?"

"Oh, lots of ways," the statue said. "Many of us hid, but it would have been impossible without our lady who protected us."

"Your lady?" I asked, confused.

The statue nodded. "She animated us and allowed us to have a fighting chance during the Apocalypse."

"Who is this lady?" I asked.

"The muse who inspired our creation, of course." She rubbed her marble skin delicately. "We are all like her children, and she didn't want anything to happen to us."

"The muse? That's great. Have you seen her?"

She nodded. "Of course, she is our patron. We are forever in her debt."

"Can you lead me to her?" I asked.

The statue cocked her head. "I don't understand. You already know her."

I shook my head fervently. "I definitely do not."

"Of course you do." The statue chuckled. "She was your tour guide this morning. We are only able to speak in her presence or the light of the moon."

"Wait, the girl who took me on the tour today was a god?"

"A muse, but close enough. About two levels down from a full-on god, but powerful nonetheless," the statue said. "She loves it here more than anything, and being a tour guide allows her to show thousands of people a year what she loves and speak about us at length. Of course, every decade or so, she has to change her appearance. I personally liked her better with brown hair, but she is still the same soul underneath."

"Someone's coming!" a male voice shouted. I turned to see a naked male statue peering down the hall. "Three galleries down."

The girl rushed back to her position and crouched down. "I'm sorry to be so curt, but we must not be found out, you understand."

"I understand."

She whispered, "If you have any sense, you would be gone from here as well.

I nodded, threw a pinch of pixie dust, and vanished just as the light from the guard's flashlight fell across the room.

***

The next morning, I walked into the Uffizi early. The boy at the ticket counter smiled at me. "Buongiorno. Back again?"

"You recognize me?" I asked, confused.

"Of course. You were here yesterday." He pointed. "Your ears are very pretty."

"Thank you," I said uncomfortably, instinctively touching my ears. They were long, pointed, and I hated them.

"Are you here for another tour?"

"Kind of. I hope you can help me. I had the most wonderful tour guide yesterday. She was tall and blonde, with a big red jacket. She was fascinating. I got separated from the group at some point and didn't get a chance to thank her. Do you know her?"

"Of course I do, and I have good news," the ticket agent said. "Susan is set to give the first tour of the day. If you buy our VIP pass, you can get in before anybody else."

I nodded and gave him money for a badge, which I put on when I entered the gallery. Several tour guides loped around, ignoring me or smiling absently at me while I looked for Susan. I found her sporting the same smile and oversized red jacket she had on the day before and stepped toward her.

"Excuse me," I asked. "Are you Susan?"

She nodded. "I am. Are you ready for a tour? It's gonna be real fun. The first one of the day is always the best before the gallery gets crowded with people."

"Not quite." I held up my hand. "I was on your tour yesterday, actually. I have to ask you something if you don't mind."

"Is it about the gallery?" she asked, bubbly. "I'm happy to answer any question you have about any of our wonderful exhibits. I just love them so much."

"In a way." I leaned in and whispered, "I know."

"You know what?" She frowned.

"I know who you really are," I replied. Then, more assertive, I added, "Who you really *really* are."

She backed away from me. "I don't like this game."

"I know you're a muse. I know you animated the sculptures on the second floor. I know you've been living here because I talked to your sister. Please do not deny it."

The smile fell from her face. "Why would I deny it? I'm very proud of it and this place."

"It shows. You are very knowledgeable."

"I should be," she said with a happy nod. "I inspired almost every work in this gallery, and those that I didn't inspire were inspired by a piece of art that I inspired." She took a deep breath in, looking at the paintings around her. "An entire culture, an entire movement, all defined by me. Yes, I am very proud. More of my work has survived on this world than any other world in the whole galaxy."

"And you should be proud. Unfortunately, that's not the reason I'm here."

"Of course not," she said with a sigh. "You don't look like the type."

"And what type is that?"

"The type that appreciates art and history."

"I dig art. But I've lived history. It's not so great."

"History is all we have," Susan said. "But I don't expect you to understand. So, you need something from me?"

I nodded. "A key."

"That doesn't narrow it down much." She looked away, distracted by a spot on the floor. "What kind of key?"

I sighed loudly. "The kind that would allow Surt to return if it were to fall into the wrong hands."

"Oh, that one," she said, turning back to me. "Yes, I know of it."

"Where is the key?"

She shifted her weight to her left leg. "I bound it in a painting for safekeeping many centuries ago. During the Apocalypse, it was lost to me, and I have never been able to find it again."

"So, it could be anywhere?"

"I doubt it. I know who stole it. I just don't know where it is now."

"And who has it?"

"Mammon, the fat pig, looted the gallery during the Apocalypse. He took many treasures, including the painting where I hid the key."

"Mammon is a demon, I assume?"

Susan nodded. "A very powerful one at that. He was a duke in Hell, at least back when Lucifer ruled, which made him one of the most powerful in all of the underworld." She blew a stray hair out of her face. "Not powerful enough to know what he possessed."

"What is the name of the painting?"

"The Badia Polyptych. The golden key rests in the hand of Pieter. Stare at the key, and unfocus your mind, and the real key will present itself…if you are worthy." She turned back to me. "I'm very pleased of that bit of genius."

"And what if I'm not worthy?"

"Then may the gods have mercy on your soul for trying to tamper with their will."

"I sure hope I'm worthy, then."

"So do I. You seem like a nice girl if a little rude." A group of rowdy Americans walked into the building, and Susan turned to them. "Now, if you'll excuse me, it's time to get to work."

"Of course," I replied, watching her walk away. "It really is stunning what you've done."

She smiled over her shoulder. "Thank you. I really am quite proud of it. Everybody needs a bit of beauty in their lives."

CHAPTER 30

Katrina

Location: Mephistopheles's Castle, Hell

We already knew that Asmodeus was working against us, and there was plenty of time to deal with him. I wanted to know if he was the only duke of Hell conspiring against me or if they were all in it together. That meant I needed to ask around to see just how deep the conspiracy went or if Asmodeus was just blowing smoke.

Mephistopheles was one of the last holdouts of my expansion plan. His land stretched across the middle of Hell. He didn't want to concede it to me, but it would have been impossible to build a connected superhighway without it.

Interestingly, except for its location, his land was relatively worthless. It was little more than a barren wasteland. He had very few followers, but he was proud and stubborn. Eventually, we came to an understanding. I would pay him a king's ransom to annex his land and then a large stipend every decade to maintain it. Since we agreed upon his deal, he had been nothing but cooperative. However, I had begun to feel like his cooperation was simply a ruse to hide the anger bubbling under the surface.

He had no guards at the entrance to his castle, and I pushed open the doors. His rancid stench filled the hallways and seemed to grow stronger with every step that I took. Even on his best day, he reeked of rotten corpse.

"Mephistopheles!" I shouted. "I demand an audience with you."

A small demon skittered across the floor.
Mephistopheles was known for his envy. He coveted that
which he did not have, and one of those things was height.
A few of the other dukes had picked on him mercilessly,
and they were the last ones that did. Mephistopheles was a
powerful conjuror and wizard, while the other dukes were
little more than raw, unbridled physical power.

"My, my my," Mephistopheles said, clasping his hands
together and rising into the air. "If it isn't our esteemed
Devil. To what do I owe the honor?"

"Cut the crap, Mephistopheles," I growled. "You know
why I'm here. Are you plotting to overthrow me?"

Mephistopheles thought for a moment, cocking his head
from one side and then the next. "Why, of course, my dear.
I have plans to overthrow everyone, but I am not working
any harder than usual if that makes you feel better."

"It doesn't."

Mephistopheles wagged his finger at me. "I knew it
wouldn't, but rest assured, I have every reason to continue
honoring our deal. Were you to fall, I fear our new Devil
would not be nearly as generous as you have been."

I stepped forward. "Then why do you plot against me?
What's in it for you?"

He shrugged. "Just hedging my bets, dear. I'm betting
hard on you if that means anything, but I have many irons
in the fire."

"Including unlocking the Four Horsemen and
unleashing Surt on the world."

"Gods, no. That is messy, messy business. Asmodeus
came to me with that plan, but I was not interested.
Messing with the Titans is a line I will not cross."

"But you do fund the church? The True Path?"

"Well, technically, you fund The True Path with your contributions to my coffers, but yes, I am a benefactor. They paint such lovely portraits of me."

I crossed my arms across my chest. "Why would you fund them if you don't plan to overthrow me?"

"Power. Influence. And, sad to say, vanity. Like I said, they do paint a very regal portrait." He leaned in toward me. The smell of aged cheese wafted off him. "But mostly because they are the most interesting piece on the chessboard right now."

"The church works to kill me. You must know that."

He shook his head. "Not all of them. Most are just misguided and need somewhere to direct their anger. It's only a few who work to overthrow you."

"Who are they?" I asked. "I want names."

He shook his head. "Now, now. That would spoil the fun."

"Tell me, or I will kill you," I growled.

"Tempting, but no. I think not." He turned away from me. "I am the only one on your side. You wouldn't want to kill your only ally, would you? I heard you just lost one on Mars and that your supporters are dwindling by the day. Without me holding the wolves at bay, the dam will break. You don't want that."

I scoffed. "I don't need allies."

Mephistopheles smiled. "Everybody needs allies, darling. Otherwise, all you would have are enemies, and that's no way to live."

"But you also ally with those who plot against me."

"Ally is such a…sophisticated word. They are so small-minded. Should Surt return, he would destroy this world and every world. I happen to like the world and this universe. It is, after all, the only one we have. So no, I do not want that. I simply leave my options open with them, should they succeed."

"What about returning to Earth? You must want to return to Earth."

"Not really," he said with a loud, bored sigh. "I tired of Earth quickly during the last Apocalypse and returned to Hell within three months. Raping and pillaging isn't my bag. I much prefer political intrigue, which Hell has in spades, especially since you took over."

"Why are you telling me this?"

Mephistopheles rose into the air to meet my eyeline. "Because you are hot-headed, like all Devils. It seems to be the one characteristic common among each of you, that and the glee with which you take to torture."

"I do not enjoy torture," I spat. "I find it despicable."

"Such an enigma." Mephistopheles tittered. "You hate torture, and yet, you still carry on the tradition in every pit around Hell."

I shifted uncomfortably. "I am working on a fix for that. I have the beginning of a plan."

"Yes, and I'm sure it will go swimmingly." He looked toward the ceiling.

"You're pulling me off topic."

Mephistopheles grinned. "I was hoping you would not notice."

"Just to confirm, you do not wish me dead?"

"I didn't say that," Mephistopheles replied emphatically. "But I don't wish you dead more than any other demon in Hell. Less, even, than most. You serve a purpose for me. However, people are easier to control when they have a quest, and this quest has kept both you and Asmodeus distracted for days, leaving me to concentrate on what's important."

"And what's that?"

"My side, of course." Mephistopheles conjured a small bottle out of thin air and pulled a rolled-up scroll from inside it. "In fact, I will give you a show of good faith to prove I do not wish you to lose. If your woman, Julia, should find the Mirror of Yilir—" He handed me the scroll. "This spell will repair it and allow you to speak to her again."

"Why are you helping me?" I said, unrolling the scroll and studying it.

"Because you are very, very entertaining," Mephistopheles said. "I have more money than I can ever use, and I do so enjoy a spectacle. Katrina, make no mistake, you are the best spectacle in all of Hell." He smiled. "I do hope the other dukes do not succeed in killing you…at least until you grow boring and stale."

CHAPTER 31

Akta

Location: Dis, Hell

If I was to have any chance of stopping the wraith, I had to find out what he was using to perform magic. Ghosts were not corporeal, and while they were made of magic energy, or at least the residue of magical energy, they were not supposed to be able to use any. That was likely why he was using those blue orbs he smashed on the ground. If I knew what they were, I could use them to track him down and hopefully recover the lance before it was used against Katrina—or worse, used to open the seals and release the horsemen.

Luckily, B'rahg was one of the most powerful magic dealers in the city. Unluckily, he was closely tied with The True Path church, and he did not like Katrina. There was little choice in the matter. Beatrice and Clovis were wonderful, but when it came to tracking down magical objects, B'rahg was second to none.

"I'm not helping you until I get paid," B'rahg said, turning away from the table where I sat.

"It's coming," I said to him.

"Make it come faster," B'rahg grumbled. "And you can leave until you find it."

"I just want to have a simple chat about a magical artifact."

B'rahg grabbed his wrist and winced. "Yes, I know how your simple chats go. Pay me, and then we'll talk.

I sneered at him and stood. "Fine, but then I expect you to open the door for me again."

"Gladly."

I disappeared and reappeared in front of Katrina's castle. I pushed open the black bone door and walked inside to find Katrina pacing back and forth at the end of a long line of suits of armor.

"Everything okay, boss?" I asked.

"No, nothing is okay, okay?" she said with a huff. "I went to see Mephistopheles to see if he was working with Asmodeus."

"And was he?"

"He said he wasn't, but he—I don't know. I am not good at this political subterfuge. Maybe I should have beaten the truth out of him."

"Lucifer wasn't good at it either."

Katrina stopped pacing and met my eyes. "That's what I'm worried about. He ended up dead, and I'm starting to think I'm going to end up dead, too."

I placed my hand on her shoulder. I didn't fear Katrina like the others, which made her uncomfortable. She winced at my touch, though she didn't back away. "You're damned if you do and damned if you don't. If you do nothing, you end up like Lucifer, alone and neurotic. If you keep changing Hell for the better, then everybody in power will hate you."

Katrina smiled at me. It was a rare sight these days. "You think I'm changing Hell for the better?"

"I do," I said with a gentle nod. "I have lived through three Devils—well, four if you count Thomas—and not one of them actually cared about Hell. Velaska saw her job as a burden. Lucifer was in over his head. Thomas saw us as his personal army, but you? You saw a problem and worked to fix it. That's noble, Katrina. Even if you die, believe that. Even if people don't agree with you. At least you tried something."

"Thank you," Katrina replied. She cleared her throat. "What are you doing here?"

"I need to raid your treasury."

Katrina pushed my hand off her shoulder. "Well, that was a nice moment, and now it's over. Take whatever you need."

"Really? No questions?"

Katrina shook her head. "You will use it for a noble cause because that is who you are."

***

I packed a satchel full of coin and disappeared back to B'rahg's apartment. I banged on the door three times and heard him shuffling inside.

"Go aw—" he started.

"I brought your money!" I shouted, jingling the coin purse.

"Really?" B'rahg said from behind the door. "That was quick. You must be desperate."

I leaned my head against the wall. "I am, and if you're smart, you'll take advantage of that fact."

B'rahg twisted open the door. He eyed the satchel weighed down with coin. "I'll have to count it."

"There's double what you asked because I have another favor to ask of you."

"If you have coin, I'll be your best friend. Come in."

I dragged the satchel through the front door and set it down next to a rack of dirty shoes. I turned around and found myself in an alchemy lab. There were jars filled with frog eyes and chameleon tongues and every kind of ingredient for a thousand different types of spells and potions. On a table in the living room, a cauldron bubbled, and the stench of burnt maggots filled the air.

"You have a lot of contraband in here."

B'rahg lifted his hands, palms up. "None of this was illegal in the old-world order. I was an honest trader then. I don't recognize any authority that makes me out to be a criminal when I'm just trying to earn a living."

I shook my head. "And yet, you are a criminal."

"Says you," B'rahg said. "Are you here to bust me?"

"Oh, no. If you blow yourself up with this stuff, all the better for me. Then, I can take back the coin."

"Don't you dare. It's rightfully mine, even in death," B'rahg said, though I could tell from his voice he was teasing. "Now, how can I help you?"

"I have been accosted by a ghost, twice. A ghost who can use magic. He was on loan to the demon guard because of his magical aptitude, and then he escaped. I've tracked him down twice, but he keeps evading me. He carries blue, glowing orbs, which he said were pieces of people's souls. Have you ever heard of anything like that before?"

"Hmm," B'rahg grunted. "That is dark magic, even for me."

"But it is possible?"

B'rahg nodded. "It is possible. It would take somebody journeying into one of the pits of Hell, finding a willing helper, and using black magic to harvest the souls."

"So, if I were looking for him, I would need to find a pit that was light on souls?"

B'ragh nodded. "Most demons take their jobs very seriously. There won't be many, even those that hate Katrina, who would help slaughter a soul."

"What about ones that follow The True Path?"

"Even them—us—we believe that souls need to be cleansed and returned to the Source. Nobody I know would agree to harvest a soul for magical ends. Destruction of a soul is the desecration of everything we believe."

"Then, I guess I'm going to central filing."

B'rahg shook his head. "They won't help you. They are stiff as boards over there. You need to find somebody lower in the chain of command, a lackey at a satellite office that hates his life enough to take a bribe." He shook his head. "I know a guy that can help you, but—"

"But you need something."

"You got it."

I placed my hands on my hips. "And what about all the coin I just gave you?"

B'rahg laughed. "That's not nearly enough to pay for the intel I have, trust me."

"Fine," I said, shaking my head. "What do you need?"

"Charlie…he owed me a delivery. A very powerful package bound in green leather. He stole it for me but then vanished before he could complete our arrangement. You get it for me, bring it back here, and I'll give you a name. Somebody that could tell if a file was doctored and get you the truth."

"You know I hate Charlie, right?"

"Good," B'rahg replied. "Then you'll definitely want to help me because losing this object will really piss him off."

"That does make it more appealing."

CHAPTER 32

Julia

Location: G'ru'l, Hell

I tapped on the open door to Mammon's office. His feet twitched, but he didn't stop snoring, so I knocked harder. This time, his head jerked, but his eyes remained closed. I turned back to the Gorgon receptionist.

"He's not waking up," I said. "What do I do?"

"Just push his legs off the chair," she said.

"Really?"

"Sure," she replied with a nod. "He won't mind. He can fall asleep anywhere and sleeps like the dead."

I shrugged and walked into the office. Mammon was massive. His skin oozed through his purple suit and folded into the chair under him. His mouth fell open, and his forked tongue fell out, followed by a long string of green drool that dripped down onto the floor, eating into the carpet.

I grabbed his feet with both hands, swinging them off the chair and causing the chair to spin around until he knocked his head on the side of the desk.

"Oops," I said under my breath.

The demon sprang to life, shooting upright in the chair as he grabbed the desk and turned himself around. He shook his head, trying to shake off the bruise on his head.

"Huh?" he said, confused. His yellow eyes filled with curdled sleep on their edges. "Oh, my sin, was I asleep?"

"Yes, sir," I replied.

He slammed his hand on the desk. "Well, I assure you, I am still ever vigilant working for your needs and—"

"She's not a resident!" The Gorgon called from the other side of the door. "No need for the theatrics."

"Oh…" he said. "Oh!" He shook his head. "Then why are you here?"

Lie. "Well, I'm thinking of moving to G'ru'l and was told you were the person to speak to about what it's like here."

"Marvelous," he said, banging his hand again on the desk. "We could always use more residents. Our residents are what make G'ru'l function, after all."

"How long have you been the mayor here?" I asked.

He scratched his head. "Oh, a few…decades…my opponents have a funny habit of dying or dropping out, so I keep getting reelected. It's quite an honor, of course, and one I don't take lightly."

"Except for when you're asleep."

He scoffed loudly, offended. "Being mayor is a very taxing job. It takes everything from me. So yes, sometimes I need to recover my mojo. I don't see anything wrong with that, as long as I'm doing my job and my constituents are happy."

I held up my hands, trying to indicate that I meant no harm by my observation. "Me neither. Seems reasonable to me."

"Well, lovely," Mammon said, leaning back in his chair. "So, what questions do you have for me? I have a fabulous real estate agent who is just the loveliest ghoul. She can set you up with a wonderful place at a great price.

That's the thing people love about G'ru'l. They can raise a family of little monsters on a budget."

"I'll be honest, G'ru'l wasn't on my top ten list of places to move when I started thinking about it, but when I found out there was a duke of Hell living here and running the place, I changed my mind. I have to admit; I am such a huge fan of your work."

"Really?" Mammon said, smiling broadly. "That's so flattering."

"Oh, yes," I replied. "You are my favorite duke by a wide margin."

Mammon puffed out his chest. "Wow, thank you. I thought everyone had forgotten about me, frankly."

"Not me, sir," I said, shaking my head. "Tell me, how did you end up here? Weren't you living in a castle?"

He sighed. "I was, but I foolishly sold my land to Katrina, the Devil. From there, I made a couple of bad investments, and this was all I could afford. A little plot of land, in a little town, in my little corner of the world. Which is why I can tell you exactly how wonderful it is to move here because I did it myself."

"So you lost everything?" I said, feigning interest and leaning forward, almost breathlessly.

"Well, not everything," he chuckled. He could barely contain his pride. "I brought a collection of my favorite relics from across the world and have been able to acquire quite a nice little collection of new magical objects in my time here. Most monsters have no idea what things are worth."

"That's fascinating," I said with a coy smile. "What are some of your favorite pieces?"

Watching a demon flirt nearly initiated my upchuck reflex, but I was able to keep my cool as Mammon placed his face in his hands and lowered his voice to a coo. "Oh, I have so many, but the most unique is one I picked up a couple of years ago. It's a broken mirror that contains the essence of the architect of Hell. I have no way of mending it. I would so long to have her regale me with stories about my castle and the world before this mess." He slid his fat fingers toward me. "You know, if Yilir could see this disaster, she would turn over in her grave…err…mirror. What Katrina has done is an abomination."

"I know, right?" I said, standing up to avoid his touch. "She's the worst."

"I hope she's overthrown one day," Mammon grumbled. "She deserves it. I long for the days of Lucifer, or even Velaska, when the Devil respected the land and its people."

I clasped my hands excitedly. "Oh, yeah. I mean…one day, maybe the lords will rise up and start Ragnarok, or something."

"Huh?" Mammon furrowed his brow. "You lost me."

I was probing, and clearly, Mammon had no idea about the other dukes' plans. "You know, I am a bit of a history nut myself. I would love to see this mirror of yours."

He shook his head fervently. "I'm sorry, but that's out of the question. My house is not ready for company. Of course, if you moved here, perhaps I could be persuaded to open my vault to you." He winked at me. *Flirting.* Flirting with a demon. And a slovenly one at that. My stomach turned over.

"That…is very tempting. Hey, do you have the number for that real estate agent? I think I'll give her a call."

"She's the best." He pulled out a card from his desk and handed it to me. "She's also my wife, but one thing has nothing to do with the other."

"Of course not." I placed the card in my pocket. "Well, thank you for this. You've given me a lot to think about."

He held out his massive paw. "I hope to see you around the neighborhood."

I placed my hand inside his, and he squeezed it tightly. "Me too."

***

I met the Mammon's ghoul wife in front of a single-story ranch unit five blocks from city hall. When I called and told her I had just spoken to Mammon, she agreed to help me right away. This was not my favorite part of investigating, but most of my job meant talking to people and gathering information, with a very little bit of hitting and fighting thrown in to make things exciting.

"Hi!" The glowing blue ghoul said as she hovered out of her car. Her head was nearly severed from her body, and she leaned to the left to keep it from falling down. "You must be Julia!"

"I am," I said, walking towards her. "Are you Shirley?"

"That's me," she said, holding the corners of her blue blazer. "Best, and only, real estate agent in all of G'ru'l."

I smiled at her. "Well, your husband speaks very highly of you."

She sighed, the sigh of a woman who knew that her husband's libido knew no bounds. "Yes, he is quite the charmer. Shall we go inside?"

I followed Shirley through the quaint house. One bedroom, a kitchen, and a patio outside; as she moved through the house, she told me about the construction that started G'ru'l fifty years before.

"Once the roads started coming in, developers understood there would need to be towns to give respite to tourists and commuters, so towns like G'ru'l were born. This was one of the first houses built once the town was founded, but I assure you, it's in tip-top shape." She walked out the back door and stepped onto the brick path. "So, what do you think?"

"It's nice," I said absently, following her. "However, I was hoping for something…bigger. I mean, I can get a little house in Dis. I am looking for space. That's what intrigued me about G'ru'l in the first place."

"Of course. That's very common."

"Where do you live?" I asked with a coy smirk. "Mammon raved about your house."

The ghoul pointed behind her. "Oh, well we live up on the hill on the other side of city hall. It's a small community, but if you're looking for posh, it's the best location in the whole city."

I forced my eyebrows up my forehead in faux excitement. "Are there any homes available over there?"

"You bet, and you have very good taste. This place is a dump. Come, come."

I got in the car with her and drove a short way past city hall and down a quaint little side street. At the end of it stood an imposing metal gate. Shirley placed her hand on the button of a call box. "Shirley Mammon." After a moment, a bell rang, and the gate swung open. She gave me a pompous smile, her chin in the air. "My favorite part of this neighborhood is the privacy."

"Do you ever miss the castle?" I asked, trying to figure out how long she had been with Mammon.

"I never lived there," Shirley said. "Mammon and I met here after he'd lost most of his power. Of course, I prefer him now. He was so bloodthirsty when I met him. Did you know this town was built on his land, and if you squint, you can almost see his castle rising in the distance?"

I leaned forward and squinted, but I didn't see anything. "So you harbor no ill will to Katrina?"

"Of course not!" she exclaimed. "I am absolutely in love with this town, and cars, and everything she's given us. The old Hell was so boring, and this, well, it's like living in the future."

I chuckled. "You're the first person I've heard say anything nice about Katrina in a long time."

"Well, she's done right by me," Shirley said with a bright smile. "Burn the past, I say. Tomorrow is a new day." She turned the corner and pointed to a blue house with green shutters, resting on a big plot of land. "That's our house. Isn't it cute?"

"Very," I replied. "Do you have anything that's a similar floorplan?"

"Of course. I have one that's exactly the same that I can show you. I love that everything is the same here. It means I never feel too far from home, even if I'm down the street."

I nodded. "I would love to see that house."

She wasn't lying. Every house on the block looked almost identical, except for the paint job, so when she pulled up to a yellow house with blue shutters, I nearly did a double-take and definitely blinked a few times. It was the carbon copy of Shirley's house, except that it sat at the end of a cul-de-sac instead of on the corner of the street.

"Here we are."

We walked out of the car. Shirley bent down and pulled a key out of a lockbox, and walked inside. The smell of fresh paint smacked me in the face when I walked in. Everything was white and clean and new—very different from the old house she showed me first.

"This is the best house in town, and I'm not just saying that because it's the same layout as mine. People who live here have the highest satisfaction level in all of G'ru'l."

"I can see why. It's really nice."

"And I haven't even shown you the best part." She grinned conspiratorially. "The kitchen is massive."

"Before you do that, I have a bit of an obsession with knick-knacks, and Mammon said that he does, too. Is that true?"

Shirley grumbled. "Yes, of course. He keeps them over there, in his study." I walked over to a closed door on the other side of the hallways and pushed it open. Inside, the walls were a faux wood finish.

"Ah, now this is where I'll keep the safe," I said, pointing to the far wall. "Or maybe over here?" I spun around to the wall across from a big window. "The problem is that it's so ugly it really destroys the décor of any room. What do you think?"

"I find safes ghastly, but he keeps his safe over here," Shirley said, walking into the room behind me. "This place is so big when there's no furniture or anything. I forgot how much room there is to move around."

"So he fits all his thingamajigs in here? It seemed like he had a lot of relics from how he spoke about them."

"Yes, he has a metric buttload," she said, dejected. "His hoarding is the reason for half our fights."

"I see. I have a lot of little knick-knacks, too. One of the things that's forcing me to move out of the city is that I don't have room to put it all."

"There's plenty of room in here, and plus, you don't have a wife telling you to keep everything in one room, so you can expand into the whole house."

I smiled at her, my eyes twinkling. "And you said this is the exact same layout?"

"Of course."

I smiled wider. "Because I think I'm in love with it. Can you show me the rest?"

"It would be my pleasure. I can help you decorate, too, if you decide to move in. Mammon's taste is so harsh and gaudy. I would welcome the chance to bring life to a place with a more feminine touch."

"You're too kind!"

Now Shirley was the one smiling. "Then come along. I have so many thoughts about how to make this little piece of Hell livable."

***

I staked out the Mammon household for the rest of the afternoon. Mammon arrived home early, and Shirley came home a couple of hours later. They ate dinner and watched some television. Then, Shirley went out for the night. Soon afterward, I could hear Mammon snoring from my perch across the street.

That's when I chose to strike. I closed my eyes and envisioned the room Shirley showed me, except that I

Nohelty 232

pictured it in Mammon's house. Since they were the exact same, I would be able to teleport in with no problem.

I closed my eyes and vanished, reappearing in Mammon's study, right in front of a big, oak desk. All around me were glass cases filled with trinkets. There were gold coins, obsidian daggers, and in the center of it all, a cracked silver mirror propped up on its side. I slid open the case and pulled out the mirror. Just like the banshee in the pawnshop, I could not see my reflection when I looked into it. However, I felt the magic power flowing through it.

I closed my eyes and pictured Katrina's castle, and then, in a flash of pink light, I vanished. Finally, something had gone our way.

CHAPTER 33

Kimberly

Location: Scotland

Mammon could have stashed the Badia Polyptych anywhere. A quick Google search showed that the painting was actually five paintings, each in their own wooden frame and clasped together with gold hinges. There were images of St. Nicholas, John the Evangelist, The Virgin Mary, Pieter, and Benedict. Aside from the Virgin Mary, I didn't recognize any of the other images, but the picture of Pieter showed him holding a large key, nearly the size of his whole arm, which fit the muse's description.

The Polyptych could have been anywhere in the world or even in Hell. Luckily, I knew someone who could help me. The one imp who was hooked up to everybody in Hell. I transported myself to Scotland and walked through the barrier of the neutral bar where the angels and demons hung out. I stepped inside and was surprised to find it nearly empty, except for a lone imp at the bar, sipping his drink.

"What's going on in here?" I asked Charlie as I walked toward the bar. "This place is usually hopping."

"Something big," Charlie said. "But I'm not supposed to talk about it."

"It probably has something to do with Ragnarok," I replied.

"So you know, then." Charlie rolled his eyes. "Ugh, do you know how long they've been planning to start Ragnarok? Demon factions have been working on it for the last hundred years or so, and nobody can get their shit together to carry it out properly."

"I don't know. The dukes of Hell have two of the weapons they need to summon the Four Horsemen. Julia is looking for another one." I pulled the dagger from my belt. "And I have the fourth. So, they are halfway there. They might even have the third weapon already."

"Is that why you're here then? To find the fourth weapon?"

"Not exactly. I'm looking for a painting, the Badia Polyptych. Do you know it?"

"Not ringing a bell."

I showed him a picture. "That's what it looks like. I need to find it."

"Where did you last see it?"

"I've never seen it. But it was last at the Uffizi before Mammon looted it."

"He's a dick," Charlie grumbled. "He hoarded all the best stuff while he was up here. The other demons really just wanted to fight. I gotta hand it to him, though; Mammon has exquisite taste in relics. That's the only thing I've ever liked about him."

I pointed to the picture. "Have you ever seen this before?"

"Maybe," Charlie said. "Did you deliver my package?"

I sighed. "I haven't been back to Hell yet, but I will. I swear."

Charlie took a swig of his beer. "How, if you're not in Hell?"

I pounded my fist on the bar. "I just—I need to find it, okay? Please, the future of the universe is at stake."

Charlie leaned closer to me. "And that begs the question…what's in it for Charlie?"

I turned up my nose. "Ugh, you really are the worst."

"I'll tell you what…I'll help you if you let me hold onto that nifty knife of yours while you search for it."

"Are you kidding me?" I scoffed. "I need to protect it, not hand it over to a demon. You wouldn't protect anything. You'll sell it the first chance you get, or just give it to a demon lord."

He shook his head. "I would never give up something so powerful. You should know that about me. And as for the demon lords of Hell, they can go stuff it. Besides, you don't have any bargaining chips. If you want the painting, you gotta give up something. I suppose I could take your soul and hold onto that. Your long life has made your soul especially juicy."

"You're not getting my soul," I said emphatically.

He shrugged and turned back to his drink. "Then you have nothing else I want."

I sighed. "What about the location of Aziolith's cavern on Earth? You've been wanting to raid it for a long time."

"Hrm, that is tempting. I would very much like to burn it to the ground, but no. It's the dagger for my help, or you can go to Hell and deliver my package. But either way, I'm not helping you without something in return."

"There are other demons I could ask."

Charlie looked around and chuckled. "Are there, though? I know we've had our differences, but you trust me a little bit, don't you? I mean, I've helped you, legitimately helped you, on more than one occasion. Good luck finding another demon you can say that about."

I placed the dagger on the table. "You will not use this dagger to hurt Katrina or give it to the demon lords."

"Whatever you say."

I slid the dagger to him. "Now, where can I find the key?"

Charlie grinned. "I'll write down the address."

***

Of course, it would be the royal palace of Madrid. Demons loved opulence, and there was nothing more opulent than the royal palaces around the world. Mammon, being one of the dukes of Hell, had his pick of castles, and he chose the palace in Madrid. Azazel chose Buckingham palace, and Beelzebub chose the Kremlin. After the Apocalypse, when humanity regained control of the buildings, they found precious gems from all over the world piled high. It took generations to return the pieces to their rightful owners, and even hundreds of years later, they were still working on getting the last pieces.

The Royal Palace had tours of their grounds, which was helpful. Then again, if the Badia Polyptych was somewhere out in the open, the muse would have found it effortlessly, and I wouldn't have had to bargain away my only weapon to an imp to get a clue. It seemed to me highly unlikely that it was still there.

I passed through the gates and went straight for one of the tour guides. I didn't have time for a second large-scale tour of the grounds, though the sheer scale of the castle was impressive. "Excuse me," I asked a man with sandy brown hair. "Do you speak English?"

"I do." He nodded. "How can I help you?"

I pulled up my phone and handed him the picture. "Have you ever seen this in your tours through the castle?"

He shook his head. "I'm sorry, but no. Perhaps the Prado would be better to help you. It is filled with the greatest art in all of Spain and has a detailed record of every painting in the Royal Palace, too."

"Seems logical," I said. "Thank you."

I walked across Madrid until I wound up at the Prado, the most famous art museum in Spain and one of the greatest in the whole world. I had spent days walking through its halls, though, admittedly it was a bit too stuffy for me. I preferred the Reina Sofia, which had more contemporary and modern art, or the Dali Museum in Catalonia, though I was relatively sure that it burned down in the early days of the Apocalypse.

Still, I enjoyed the El Bosque depictions of Hell and some of the more avant-garde pieces. I approached a few different tour guides, eyeing their jackets for the little pin that indicated the language they spoke. I was looking for one with a British Union Jack.

"Hello. Can you help me?"

"I can try," a young woman with olive skin and bright green eyes said.

"I'm looking for a specific piece of art that was in the Royal Palace over 200 years ago. Is there somebody that could help me?"

She considered this for a moment, then offered, "There is an art historian on staff. He might be able to help you. He seems to know the history of every significant piece hanging anywhere in Madrid."

"Thank you. Where can I find him?"

"At this time of day?" she said, looking down at her watch. "He's generally in the Café Prado having a sangria. You can't miss him. He has a long white beard and a gray tweed jacket. He is called Jacamo."

"Thank you."

I twisted my way around the museum until I reached the Café Prado in the middle of a courtyard. Sure enough, I saw a man sitting alone with a long beard and smile on his face, sipping on a cup of sangria. A look of contentment and peace rested across his face, and for a moment, I desperately wished I could feel that way, even for a fleeting second.

"Excuse me, Jacamo?" I asked, walking up to him.

"Why yes," he said in a thick Spanish accent. "How can I help you?"

I pulled out my phone. "I know you are busy, so I will get to the point. Have you seen this painting?"

Jacamo reached into his pocket and pulled out his glasses. He squinted at the image. "Why, of course, dear, that is the Politico di Badia by Giotto, painted around 1300. It's one of the most famous paintings in Italy. What do you want to know about it?"

"I was told that it ended up here after the Apocalypse of 2020."

"Yes, yes. Many of our paintings were stolen then as well and ended up all around the world if they weren't destroyed." He looked up in the distance for a moment and then took a sip of his wine. "And many pieces from other countries ended up here, including the Badia. It took nearly 200 years, but we were finally able to return every piece of art to its rightful place. We shipped that Badia off a decade ago, back to the Uffizi so that it would hang there once again."

"Wait," I said with a growl. "You're saying this painting is in the Uffizi?"

He nodded. "That's exactly what I'm saying."

I snarled. "I'm going to kill that god."

***

I flashed again to the Uffizi in Florence, sick of being jerked around. I stormed into the museum just as a big tour group filed out. I swam against them until I reached the entrance. The sun was setting, and the Uffizi was emptying of tourists.

"Scusi!" A guard shouted. "Mi dispiace, siamo chiusi."

"I don't speak Italian," I said to him, pointing to my ears.

The guard gave me a blank look. "Closed!"

I held up my arm. "This will only take a minute."

"NO!" The guard said, pulling out his baton.

I didn't want to get into a fight, so I threw up my arms. "Fine!"

I found a stoop outside the museum and waited for the blond muse. It took two hours, but finally, I saw her walk across the entranceway and out into the street, letting down her hair as she went.

"You lied to me, Susan," I said to her as she passed me.

Susan spun around. "You're back."

I stood up. "You had to know I would be back."

"I thought it was a possibility," she replied. "Not this quickly, though. What are you, a pixie?"

I nodded. "That's exactly right."

"Damn," she said. "It's supposed to take people a lot longer to realize I sent them on a wild goose chase. Usually, they just give up. In fact, they always give up. Nobody has ever come back. Wait, how did you even find out that it was—ah, you know a demon. Of course, you do. I could smell the sulfur on you."

I smelled my shirt. "In fairness, that might be because I was recently in Hell."

She sighed. "You understand why I had to do it, right?"

"No, I don't."

Susan stood silently for a long moment, looking off into the distance. "That key, it's the last failsafe that protects us from Ragnarok. If you find it and take it, who knows what will happen?"

"I won't let anything happen to it."

"You'll want to protect it, but what if you fail?" She eyed me up and down. "After all, it looks like you lost the dagger."

"Didn't lose it," I replied. "Gave it to someone for safe keeping."

"I hope you didn't give it to your demon friend." There was a long silence while I avoided eye contact. "See, and that was just the dagger. If I gave you the key, you could destroy everything."

"Somebody else will come for it, if not me. And they will not be so kind," I replied. "They have already stolen two of the horsemen's weapons. They're not going to stop until they find the last two and the key. The best chance to prevent Ragnarok is to let me have the key, so I can keep it safe. Trust me, whoever comes looking for it will be vicious, and they will stop at nothing to capture it, including killing you."

"Death is not so bad," Susan smirked. "I will deal with them on that day. Right now, I'm dealing with you."

I pinched the bridge of my nose. I was getting a tension headache. "Listen, the only way you can stop me from getting that painting is if you kill me."

"I could do that, easily," she replied, her eyebrows raised. "I am a god."

"I know, but you are not a killer, are you? You are a creator, and killing is the opposite of creating. And if you won't kill me, you won't kill somebody who comes to do you harm, either. Again, they will not be as kind as me. So, please, just make this easy on yourself and me, and give me the stupid painting."

She shook her head. "I can't give it to you, but I will show it to you and let the painting make up its mind about you. Follow me."

***

Susan led me down a series of small alleyways and cramped corridors until we reached a small restaurant in the middle of a long-forgotten square, where a cherub fountain spat water into the air.

"I'm less than impressed," I said. "I've taken walking tours of Rome before, and I've seen better simply taking a stroll by myself."

The bay windows of the wine bar were open, and you could see all the way through to the back of it, where a painting hung; five of them, actually. They didn't look like the painting I was looking for, but the paintings had a striking resemblance to the Badia Polyptych.

"I'm not playing around," I said.

"Me either," she replied. "Look closer."

The place was empty, except for a small, bearded man cleaning the bar. I stepped through the tight walkway between the tables and chairs and up to the paintings. The first showed an old man looking up into the sky. The second, a young man reading a book. The third, a woman holding a baby. The fourth, a priest praying to Heaven, and the fifth, a man, holding a key in his hand. I stared at them until my eyes crossed, and when they did, I realized that there was a painting underneath the one on the wall.

"You hid the paintings."

"I did," she said with a smile. "In plain sight. I couldn't send them away, and I couldn't risk somebody finding them. So, they stayed close to me, at my favorite bar in all of Italy."

"Thanks, Euterpe," the bartender said with a gruff smile. "And you're my favorite customer."

"Thanks, sweetness," Susan said, smiling at him.

I pointed to the man behind the bar. "Is it safe with—"

"He's with me. He's a cherub who has protected me since the time when gods roamed freely. I trust him with my life."

I turned back to the paintings, and specifically, the one with the key. "What do I do?"

"You don't have to do anything. The painting will do it all."

I took a deep breath and closed my eyes. When I opened them, the key was gone. I felt something cool in my hand, and I looked down to find a long golden key clutched in my palm.

"You were not wrong. You are worthy," Susan said. "I just hope you are less careless with the key than you were with the dagger."

"I wasn't careless. I'm about to get it back. Had you given me the key the first time and not lied to me, I wouldn't have made a deal with a demon."

"Silly child," Susan said. "I felt its power vanish from this plane of existence the moment you came to Rome. It is gone. If I had to guess, it was taken back to Hell and to the very people you have tried to protect it from."

"Shit."

Her face fell. "But at least you now have the key. I suppose that is something."

It wasn't much. It was exchanging one piece of the puzzle for another. I was no closer to saving Hell than when I started my mission. If I lost the key, I would be much further away.

CHAPTER 34

Akta

Location: Dis, Hell

Charlie's apartment was just north of the downtown area of Dis. I had kept tabs on him for most of my afterlife. He made a decent informant because he had his fingers in a lot of pies, but he was also shifty and manipulative. It was better to be on his side than not, but I still wondered if knowing him was worth it.

Charlie had two children, so when I knocked on the door, I wasn't surprised to find a pock-faced pair of twin imps opening the door and staring at me.

"What do you want?" one of them said through a lisp.

I leaned against the doorjamb. "Your father has a package for me. I'm here to pick it up."

"He's not here," the other said, trying to push the door closed. "Come back later."

"It's kind of important," I replied, holding the door open. "Can I come in and look for it?"

"Whatever." He let go of the door and hopped back in front of the TV. The other one joined him, and they picked up two controllers and started playing a racing game on their television.

I moved past them and rifled through cabinets in the kitchen before looking under the sink, the refrigerator, and the freezer. B'rahg told me that the package would be green and roughly a foot across. It would be enchanted with wards and runes, which would be carved into the leather that encased it. I moved from the kitchen into the living room, where I looked under the television, blocking the TV.

"Move!" the boys shouted at me in unison. "You're totally killing me!"

"Sorry!" I said, intentionally standing between them and the television. "Maybe you can help me? Have you seen a big box made of green leather?"

"What?" one said. "No. Now get outta the way."

I kept my anger contained content in the knowledge that their lives hung in the balance, and I could slice them open in a second. "Which of these is your dad's bedroom?"

"End of the hall. Gods!" one of them exclaimed. "Go away."

I wondered if they knew how easily I could snap their necks. *Unlikely.* Children were never aware of how close they come to death on a regular basis. Although, since it was impossible to kill a demon without a magical weapon, and Kimberly had mine, the most I could do was put them in a lot of pain.

Usually, though, that was enough.

I pushed open the door to Charlie's room and turned on the lights. Even then, it was nearly dark in the room. Immediately, I felt a great heat coming from under the bed. I reached underneath and pulled out a green leather box covered in runes. Whatever was inside made my fingers tingle just holding it.

"This must be it," I said.

I closed my eyes and disappeared back to B'ragh's apartment. I appeared in a purple flash and rapped on the door. The box in my hands grew heavier by the second, and I dropped it on the ground before collapsing from the sheer power of it. There were two voices inside the apartment, screaming at each other. I reared back and kicked the door open with all the force I could muster. I managed to kick the box into the door and then walked inside.

Inside, I found Charlie holding the Dagger of Obsolescence at B'rahg's throat. "This is for threatening me."

"NO!" I shouted, but it was too late, Charlie sliced through B'rahg's throat, and he exploded into a million pieces. "You idiot!"

Charlie turned to me. "Oh, hi, Akta. Nice knife, isn't it?"

"Where did you get that?" I asked.

He stared admiringly at the knife. "A pixie I know gave it to me."

I stepped forward. "Gave it to you, or you tricked her out of it?"

"It's all one and the same to me." He looked down at the box. "Oh good, you have it. Hand it over."

"What's inside?" I asked.

"None of your business. Or should I say it's irrelevant to your current quest? Don't worry. There'll be plenty of time to stop me later if you save the universe, that is, and if you don't, then it won't much matter."

"Why did you kill him?" I asked.

"He blackmailed me, for one, and for another…I know he helped you take the dagger from me before. I have a long memory. I bided my time and look at me now. I have it again. Only took a few thousand years."

"Drop it."

"Relax, toots," he said, holding up his hands. "I'm not going to give it to Asmodeus. He has no class anyway, and I have no interest in the universe ending. You can have it. You give me the box, and I'll hand it over to you."

"Fair," I replied. "But you have to help me first."

"That's not part of this deal."

"It is now," I replied, maintaining eye contact with him. "There's a ghost who's been stealing souls and using them to perform magic. I need to know where they are getting the souls. B'rahg was supposed to—"

"—Lead you on a wild goose chase. He didn't know nothing about anything. That's the thing I hated most about him. Give me the box. I'll give you a name where you can find a lead, and I'll give you the dagger on top of it."

I nodded. "And you won't hurt anyone with it?"

"I didn't say that. I said it's not your concern." He dropped the knife to the ground. "On three. One, Two. Three."

I kicked the box over to him, and he did the same with the knife. I dropped down and picked up the knife, and he scooped up the box.

"Pleasure doing business with you."

"Give me a name."

"V'irl't," Charlie replied. "He is an imp working in the fifth pit, outside of a small town called Ftwix by the gates north of here. He has been a corrupt little bureaucrat for years. That's what I love most about him."

"How do you know?"

"He's one of my best customers," Charlie replied with a smile. "Now, I must be going." He thumbed the leather box. "There's so much to do."

He snapped his fingers and was gone. I looked down at the dagger, worrying about what it meant for Kimberly on Earth. I hoped she had just been suckered by Charlie and wasn't dead by his, or any other, hand. However, if she were dead, she would show up in Hell soon, and we could use all the help we could get.

Conquest 249

CHAPTER 35

Katrina

Location: Gateway to Hell, Hell

I knew where the Gateway to Hell was, and it seemed like the dumbest thing ever. It was a flaw in the system that had existed since the dawn of Hell. Who would be idiotic enough to come willingly into Hell? You needed a body to get back out onto Earth, so souls couldn't get out. It was only a matter of time before Kimberly crawled back into Hell through the tunnel, and I needed to talk to her when she did.

"You had one job," I said with a sigh when she finally crawled through the hole and stood up, confused and shocked that I was sitting there waiting for her. After a moment, she regained her composure.

"Actually, you gave me two jobs. Find the key and protect the dagger."

"And you lost the dagger, which means you failed. Fifty percent is failing."

Kimberly shook her head. "I didn't lose it. One of your demons stole it after I let him hold on to it for a moment."

I hopped to my feet. "You trusted an imp. I would say that makes you an idiot but crawling into Hell twice pretty well already makes you an idiot."

"Does that mean you found the dagger?"

I crossed my arms. "With no help from you. Did you get the key?"

Kimberly rooted into her jeans pocket and pulled out a key. "Right here."

"And thank you for bringing it back into Hell, where any demon could steal it from you."

"You're welcome," Kimberly replied with a smile. "And yes, I know you're being sarcastic, but what else did you expect me to do with it?"

"Keep it safe on Earth, not bring it closer to the demons who want me dead, obviously."

"Well, you weren't specific, now were you?"

"I'm pretty sure I was." I sighed. "Let's just go."

Kimberly placed her hand on my shoulder, and I snapped my fingers to vanish. I tasted burnt toast as we disappeared. It always tasted like burnt toast when I traveled that way. I'd hoped for something better, eventually, but the burnt toast taste was all I ever got. We reappeared inside my throne room. Julia and Akta were there talking with Carl, and I walked past the cracked, black skulls of my throne room to join them.

"Welcome back," Julia said, pacing back and forth. "I hoped I wouldn't see you again for a long time."

"Sorry to disappoint," Kimberly said, shaking her head. "Did you find the fourth weapon?"

"Not yet," Akta said, holding the dagger. "But I did find this."

"Oh good," Kimberly said with a smile. "Please tell me you made Charlie suffer to get it back."

Akta shook her head. "No such luck. And he killed my best lead in tracking down a ghost that's been hunting me, so there's that."

"Enough," I snapped, waving my arms in the air. "Catch up on your own time. Tell me where we stand now."

"Well," Julia said. "We have Yilir's mirror and a map which apparently shows the original architecture of Hell."

"I have a scroll that's supposed to fix the mirror and allow us to talk to Yilir," I replied. "So, at least something is working for us."

"And we have the dagger," Kimberly said with a firm nod. "If we can find the other two weapons, then we can prevent Ragnarok."

"I have a question," Julia said, scratching her head. "Why don't we just destroy the key and the dagger right now? I mean, if they don't have the key, they won't be able to open the shackles that bind Surt, and without all four weapons, they can't summon the horsemen or break the seal."

Carl pulled up his tablet. "It's because there is no way to destroy the dagger, apparently. I have tried a hundred ways to destroy it over the years, and they've all failed to even dull the blade, let alone destroy it. Based on the chemical composition of the key, it was forged by the same material. If it were capable of being destroyed, the gods would have destroyed it. The only chance we have is finding the weapons and keeping them safe."

"I guess that makes sense," Julia said, crossing her arms. "It still feels like it's easier to just sit on these weapons and wait for them to come to us."

"I hate waiting," I grumbled, wringing my hands together. "And I'm not going to sit here and wait for some stupid conspiracy to kill me."

"Fine," Julia said, throwing up her hands. "It was just a suggestion."

"And your suggestion is noted and summarily rejected," I replied. "Now, how about we fix this mirror and talk to this ghost architect." I passed the scroll to Akta. "You were friends with her, so you do it."

Akta walked over to Julia and took the mirror from her, then placed it on the floor. She sat next to it and unfurled the scroll.

"*Quod confractum nunc flectantur.*" Akta made the sign of a pentagram over the mirror and then traced the cracks in the mirror. As her fingers ran over the mirror, the cracks resealed themselves. "I remember the battle when these cracks happened, sealing Yilir away forever."

"Clearly not forever," I mumbled.

"True. It will be good to see my friend again," Akta smiled. "*Quod confractum nunc flectantur.*"

The mirror mended itself into one smooth piece of glass until a blue light radiated from it when it was completely fixed. Akta's reflection shimmered in its face. However, even with it fixed, nothing happened to bring forth Yilir.

"What now?" I asked. "Shouldn't she just come?"

Akta shook her head, lost in thought. "Not yet. Hang on one..." She vanished in a haze of purple smoke. Before I could ask a question as to why, she returned, this time holding two white flowers in her hand.

"Where did you go?"

"Your garden," Akta replied, sitting down again. "I hope you don't mind, but there is a ritual that you must perform to call forth Yilir."

Akta placed the two flowers on the mirror and sat down next to it. She closed her eyes, and for a long time, all she did was breathe.

"What are you doing?"

"I haven't performed this ritual in over two hundred years, and it needs to be done correctly to evoke the architect." After another breath, she opened her mouth again. "*Evestra Italhir Megastin. Evestra Italhir Megastin. Evestra Italhir Megastin*. Dark witch of the sacred forest. Come. Come. *Evestra Italhir Megastin. Evestra Italhir Megastin. Evestra Italhir Megastin*."

Her hands circled the mirror as she spoke the words, and with every incantation, the blue glow increased until it forced a blinding beam from the mirror into the ceiling, and then, with an explosion of light, a beautiful woman stood in front of me. She had long, elven ears and was dressed all in white. Her white skin glowed, and her blue eyes shone brighter than lightning.

"Yilir," Akta said, standing up. "Welcome back."

Yilir turned to her. "My friend. If there was one who would bring me back, I hoped it would be you. You, or my darling Charon."

"Charon?" I asked.

"Yes. He is my love." Yilir said. Her robes rippled elegantly when she turned to me. "I recognize this castle, but not you. Are you the Devil?

"I am."

"Then he would be your boatman."

"Oh." I dropped my eyes. "I'm afraid he was killed by an impetuous child some time ago."

"No!" Yilir said, dropping to her knees. She turned back to Akta. "Say it is not so!"

Akta dropped to her knees. "I'm afraid it's true, my friend. He thought of you often until the end of his days."

Yilir began to sob and fell into Akta's chest.

"I'm sorry for your loss, Yilir," I said after a long silence where the only sound was her sobbing. "But we did not bring you back to tell you of Charon's death. We need your help."

Yilir dried her eyes. "Of course you do. That is all you Devils do is want, want, want. Not caring about anybody else but your own desires. I can't even have a moment to lose myself in grief." She took a deep breath. "How may I serve you, mighty Devil?" Sarcasm oozed from every word. "After all, I am but your humble servant."

"You don't have to say it like that," I replied.

"Yilir," Julia said, walking forward. "I know you designed most of Hell for the gods, and now, somebody is trying to unleash Surt from his final resting place."

Yilir sneered. "Stupid gods. They were so sure that it would be impossible to raise the Titan, but I knew it wouldn't be. I begged them to toss Surt into another dimension or cut him into a million pieces and scatter him throughout the universe, but they were brazen and bold. They wanted him close and alive, in case they ever needed his power. All I could do was construct his prison and lock him in it."

"With this key," Kimberly added, holding up the golden key.

"Yes," Yilir said with a slow nod. "That key binds his hands to the world chains, the Four Horsemen guard his path to freedom, and the blood of a pixie breaks him free of Hell. Have you found the four weapons yet?"

"No," Akta said, pulling out the dagger. "We have the dagger and the key. The conspirators hold the bow and the lance. We have yet to find the fourth weapon. We were hoping you could help us with that."

"I can and will help you. There was a map…"

Julia held it up. "I have the map."

"Then this will be simple, though the path forward will be treacherous. I did not make it easy to find the weapons. I hid them for good reason. The horsemen have been waiting since the dawn of time to bring back Ragnarok. I hope you know what you're doing."

I shook my head. "We definitely don't."

"That's comforting."

"Julia, you, and Kimberly, go find the fourth weapon, and don't get caught this time." I turned to Akta. "Meanwhile, you need to figure out who's really leading this conspiracy against me."

Akta nodded. "I will speak to Asmodeus and track down the ghost who imprisoned me to start this whole thing. If there is a culprit, I will find him."

"And I will protect the dagger personally," I added, taking the dagger from Akta's outstretched hand. "If any of these items fall into the wrong hands, then all of this is for nothing."

"What will you do if we find them all?" Kimberly asked. "If you can't destroy them."

"I don't know," I replied.

"There is a way to destroy them," Yilir said.

"Excuse me?" I replied.

"They were all forged together, and they must be destroyed together by the same flame that made them. The Sword of Damocles."

"The sword made the key and the other weapons?"

"Not by itself, but a spark of its flame created the Four Horsemen, who chose to bind themselves to the seals to protect humanity, and the flame re-forged the dagger from Death's scythe. The gods did not want the weapons destroyed, in case they ever had to use them on each other, but…they can be destroyed, if you can find them all."

"Then that's exactly what we will do," I replied, slamming my fist on the edge of my throne. "That's exactly what we'll do. Meanwhile, take Yilir somewhere for safe keeping."

Akta nodded. "I know just the place. I'll drop her off on my way." She turned to Yilir. "I hope you like the smell of leather."

CHAPTER 36

Akta

Location: Katrina's Castle, Hell

I didn't like torture, but I didn't detest it like Katrina did. I had witnessed plenty of it and been the recipient of it enough that I developed a hard stomach. That didn't mean I reveled in it. Just talking to a prisoner was often enough to get them to cough up information, and if you did it right, they wouldn't even know they'd implicated themselves.

I pushed open Asmodeus's cell. He was shackled and dangling from the ceiling in the middle of the room. Blue goo dripped down from the bottom of his torso and pooled on the floor under him.

"Of course, Katrina would be too chicken to torture me herself." Asmodeus let out a growl. "She is human. By definition, she is weak."

I shook my head. "She is the strongest Devil I have ever seen. She didn't run away from Hell's problems. She tried to change them for the better. She has brought real change to Hell, some for the worse…"

"Much worse."

"…and some for the better, but she has always taken responsibility for them, and that is strength. That is courage. She would never lurk in the shadows, working in secret like you have."

"Hrm," Asmodeus sighed and rolled his eyes, looking up at the floor. "Is that why you are here? To lecture me?"

"No," I replied. "I'm looking for your boss."

"I have no boss!" he spat, jerking his arms against his chains. "I told *your* boss the same thing."

I leaned in toward him. "I don't believe you. You aren't smart enough to carry out an attack on your own."

He laughed. "This is bigger than any one demon. It is all demon-kind who wish to do Katrina harm."

"Yes, yes, but who is *funding* this enterprise?" I recounted in my head. Beelzebub and Azazel were dead, and Lucifer was in Heaven. Asmodeus was too dumb, Mammon too poor, and Mephistopheles too obvious. "Who paid you?"

"Nobody paid me!" Asmodeus shouted. "I am my own demon!"

I shook my head. Asmodeus was one of the last holdouts of Katrina's expansion plan. He squandered all of his payouts, just like Mammon. "You're out of money, yet you are still able to live lavishly. Who is paying you?"

"I make my own coin."

I shrugged. "I didn't think you would help me. I'm sorry you didn't. I don't envy what is coming for you."

Asmodeus started to laugh. "My dear, this is only the beginning. Everything is going according to plan."

I closed the door. "Then you have a horrible plan."

***

Asmodeus's lack of helpfulness didn't deter me. I still had a series of clues to lead me to the wraith who attacked me. If I could find him, then I was on my way to finding out who hired him.

Charlie gave me a name, V'irl't, and a town, Ftwix. A small community of demons founded it a hundred years ago to get away from the Gates of Abnegation barracks. It was one of the first attempts before Katrina's time to create a life in Hell.

V'irl't didn't work in the pits himself but in a county clerk's office, filing paperwork. The best corruption happened at the local level, where money stretched further. Every step up the chain cost more but bribing a county clerk could be done for a few shekels or maybe tickets to a good concert. The trick was finding the right official, one with enough power to change things but not enough to know he had any real power, somebody put upon by an outside force and desperate for relief.

In that, V'irl't seemed perfect. He handled every soul transfer and request that came from the pits in the northwest quadrant of Hell. His job was important but low level, and he hadn't had a pay raise in over a century.

He wore thick glasses and a thin, black tie. With his sleeves rolled up, his face was contorted in a look of consternation as he stared at his computer, surrounded by stacks of papers.

"Excuse me," I said. "I'm looking for V'irl't."

He grunted and pointed to the name placard on his desk, hidden by a mess of papers. The placard read V'IRL'T in big, block letters.

"Wonderful," I replied. "I am afraid I have a delicate matter to discuss with you."

He looked at me over his glasses. "Do you really think I have time for this?"

"Excuse me?" I replied. I hadn't counted on him being so aggressive at the onset.

"I have a hundred requests to process today and more coming in every hour. I don't have time for 'delicate.' You can make an appointment or come back once I'm done with this paperwork…in about a decade."

"Well, it's those papers that I want to discuss with you."

"Really?" He pushed the glasses up to his nose and pressed back from his computer, looking at me with slightly more interest, if not suspicion. "Nobody ever asks about my work."

"Now, that's not true," I said, crossing my arms. "I happen to know that many unsavory characters have come through this very office inquiring about your work. A friend of mine told me as much, and he's as unsavory as they come."

V'irl't scoffed. "Oh yeah, who's that?"

"Charlie." I waited for the name to land on his ears before I continued. "A little imp. You must remember him. He's too irritating to be forgettable."

"Oh, shit," V'irl't said, gulping loudly. "Not him."

"Yes, him." I poured out my syllables slowly. "I'm not here to bust you. I just need a name. A wraith who asked you to make some souls disappear."

V'irl't hunched forward and pulled at the tie around his neck. "I—I can't—He'll—he'll eviscerate me. He'll break me into a billion pieces and shoot me into the sun."

I smiled. "I'll do just as bad, and if your boss finds out, you'll be stuck in that pit instead of pushing papers around. If you think this is Hell, wait until you see what actual Hell is about."

V'irl't started typing on his computer. "There's only one guy I know like that, and you do not want to be on his bad side."

"And he doesn't want to be on mine." I clicked my tongue. "And yet, here we are."

***

V'irl't's information led me back to a small parish of The True Path in the northernmost tip of the city, right before you crossed the ancient wall that was torn down to make room for Katrina's expansion. Of course, it did. The True Path might not have been funding the conspiracy against Katrina, but its members were intimately tied to it.

At first, I thought that V'irl't had led me on a wild goose chase, but after staking out the place for a couple of hours, I noticed a faint blue light coming from a window in the church's steeple. The church was giving my wraith sanctuary, which meant they were more deeply connected to this whole plot than any of the demons let on. It also meant that I would start a war with the church if I stole him. Unfortunately, there was no time to handle it with tact. I had to confirm the wraith's existence and then take him down.

As the fire set on another day, dozens of monsters made their way down the street and into the church. I couldn't inconspicuously capture the wraith with so many bystanders, but perhaps he would be inside the church. I could get a look at him without him noticing and make sure raiding the church was worth it. I made my way across the street and into the old church. The pews were near full, and an orc in a clerical collar smiled at me as I walked inside with the steady stream of people filing in.

"Are you here for mass?" the orc asked.

"I—guess so?" I replied.

"Then you're just in time. We always welcome new members into the congregation. Please, take a seat."

I didn't want to make a scene, so I sat down in the back row, waiting for my chance to disappear up the stairs when nobody was watching. I had just slid into my seat when the organ began to play, and the din of the parishioners quieted down. The congregation turned around to watch the orc walk down the middle aisle, holding a ball of incense. As he passed, there was a flash of light behind him, and when it dissipated, I saw the wraith at the back of the church, dressed in a blue clerical collar. Recognition crossed his face when we made eye contact, but he just smiled a faint smile and walked down the aisle. When he reached the lectern at the front, he raised his hands in the air. "For the glory of Hell, forever and ever. Amen."

"May the kingdom never waver in its greatness, Pastor Bill," the crowd chanted in unison.

"Please be seated," the wraith, Pastor Bill, said solemnly. "We gather here today to celebrate the glory of Hell and each other. Please, look around, and find a fellow soul. Welcome them to the parish and wish them well."

I turned to a pig-faced monster, who snorted at me. "I wish you glory and honor."

"And I you," I replied, shaking his sweaty hand.

Once the noise quieted, Pastor Bill continued. "I am happy to see your faces here tonight, and I notice some new faces. There is one face that is both recognizable to me and new to the church. Would you please stand up, Akta of the Forest?" The parishioners looked around the room at each other, wondering who he was talking about.

"No," I called out. "That's okay. I don't think I will."

"We're not going to bite," Pastor Bill replied, a simpering smile on his face. "I must insist." A few of the orcs and demons smiled dumbly at me in encouragement.

Most of them just looked around, confused by the disruption.

"So that's an order?" I asked, my tone full of indignation.

"Whatever you'd like to call it, but we can't continue until you do, I'm afraid."

I pushed myself up. "Fine."

"Akta works for Katrina, the Devil." A chorus of boos echoed through the room. "Please, fellows, it's not her fault she has been misguided for so long." He leaned forward on the lectern and addressed me directly. "I believe, if I have this right, you have worked for every Devil since Velaska. Is that correct?"

"Yes," I said, looking around at the other parishioners. "Though Thomas's reign was so short, it was almost as if I never worked for him at all."

"It's a shame, for he would have been a magnificent Devil."

"You're not the first person to tell me that today."

"And why are you here, Akta of the Forest? Have you had a change of heart? Are you ready to repent for your past?"

I shook my head. "I have nothing to repent for. You, on the other hand, have been stealing souls and molding them into weapons." The crowd gasped, looking from me back to the wraith. "That is against the teachings of the church, is it not?"

"That is a serious accusation, Akta," Pastor Bill said, his syllables carefully measured. "I hope you have some proof."

I stepped forward. "I don't have proof, but you've used them on me twice. I know that The True Path values souls more than anything. They believe their job is to cleanse souls and send them back to the Source, isn't that right?" The monsters around me agreed, nodding their heads. "So, how do you think they'll react to you destroying souls to create magic?"

"Lies!" the wraith shouted.

I held my hands up in the air. "And what do you think they will say to you trying to unleash Ragnarok and destroying Hell?"

"Is this true?" a minotaur shouted through the crowd.

"Of course not!" Pastor Bill answered, hardly containing his anger. "You know the Devil is the queen of all lies, and this pixie has been twisted by her words for too long."

I stomped my foot. "I have never lied, not in my whole life or afterlife, and I'm not lying now. We can settle this right now, can't we?" I looked around at the faces in the congregation. "Let us all go upstairs to your rectory and see if you have any souls there."

The eyes of the other monsters fell on their pastor, who squirmed. "That is a holy place, and you are unclean, pixie. I would never let you into my private sanctum."

"Then let me go!" an ogre said, standing up. "We can figure this out right now."

"And me!" A chameleon lizard also rose to its feet. "If we can prove you are innocent, let us."

"These are good monsters," I said. "But you know they can't prove you innocent. So, tell me who you work for, and I will let you live."

Pastor Bill reached under the lectern and pulled out four glowing blue orbs. "I was prepared for this."

The crowd gasped. "Then it's true!"

"He really is harvesting souls!"

"Get him!" a sentient centipede shouted from the back row.

"No!" I shouted, raising my arms to quiet them. "He is still of use to me." I turned back to the wraith. "Tell me who is funding you, and this will all go away."

Pastor Bill smiled. "Tell you? Why don't I show you?" He smashed the blue orbs on the ground. "*Adducere ad dominum meum*!" A flash of blue rang through the church, and I knew we had disappeared into the abyss, but for the first time in a long time, I had no idea where we were going.

CHAPTER 37

Julia

Location: Yilir's Cave, Hell

Yilir took us to the Dragon Cave in the northeastern-most cliffs of Hell. The dragons who lived in and around there were fanatically protective of their possessions. They would rather rip a person to shreds or eat a trespasser whole than negotiate with them.

To bargain with them, you needed an object of incredible power and prestige, something that was undeniably personal and important. I kept all sorts of those things in Aziolith's cave on Earth, but Kimberly wasn't willing to crawl back through the gateway, so I was running light on trinkets in Hell.

"I think it's that one," I said, looking down at the map and then up at the alignment of caves dotting the cliffside.

"Third from the left and third row from the bottom," Kimberly muttered, tracing her finger along the map. "I think you're right."

"I hope so." I rolled the map up and placed it in my back pocket. "I don't want to negotiate with the wrong dragon. It's stupid enough for us to talk with the right one."

"Why don't we just get Aziolith to do it?" Kimberly asked.

"Are you kidding me?" I exclaimed. "Do you know what would happen if a dragon went to negotiate with another dragon?"

"No, obviously."

"There would be a war," I replied. "Dragons are incredibly territorial and possessive, especially with other dragons. We're just magical enough to pique a dragon's interest but not powerful enough to threaten them. It has to be us."

Kimberly unfurled her wings. "Then let's go."

She rose into the air, and I followed behind her. The grumbles from the dragons around us quaked the mountainside, and the fire from their breath flashed in the darkness, giving me a small understanding of their power. Aziolith was small compared to these dragons, whose lives spanned back to the beginning of Earth. Many of them were so old that they predated the angels and demons to before Lucifer fought against the gods and took over for Velaska. Back when Hades and Anubis ran things.

They were the original inhabitants of the caves and would be powerful allies in the battle to control Hell, but as of yet, they had not chosen a side. They seemed to be content in Hell and made little attempt to return to the surface even during the Apocalypse. It was cold on Earth, they said. Aziolith was one of the few that preferred Earth to Hell, but ice ran through his bones.

I landed on the edge of the dragon's lair. "Remember, respectful."

"I know," Kimberly said with snark oozing from her voice. "I'm not a child."

"You will always be a child to me," I replied. "Now, wash the tone out of your voice. It will get you killed."

"Do not step further, pixie," a deep voice grumbled. The bass was so low I could barely understand the words it spoke.

"My apologies, great dragon, but we come with a matter of great import." I tilted my eyes down.

"Hrm," the dragon muttered. "It must be important if you choose to rouse the great black dragon Ghortho from his slumber."

"It is," Kimberly said. "We swear it."

Two giant yellow eyes popped open in the darkness. They were easily ten times bigger than my whole body, and I quivered in my shoes as one of them closed in on me.

"I have not eaten in a long time," the dragon said, its eyes bouncing back and forth between us. "You have great power, and power tastes delicious."

"Please," Julia said. "Just listen to our offer, and if you do not like it, then you can eat us. Both of us."

"Speak for yourself!" Kimberly shouted. "I do NOT want to be eaten."

Ghortho's eyes narrowed. "I smell ancient magic on you. Before the age of pixies and monsters. Back when all of this was a faint memory, and I was young to this world."

I stepped forward slowly and unrolled the map for him. "This is the original map of Hell, drawn by Yilir when she constructed it for Anubis."

"It takes me back to a time when I first came to Hell," Ghortho said. "Yilir was a friend to me then and made me feel safe. She built these caves for me and my kin."

"She is who sent me here," I replied. "She said you guard the entrance to a cave which holds a powerful weapon."

A deep laugh came from the cave. "Yes, this is true. She asked me to guard it for her, and here I am all these years later, still fulfilling my charge. So many of my kind would have given up on it."

"You are truly loyal," Kimberly bowed her head for a moment and then looked up. "We really need what's in that cave."

"Many do," Ghortho said. "And what do you offer me in return?"

I laid the map down on the ground. "This map, for your collection."

The dragon blew fire out of his nose, and it singed the edges of the map. "That map is nothing but a relic from a previous time. It means nothing to me."

"It is all we have to give."

"Then I believe we are done here."

"Wait!" Kimberly said. "Is there something you want, anything we can retrieve for you?"

Another groan came from the cave. "Perhaps. Not long ago, something was stolen from me...a box, green leather, containing more power than you can imagine. If you can find it and return the magic inside to me, I will let you enter the cave."

"That's not very much information to go on."

"It is precious to me. It was given to me by a dear friend for safe keeping," Ghortho said. "A small imp took it from me."

Kimberly and I glanced at one another. "I happen to know somebody who fits that description," Kimberly said. "And he was after me to deliver a box for him."

"Then perhaps it is kismet we met," Ghortho said. "And that I have not eaten you yet. Return without the box, however, and I will change my mind."

***

"I mean, how is it always *this* demon?" Kimberly asked. We were standing outside of Charlie's apartment. "Can't we just kill him and be done with it?"

"He does seem to be at the center of everything, doesn't he?" I shook my head. "We would need the dagger to kill him, and I frankly just don't have the energy to kill him."

"But you have the energy for this bullshit?"

I shrugged my shoulders. "Look at it this way, if he didn't steal from the dragon, then we would probably have to give the dagger away, so maybe he kind of did us a favor."

Kimberly sighed. "I just hate this so much."

I knocked on Charlie's front door. "MOOOOOM!" I heard a whiny voice inside. "MOOOOM! DOOOOOR!" I knocked a second time. "Ugh!"

There was a shuffling behind the door and feet clomping to the door. The door swung open hard, and a pimply-faced imp blinked at me. "What do you want?"

"Your dad. Is he here?"

The imp sighed. "No, he's not here. He hasn't been back since that other one of you came here."

"Other one of us?" I asked. "Who are you talking about?"

"I don't know. She was a pixie. She looked like Link or something. Definitely not stylin', ya know?"

Kimberly grimaced. "Akta."

He shrugged. "Sure, whatever. But he's not here. He hasn't been around for a long while."

"Do you know where he went?" I asked.

The imp scratched his head. "Earth, maybe? Or church? Or, you know, literally anywhere. He's always leaving for weeks on end and not telling us. He could be anywhere. That it?"

I nodded. "I guess so unless you have a cell phone number or something for him."

The imp reached into his pocket a pulled out a cell phone. "I mean, I guess I do. It's a burner, though." He flipped through his contacts. "If you catch him with another woman, tell my mom so she can roast him on a spit."

I chuckled. "That I can do."

***

Having the backing of the Devil meant I had access to all the goodies at the police department's disposal, including the ability to track phones. Assuming Charlie was still in Hell, we could track him down. It was one of my favorite advancements in technology since before the Apocalypse.

"Have you found him yet?" Kimberly said.

"Not yet," a lizard computer tech said as he stared at his screen. He licked his eye with his forked tongue as he worked. "You know, he could have put this phone down anywhere if he left Hell, and if it's off, we can't—wait a minute. He's turning it on, and it looks like he's placing a call."

I put my hands on the desk and studied the screen. "Can you tap it?"

"Give me a second." He typed furiously on his keyboard. "There we go. Coming in now."

"I'm here," Charlie's voice said over the tinny speakers of the tech's computer. "Where are you?"

"Relax," a voice said. "I'll be there soon."

"I don't like this," Charlie's said. He was out of breath. "I peddle in information, not magical artifacts, and I'm not an errand boy."

The voice on the other end of the line snorted. "Don't pretend like this is beneath you, Charlie. I know where you came from."

"I'm not that guy anymore. I'm more or less legit."

"And yet you have my box, and I have your money. So much money, Charlie. Enough money for you to buy your way into polite society."

"That's the only reason I did this for you."

"It's the only reason anyone does anything. Now, stay there. My man will be there shortly to collect."

The phone went dead. I bent down to the tech. "Get me that address."

*　*　*

We dropped some pixie dust and vanished from the precinct, reemerging outside a train station in the bowels of Dis. This was one of the few still ravaged by time. Katrina hadn't managed to repair or replace it yet.

"There he is," I said, pointing to a small imp in a trench coat. He was thumbing a green box in his hands.

"How do you want to play this?" Kimberly asked. "Fast and loose?"

"No, we have to know who is paying him before we can—" A black sedan pulled up and out stepped a ghoul, glowing slightly blue. Instantly I recognized her as Mammon's wife, Shirley, the one I'd met in G'ru'l. "What is she doing here?"

"Recognize her?" Kimberly asked.

"Oh my gods...I know what happened." And it was true. At that moment, I knew exactly who was responsible for the attempts on Katrina's life. Everything fell into place. "We need to move now."

"What is it?" Kimberly asked.

"I'll tell you in a second," I said, moving toward the car. "Wait here."

I dropped some pixie dust and flashed away, reappearing between the ghoul and Charlie just as they were about to make the handoff. "Hi, Charlie." I grabbed the box, and it tingled in my hands. I tried to flash away, but I couldn't. The power of the box overtook me, and I dropped to my knees.

"Hi, Julia!" Charlie said. "So nice that we can kill two birds with one stone."

I rose and started to run, with Charlie and Shirley chasing after me. I managed to make it across the street, but they were fast on my tail, and the box weighed me down more with each passing second.

"Go!" I shouted at Kimberly, who raced forward to grab me. She picked up the box just as I fumbled it. Free of the box, I suddenly had strength again, though not much. "It was Mammon. Find me at his house in G'ru'l."

"Who's Mammon?"

I rubbed my hand with pixie dust, pressed my hand to her chest, and closed my eyes. I imagined Ghortho's cave and sent her there. She vanished from sight, fear in her eyes, just as I fell once again onto the ground. I turned to see Charlie grinning over me. He drew back his fist and smashed me across the face, and everything went black.

CHAPTER 38

Kimberly

Location: Dragon Caves, Hell

In a flash, I appeared before the dragon's cave, holding the green box. It tingled, and I could barely feel my hands by the time I dropped it to the ground.

"You've found it," the dragon grumbled. "Bring it to me."

"I'm not touching that thing," I replied, trying to catch my breath. "It tried to kill me and weakened my friend enough to get her caught."

Ghortho chuckled, rumbling the cave. "The box is just a box. It's not trying to do anything but exist. The magic inside, however, is a different story."

I took a step closer and crouched down to study the box. "What's in that thing?"

Ghortho shook his head slightly. "I honestly do not know, but it is powerful magic forged from the first crucible of the universe."

"Who gave it to you?"

"My, you have many questions." There was a long pause. "I do not like to be questioned."

I stood up and faced the great, black dragon. "My best friend just got captured to get this to you, so excuse me for being curious."

"Curiosity killed the cat, they say."

"And satisfaction brought it back," I replied. "I hate when that quote gets cut off."

"Hrm," the dragon said. "I have never heard that part of it, only the first part."

I stared straight into the dragon's massive yellow eye. "Well, that's the whole quote, so please, tell me."

"Fine," Ghortho replied. "It was given to me by my friend, Pandora."

"Pandora?" I breathed, my eyebrows shooting upwards at him. "As in, Pandora's box?"

The dragon's eyes traveled to the box and then back to me. He seemed to make some mental calculations. "Well, that is a box, and it was given to me by her, so I suppose it is Pandora's box."

"What happens if you open it?"

"There are many theories. Pandora only opened it once and could never get the courage to tell me what she unleashed. She assured me there was something horrible inside that could destroy us all. It matters not to me. I simply like to keep it close because it reminds me of her, and it provides warmth to my ancient heart."

I picked up the box and walked it quickly over to the edge of the cave, placing it in front of the entrance before my arms went numb. "I'm already dealing with one Apocalyptic event right now. I can't deal with a second."

"I will keep it safe. I am old and have grown soft. I even made a bargain with you. In my younger years, I would have simply eaten you."

"Please don't eat me."

"I'm not going to eat you, pixie," Ghortho said. "We have made a deal. However, I will not trust as easily in the future, and any new callers to my cave with be dealt with…harshly. Now go before I change my mind. The cave entrance is just there." He nodded his massive head behind him.

"Thank you." I could no longer see the great dragon as I walked past his ancient body into the darkness behind him, but I felt his breath. His simple act of inhaling shook the foundation of the cave.

"Do not thank me," Ghortho said. "For none who have entered the cave have come out alive."

***

The cave narrowed until I reached a wooden door with a metal lock. Resting on a smooth rock next to the door were three lockpick sets lit by a pinprick of light from above. I picked them up and stuffed them in my pocket. When I did, a note appeared on the door, written in calligraphy. The handwriting matched the script on the map, so it must have been written by Yilir.

Three chances. Make it through, and it is yours. Fail, and you will never see daylight again.

"Cute," I muttered to myself.

Lockpicking had never been my forte, but Julia taught me how to do it when I was a child, and I had used the skill throughout my long life. I was likely one of the best lockpickers in the world, even if I was out of practice. Really though, I preferred smashing my way through.

I knelt in front of the door and slid the tension wrench into the lock before inserting the hook and searching for the first binding pin. I twisted it right and then left until it gave. The old lock, having been manufactured thousands of years ago, was a bit clunkier than the ones I was used to. The pins were heavier and clumsier, but it was also crude construction and magic, the simplicity of which let me quickly make my way through the first three pins.

On the fourth pin, the lock jammed. I tried to slide out the hook, but it wouldn't budge. When I exerted a bit more pressure, the hook snapped in my hand and fell to the floor. "Shit," I muttered. "Two left."

Before I could pull my hand away, I heard the buzz of a saw, and a blade appeared on the door. It zipped up so fast that even when I tried to pull my hand away, it nicked the tip of my pinky finger and sliced the tip off.

"Ow!" I shouted, blood spurting out all over the place. I reached into my bag and pulled out a handful of pixie dust. It was good for many things, but one of its most important uses was as an anti-coagulant. I sprinkled a pinch of dust onto the nub of my finger, and the blood began to sizzle. It hurt something fierce, but the blood soon stopped, and the pain subsided.

I turned around, looking for the tip of my finger, hoping that maybe I could reattach it, but all I found was a shadow come to life that looked exactly like me. It held daggers in each hand, and its glowing red eyes stared deep into me.

"Not good," I said, rolling out of the way as the shadow charged.

I pulled out my daggers and ducked to avoid the shadow's slashing knives. I had dealt with shadow creatures before, and their one weakness was the light. Unfortunately, there was no light that I could see, save for the pinprick from the ceiling, which wouldn't do anything but irritate the beast.

I kicked into the air as the pixie sliced again. As I rose, I saw a mirror resting on a ledge in front of me. I flew over to it and picked it up. The second it was removed from its place in the wall, a rush of light shot through the room.

The shadow creature pulled out another set of daggers and hurled them at me. I tilted the mirror toward the light, and when the beam reached the daggers, they disappeared in a cloud of smoke. The pixie shadow rose into the air, and I moved the light to reflect onto her. She screamed and melted into the darkness.

I floated down to the ground and caught my breath before I pulled out the second lockpick set. "Do not screw it up again."

The lock seemed to give quite a bit easier than before; the pins felt lighter on my lock pick. I tapped the last two binding pins into place, and the door clicked open. I pulled it open and, sighing with relief, delved deeper into the cave.

***

I walked through the tight corridor until it broke wide open into another room, empty save for the skeleton of a huge creature in the center of it. I stepped carefully through the room, never taking my eyes off the skeleton until I came upon another door.

"Great."

I knelt again and tried my hand at the lock. It was much more difficult to move the pins than the previous door, and I only got to the second one before the lockpick snapped in half.

"Shit," I muttered under my breath. I whipped around, scanning the room for movement. "What now?"

A blue light hit my face. I watched the giant skeleton rise into the air and the soul of a huge snake uncoiled and screeched. When the tail closed itself around the last bit of the bone, it hissed and lunged toward me.

A wraith. Wraiths could hurt you and take corporeal, though translucent, form, but at the end of the day, they were a lot like ghosts. That meant you could reach inside of them or run through them, as long as they did not attack while you did. I was not in a position to do so at the moment. I needed to maneuver into a better position, so I threw a bit of pixie dust and disappeared across the room.

The creature was fast, but I was faster, if just barely. It turned on a dime and lunged again, and I dove out of the way to avoid getting hit. I reached into my boot and pulled out the small silver knife I kept there.

It didn't look like much, but it was made with pure silver, the only known substance to kill a wraith. However, the knife was only three inches long, and the snake was ten times that and as thick as my body. I doubted the little dagger would do much, but it was all I could muster on short notice.

The snake snapped again, and this time when I jumped aside to avoid it, I managed to stab the snake in the side of its face. It screamed out in anger and recoiled. It was then that I saw the remains of a knight inside its belly, and as the wraith rose, the sword the knight carried glinted like silver. His armor was long-rusted, but the sword was perfectly intact. I rolled forward as the snake reeled and dove toward the sword.

The snake glared and dove to attack. I jumped toward its ribs and pulled the sword from its bowels as I swam through the goopy, gelatinous entrails of its stomach. The snake reeled again, and when I stood up, holding the sword, it had punctured a huge hole in the snake's stomach. The sword was made of silver, too. It could defeat the wraith.

When it lunged for a third time, I ducked under its head and stabbed the beast through the head with a vicious uppercut. The snake reared once more with a scream, then fell to the ground in a violent thud before disappearing into the ether, leaving nothing but its bones behind.

The sword clattered on the floor when I dropped it on my way back to the door. Like the first door, it gave more easily than it had before the fight as if destroying the snake had broken a spell. I finished picking the lock, and once again, the door swung open, and I walked forward. I silently hoped there were no more trials but knew that was foolish. The gods worked in threes.

***

When I passed into the third room, a gate immediately slammed down behind me. Gears whirled all around me, and the walls began to close in, revealing large spikes with the bones of adventurers on many of them. I rushed through the room toward the exit but saw a gate coming down to block my egress on the other side as well. The answer had to be in the room. I looked at the floor, checked with white and black tiles except in the middle, where it was locked just like the other doors.

I pulled out my last lockpick. There was no room for failure. I took a breath and placed the tension rod into the lock. I eased in my hook and slowly, methodically, found the first tension rod and pressed it into place. The lock worked against me, but I did not press it. I took my time, even as the adrenaline filled my blood and made my hands shake. The walls were closing in on me, but I pushed the spikes out of my mind and moved to the second pin, which gave easier than the first. The third wouldn't give until after the fourth did.

I took a deep breath as the spikes grazed against my knee. I gritted my teeth, pushing the fifth pin into place. The lock gave, and the panel opened to reveal two large buttons. I pressed one of them, and the gates on either side of me opened. When I pushed the second button, the gears around me stopped for a moment, then started again. This time, instead of pushing in toward me, the spikes receded. I leaned back and let out a deep breath.

The gash on my leg bled, but the wound was superficial. I rubbed in a bit of pixie dust, and it closed. I stood up and hobbled toward the gate, into the darkness once again.

***

In the center of the next room, a light shone down on a giant, golden cage. It was large enough to walk inside. As I approached, I saw a golden, two-sided war hammer resting inside the cage. Its long wooden handle was bound in red leather and curved gracefully at the end, with runes etched down either side.

The door of the cage was locked. In front of it, on a small table, rested a single, golden lock pick. *One more challenge.*

The pick felt frail and fragile in my fingers. One false move, and it would break. This time, though, my hands were still as I slid the hook inside and confidently clicked each pin into place. The door swung open.

My fists clenched instinctively, but after a moment when no fight came, I walked inside the cage and picked up the war hammer. It was lighter than I expected. A surge of power ran through me as I lifted it into the air, and I vanished, reappearing at the front of the cave. The smell of charred bones seared my nostrils as I rushed to the entrance. The ashes of several bodies, still smoking, were piled there.

"You should hurry, little bird," the dragon said, still concealed in the darkness. "Your friends are in grave danger…and I fear they do not have a dragon to protect them."

I smiled at him. "Actually…"

CHAPTER 39

Katrina

Location: Devil's Castle, Hell

I hated waiting. I was so sick of not being in control of what was happening in Hell, so I decided to do something about it.

"Asmodeus!" I shouted as I entered the dungeon. "We need to talk. Now!"

I stomped to his cell and swung open the door, but when I entered, he was not shackled to his chains. The only thing in the room was the drippings beneath where his body used to hang.

"You really are very predictable," I heard behind me. I wheeled around to find Asmodeus strapped to the back of a blue troll, his torso having been ripped from his body, by me. He was holding the Dagger of Obsolescence.

"You have made a formidable enemy," I snarled, but I dared not charge. I was powerful, but he had the dagger.

"You have made enough powerful enemies for a thousand lifetimes," he replied, waving the blade toward me. "And now you will die!"

"I don't think so!" I heard a voice call out. A breath of fire rushed down the hallway, and the blue troll leaped back into the cell. Kimberly moved into the doorway with a hammer, Aziolith standing next to her in his human form.

"Sven?" Kimberly asked, confused. "What are you doing he— You know what, I don't care. Drop the dagger, Asmodeus."

"Fool!" Asmodeus screamed. "Dozens of demons are rushing through the door where the brambles once stood and into the castle from the lava. They're coming from every direction, ready to take you down. You won't be able to stop them all."

"Says you." Kimberly lunged, and the troll backed up again.

I spun to avoid them and turned toward the door, nodding to Kimberly. "Thanks."

"Any time," Kimberly smiled. "Now, what do we do with them?"

"Kill 'em, and let God sort it out."

"Sounds good to me."

Asmodeus reached behind him into a purse the troll kept on his belt and pulled out two blue orbs. He smashed them on the ground and disappeared in a haze of blue smoke.

"No!" I shouted. When the dust cleared, both he and the troll were gone. "Now, where did they go?"

"I think I know," Kimberly replied. "Before she was captured, Julia told me who funded this whole operation."

"Who?"

"Mammon. Does that word mean anything to you?"

I chuckled. "She must be mistaken. Mammon isn't smart enough to plan anything. Besides, he's broke."

"Julia is not often wrong," Kimberly said.

I scoffed. "Hasn't she been captured like, twice in the past couple of days?"

Kimberly nodded. "Yes, but that doesn't make her wrong, just sloppy."

A dozen soldiers ran down the hallway, coming from either direction. They snarled at me when they stopped in front of me, all weapons, claws, and teeth. I was ready for them. They would not take my castle, or me, this day.

"Then you should check it out," I replied, clenching my fists. "I have to defend this castle."

"Do you need help?"

I reached for the hammer. "No, just leave me this, and I'll be fine."

"I will stay here to help you, just in case," Aziolith said before turning to Kimberly. "If that's okay with you."

Kimberly nodded. "Fine with me, if you think you can help take them."

Aziolith smirked, fire escaping from either side of his grin. "I've had worse odds."

"Then, I will go and find Mammon," Kimberly said.

I waved the hammer back and forth to get a feel for it. "The last I checked, he was in a town called G'ru'l in the south. It sounded horrible."

Kimberly grabbed a pinch of pixie dust and threw it onto the ground, disappearing from sight in a cloud of purple smoke.

"Ready?" I said as the demons charged towards Aziolith and me.

"I was born ready," Aziolith said.

"Awesome," I said. "You go down the hall. I'll stay here."

"Right," Aziolith said, rushing forward, breathing a stream of fire at the demons.

I planted my feet and swung the hammer hard, connecting with the chest of a demon and breaking him into a million pieces. I spun around and hit another one in the side of the face, dusting him into oblivion. I shot my own stream of fire out of my hands, and it streaked down the hallways, destroying a cadre of demons on its way. I made my way down the corridor, destroying demons as I went. When I finally reached the end, another cadre of demons made their way to me, this group led by General K'bab'nik.

"So, it's true," I said to him. "You really are a traitor, General Kebab. I didn't want to believe it."

"Traitor?" he said. "No. I am loyal to Hell, and you have desecrated it." His arm rose high into the air. In his hand, he held a longsword seeping with black ooze. When he dropped the sword back to his side, his soldiers charged at me. They were bigger and more muscular than the last set, but no less dumb.

I took care of them in short order, destroying each of them with a combination of my hammer and my flame, until only General K'bab'nik remained. He had been in the army of Hell for hundreds of years, and his technique showed a demon with complete command of his body. He held out his black sword and charged me.

I swung, and he ducked. I shot fire, and he avoided it. I spun around to make another hit, and the general's sword stuck into my stomach. He pushed it forward until the hilt dug into my abdomen, and the tip came out the other side of me. I had never been beaten in battle before, and the sweet sting of the blade hurt enough that I dropped my hammer.

General K'bab'nik picked it up and hovered over me. "That blade won't kill you, but it will sting your stomach for a hundred years. This hammer, though, will kill you quickly. The hammer rose above his head, but before he could drop it down on my head, a flame licked his face and sent him careening down the hallway.

He rose and looked to where Aziolith was standing, then over to me, then down at the hammer, and smiled. "I was supposed to kill you, but I'll let Surt take care of you himself." He pulled a blue orb out of his pocket and smashed it to the ground, vanishing. Kebab had come to kill me, but he got an even better prize. Now they had all four weapons and could summon the Four Horsemen to break the seal. All they needed was the key…and I had just sent Akta with it directly into the belly of the beast, The True Path church.

I looked down at the sword still embedded in my stomach. Black, inky liquid drained out of me and soaked into my clothing. Aziolith rushed over and knelt beside me.

"I'm sorry, my Devil. I could not protect you."

"It's okay. I can't die from it, I don't think, but it hurts like a bitch." I looked into his eyes. "We lost, Aziolith."

He shook his head. "Nothing is lost yet. There is still hope, and while there is hope, we will keep fighting."

BOOK 3

CHAPTER 40

Akta

Location: Hell

In a flash of light, the entire congregation from the church reappeared at once, shaky-legged and wobbling, in the darkness of an unknown location. Most monsters had never teleported before, which was clear by the sheer number of them that vomited and fell over when we rematerialized.

I wasn't nauseous, necessarily, but I felt violated. I had never been transported without my consent before. I did not like it. In fact, I vehemently hated it, and the wraith would pay for his impudence.

"I'm sorry," the blue wraith said. His light shone on the wooden beams around him, and as my eyes adjusted to the darkness, I realized we were in an unfinished basement with cinderblock walls and exposed wooden beams buttressing the ceiling. The light flickered on from a swinging bulb that swayed back and forth in the aftermath of the wraith giving it a harsh tug.

"Why, Pastor Bill?" a sentient monkey asked, tears in its eyes. "Why would you do such a horrible thing?"

"The ends justify the means, Yvette," Pastor Bill said. "They are sacrifices for the greater good."

"But harvesting souls, Pastor?" Yvette said. "Destroying them…that goes against everything the church stands for, everything we stand for. We are trying to free souls, not weaponize them."

"That is one interpretation of our goal," Pastor Bill smiled. "It's not personal, Yvette, but we have reached the endgame of our little battle with the Devil, and it is time to finish it. You will be a great boon to our cause."

"You're insane," I said.

Pastor Bill swung around to face me. "Hell is insane, and perhaps it takes a madman to understand the truth of it all."

"Bill?" a soft voice came from the stairwell. "Is that you?"

"Yes, Shirley," he hollered up to her. "Sorry for barging in like this, but we have a problem."

A door creaked open at the top of the stairs. Gentle feet pattered on the stairs as something or someone descended. It was only when she turned the corner that I saw that she glowed the same blue as Pastor Bill.

"Drat. I hate complications." Her hollow eyes glided back and forth between all the monsters in the basement. She shook her head and pressed her hands against her mouth. Then she let out a deep, disappointed sigh. "He's not going to be happy about this."

"Perhaps this is a blessing in disguise," Pastor Bill said. "After all, we need a lot of power to call the horsemen. I have been stealing a soul here and there trying to gather enough energy for the spell, but monsters have magic in their blood. Harnessing them all at once would give us the juice we need in one fell swoop."

"These are monsters, Bill," Shirley said. "We're trying to help them, not kill them."

"I know, sweetheart." He glanced at the group of monsters watching him and stepped toward her. "But...what is the sacrifice of a few to save the many?"

Shirley sighed again. "This is not the way. He's really not going to like this."

"He doesn't have to know," Bill replied, the sides of his mouth curling upwards. "After all, what Mammon does not know could just about fill the deepest pit in Hell."

Shirley smiled, moving close to Bill and squeezing his hands tightly. "You're so bad."

Bill kissed her on the cheek. "This is Hell. Only the bad survive."

"Okay, let's do it." Shirley looked at the monsters and addressed them for the first time. "I'll get snacks! We must make sure you are all well fed before you meet your final ends."

Shirley clomped up the stairs, and Bill floated behind her. He stopped halfway and turned to point at me. "And don't try using magic. This has been very well insulated to prevent you from flittering away. You can ask your friend. She has been trying all afternoon."

Friend? Who could—? I spun around as Bill ascended the stairs. I pushed my way through the monsters, who were standing around petrified. At the back of the room, I found Julia chained to a wall, her hands and wrists raw and bruised from the shackles.

"Julia!" I shouted.

"Akta!" Tears jumped into her eyes. "I thought I would never see you again. I'm so sorry, I—"

"Please, don't apologize," I replied. "I didn't even know you had been captured again."

She looked down. "Don't remind me. It is embarrassing."

"Hey," I said. "They got me, too. There's nothing to be ashamed about."

"So, you know about Mammon then?" she asked.

"I just heard. How could he—"

"I don't know," she said, shaking her head. "And it doesn't matter. The only thing that matters is that we stop him before he can call the horsemen and open the seals."

I heard the murmur of the wraiths talking to each other on the floor above us. "That's going to be hard from down here. We need to get out of here, but I don't know how."

"If we could get upstairs," Julia said, "we could teleport, but this basement is warded up the ass. I can't even use my pixie dust to escape. We're locked in."

I traced her hand across the wall. Every inch was grooved with runes. I pressed my hand against them and ran my fingers down the indentations. They were chiseled deep into the stone and impossible to remove.

"We'll get out of here. First, we have to get you out of these chains." I looked through the crowd, who had turned to watch us. "Can anyone help me break these chains?" The group turned from me, almost in unison. "Are you kidding me? Do you understand what will happen if you don't help me?"

"Yes," an ogre with a guttural voice said. "She will die. We will die."

I pushed myself to my feet. "Then come here and help me."

"Maybe it's for the best," a black-clothed elk replied, her head hung low. "Pastor Bill has never led us astray before, and if we can help return Hell to its former glory—"

"Hell was never glorious!" I shouted, rising to my feet. "It has been an insufferable mess for the past three thousand years. Katrina has made it livable, sufferable even, at least on its best days. She has given you hope."

"And what good is hope in this place?" a wood nymph called out from the other end of the room.

"Hope is everything!" I answered. "It is the only thing we have. A little sliver of hope is all that I've held for three thousand years. If you lose that hope, then Hell has won. It is only through hope that we have any agency in this world."

"We are nothing but slaves," an ogre replied. "It is better to die than live as a slave."

"I don't believe that," I said. "Hell is eternal. In the last hundred years, you have gained the right to change jobs, form a union, and take time off. You can advocate for yourself in a way that is unprecedented. Do you know what I would have done to get two weeks of vacation, three-thousand years ago?"

"Yeah, but you can only vacation in Hell," the pink antlered deer pointed out.

"At least it's not the pits. Have any of you ever worked in the pits?" I scanned the room slowly. One by one, all the eyes looked away from me. "I have. Julia has been in them. This is so much better. Right, Julia?"

"A million times better," Julia said, nodding her head emphatically. "Probably more."

The ogre crossed his arms. "But it is not Heaven, and we have no ability to get to Heaven."

"That's not the Devil's fault," I said, throwing my hands in the air. "That's a flaw built into the system by the gods. Besides, I've been to Heaven. I've met God, felt the warmth of the celestial fire, all of that. Honestly, I would rather be here than there."

"You're crazy," the dryad said dismissively. She crossed her arms and rolled her eyes.

"I'm serious," I said. "Bacchus hates you. He thinks you monsters are subservient to him. Katrina actually cares deeply about each of you." I lifted my finger in the air. "Bacchus would rather watch you all die than raise a finger to help you. So no, I'm not crazy. I would take the ruler who tried to make my life better over the one who couldn't care less about me."

The ogre raised an eyebrow. "You have really been to Heaven?"

I nodded. "Well, in my day, it was called Mount Olympus, but I've been there and seen the majesty of Valhalla. I would rather be here, now, no matter how insufferable it is here." I didn't believe the words I was saying. I was happier in Valhalla than I had ever been, but Hell was a close second, and when I looked around the room, I saw that my words were sinking in. "I'm serious."

The pink-horned deer frowned and gave a little nod. "Perhaps it is not so bad."

"It's really not. In fairness, it is still Hell, which means the floor is pretty low, but it is so much better here now than it has ever been. So please, help me save Hell and my grand-niece." I gestured toward Julia.

The ogre looked at the deer and nodded. He stepped forward and grabbed the chain that held Julia. With a single yank, he snapped the chains in two, and then he ripped the chain from the wall.

"Thank you," I said.

The ogre looked me in the eyes. "I still do not believe in this place, but I believe in you, at least."

"Fair enough." I spun back to Julia. "Can you stand?"

She pushed herself to her feet. "I can. Now, how do we get out of here?"

I smiled. "I think we should take a page from Katrina's playbook and just bum rush them."

"Do you think these guys will be into it?" Julia asked, looking around the room.

"Let's see." I turned to the monsters. "I have a very stupid plan."

"I like stupid," the ogre said. "Stupid is good."

"Then follow me."

I moved to the stairs and unfurled my wings. I floated up to the top of the door and held my head to it. "When this door opens, we rush them. They can't stop us all."

Julia floated up to the top of the stairs to join me. "Are you sure about that?"

"No," I replied. "But hopefully, we'll have the element of surprise, and that will give us a momentary advantage." After a moment, I heard footsteps moving toward us. "They're coming."

The door creaked open. "I have treats!" Shirley's eyes went wide when she saw two dozen monsters staring back at her from the bottom of the stairs.

"Now!" I shouted, flying forward. The other monsters screamed and charged up the stairs behind me. Their feet made thunderous echoes on the floor, shaking the house.

"For Hell!" the ogre screamed. When we reached the top of the stairs, Pastor Bill met us. He pulled four blue orbs from his pocket and slammed them down on the ground. *"Daemonum inferni vocat mea!"*

From the blue mist, ten demon dogs appeared, each with three heads snapping at us as they charged. I rose into the air to avoid them, and Julia spun to the side. They attacked the group of monsters instead.

"No!" I screamed. "Watch out, everyone!"

"We can't wait!" Shirley shouted over her shoulder at Bill, trying to wrangle the congregation. "You have to do it now!"

"Not without you!" Pastor Bill shouted.

"What is one life—" Shirley said meekly, her voice drowned out by the howling of the dogs.

"There are too many of them!" Pastor Bill said. "I can't save you!"

Just do it!" Shirley shouted, kicking an ogre into a demon dog. "I gladly give my life for the cause!"

"I'm sorry." Pastor Bill placed a blue orb into his mouth. He bit down on it, and the blue bile dripped out of it, leaking onto his chin. *"Conforta me tradam potentia inferni!"*

Bill glowed brighter. He smashed his hands together, bent down low, and slammed them onto the floor. A great pentagram appeared from the cracks in the floor that rippled through the kitchen and sent the monsters sprawling.

"Animam meam: Adiuro te. Adiuro te animam meam. Animam meam: Adiuro te. Adiuro te animam meam!"

I watched Shirley mouth "I love you" to Bill as blue flames rose from the ground and consumed her alongside the monsters. Julia and I nodded to each other and flew toward the wraith.

"*Clypeus*!" A shield rose in front of him and sent us falling backward.

The monsters were screaming out in pain, clawing each other, trying to free themselves from the flames. I looked over at Julia, who crawled away from the sigil. There was nothing we could do. I grabbed her and pulled her toward me.

"Vanish us!" I shouted.

"What if it doesn't work? What if the wards aren't down?"

"Then we'll die here! Do it!"

She pulled out a pinch of pixie dust and slammed it on the ground between us, and we vanished from sight. We reappeared in front of the house and watched as the blue light crashed through the windows and the house imploded on itself. In the dust, only Pastor Bill remained, a cavalcade of blue orbs next to him.

"*Veni ad me*," Bill spoke softly, and the mountain of blue orbs rose into the air and fell into a small pouch in his hand. When they were all inside, the pouch was no larger than when he started, and he placed it back around his belt. "It is done."

"You...killed them all," I said. "They trusted you. They loved you."

"I had to do it." Bill looked at me. "For the greater good."

"Your greater good!" Julia shouted.

"You are blind to the truth, and that is why you will fail." Bill pulled a ball out of his belt and slammed it onto the ground, disappearing from sight.

"He's gone," I said, staring at the spot where he'd disappeared.

"What do we do now?" Julia asked.

I opened my mouth to answer, but there was another flash of light. This time, Kimberly appeared in front of us. She held her dagger tightly, ready for a fight, but when she saw us standing around casually, her posture dropped, and she relaxed. "Oh, you're free. I was just coming to save you."

"No need," Julia said, still staring at where the house had been. "We saved ourselves."

"Good," Kimberly said, stowing her daggers. "We don't have time to spare. Asmodeus attacked and took the last weapon. He's going to call the horsemen, and this will all be over."

"Then we have to find out where he's going," Julia said.

"That's not all," Kimberly said. "Katrina's hurt. Really badly."

"I'll go to her," I replied. "Julia, you take the map to Beatrice and Clovis. I left Yilir with them for safe keeping. Maybe one of them will have an idea."

"Smart," Julia replied. "When did you do that?"

"I don't have to explain my every action to you. Just know it happened."

"What about me?" Kimberly asked.

"Do you still have the key?" I replied.

She fished it out of her pocket. "I do."

"Then guard it with your life. Return to Earth. If they capture you, they'll use your blood to unleash Surt and the key to unlock his chains. You are literally the most important being on the planet right now."

"If I go to Earth, they'll find me," Kimberly said, shaking her head. "There are at least a hundred demons there, and who knows how many of them are working with the dukes of Hell. I'll be the biggest threat on the planet, and they'll hunt me. I need to go somewhere demons can't follow me."

A lightbulb went off over my head, and I knew what to do, even though the odds of success were minuscule. "You're right. We need a better plan, and I think I have one, but we're going to need Katrina's help. You come with me. Julia, you—"

"Talk to Yilir." She held up her hand. "I got it. You don't have to tell me twice."

I smiled. "I was going to say not to get captured again. I don't have the energy to save you a third time."

"Touché," Julia replied with a smile. "Now, let's go save the world."

CHAPTER 41

Julia

Location: Dis, Hell

I walked into Beatrice and Clovis's shoe shop with Yilir's map clutched tightly in my hand. The shop was less crowded than I had seen it on my last visit, but customers still roamed around the aisles. However, Beatrice wasn't on her usual perch, and I didn't hear her barking orders, either. I entered the back room, where elven cobblers sat making the custom shoes that were the shop's staple.

"So you designed the mountains, too?" I heard Beatrice ask from down the hallway. A faint blue glow shone from under the doorway. I walked back and pushed open the door. "We're closed—oh. It's you."

"It's me," I replied. "Sorry to barge in on your play date."

"Apology accepted." Beatrice turned to Yilir. "Continue."

Yilir smiled at Beatrice, who was sitting behind the desk. "Actually, little one, it was easier to hollow out the core of the Earth, so all of the cliffsides around Hell are natural formations, in a way, though I did mold them to the right specifications."

"I'm sorry for intruding," I said to them. "But I need your help, Yilir."

"This cannot be good," she replied, shaking her head.

"It's not, unfortunately. Mammon has the four weapons. All they need is the key and the pixie blood, and they can unlock Surt and let him loose across the universe."

Yilir shook her head and began pacing the floor of the office. "They won't wait another moment. They'll summon the horsemen first. The horsemen can sense the key, and they can move between worlds. They'll be able to track the key wherever it lies, as long as the key lies in a live being."

"It…lies with Kimberly."

Yilir stopped in her tracks. "Then she is in grave danger."

"How do I stop them from calling forth the horsemen?" I asked.

"Four seals, placed in Hell, prevent the Four Horsemen from returning. They were banished to another universe. They can only be called back by breaking the seals."

"What do they need to break the seals?" Beatrice asked before I shot a look at her. "Sorry. This is all just very exciting."

Yilir balled up her fist and raised it to the sky. "Incredible power. The likes of which I've never seen before."

"What about a bunch of souls? Magical souls. Would those work?"

Yilir scratched her chin. "That depends on the number, but it could work, in theory. I weep for the souls that would have to be lost to make such a weapon."

"Weep later," I replied. "Let's just assume it's already happened, and there are now a ton of dead monster souls giving power to the bad guys. What will they need to do to call forth the horsemen?"

I rolled out the map on the table. Yilir looked it over. "Break the seals that ward them from this place." She pointed to four points in the middle of the map. "Here, here, here, and here."

I shook my head. "That's impossible. That would put the seals right on top of Dis."

"That's right." Yilir nodded. "This city was the magical epicenter of the Underworld. All creatures felt a pull to come here. That wasn't part of my design, but yes, there is a reason Dis is located here. The Titan Surt rests under the bowels of the city."

"So if he's released…"

Yilir nodded. "The city will be destroyed, along with everything else."

I shook my head. "I can't let that happen. I need your help stopping the horsemen from being summoned." I walked toward the desk. "Can you lead me to the seals?"

"Of course," Yilir said, disappearing into the mirror. "This is much more portable for you. Let's away."

"So you're just going off to die?" Beatrice asked sadly.

I smiled. "We're already dead."

"You know what I mean. I'm sick of saying goodbye to you."

I placed my hand on her shoulder. "I'm sorry, but that's the job."

Beatrice crossed her arms. "This sucks."

"A far cry less than the destruction of everything, I assure you," Yilir replied from inside the mirror.

"You will come back, though," Beatrice said.

"If I am able," Yilir replied. "Now, let's get to Dis."

If we couldn't stop the horsemen from being called, I feared that the end was inevitable. I grabbed the mirror, dropped a pinch of pixie dust, and disappeared.

***

I reappeared at the top of the highest tower in all of Dis. I had come there often to find my bearings and to stare out into the abyss of Hell. In the distance, I could see Katrina's castle and the gate that guarded it. On the other side were the Gates of Abnegation and the dragon cave that rested on the cliffs to the right of them.

I held up the mirror and pointed it forward. "Where are we going first?"

"I don't know," Yilir replied, pulling herself out of the mirror. "This is not at all the same as when I designed it. There has been so much construction."

"Take your time." I paused, then added, "But not too much time."

Yilir looked across the horizon. "That church in the distance is about the right place for Death's seal, but if something was built upon it, I can't be sure—"

As we stared at the church, it exploded in blue fire. The shockwave knocked me off my perch, and I tumbled toward the ground. The mirror fell from my grip. Instinctively, I unfurled my wings and dove toward the ground, swooping under the mirror and catching it just before it hit the pavement.

"That was close," I said, skidding to a stop along the ground. "What do you think—"

In front of me, another explosion rocketed through the streets. I looked up to see the fire consume the sides of a skyscraper, eating the glass until the building collapsed upon itself in a plume of smoke and ash.

Yilir watched the explosions beside me. "It's happening," she said.

Before I could catch my bearings, two more explosions rocked the ground. Everybody around us screamed and started to run for cover, as two more buildings shattered and fell to the ground. The blue flame from each explosion rose higher into the air until they converged on each other in the middle of Hell. The fires coalesced into a ball of energy right above the center of Dis. A great black void ate the blue flames until it was large enough to dominate the sky and turn the orange hue of hell into blackness.

"Oh no," Yilir said. "We must go."

"Where?"

"There is a meeting place of the four horsemen, where they gather to ride again. Look into my mind and find it."

I placed my hand on Yilir's mirror. Her energy pulsated through me, and I saw an image of a place long lost to time. I pictured it in my mind and hoped it was still standing. Then I vanished.

***

I reappeared underneath a busy overpass with dozens of cars passing overhead. It was nothing like the calm meadow Yilir imagined in her mind, but it was the right place. Pastor Bill and Mammon stood with Asmodeus, who was strapped to the back of Akta's friend Sven, atop a giant pentagram.

When I rose to my feet, Pastor Bill smiled at me. "You're too late!"

Mammon stood next to him, in front of a cadre of soldiers. He held the lance and the hammer, while Asmodeus held the dagger and the bow. "Thank you for your part in this, Julia. I knew that Yilir would never help me without you."

"You're damn right I wouldn't!" Yilir screamed from inside the mirror.

"So that's why you let me steal the mirror?" I asked.

"Of course, and you fell for it perfectly."

"What about the box? Pandora's box?"

Mammon shrugged. "We thought it would have enough power to break the seals, but we managed without it. We just needed a whole bunch more souls, which the pastor's congregation provided."

"You destroyed the church!" I shouted. "You destroyed everything!"

"No!" Mammon corrected me. "We are saving everything! There is no cost too great to save every soul in Hell."

"He killed your wife!" I pointed at Pastor Bill. "Did you know that? Ask him!"

Mammon turned to Pastor Bill. "Is that true?"

The blue wraith shrugged and held out his hands. "She begged me to do it. It was the only way we could get enough souls for the ritual."

Mammon dropped his head and was silent for a moment. "A sad pity, but for a noble cause. She would have approved, and it is a small price to pay for salvation!"

A lightning bolt cracked through the overpass, sending concrete falling on us. I disappeared to avoid the avalanche of stone, reappearing closer to Mammon, whose men had ducked to avoid the blast.

When I turned around, four figures stood in front of me. The first one was dressed in a black robe, his fingers boney and gaunt. Two yellow eyes stared out from the darkness of the robe. "That must be Death."

"It is," Yilir replied.

The second was dressed in a robe of green, with streams of green smoke rising from her. Her face was rancid with death, and her eyeballs hung halfway down her face.

"Famine?" I asked.

"The archer. Don't let her sunken eyes fool you. She is deadly with a bow."

The third was dressed in red, bulky and strong, unlike the other two, with chain mail strapped across his chest. His burgundy robe fit tightly and cinched across his chest. "War?"

Yilir nodded. "He wields the Hammer of War."

A shining figure dressed in white and wearing a crown pushed through the rest. He held his head high and stepped with confidence across the field as cars honked above him.

"Conquest," Yilir said. "The most arrogant of the siblings."

"Siblings?" I asked.

"Four gods, birthed by the gods. Their sacrifice allowed us to contain the beast Surt and keep him locked up. Only they had the power to release them, and their purity was unmatched for a time. However, they became consumed with power and were banished."

"Who summons us?" Conquest barked, looking around.

Mammon and Pastor Bill knelt. After a moment, Mammon rose again. "It is I, your humble servant, come to bid you reverse your charge and release Surt into the world once more."

Conquest cocked his head and studied the creatures in front of him. "You do not look or smell, like the gods." He studied the weapons. "And yet, you have our weapons and know our charge."

Mammon handed the lance to Conquest. "We were given your charge by the gods when they left Earth to find their next settlement among the stars."

"That's a lie!" I shouted. "He doesn't—"

"Who dares speak to me?" Conquest said, whipping around.

"She is nobody," Mammon said.

"I can prove that it is a lie." I held up the mirror. "It is true, Conquest. You have been called forth—"

"*Fractus!*" A blue orb slammed against the mirror, fracturing it in half. Pastor Bill shouted, and the mirror shattered into a hundred pieces, exploding from my hand.

"No!" I screamed. Yilir's sad face looked up at me from the dozens of mirror fragments, reaching her hand out as she disappeared from sight. The glass shards went dark.

Conquest cocked his head. "What was she about to say?"

Mammon smiled. "That you have been called forth to open the gates of Ragnarok."

The crowned horseman spun the lance in his hand. "I never thought I would feel it again. After I was banished, I longed for it."

"It is a magnificent weapon," Mammon said, tipping his head to grovel even lower.

"All we ever wanted to do was serve the gods," Conquest said. "And they turned us away the moment we were no longer useful to them. I've been looking forward to the day we'd make them quake in fear once more."

Mammon smiled. "And this is the perfect revenge."

"It truly is, to release that which we bound." Conquest smiled and turned to the others. "My siblings, it is time to ride again."

The Four Horsemen gathered in a circle. Death grasped the dagger in his hand. Famine felt the string of the bow. War swung his hammer. Then each of them lifted their weapon above their heads, and a surge of power crackled through the air.

"Have you the key?" Conquest asked when he had finished admiring his weapon.

"We do not. A cowardly pixie has taken it. She works to undermine us, even now."

Conquest turned to Death. "Can you find her?"

Death nodded. "I smell her, even now. It is a familiar smell."

"Get her."

"Yes, brother." Death let out a shrill whistle, and moments later, a huge white horse materialized in front of him. It was double the size of any I had seen in my long life. Even the unicorns in Hell were not as big. The horse reared back, and two large, glittering wings extended from its body.

"Stop!" I shouted, but it was no use. Death was on the horse, galloping off into the abyss.

"We will make arrangements to open the gate while he is away retrieving the key."

"Lead the way," Mammon replied, then pointed at me. "But first, kill her."

I wanted to stay and collect the pieces of Yilir's mirror, but I knew that would be a fool's errand. Nothing could save us now, not even Yilir. I had to make it to the Devil's Castle and warn Katrina.

CHAPTER 42

Katrina

Location: Katrina's Castle, Hell

The inky blackness oozing from my stomach wound had risen through my chest and into my face, spidering across my neck and into my cheeks. I looked like Venom, transitioning from Eddie Brock into his ugly, alien form.

"How does it look, Carl?" I asked the imp sitting at the foot of my bed. "Be honest."

"Horrible, ma'am."

I nodded solemnly. "Thank you for always being honest with me. I don't suppose you are trying to kill me."

Carl smiled. "No, ma'am. I don't suppose I am."

"I believe you."

Aziolith knocked on the door to my room as he entered. "Are you feeling any better?"

"Do I look any better?"

He shook his head. "No. I brought somebody to see you."

Aziolith moved out of the way, and my dad walked forward, smiling. "Hi, kiddo." He sat on the edge of my bed and took my hand.

"Hi, Dad," I said, squeezing his hands. "I really stepped into it now."

"You'll figure it out," he replied, brushing some hair out of my face. "You always do."

"I always have, but that doesn't mean I will. Everybody has a 100 percent survival rate until the day they die."

"I don't think this poison will kill you," Aziolith said. "It's just meant to incapacitate you for a time."

"Oh, so I'm just going to be tired and in pain constantly?"

"Basically."

"That's no way to live." Pain sliced through my body, and I nearly lurched off of the bed. "This is worse than death."

"You don't know that," Aziolith said. "You have never died."

"And yet, I'm praying for it right now."

Akta and Kimberly rushed into my room. "Devil," Akta said. "We have news."

"Something good, I hope."

"Nothing good, I'm afraid. They have broken the seals in Dis and have unleashed the horsemen. All they need is the key to release Surt."

"Luckily, we have the key here," I coughed inky blackness into my hand. "Though, that hasn't been very helpful as of yet."

"No, it hasn't," Kimberly agreed. "And if Mammon gets the key, he'll be able to release Surt and attack Heaven."

I tried to shake my head and stopped. Every movement sent pain shooting up and down my spine. "Then we shouldn't let him do that."

"I was thinking," Akta said. "What if we sent Kimberly to Heaven?"

I thought for a moment before turning to Kimberly. "Were you a good person on Earth?"

"Not particularly. Besides, I'm not a human."

"She's at least half-human," Akta offered.

I started thinking my way through the plan out loud. "I doubt Heaven would take you, but if we can somehow get you in the judgment line, that will buy us at least a couple hundred years while they process your paperwork. I'll have to incinerate your body to make sure that the key travels with you to Heaven."

Kimberly stopped me. "Wait, you can do that?"

"I told you. I only control your soul." I nodded. "If there's one thing I'm very good at, it's burning things."

"And how do we figure out if they'll let me into Heaven?"

"Let me make a call."

"I'll set it up," Carl said, scurrying out of the room. What I wouldn't give to be able to scurry.

***

Aziolith helped me hobble to the throne room, where I sat down on my throne. When I was seated, Carl pushed the blue button to call Heaven. Michael came up on my screen and sneered at me.

"Would you please stop calling here?" he said. "I'm about to block this number."

"They have the weapons," I said pointedly. "We have the key, for now at least, but it's just a matter of time until they come for it. I have somebody that requires asylum from the horsemen."

"We don't care," Michael replied. "We don't take asylum seekers from Hell."

"You should. What do you think happens if Surt gets loose? He will attack Heaven. He will steal back his sword, and he will destroy everything. This is not just a 'me' problem, you obtuse asshole. Can't you see that?"

Michael grumbled to himself. "I suppose you're right, loathe as I am to admit it."

"I know I'm right!" I said, raising my voice until the pain in my stomach caused me to double over.

"What's wrong with you?"

"I don't know. I was stabbed by a traitorous sword. It won't kill me, but I don't know how to fix it."

"So you're in pain?" Michael said with a smile.

"You don't have to take so much pleasure in it."

"It's a good look on you."

"Don't get used to it," I growled. "I'll be back to my old self in no time. Or I'll be dead. One or the other. Now, will you help us or not?"

He shook his head. "I can't do anything unless they are dead, but if they should die, I would be able to place a tracker on their souls and bring them here, I suppose."

Kimberly stepped closer to me so that she was in view on the screen. "Isn't there another way? A way…without me dying?"

He shook his head. "Not without a bunch of red tape, and I hate red tape. Plus, that would add a few years to the process."

"Years!" Akta said. "We don't have that kind of ti—"

"I'll do it," Kimberly said. "I'll do it."

"Are you sure?" Aziolith said. "You can't take back death. I know. I tried."

"I have to, man," Kimberly said. "And if I sacrifice myself, maybe I'll actually deserve Heaven."

A bright flash appeared in front of us, and Julia fell to the ground. "He's coming for the key. Death is coming."

She didn't get a chance to stand before a black rider riding a pale horse kicked through the door and rode into the throne room. The giant wings on his horse flapped forward, and he bore down on us.

I pushed up from my chair and leaped into the middle of the room. I threw fire at the horse for a moment but keeled over from the immense pain that overtook me. The horse smashed through me without breaking its gait and rushed toward Kimberly.

"Do it!" Kimberly shouted.

Akta brought out her dagger and stabbed Kimberly through the heart. "I'm sorry."

"No!" Julia shouted.

Kimberly's eyes went wide, and she fell to the ground. I reached out with my hand and engulfed her in flames. Death's horse flapped its wings, extinguishing the fire, and I collapsed. The last thing I saw was Death scooping up Kimberly's body and dragging it out of the room. The light went from my eyes, and I fell into darkness, pain coursing through my body, having completely failed.

CHAPTER 43

Kimberly

Location: Heaven

A burning pain ripped through my body as I shed my mortal coil. I felt all the color drain from my body until there was nothing left but a dull whiteness, and as I closed my eyes, I drifted off into the nothingness. Even though I was unsure of what would happen next, I was at peace.

I woke lying on a bed of clouds. A blond-headed angel was looking down at me with a grimace on his face, his wings unfurled, blocking out the sun.

"You her?" he asked.

"I think so," I said. I tried to right myself, but when I pushed against the cloud for leverage, it gave way. "I'm Kimberly."

"I'm Michael, the archangel." He gestured toward my wings. "It's easier to fly here rather than walk."

"Thanks," I said. I flapped my wings and rose into the air. They weren't the same bird-like ones that Michael had, but the fairy sort that resembled dragonfly wings.

He spun around. "Follow me."

We flew through Heaven until we reached a great golden gate, where a line of people extended into the distance. An old man sat behind a podium, paging slowly through a ledger. In front of him stood a man with a long beard and sunglasses. He wore ratty jeans and a baseball hat with "lousy" stitched across the front.

"Aberforth Macgillicutty?" the old one said. "Oh my, no no no. They definitely sent you to the wrong place. I'm sorry about that, but you'll have to queue in line downstairs."

"What's happening here?" I muttered to Michael.

"When a soul's balance tips toward Heaven, they end up here. When they tip toward Hell, they are sent below, and then a final judgment is rendered."

A hole opened in the floor of Heaven, and the man screamed as he fell into the depths. Michael pointed down to the line of souls that extended into the horizon.

"You queue up there, at the end. When you get to the end in a few hundred years, I'll come for you again and send you to the back of the line."

"So, I just stand here, in this line, for the rest of eternity?"

"Seems that way," Michael said. "It's a far cry better than being in Hell; I will tell you that. Frankly, I don't know why more people don't do it. While you're out here, at least you haven't been judged yet. The odds of getting inside are astronomical."

I shrugged. "Everybody thinks they're a better person than they are, I guess."

Michael nodded. "Ego is a very human emotion."

I flew closer to Michael. "Listen, I know the deal you made with Katrina, but I really think I should talk to God about this whole Ragnarok situation."

"There you go again with the ego." His eyes narrowed. "We have it under control."

"Obviously, you do NOT have it under control. The demon lords have summoned the Four Horsemen, and they have the weapons to unleash Surt."

"But they do not have the key or the sword?"

"I don't know about the sword but—" I reached into my pocket, searching for the key, but I didn't find it. "Oh no."

"What?"

I gulped. "I have bad news for you. Katrina was supposed to incinerate my body, and then the key would arrive with me in Heaven, but it's not here, which means she failed, which means they probably have the key—and my body. If that's the case...they've won."

Michael grumbled under his breath and spread his arms wide. As he did, a hole appeared in the clouds at our feet, and a shimmering lake filled it. When the lake grew still, I could make out an image. It was Death's reflection—Death was riding across Hell on his pale horse, carrying my body.

The angel sighed. "This is not good."

"That's what I'm saying," I replied. "We have to get to God and tell him."

Michael held up his hand. "I will do that myself. You are inconsequential and unnecessary to the equation now that you have failed."

"Inconsequential? Unnecessary? You have no idea what's going on down there." I pointed to the clouds below me. "I've been down there since the first minutes, figuring this whole thing out. You're going to muck it up. You need me."

"I am the archangel Michael. I don't muck things up."

"Yes, you do." I floated closer to him. "You should have told God about this already, but you've been holding out, and now it might be too late."

His eyes narrowed. "I don't like you. You remind me of Katrina."

I smiled. "Those are two of the best compliments you could ever give me."

"Peter!" Michael said and turned to him. "Open the gates."

The old man turned to me. "Of course, as soon as I verify your friend, here."

"She doesn't need verification," Michael growled. "She is with me."

"I'm sorry, but—"

"Open the gate!" Michael shouted. "Or I will flay you as I did the great boar of Exedor."

Peter let out a low whistle. "My, you are grumpy." He waved his arms and the door open. "Very well. I have too much to do to argue with you. We are very far behind. One less soul to judge would be welcome."

Michael turned to me. "We're never going to catch up."

I stared at the long line behind him, then said, "You should change to computers. Katrina did, and it seems to be working wonders."

He scoffed. "I will never do anything simply because a human Devil is doing it."

"Whatever." I fluttered toward the open gate. "I don't care. Let's go."

***

I couldn't believe how dead and lifeless Heaven was beyond the pearly gates. Hell was full of monsters, demons, and people. Giant superhighways raced across the countryside, and there was a vibrant energy about the place.

Heaven, in contrast, felt empty. Few angels fluttered across the landscape, and those who did were somber or downright morose. There was no laughing or chatter of any kind. Everyone went about their time with dead eyes. Nobody looked energized by being in Heaven.

"Heaven seems lame," I said to Michael. We were flying across the Elysian Fields, headed toward an agora on the horizon. It seemed to be the only structure around for miles. "Maybe Akta is right about Hell being better."

"Not bloody likely," Michael said. "These people have all their needs met. They are content. Maybe that looks boring to you, but I assure you these people are very happy. There is no need to innovate. This is perfection."

We flew past a couple, holding hands with each other. "Is that true?"

The woman turned to me. "Excuse me?"

"Are you happy?" I asked her.

She glanced at Michael and then me again. "Of—of course. This is paradise."

"If this is happiness, then I would gladly kill myself again to be rid of it." I turned back to Michael. "I hate this place."

Michael chuckled. "So did Katrina, but I assure you, for the right temperament, it is bliss."

"Is that why you don't let anybody in?" I asked as we continued.

"We let many people in over the years."

"Discounting the Rapture, how many people have you let into Heaven for the past two hundred years?"

Michael scratched his chin. "I do not have a calculator on me, and it's not my department, but a fair few, I would think."

I held my arms out wide and spun around. "Then where the heck are they?"

"Enjoying eternity," Michael said, speeding up. "We should go more quickly. I tire of this conversation."

"Whatever you say."

Michael lowered himself to the ground before a large open building. Great columns extended high into the air but held up nothing but the sky. Stairs, bound to nothing, hovered on the edge of the circular structure. Michael stepped onto the first one, which gave ever so slightly under his foot.

When we reached the top of the stairs, I found two beings. One was red and scaly, with giant horns growing out of his head and yellow, glowing eyes, and a thin beard. The demon turned to me, his pot belly bulging from under his stained T-shirt.

"You're back already. And you brought a friend."

"Shut up, Lucifer," Michael snarled.

Sitting across from him was an older man with a thick white beard and glowing white eyes. In fact, his whole body, robes and all, seemed to glow and pulsate. He looked over a chess board intently.

"Be nice, Michael."

Michael grumbled under his breath. "You didn't hire me for my table manners, sir."

"No, I didn't," the man said, barely acknowledging him. "But that does not mean we can't all be civil, even if you don't like each other."

"Yes, sir." It didn't take a genius to infer that he was God. "I come bearing news from Hell."

God turned to him. "You know I don't want to hear about that dreadful place."

"I know, sir, but this is urgent. You know I would never interrupt you if it weren't."

God crossed his legs and turned to Michael. "Very well. If you insist."

"I do, sir, it seems—"

I stepped forward between Michael and God. "The demons have summoned the Four Horsemen. They have the key and are on their way to break the seal and unleash Surt. They only need the Sword of Damocles, and they will be able to unleash the Titan back on the world."

"Surt!" God said, shocked. "Why was this not brought to my attention before? Do you know what the other gods will do to me if I unleash Surt back on the universe? I cannot go to jail, Michael. I'm not built for it."

"Then help us stop it," I replied. "You can—"

"I can't," God said. "I'm not allowed to meddle in human affairs."

My mouth opened and closed several times before I finally managed to say, "Haven't you been meddling in human affairs for like, literally ever?"

"That's different," he said. His lip wrinkled into a pout.

"How? This is the single most important thing you could possibly do. Help us stop Ragnarok."

"I—I—I need to confer with the other gods. Shouldn't take more than a couple hundred years."

"We don't have that kind of time!" I shouted. "We'll all be dead by then. Once Surt escapes, you won't just be able to sweep this under the rug. Everybody will know."

"Not if they don't have the sword, and it's sitting right there." God pointed behind me, where a flaming sword was held inside a stone embedded in the base of the floor. "No demon can come to Heaven. You must be gods' touched for that."

As if on cue, a bolt of lightning struck the furthest column, which came crashing down upon the chess board. Both Lucifer and God jumped to get out of the way. A thunderous boom quaked through the agora, and in its wake stood a shimmering white being, which pulsated in rhythm with God.

"Hello, Bacchus."

"Logos…"

The white horseman trotted forward. "I prefer Conquest now, or I believe they once called me Pestilence, which I also quite enjoyed."

God stood. "We banished you to the nether realm."

"Yes, you did." Conquest walked toward the sword. "And the demons of Hell brought us back. All four of us."

"You can't be here," God said. "The gods—"

"Are useless," Conquest said, moving forward. "We were faithful servants, but you feared our power, so you banished us. That is not fair, brother. All we wanted was your love, and you exiled us. Now, we will have our revenge."

"Don't do this. You have no idea what you will unleash upon us."

"Sure I do," Conquest replied. "I was stupid enough to banish him once in service to the gods, back when I was foolish and naïve, and now I will bring the Titan back to exact vengeance on the universe. He will destroy you and our father."

"Surt will rip you apart. He has no loyalty to you. He has loyalty to nothing."

"And you do!" Conquest shouted. "You made us from nothing, raised us like lambs to the slaughter, and then forced us to die for your sins. Why should I listen to you?"

"Because I am your kin."

"Then I renounce you," Conquest said.

I pulled out the daggers in my belt and rushed Conquest, who raised his arm in the air and flung me backward. I crashed into another column and rolled out of the way as it came crashing down upon me.

"Sending someone else to do your dirty work, Bacchus?" Conquest chuckled. "So like you."

Michael reached into the air and grasped high above him. As he did, a flaming sword materialized in his hand. "If you touch that sword, it will be over for you."

"You and what army?"

Lucifer rushed forward and bared his claws. "And me."

Conquest raised his lance into the air toward them. "I defeated Surt once, the Titan lord, with nothing but a lance. Do you really think I can't take all three of you pitiful beings at once?"

"You can try," God said. A black war hammer materialized in his hands, and he gave it to Lucifer.

Conquest sighed deeply and raised his lance into the air. "This shouldn't take long."

Michael rushed forward, and Conquest swung his lance toward him. Michael blocked the blow, but the force caused a shockwave that knocked him across the agora. Lucifer slammed his hammer down toward Conquest, but the horseman slid out of the way easily. He raised his hammer again and tried to upper cut Conquest with it, but again, Conquest turned out of the way with ease.

"I expected more of my family's favorite angel," Conquest snarled. "A pity."

Faster than I could see, Conquest sliced Lucifer across the chest and kicked him off the platform. Michael flew forward, and Conquest ducked under him, then swung upward and knocked Michael far into the sky. When the angel fell back down to Heaven, Conquest slammed him into the ground, embedding him deep in the platform.

"Enough of this!" God shouted. The sky darkened, and lightning filled his hands. He fired it at Conquest as the horseman charged. Conquest held up his weapon and absorbed the lightning, sending it back at God and electrocuting him, his glowing white eyes fading to a dim blue.

Conquest spun his lance and brought it down upon God's neck, stopping it within an inch of his throat. God collapsed onto the ground. "I would kill you now, but I want you to see the destruction that your ineptitude has wrought. Only once Surt has destroyed the whole of the universe will you die after you have watched everything you love burn around you."

God chuckled. "You act as though there are things I love."

Conquest walked toward the sword. "You love humanity more than you should. You want them to idolize you. That is why you made them worship you." With one hand, Conquest pulled the Sword of Damocles from the stone, smiled, and then vanished into a ball of lightning.

I rushed over to God. "Are you all right?"

"No," God said. "Nothing is all right. We have failed."

"There must be something you can do."

God shook his head. "Only the horsemen are powerful enough to stop Surt, and they have chosen their allegiance."

"What if they haven't?"

"I saw it with my own eyes."

I shook my head. "No. I met Death once. He made me immortal. Perhaps I can still reason with him, make him see the truth."

"It will never work."

"The only thing that will never work is doing nothing. Send me back to Hell. Let me try."

God smiled at me. "You are persistent, like Katrina. That will serve you well in the battle to come. Very well. I will send you back."

"You can come with me."

"No," God said. "I cannot step foot in Hell, and I would not try even if I could."

"Then we are on our own."

God grabbed my shirt. "Hold out your weapons."

I held my daggers toward him, and he touched them. He screamed out in pain as the blades began to glow blue and then back to their metal.

"What did you do?"

"I imbued them with a bit of my essence. If you can get close enough, this will kill Death. I hope you don't need it, but just in case. It's only good for one hit, and you have but a short time to use it."

"Thank you."

God snapped his fingers, and I was gone. In the darkness, I tasted maraschino cherries.

CHAPTER 44

Julia

Location: Dis, Hell

"On the left!" I shouted to a fat demon crossing the street. Akta and I had chased Death into the middle of Dis and were speeding through a downtown intersection, trying to catch him before he delivered Kimberly to the other horsemen. We had been taking turns fighting Death, but he had managed to fend us off.

"We're running out of time!" Akta shouted next to me. "Surt's cell is under the city. If the horsemen find it, we're all doomed."

"Right!"

I disappeared and reappeared in front of Death yet again, swinging my daggers at him. The horseman dodged them easily. As I struck at him, his pale horse kicked me, and I fell out of the way.

From above, an arrow flew through the air. Famine, riding a yellow-tinged horse, looked down at us from the top of a building. "Over here, brother!" Famine's cracked voice shouted.

Death turned down a busy street and pulled the reins of his horse, rising into the air. Akta rematerialized on top of Death, kicking him off the horse and sending him crashing into the sidewalk.

"You got him!" I shouted.

"Save Kimberly's body!" Akta shouted back.

I rushed forward and grabbed onto the horse, slicing through the rope with my daggers to release Kimberly. Famine pulled back her bow and fired another arrow at me. I jumped to avoid it, and Kimberly's body tumbled out into the air. I raced down to gather it and clung to her arm just as she was about to splatter onto the ground. "Got her!"

"Good job!" Akta screamed.

I slid to the ground and frantically searched through Kimberly's pockets for the key. As I did, Akta crashed against the building next to me, having been punched by Death.

"It's not in here!" I screamed.

Akta rose to her knees. "What do you mean it's not in there?"

"Looking for this?" Death reached into his robe and pulled out a golden key. "You have lost."

I stood up straight. "Never!"

Lightning crashed into the building above us, and a shimmering white man sat atop a black horse, holding up a flaming sword above his head in one hand, a lance in his other hand. "I have it, brother! Bring the pixie's body."

Death marched forward and grabbed Kimberly's body. I tried to hang onto her, but she slipped out of my grip. Death yanked her body from me and turned around, just as the pale horse swooped down to pick him up. As he dropped the body onto the back of the horse, there was a sudden wail. Startled, Death dropped Kimberly's body to the ground, which rolled over to us. Her eyes popped open, and Kimberly looked at me, blinking her bloodshot eyes.

"Kim!" I said. "You're back. How are you back?"

"Help—me—up."

Kimberly stood on shaky legs as Death took a few imposing steps toward her. "You are stronger than I thought."

"Do you remember me?" Kimberly asked. "You...gave me immortality."

Death cocked his head. "Yes, I thought you smelled familiar. Ha! My magic is more powerful than I thought. Even the Devil cannot kill you easily. No bother, you will die this day."

"Don't do this," Kimberly said quietly through gritted teeth. "Death, I know this is not you. You hold no ill will to humanity. You unshackled them from life and provided a respite for their death, like an old friend."

Death looked down. "That was a long time ago."

I reached out and touched Death's bony wrist. "You don't have to follow your family. Don't give them the key. Don't let them unlock Surt. Be better."

"I...can't..." Death looked at his brother, who was cackling up above us. "You don't understand."

"No, I don't. I'm just an immortal pixie, not a god, but...I know that the universe is better without a psychopathic Titan rampaging through it, you know?"

"What do you know about the universe, human? Have you ever been told you were worthless? Had your sacrifice negated by those you loved? Told that you were dangerous? That you had no value? Do you know what it was like to be thrown into the void, cast off from everything that I loved?"

"No, I don't," I said, shaking my head slowly.

He brushed my hand away. "It was Hell."

"No." I pointed to where we were standing. "This is Hell, and you can escape it. Just go. You can change your destiny. Don't be responsible for bringing doom to the universe. Be responsible for saving it."

Death looked over at Famine, who held up her bow. "Nobody can escape their destiny."

Kimberly sighed. "I'm sorry you feel that way." In one rapid motion, Kimberly plunged her daggers into Death's chest, and the black hooded figure began to convulse. It looked as if he was being sucked in by a great vacuum from the inside out. In another instant, a shockwave quaked through the air, and nothing remained of Death except a pile of ash.

Kimberly fell to the ground, and I ran to her. "You did it."

"Ow." Kimberly breathed heavily. She collapsed on the ground. "I think I'm dying. For real this time."

"No, you—"

"Ow. It's so painful." Kimberly said, her words coming slowly and weakly. "Ow, ow, ow, ow, ow."

A shimmer of light caught my eye. From the ashes of Death, a pulsating purple light rose into the air, tendrils climbing higher and higher. It snapped and pointed to Kimberly, lowering quickly and viciously until it pierced through her skin and shot through her body.

Kimberly arched into the air and screamed to the Heavens. Then, the black mist was gone. Her eyes opened, but this time they were not the old familiar brown, but yellow. She rose to her feet, and as she did, a black cloak formed around her. She looked back at me without a hint of recognition. Famine and Conquest dropped from their building on their horses and met her.

"Brother?" Conquest said.

"It is I, still," Kimberly replied. "Come. We have work to do."

"No!" I screamed. "Kimberly!"

But he didn't stop. He simply got on his pale horse and rode away on it, with Conquest and Famine riding behind him, using Kimberly's body as his vessel.

CHAPTER 45

Kimberly

Location: Dis, Hell

I saw and heard everything that was happening, but I wasn't in control of my own limbs. I tried to fight, but my body kept moving forward, flying through the air until it rested on the top of a tall building. I watched through Death's eyes as Conquest and Famine got off their horses, and then my body dismounted as well. The door to the building swung open, and War exited, holding his hammer.

"I found the seals and the prison." His voice was like gravel. "They are in the basement of this building. Come on."

Conquest walked into the building behind War, carrying his lance in one hand and the sword in the other, followed by Famine and then me. I concentrated all my energy to make my legs stop, but they wouldn't stop moving.

"Stop struggling," Death's voice cooed at me from inside my head. I could hear it vibrating through me. "You'll only make it worse."

"Death?" I uttered.

None of the other horsemen could hear the voice as they stared blindly forward, concentrating on the task at hand. "They once called me Thanatos," the voice continued. "Did you know that?"

"I didn't."

"I was much like you. Headstrong, bold, confident— loving even, back when I had people to love. Until they were taken away from me. That's why I gave you eternal life, you know? Because you reminded me so much of me."

"Revenge is not good fuel," I said. "It burns dirty."

"That is funny, coming from you. When we met, you were filled with righteous anger. Tell me, did you ever get revenge on those that killed your mentor?"

"Yes, I got it," I said quietly, inside my own head so the others could not hear. "And I've taken revenge for decades since on anyone that wronged my kind. Spite fueled me, and hatred lit a fire in my belly. That doesn't mean I was right. Dying, twice now, showed me that. Going to Heaven—"

"That place isn't Heaven. It is an abomination. This whole planet is an abomination. This universe was created by Titans but ruled by lesser beings."

"The universe has a lot of good in it, too."

Death walked behind the others through the hallway of an office building. "You are so naïve, my child. I kept you alive for so long, hoping I would have a chance to see you again. You were the first person I connected with in a thousand years, and to see you again brings joy to my heart. I am glad you can be a part of this historic moment."

I looked again through Death's eyes and saw that we were now in an elevator, descending through the floors to the basement, which was the only floor highlighted.

"It will soon be over. My charge will be complete, and I will return to the quiet. Once Surt comes back to the world, there will be no use for me, and I can rest."

"I can't let that happen, Thanatos. You know I can't."

"You don't have much of a choice. You are, after all, only human."

"No, I'm not." I concentrated hard. "I am a fairy. I was touched by Bacchus. I consorted with Katrina. I am more than a human." My eyes tracked down to my hands, which were shaking, as I tried to regain control.

"You are only half fairy," Death said. "You are half mangy human."

"Are you okay?" War grunted, looking over at Death.

"Fine," Death answered. "Just adjusting to this new body."

But he wasn't fine. He was barely holding on to control. I focused even more of my energy on breaking the bond between us. "Humans are more powerful than you can ever imagine. Humans power the Source of all creation. We are the battery. We are the light. Without us, none of this could be."

The elevator dinged, and the other three horsemen left the elevator. Death tried to move with them, but I held him back. I reached out my shaky hand and pressed the button to the lobby.

"No!" Death shouted. "Stop this."

"What are you doing?" Conquest wheeled as the door closed.

"How are you doing this?" Thanatos asked.

"Strength of will, and hope. I told you that hatred burns dirty, but hope and free will? They burn clean. They are renewable. I believe I can defeat you. I believe I am stronger than you, and my will makes it so. Now, sit back. It's my turn to drive."

I felt a great power surge through me, and suddenly, my body moved to my whims. I could no longer even hear the words of Death, and as the elevator dinged for the floor, I saw Julia and Akta. I smiled at them.

They drew their daggers into the air and charged me. "Wait!" I shouted. "It's me."

Akta dropped her dagger and squinted. "Kimberly?"

I nodded, lowering my hood. I stepped out of the elevator and caught my reflection in the mirror on the wall next to me. My eyes had turned back to their brown, but my skin was still completely charred.

"Prove it," Julia said.

"Besides the fact that I'm not trying to kill you?"

"Yes?"

"Fine," I replied. "When we met, you saved me from a banshee. I never told you, but as she led me through Hell, I was captivated by it as much as I feared it. When you found me, you told me it was all going to be all right, and I believed you." I stepped closer to her. "I'm telling you now; it's all going to be all right."

Tears fell from Julia's eyes as she wrapped her arms around me. "It is you."

After a second, Akta pulled us apart. "I hate to break this up, but we still have to save the universe."

"Right," I said, putting up my hood. "Let's do it."

CHAPTER 46

Akta

Location: Dis, Hell

I was riding an elevator with Death down to the basement of a skyscraper to stop Ragnarok, and none of that surprised me. It wasn't a normal Tuesday, but in my thousands of years in Hell, I had stopped my fair share of Apocalyptic events. In fact, in my whole time in Hell, I had only ever failed to prevent one.

And I couldn't really fault myself for that. Frankly, I thought it needed to happen. Hell was overcrowded and stunk more than usual, which was saying something because even on a good day, it stunk something fierce. That apocalypse got the powers that be to take notice and allowed Katrina to assume control. I liked Katrina and the boldness with which she enacted her vision. It upset me that so many hated her and wished ill on her. I was one of Hell's oldest residents, and if I could see the advantages of modernization, I wondered why nobody else could.

"When we get down there, we have to work fast," Kimberly said with Death's mouth. "I'm going to try and kill War right off the bat since he's the strongest. Akta, you take Famine, and Julia, you handle Conquest. With any luck, we should be able to neutralize them with little resistance."

"And if we can't?" Julia asked.

"Let's not think about that," Kimberly replied, staring forward. "Positive thoughts lead to positive actions."

The elevator doors slid open, and we charged. The remaining Horsemen stood on red circles in the corners of the room. In front of them was a larger circle, glowing blue, and a final blue circle equidistant from them on the near side of the room. The sword laid against the wall next to them, waiting for its bearer.

Julia flew across the room and took on Famine, who fired with her bow. I couldn't concentrate on them as Conquest's lance swung with effortless grace toward me. I parried it with my daggers and then kneed him in the stomach.

"You will pay for that," Conquest said to me as he rose from the ground. He turned his lance over in his hand and twisted it around until it moved faster than I could track. I held up my daggers, but the speed of the lance knocked them out of my hand, and they flew across the room.

As I rushed to retrieve them, I saw Kimberly in battle with War, who swung his hammer so hard that its impact with the Earth quaked the building, causing cracks to form in the foundation.

"Be careful!" Famine shouted from across the room. "You'll cause this whole place to come down!"

"So what?" War replied. "A little destruction never hurt anybody!"

"Yeah?" Famine said. "Do you want to excavate this cave for the next hundred years?"

"No…"

"Then watch it!" Famine screamed, her shrill voice cutting through the air.

Just as I reached my daggers, the hard metal of the lance's hilt knocked me across the head. The impact caused my eyes to cross, and my knees buckle. The last thing I saw before I blacked out was War smacking Kimberly with his hammer hard enough that she flew backward, embedding into the elevator doors.

***

I came back to consciousness tied to a sewer pipe, Julia bound next to me. The other three horsemen were trying to unwedge Death—Kimberly—from the elevator doors.

"Pull!" Conquest shouted, and with a final tug, she was released.

"This is not good," I said to Julia.

"None of this has been good."

I kicked my legs out into the hallway, trying to find War's foot, but he just stepped over me. Famine smiled, her teeth visible through a hole in her cheek. "We were going to kill you, but we thought you should watch this. After all, Surt will be hungry after his long imprisonment, and he loves to devour magical beings, especially ones the gods once loved so dearly."

They dragged Death to her place in the fourth circle, then took their own places. They placed their hands together at their chest and bowed their heads. "*Vinculum rumpitur. Sit vetus confractus est liber. Vinculum rumpitur. Sit vetus confractus est liber. Vinculum rumpitur. Sit vetus confractus est liber.*"

The blue circle in the center turned red then cracked in half, ripping the foundation of the building from its moorings. The walls began to break apart as the crack opened below us. As it did, Death stirred and opened her eyes.

"Kimberly!" I shouted.

"What—what is happening—" Kimberly replied. The crack forming underneath brought her back to reality. "Oh, shit."

She jumped out of her circle to avoid being swallowed, but the other horsemen just laughed. "It is too late!"

The building rumbled and quaked as Kimberly made her way over to me. "We have to get out of here."

"The pixie dust, in my pocket." Kimberly reached down and grabbed it. She pulled a pinch and placed it in my hand. "Get us out of here."

"Wait," I said. "The sword."

Kimberly looked over at the Sword of Damocles on the ground next to Conquest, across the cracked foundation of the building. She nodded and leaped across the hallway.

"No!" Conquest shouted, but it was too late to stop her. Kimberly grabbed the hilt of the sword and pulled it toward her. Conquest swiped at her, but she ducked his blow and rushed back to my side.

I reached out to grab Julia's hand, and Kimberly took mine. I closed my eyes and thought of Katrina's throne room, the safest place now that Surt had been unleashed. The three of us vanished from the basement just as the ceiling collapsed.

There was only a glimmer of hope, but it was there: Surt would be free, but we still had the sword, and Kimberly's blood, so he couldn't leave the boundaries of Hell…yet.

CHAPTER 47

Katrina

Location: Devil's Castle, Hell

I watched from the window of my castle as the great city of Dis fell. Though I could not hear the monsters scream as they fled the rubble, I felt their pain in the core of my soul.

"This is it," I said to Aziolith, who sat on a chair by my bedside.

"Maybe it's for the best."

This was the end times, and I was officially no better than Lucifer. I had brought this on, with my ineptitude, with my desire for modernization, with my unrelenting quest to improve Hell. Could I have been more diplomatic? Had I been comfortable to let things continue as they were, perhaps I would have been able to stave off this coup. Maybe I could have saved Hell. Maybe I could have saved the universe.

"It's definitely not for the best," I replied.

Or, perhaps if I just died like a good little girl during the Apocalypse, the demon lords of Hell would have been satiated. There would be no more expansion. There would be no ill will. They would be free to rule Hell as they saw fit, and I wouldn't have cared because I was vapor.

But I did care.

I cared desperately about Hell and making it livable for monsters and humans alike, and it was working, damn it. It was working. Monsters had better lives now than they did two hundred years ago. The pits on Earth, Venus, Mars,

Europa, and even Pluto were more humane and ethical than ever. Monsters and demons were no longer slaves; they finally had a say in their lives, and yet they were more miserable than ever.

It saddened me that their say was to make things go back to how it was before when they were blissfully ignorant of choice, but that was a choice in and of itself. Of course, now the whole universe was in jeopardy.

A surge of pain ran up my leg, and I collapsed onto the ground. The inky black had covered my arms and legs, but it had yet to overwhelm my face. Only spindles of the blackness rose from my chin into my cheeks. There were none I trusted to help me, so I suffered alone, knowing that I could not die, still fearing the destiny waiting for me when Surt came for my soul.

"Lord Katrina," Carl said, opening the door. I looked up. "They are back."

"Help me," I whispered, leaning toward Aziolith.

Aziolith picked me up in his arms and carried me to the throne room. He laid me on the throne, where Akta, Julia, and a death-shrouded Kimberly stood.

"My gods," Akta said. "Are you okay?"

"Not even a little bit," I wheezed. "But we have bigger fish. You have failed, I see."

"We did our best," Julia said. "The horsemen overpowered us. They were too strong."

"And what happened to you?" I said to Kimberly. "You died, went to Heaven…?"

"Then I came back and became Death, one of the horsemen." She pulled a dagger from her pocket. "I have his dagger." She held up the Sword of Damocles. "And this."

"Lot of good they do us now."

"Actually," a voice boomed from the back of the room. I looked up to see Lucifer, clad in full metal armor, walking toward us. "It might do us some good yet."

"Lou!' I croaked. "What are you doing here?"

"God realized that if Surt were to get out of Hell, he would have to answer to the old gods. He didn't want his mother to find out. So, he sent an army."

"An army?"

"There is a legion of angelic guard waiting outside the gate." He reached into his pocket and pulled out a glowing, white vial. "Meanwhile, drink this."

I took the vial from Lucifer's hand. "What is it?"

"Purity," he replied. "Or the concept of purity, distilled into a potion. Darkness has caught you in its clutches. This should wash it out of you."

I studied the glowing bottle. "And what if it kills me since I'm the Devil and thus the antithesis of purity?"

Lucifer placed his hand on my shoulder. "You should know more than anybody that the Devil is not one thing. It can be anything. Now drink, and if you die, well, at least you don't have to suffer."

"Fair enough." I pulled the stopper off the bottle and drank the potion in one gulp. A cool sensation washed over me, and I could breathe for the first time in days. The darkness in my arms receded into my chest. After a few moments, a chill filled my bones, and then a pulse rocketed through me. When it dissipated, I felt better than I had since I remembered.

"Better?" Lucifer asked.

"Wow, a lot." I shook out my arms and legs, enjoying the new life in them. "Now, what was that you were saying about the weapons?"

He nodded. "I was here when we beat Surt back last time. He was defeated by three gods giving up their life force and using it to create a sort of bomb that sapped him of his power."

"That's great, but we're running short on gods to use for power unless God is volunteering."

Lucifer shook his head. "He is not, but I think we can use the horsemen's weapons to replicate that energy blast. They were forged in the death of the gods who gave their lives to protect this realm. All we need to do is capture the horsemen and destroy them."

"Excuse me, but won't that destroy me?" Kimberly asked.

Lucifer looked back at her, sadly. He opened his mouth and then closed it again.

"Not gonna happen." Kimberly stamped her foot. "NO! I already died once. Figure something else out."

"Fine," Lucifer sighed. "We'll just destroy the other weapons and hope it's enough, okay?"

"That works," Kimberly said. "As long as I don't have to sacrifice myself."

"How do we even do it?" I asked. "These weapons are supposed to be indestructible."

"That's not true," Akta said. "Yilir told me they can be destroyed with the Sword of Damocles."

"Right!" Julia nodded. "They were forged by the sword and can be destroyed by the sword."

"And we have the sword with us." Kimberly held it up and looked at it, her eyes shining.

"We have to hurry, though," Lucifer said. "Right now, Surt is bound to Hell, but destruction fuels him and his flame. If he spills enough magical blood, the rift between Hell and Earth will shatter whether or not he has the sword, and he will once again roam the universe."

"So we have a plan," I said. "Kimberly, you'll have to go with each team as they try to recover the weapon. Once they lose their weapons, kill them, like you did with Death."

"I can do that."

"Akta, you will lead a team to take the bow. Julia, you lead a team to take back the lance. I'll lead a team to take back the hammer. Keep your horseman distracted until Kimberly gets there, and then we'll give a final attack, and hopefully, be able to make this work."

"Got it," Kimberly said.

"The gods' speed to us all," I replied. "Everything is on the line. If we blow this, the whole universe will be destroyed."

"No pressure," Lucifer said with a smile.

"I thrive under pressure." I smiled back, and it was the first genuine smile I'd felt in a long time. This was when I was at my best, charging headlong into certain death with the bare inkling of a plan.

CHAPTER 48

Kimberly

Location: Hell

When we exited Katrina's castle, we were awash with the glow of angels shimmering across the lava sea in their full battle regalia, waiting for us. Katrina snapped her fingers, and we appeared on the other side of the molten lake. She trudged up to the gate, which opened for her.

Michael stood in the center of the angels, holding a flaming sword. Behind him, a gigantic monster rose, red and black, with horns growing from his head. His gigantic sword slashed through the air as he pushed against the roof of Hell.

"You've come," Katrina said. "I'm surprised."

"An alliance between demon and angel, for the good of the universe," Michael said. "I can't believe God suggested it, but I do love a good battle."

Katrina nodded. "Divide your men into three battalions. We're going to split up and take on each horseman separately. The goal is to get their weapons and destroy them to send Surt back to his prison."

"A bold plan. We will be with you...until it fails."

Katrina gave him a hard stare. "Thank you for the confidence."

I turned to Aziolith, who had transformed from his human form into the red dragon form I preferred. "Can you find the dragons? Get them to work with us?"

"I will try, but they are stubborn."

"They have just as much to lose as anybody."

He nodded in agreement and then took off into the sky. When he had disappeared from my sight, I turned to Akta. "Can we really do this?"

Akta smiled. "Maybe, with your help. You're our secret weapon."

I looked down at my black robe. "I don't feel very secret. Or much like a weapon."

Akta unfurled her wings and lifted into the air. "Let's go. There's a lot of work to do."

I whistled, and my pale horse flew down from the sky. I hopped onto its back as if I had ridden it a million times. Gripping the Sword of Damocles tightly, I rose into the air to meet Akta, with the rest of our battalion floating behind us.

***

Akta and I flew at the head of the formation in front of a thousand angels. We were the first wave, and our job was to find Famine and take down the bow. As we entered the rubble of Dis, a wave of arrows riddled through our numbers.

I looked up to see Famine riding her yellow horse, firing arrows at our line. Behind her, the fiery body of Surt masked her movements. His flames seemed to engulf the horseman.

"Split up!" I shouted. The angels broke formation, flying into the air toward Famine. As they neared, Famine's rate of fire increased. She was deadly accurate with her bow, and the angelic host fell into oblivion at her hand.

"Let's hope the angels keep her confused," Akta said, flying high into the air. "I'll take her high. You take her low. Hopefully, she'll be too distracted to see us coming."

Thousands of monsters screamed beneath us, running through the streets for safety, abandoning their cars, and trying to avoid the burning buildings all around them. The flames licked at me as I passed through them, but they didn't burn my immortal body.

I landed on the ground and dismounted my trusty horse, then studied the carnage above me. One set of angels kept Famine busy, while another group headed across the plains gunning for Conquest.

"Wait here for me, girl," I said softly, and the horse whinnied back to me. It was too fast, and I would arrive in Famine's face too early if I used her to assist my flight. I kicked off the ground with as much force as I could muster. If we planned this right, then Akta would grab the bow as I ran Famine through with the sword. Both of us had to hit her at the same time.

I rushed forward as fast as I could, faster than I remembered being able to move in my whole life. I saw Akta emerge, soaring far above me. I stalled for a second to match her pace and then started my ascent again. As Famine shot the angels, we approached silently, and when she saw us, it was too late. Akta grabbed the bow from her hands, and I sliced her from naval to neck, dusting her into a million pieces.

Yellow tendrils escaped from Famine's body and headed in my direction. I tried to avoid them, but they hunted after me until they latched onto my leg and disappeared into it. The energy burned up my leg until it consumed my whole body and exploded through my veins.

It was too hard to maintain my momentum, and I fell and fell until I crashed into the ground.

**

"You made a mistake, killing me," Famine's voice echoed in my ears. "I am not as weak as my brother, nor do I have a soft spot for humanity."

"Would you shut up?" I mumbled to myself.

"Do you know what? They were right to bind us into another universe. We were too powerful, and I would have slaughtered them all if they let me stay."

"I said SHUT UP!" I bellowed.

I broke through the inky blackness, and my eyes shot open. I no longer heard Famine's voice, and my arms moved of their own volition. My pale horse was licking my face as I lay on the asphalt.

"Kim!" Akta shouted when I finally regained consciousness amongst the carnage. "Are you okay?"

"I think so," I said.

"What happened?"

I sat up and rubbed my head. "I don't—I think I absorbed Famine's essence like I did Death's. Is it possible to have the power of two horsemen flowing through you?"

"I don't know," Akta replied. "Magic is weird. I learned a long time ago not to ask questions."

"Can I see the bow?" I asked her.

Akta handed it to me. It felt natural in my hands. When I held the bow, a quiver materialized on my back. I took an arrow from it and pulled back the bow to unleash it. I did this over and over again, and each one shot straight, piercing a building in perfect succession, one snapping the other in twain.

"That felt pretty good," I said.

"That will do well in your battle against Conquest." Akta pointed up to the top of a skyscraper. "Julia has found her target. Let's go help her."

I kicked into the air as Famine's yellow horse swooped in to grab me. It knew I was its master instinctively, and I moved onto its back. The swarms of angels were attacking Conquest, but he fought them off with ease. I nocked an arrow in my bow and aimed it at Conquest. I fired and fired and fired, throwing him off balance, even though he was able to fend them off.

"You'll never defeat us all," I heard Famine shout into my ear, but I had enough experience with horsemen trying to take over my body that I paid her no mind. I was stronger than they were, much stronger because I had hope and a will unmatched by any deity.

I pulled another arrow, firing once again at Conquest. Again, he deflected. I broke through the legion of angels floating around the skyscraper and leaped off the yellow horse, landing on the top of the burning building swarming with angelic guard.

"You killed two of my kin," Conquest growled. "You'll pay for that."

He charged at me, and I ducked to avoid him. "You let loose Surt. You'll pay for that."

Akta and Julia flew toward Conquest, swiping at him as he fended them off with his lance.

"Don't get too close!" I screamed. "I'll take care of him."

Conquest spun around to ready another attack, grinning at me. "You know it's funny, I never much cared for family anyway, and now I can defeat you and absorb their energy. You've done me a great favor."

He swung his lance, and this time instead of ducking beneath it, I grabbed hold of the weapon. He tried to yank it away, but I had control of it. I pulled it hard, and it fell out of his hands. I twirled it a few times before sticking him through the stomach with it. He stared at me blankly for a moment, then fell to the ground, collapsing in a million pieces of white flecks.

Just like the others, tendrils rose from him, but this time I did not fight them or run away. I closed my eyes and extended my arms, and as the energy took over me, I took a deep breath and savored the sensation of burning hot energy coursing through my veins. My body throbbed with energy, and I felt like I could do anything, say anything, be anything. Under me, the ground shook. I looked over the side of the building and saw War with his hammer, slamming it against the building, trying to get our attention.

"Holy shit," Julia said. "That was awesome."

"Send the rest of the angels to distract Surt." I slung the bow over my shoulder and held the lance and sword in either hand. "Don't let him escape. We're so close."

"I won't," Akta replied.

"We'll try to keep the destruction to a minimum," Julia added. "If we can."

I leaped onto the horse and flew to the ground, extending the lance in front of me like I was about to joust. Just as I bulleted toward him, Katrina slammed her fist into War's face and sent him stumbling backward. The angelic guards swooped around us.

I leaped off my horse. "Go distract Surt with Akta! We have this!"

Katrina looked back at me. "We do?"

I spun the lance in my hand. "Well, I do." I handed her the sword, and I walked toward War. He swung his hammer at me, and I moved my lance to parry. Katrina came up behind and slashed at him with the sword, but War's hammer deflected the blow. He struck her with a vicious backhand, knocking the sword from her hand. Then he turned to me, and for a moment, I thought I had made a massive mistake.

"You killed my family," War growled.

"You're next," I replied with a smile. "If only you were nicer."

I readied the lance as War pulled back on his weapon. He started to drive it down, but he couldn't. He looked back to find Katrina holding the hammer with her hands. She yanked it from him and gave me an opening where War was unprotected. I stabbed the lance through his chest, and he exploded into a flurry of red ash. Once more, the tendrils of red escaped the dust and slammed into me. I felt an angry rage moving through me as I stepped to Katrina.

"Are you okay?" Katrina asked. "That was bonkers."

"No, I'm not okay. The Four Horsemen are inside me, trying to break my brain and escape. So, let's end this quickly." I gestured to the weapons. "Give them to me."

"Are you sure?" Katrina said, cocking her head.

"I have the combined knowledge of the Four Horsemen coursing through my veins. I know what to do."

Katrina handed me the sword and the hammer. I rose into the air and flew through the remainder of the angels. It was time to meet Surt face-to-face.

"It's not going to work," Conquest said in my ear. "It is folly to try."

"You will destroy us all!" War shouted.

"Don't be a fool," Famine added.

The only one who remained silent was Death because he knew the truth. He knew it would work, and he knew for it to work, I would not be able to kill him. He served a vital purpose shepherding life from one world to the next and had been gone from the universe for too long, but the others, his siblings, brought nothing to the world. Their destruction could only improve the outlook of the planet. I landed on top of the tallest building left standing in Dis that Surt hadn't destroyed.

Surt stood tall, nearly as tall as the tip of Hell. He swiped his flaming arm along the ground and destroyed a whole street with one slice of his monstrous body.

"Do you see this!" I screamed at him, dropping the lance, bow, and hammer on the ground. "I bind you!" I looked down at the weapons. "Three souls to bind the beast."

Surt turned slowly toward me, the power of the weapons in front of me drawing his attention. His foot smashed into another building as he moved, and he leaned forward until his flaming eyes found me. He gave a pained look as I raised the sword into the air. When the sword dropped, the Titan's expression changed to horror.

"No!" Famine shouted as her yellow aura shot out of me.

"What have you done?" Conquest screamed as the sword connected with the hammer, snapping it in half. I felt the tug of his body explode from me.

"YOU FOOL!" War cried as his red aura rose into the air.

The sword connected with the other weapons, and they each broke in half, shattering around me into a thousand pieces.

Surt looked down and screamed. He clawed at the roof of Hell, but it was no use. He fell, lower and lower, until he dropped into the hole he had created upon his escape. I flew down into the hole, where I was met by Michael and Katrina.

"Give me the dagger," he said. I handed it to him, and he nicked Katrina with it.

"Hey!" She rubbed her hand defensively.

"Sorry," Michael said. "But blood magic is the most powerful magic in the world. He bent down and drew a circle around the main seal. "*Titan constringo vos ad locum istum semper.*" The crack around the seal quaked until it smashed back together. "Take a spot at one of the four corners."

Michael bent down and drew the knife across his own hand. He drew a circle around himself with the blood and then told us to do the same. Lucifer flew down into the pit and took his turn with the dagger as well. He drew a circle around himself.

"All together now," Michael said.

"Titan constringo vos ad locum istum semper."

Around us, the circles glowed red and then blue, in harmony with the seal in the center. As we spoke the words, the crack in the concrete mended back together, finally sealing completely. The walls of the building reformed as if there had never been a crack at all.

"We four are bound to keep Surt locked up forever. Understood?" We nodded our heads solemnly. "Good. It is an awesome responsibility and not to be taken lightly."

"I won't," I said.

"Me either," Katrina replied.

"I might," Lucifer said with a coy smile. "But probably not."

Michael nodded. "And I certainly will take this responsibility with the level of importance it deserves. We are four of the most important beings in the universe now."

Katrina grinned. "That won't do anything for my ego."

CHAPTER 49

Julia

Location: Dis, Hell

Dis was destroyed. Hundreds of buildings sat in ruins. Thousands of monsters had been killed, even more displaced. As I walked through the cracked streets, I heard the screams and cries of the monsters that had lost everything.

What was even the point of it all? What was the point of trying? Emotions overcame me, and I dropped to my knees in a fit of tears. After a long moment, I felt a hand on my shoulder. I looked up to see Akta, who sat down cross-legged next to me.

"What's wrong?" she asked.

"All of this is our fault."

"No, it's not," she replied. "We saved everybody today. You should be thankful for that."

My whole body shook. "I can't be thankful. All I can think of is that we should have been better. We should have done more earlier. We shouldn't have been so careless."

"The world's entropy is chaos," Akta said. "It does not want order, and those who try to give the world order will always have a harder time than those who seek to destroy it. That does not mean what we're doing isn't the right thing. It's a noble thing, and on this day, we won. All we can do is try to do better the next time."

"But it's not the last time. It feels like we're constantly defending something from someone. How many times have we stopped Katrina from being assassinated?"

Akta gave a little snort, laughing. "Seven. I guess eight, now? Or maybe a hundred, depending on how many times you consider this whole fiasco. Evil will always be there. It's our job to stop it. That's what good people do."

"I don't even know what that word means anymore."

Akta stood and held out her hands to pick me up. "We did good today. That's all we can hope for—that when we look back, we are on the right side of history."

"And what if we're not?" I asked.

"Then we course correct and try to do better the time after that. Our lives are long, and there is time to fix our mistakes."

"And make new ones." I reached out for Akta's hands, and she lifted me up. "That's not good enough."

She smiled at me. "It has to be."

I pulled Akta close to me, and she begrudgingly wrapped me in her arms.

"Can I get in on that?" Kimberly said, wrapping her arms around both of us. "I could use a hug after all this."

I wiped the tears from my eyes. "I'm so sorry, Kimberly."

"Why?"

"Look at you!" I gestured at her. "You are…Death."

She shrugged. "Don't worry about me. I'm going to be just fine, I think."

Akta nodded. "I see many great adventures for you."

"I can't wait."

As we hugged, I heard a great shriek in the air. Aziolith descended on us with a dozen dragons following behind him.

"What happened here?" he said when he landed. "It's over? Already?"

Kimberly nodded slowly. "It's over, buddy. I'm sorry."

"Well, that's a bummer. A bit anti-climactic, if you ask me. Do you know what I had to promise to get these dragons to help us?"

Kimberly pulled a dagger from a sheath across her back and handed it to him. "Maybe this will make it up to you."

"My dagger!" Aziolith shouted.

She nodded. "Keep it safe. If it's destroyed, then I'll die, too."

The great dragon nodded. "I will guard it with my life."

"YOU!" We all turned to see the blue wraith, Pastor Bill, walking across the disaster zone toward us, his body smoking in the rubble. "You ruined everything! All of you!"

"I'm sick of you, alright." Akta turned to Aziolith. "Can I borrow that for a second?"

"I don't think so."

The wraith slid forward toward us, pulling two blue orbs from his pocket. "I curse you. I curse you all!"

Akta looked up at Aziolith. "I promise I will give it back."

"Just do it, buddy," I said. "Please."

"Very well," Aziolith said with a sigh, handing her the dagger. "Be careful with it."

"No," Akta stepped forward and flung the dagger at the wraith, who exploded into a million pieces. "There, that's better." She walked over and pulled the dagger out from where it had embedded into the ground. After she'd wiped it off across her pant leg, she handed it back to Aziolith. "I believe this is yours."

Aziolith let out a low chuckle. "About time. Don't think this means I like you."

Akta smiled. "I would never think that."

Somewhere in the bleak darkness of Ragnarok and the horribleness that we endured, I had found a family I never knew I needed, and I smiled at the thought. Yes, it seemed, Death could smile.

CHAPTER 50

Katrina

Location: Dis, Hell

The angels of Heaven stood waiting at the Gates of Abnegation. They slowly funneled out of the gates to a large white portal that rested above a cliff on the other side.

"You know," Michael said. He held the Sword of Damocles in his hands. "I must say, this place is nowhere near as bad as I thought it would be."

I smiled. "I told you I was fixing Hell."

He nodded appreciatively, looking around. "I'm kind of impressed."

"I have a plan to fix a lot more than this. I've been working on it for a while now."

"When you finish it, let me know, and I'll try to get it in front of God."

I raised an eyebrow. "Don't say something like that if you don't mean it."

He shook his head. "I would never do that to you or me. I know how tenacious you can be."

Michael flew off, replaced by Lucifer. "You've done well today," he said.

"Thank you."

Lucifer looked off into the distance, at the ruins of Dis. "What will you do with the traitors, the ones who are still out there?"

I shrugged. "I'm going to do what I do."

"May I suggest…some tact. Let your enemies know you are open to hearing their ideas. Otherwise, their bitterness will fester. Doing what you do is what got you into this mess. Maybe try being better than what you do, or what I do for that matter."

"I'll take it under advisement."

Lucifer hugged me and then flew into the air toward his eternal salvation, leaving me to clean up the pieces. I didn't mind. I created Hell in my image once, and it was a disaster when I started. Perhaps he was right. Maybe it was time for a new way.

***

I pushed open the door to Mephistopheles's castle and stomped through the halls. The impish demon lord floated toward me before I could get past the foyer.

"My, my, Katrina. You've had quite a day, haven't you? To what do I owe the pleasure?"

I smiled. "It's weird. Every other demon lord left in Hell was part of this plan to start Ragnarok, except for you."

"I told you I was on your side. The others are misguided."

"Yes," I reached into my back and pulled out the General's sword, still oozing with inky blackness. I tossed it to him. "We caught the general trying to escape Hell through the Gateway like a cowardly idiot. I asked where he got the magic to poison me. He didn't say anything, even under extreme torture. However, the magic is very complex and very powerful. Did you know there are only about three magicians on the whole planet that could make something like that?"

"I…I didn't…"

"I'm not going to insult you by saying out loud who it was that made the blade, but just know that I know."

"And what are you going to do with this magician?"

I sighed. "I have been thinking about that a lot. It seems that everybody in Hell hates me."

"Not everybody—"

"Shut up! I'm talking now!" I said, my eyes flashing with fire. I took a breath and calmed myself down until I could talk without rage consuming me. "I'm sorry. That was uncalled for. I'm trying to be better about my anger issues."

I cleared my throat and started again. "What I meant to say was…I would like to change that. I would like to extend the olive branch. You, Mammon, and Asmodeus will join my small council. We fix Hell together."

"That—I don't know where they are—"

"I didn't say it was a choice," I growled. "Please, don't insult me, and I won't insult you. I know you are hiding them. I could rip you in half. I could raze your castle to the ground, but there would be others to take your place, and then more after them. We need to cut this hostility off at the pass right now. Join me willingly. I will let you keep your power, and in return, you recognize that *some* modernization is important. For my part, I'll admit that I might have gone too fast with implementing it."

"And you'll make everything go back to normal?" he asked.

I shook my head. "No, but we have to rebuild Dis, and we can either rebuild it in my image or our image. Be the change, with me."

Mephistopheles sighed. "I can't guarantee anything, but I think I can sell that to the others."

"I hope so," I said with a smile. "Otherwise, I'm going to have to kill you." The smile drained from my face. "And I will make it very, very painful."

Mephistopheles gulped. "Noted."

I walked out of the castle, whistling to myself. It was the dawn of a brand-new day, and I was going to make sure the new day went differently from every day that came before it.

***

If you loved this, keep reading after the author's note for a sneak peek at *Darkness,* which features three stories following Kimberly during her long life, including our first story set *during* the Apocalypse.

AUTHOR'S NOTE

I never thought this book would exist. When I first launched the Godsverse, it was a disaster, and a debacle rolled into one. Every book launched worse than the one before it. I was so far in the red on the production of the first four books that I thought it would take me a decade or more to crawl out of it.

Even though I had the plot for this book, and the outline, sitting on my hard drive, I was considering giving up writing altogether, truth be told. It was hard to keep my head up.

Then, I ran a Kickstarter for the first four books in the series, and it went gangbusters. I paid off all the costs for the books **_and_** made enough to pay for most of the production costs for this fifth book. In two weeks, I went from never writing another book in the Godsverse again to making the fifth book the very next one I wrote.

It was an amazing turnaround, and I owe it all to the 264 backers who helped make this book possible. This book would literally not exist without them.

When the Kickstarter exploded and we unlocked the next book in the series, I knew that I would be delving deep into Ragnarok. I was so excited. After Greek and Roman mythology, Norse is my favorite. Really though, I just have a thing for apocalypses, and Ragnarok is such a good one. I love it so much, and it dovetails so nicely with the Christian Apocalypse, and the Greek/Roman pantheon, that melding them all together made perfect sense.

Doom hinges quite heavily on Norse mythology, and making this book about Ragnarok made perfect sense, especially with how I weaved Norse mythology into the universe in my previous work in this universe.

I hope you enjoyed this book. If so, I hope you'll check out more of *The Godsverse Chronicles* or my other work, like *The Obsidian Spindle Saga,* which is mythology meets fairy tales, set in a place called The Dream Realm. Check out *The Sleeping Beauty*, the first book in that series.

***

Keep reading for a sneak preview of Kimberly's journey in *Darkness.*

DARKNESS

Book 10 of The Godsverse Chronicles

By:
Russell Nohelty

Edited by:
Leah Lederman

Proofread by:
Katrina Roets
Toni Cox

Cover by:
Psycat Covers

Planet chart and timeline design by:
Andrea Rosales

CHAPTER 1

It was five years ago when a bloody cult murdered my best friend and mentor, Julia Freeman.

No. That's not true.

She wasn't murdered. She was sacrificed at the altar of a demon, a mhrucki, so the cultists could attain longer lives and fill their coffers.

The only bright side to the whole affair was the mhrucki lied about helping their cause and, after being brought to Earth, she slaughtered each and every one of them and escaped, but not before sucking the soul from my body, leaving me in a coma.

I shouldn't have survived. I wouldn't have survived, except that Julia somehow came back from the bowels of Hell, possessed my comatose body, and used it to track down the mhrucki and kill it, sending my soul back into my body and jolting her back to Hell. I can still feel her sometimes, in the darkness—or at least the remnants she left behind inside of me. Just a hint here, or a moment there, but I always smile when I feel her.

I should be dead, but she gave everything to save me. Since then, I have been obsessed with finding her and saving her soul from the pits of Hell. I don't have any problem saying that I'm obsessed. What would you do if somebody came back from the dead to save you from eternal torment? If you wouldn't give up everything for them, I question your morality.

I still wake up in the middle of the night, remembering the feeling of a million pins and needles ripping my soul apart inside the stomach of the evil mhrucki. I've never been the same since that horrible experience, never had a worse experience than that—and I've been to Hell.

Yes, that's right. I've had a crappy life, all things considered. I've quite literally been to Hell and back.

I was only a child when a banshee kidnapped me and brought me to Hell as an offering to Lucifer. I was lucky there, too, because Lucifer did not accept me as a sacrifice. It was better than I deserved and more decency than I thought Old Scratch capable of, given the stories about him.

I was lucky because Julia came for me then, too.

She'd saved me twice, which is all the more reason why I won't rest until I rescue her.

After she saved me from the banshee, she took me under her wing and taught me all she knew. She showed me how to fight and how never to be scared again.

I was a violent child, filled with rage, and she showed me how to channel my righteous anger and turn it against the demons who deserved it. We saved a lot of fairies together. I still work to save fairy kind every chance I get. I carried on Julia's legacy or tried to, and I hoped she would be proud. Still, I wouldn't rest, I couldn't truly rest until I knew Julia was safe, and she could never be safe in Hell.

After I graduated high school as valedictorian of my class, I went to North Larchmont University in Havenbrook, Connecticut, to study under Doctor Reginald Dankworth, the foremost occult scholar in the world. My mother thought I was crazy for turning down scholarships to Duke and Notre Dame. She told me a thousand times that I was throwing my life away, but I knew what I was doing. By all rights, I shouldn't have even had a life. Julia saved me twice, so I made my decision about where and what to study based on what was the best way to help her.

The least I could do was save her, just once. If it took the rest of my days—if I died without finding her, then at least I could die knowing I tried to help her. I couldn't let her burn in the pits.

I could have been a normal kid. I could still be normal, I guess. I heard people talking about the new *Batman* movie directed by the guy who brought us *Peewee's Big Adventure*, and I just couldn't care about it at all. I didn't care about watching the Ghostbusters jazz up the Statue of Liberty, and I certainly didn't want to talk about whether George Bush was going to raise taxes or not. I didn't care about any of it. I only cared about getting Julia back and protecting magical creatures from demons and other things that went bump in the night.

My life became a cycle. I spent my days studying every bit of demonology and Christian theology I could find while I spent my nights tracking down leads, protecting fairy folk, and looking for anything that could give me a clue on how to summon Julia from the abyss or bring her back from the dead.

I was set to meet one of my informants later in the evening for intel on where to find Julia, and I was frantic to finish a paper on microeconomics before then. It was a class I didn't even care a little bit about, except that it was essential to graduate.

In my first semester at school, I forced my way into an independent study degree with Doctor Dankworth on occultism. I quickly rose to become his star pupil and most trusted aid, but I still needed a lot of gen ed classes to graduate, even though I hated them. I mean, when would I ever need to understand the efficacy of the stock market, really? It's not like money was even going to matter once the Apocalypse descended upon us, and it would descend on us eventually, but until then…I had to act the part of a good student if only to make my mother happy.

"How is the paper coming, Kimberly?" my roommate, Molly, asked as she passed my room, her body and head wrapped in two different white towels that accented her dark complexion. She had just finished a shower, and her skin glistened from the water. Her bright smile filled any room she entered. Everybody loved her. Somehow, she tolerated me, even though I hated everybody she liked.

"It's going," I said. "Honestly, if I have to look at stock symbols for one more minute, I might scream."

She smiled even wider when she laughed, which she almost always did like the world was filled with overabundant joy. Everything seemed to work in her favor without her even trying. Nothing seemed to get her down. "At least wait until my date gets here before you go postal. I don't care that you scare off any boy who gets close to you, but I do care if you scare them off when they come around for me."

I couldn't help but chuckle. I wasn't much of a laugher, but Molly brought it out of me. I hadn't gotten close to anyone since Julia. If I didn't scare Molly off pretty soon, maybe she would even succeed at winning me over. "Deal. Where is Ted taking you?"

"Ha!" She belted out a laugh. "That boy is last week's spoiled potatoes. I think this new guy's name is Ernie or Jordan. I have it in my planner. I have a date with one of them tonight and the other one tomorrow." She leaned in closer and whispered, "I can't really tell them apart."

Molly went through boys like I went through knives, and for the same reason—because they became dull and uninteresting. I hadn't been on a date since high school, and then just barely. In high school, it was hard enough to be that girl who got abducted by a cult and used in a ritual sacrifice. I didn't want to be a freak because I didn't date, too. Eventually, I grew out of caring what other people thought of me.

"If you get done, I'll probably be at Patty's later." Patty's was a bar and a diner, the kind that only existed in college towns. They served terrible food and watered-down drinks, but they were cheap, making them a popular hangout. It was the kind of place that sounded great while you were in school, but you quickly realized it was a sty after you graduated. I realized it earlier than most, but Molly loved it because it was always filled with drunk boys, and drunk boys showered her with attention. Molly's battery ran on attention.

"I'll think about it," I said with a polite smile. I knew I wouldn't be showing up. She knew it too but was too kind to say anything. Instead, she left with a knowing nod. The door to her room slammed a couple of seconds later, and I heard loud bass thumping through the walls as she got ready for her date.

It had been a lonely road since Julia left. It's not that I didn't try to get close to other people, but every time I did, my stomach curled up in knots as I realized what horrors they would experience if they got close to me.

My life was filled with demons, hellhounds, and all manner of undead creatures hunting me as I hunted them. I couldn't subject anyone to that, no matter how much I yearned for connection. I had already lost one friend to the darkness, and I wasn't about to lose any more, which meant I needed to close myself off.

Molly was the exception. She had been my roommate since freshman year, and when she wanted to move off campus junior year, it made sense we would room together. We lived two separate lives, but we could cohabitate well enough together. Still, even after three years, I wouldn't call us friends.

Fifteen minutes later, I heard a knock. Molly turned off the music and skittered to the front door, where a deep male voice greeted her. They exchanged muffled pleasantries, and a moment later, I heard the door close again, this time with Molly on the other side of it with her date. I was alone in the dark silence, which had become the only true friend I had left.

***

My meeting was at 2 am. Demons did not like the heat of the sun. I always thought that was weird, as they were creatures born and molded in Hell. Maybe it was because the night bred mischief, and demons oozed chaos out of every pore.

Charlie was no different. I met him a year ago, and he'd helped me slowly piece together Julia's life in Hell. He would have been a friend if you could make friends with demons without them stabbing you in the back, literally. He understood how the world worked and knew a lot about the occult, a subject more people shied away from in polite society.

I met him outside the large library that dominated the middle of the campus. I spent many hours in the basement of the library, which housed one of the greatest collections of occult literature from the 1600–1900s, culled from decades of Doctor Dankworth's obsessive quest to track them down.

"You're late, Kimberly," a gruff grumble came from behind a giant bronze statue of a hippopotamus, the school's mascot.

He startled me, and I instinctively went for the daggers I kept sheathed on my hip. When I saw the yellow of his eyes, I softened and looked down at my watch. 1:55 am. "I'm five minutes early."

"That's not what my watch says," Charlie grumbled, choosing to stay in the shadows instead of stepping into the soft light shining through the library windows. "You know how I feel about punctuality."

I looked up at the top of the library, which steepled in a clock tower. The tower read the same time as I had on my watch. I let it go. It wasn't worth the argument. I let most things roll off my back. It made getting through life easier.

"I'm sorry, Charlie. I'm here now."

"I guess that's something. Do you have it?"

I reached into my leather coat and pulled out a vial of ashes from the grave of Peter, the first pope of the Catholic church. As a pixie, I was able to teleport anywhere in the world as long as I could paint a complete picture of it in my mind. That made me valuable to Charlie, especially since he liked to collect weird pieces of Catholic theology. Demons couldn't step into churches, especially the Vatican where Saint Peter was buried. It was dirty work, digging up a two-thousand-year-old grave, but I was used to dirty work.

Charlie held out his thin, red, clawed hand and snatched the vial from my hand. "Not very much, is there?"

I scoffed. I'd spent four days trying to get that tiny vial. "You asked for ashes. It was hard enough to get that much."

"Yeah? How'd you get them, anyway?"

I didn't want to think about it. "What matters is that I got it. Do you have what I need? I didn't just dig that vial up for my health."

The light hit Charlie's bald, red head as he moved reluctantly into the light. He was short, barely waist-high, with a bulbous paunch and two little horns poking out from his forehead. His teeth were yellow and pointed, and his arms dangled low on his body. He pulled out a piece of parchment from his belt. "It wasn't easy to get this either, you know. I hope you appreciate it."

The corners of my mouth twisted into a scowl. "Just give me the paper."

He handed the paper over, and I unfolded it. It was an address in Queens. "You sure about this?"

"Who you askin'?" Charlie said with a growl. "Of course, I'm sure. That demon worked the same pit Julia was assigned. I'm sure of it. If imps know anything, it's bureaucracy."

I clasped the paper close in my hand. "Finally. Thank you, Charlie."

"Don't thank me yet," Charlie said, holding up his hands and backing away. "That demon's a real asshole."

I smirked. "Aren't they all?"

CHAPTER 2

Julia taught me to travel without using pixie dust. It wasn't quite as accurate, but it was a whole lot more convenient. The pink powder was temperamental and stuck to your fingers, and in the middle of a fight, it was a pain to have to go digging in your pocket for it. It was even more annoying to carry it around your belt.

To teleport between locations, it helped if you'd been to your intended destination before. A picture would do in a pinch. I spent years training myself on landmarks around the world, from luxurious places like the Eiffel tower to the more unimpressive First Reformed Church in Jamaica, Queens. You never knew where you would have to travel and needed to bank and recall as many places as possible quickly. I spent many nights with cue cards quizzing myself on the landmarks of the world…because, of course, I did. I was always a good student. Before she died, Julia taught me to study and analyze every situation. I did this obsessively to always make sure that I wasn't walking into a trap.

I closed my eyes and pictured the town hall in Flushing, Queens. When it was vivid in my mind, I vanished in a puff of purple air. A moment later, I was standing outside of the town hall. The building looked a bit like a medieval castle, replete with towers around it that, in a different time and place, could have housed little imps with arrows.

The address I was given was a half-mile away. I could have pulled out my wings and flown, but I liked to keep a low profile, even in the dead of night. It would be light soon, and that meant the demon would likely be home, safe from the breaking of the dawn. Their apartments were filled with blackout curtains to blot out the sun, and they kept their lairs dark.

The fact that this particular demon had an apartment meant he probably had a job nearby. Perhaps he was on a mission for Lucifer, or the ever-elusive Lilith, queen of the demons, whom I had been trying to track for half a decade. She was my white whale. There was no one as knowledgeable as to the workings of Hell as she was. Since being kicked out of the Garden of Eden, she had seen thousands, perhaps millions of demons pass through Earth. Her writings became the cornerstone of everything else I knew about demons, the bedrock of my studies.

After about ten minutes of walking, I arrived at a dump of a building. The façade was cracked, and the walls seemed to sway in the stiff breeze of the autumn evening. It didn't surprise me that a demon would choose a rundown hole. They preferred decrepit places.

I expected it to be locked, but when I tried the front door, the knob turned for me. I pushed open the door and strode inside. When I took another step, my foot brushed past something that tugged at the cuff of my pants. I heard the "click" and looked down. A tripwire. *That's not good.* I closed my eyes and vanished just as the flames licked my face, and an explosion rocked the walls.

I had been set up, and that little imp Charlie was going to pay for it.

***

In a small town in Scotland, there was a bar. The place looked like a plain house, like any other house on any other unassuming block in the country, except it was filled with angels and demons drinking themselves stupid. Legend had it that hundreds of years ago, a man accidentally summoned a demon while making his dinner. He and the demon got to talking and became friends over a beer. That beer led to another, and those beers led to dozens more over the next few years. Eventually, the word got out that the man was a hospitable host and more demons showed up. Those demons brought the suspicion of angels, who came to investigate and ended up joining in on the fun. They were all having such a good time that it became a sort of neutral zone for demons and angels visiting Earth.

A forcefield protected the house, turning away anybody who didn't know the place existed. In order to move through the forcefield, you had to hit it head-on at full gait, brimming with confidence. Even then, it stung.

I took a running start and passed through the forcefield without incident. My hands and feet went numb from the intense shock, but after a minute, I could feel them again, and I marched inside the house. The place also happened to be the favorite hiding space of an imp who I was about to send back to Hell in a body bag.

A group of angels was shouting off-key, "You take a whiskey drink, you take a lager drink!" Some gruff demons joined them, growling, "You sing the songs that remind you of the good times, you sing the songs that remind you of the best times!"

As they splashed their drinks together, their arms flailing in the air, I craned my neck, looking for the imp in the sea of demons and angels. Their commingling was really a mind screw if you hadn't seen it before. Mortal enemies sharing a drink like they were best friends, even though their job was basically to kill each other.

I walked up to the wooden bar at the far end of the pub. A ginger-haired man with a thick, bristly beard smiled at me.

"What can I get ya?"

"Charlie," I hollered clearly over the screams of the denizens.

He shook his head. "Don't know that drink, I'm afraid."

"It's not a drink." I pressed my hands on the bar. "He's an imp. A real squirrely one. Likes to hang out here."

"Oh yeah," the barkeep said. "He's got quite a tab. I haven't seen him for a while. If you find him, send him this way before you kill him, will ya? He needs to settle up."

"I'll do that," I said, my eyes narrowing. "You sure you haven't seen him?"

The barkeep shrugged. "There's a lot of demons that come through here, but Charlie's a right git. I try to keep track of him whenever he's around. I'm telling you I ain't seen him for a fortnight, maybe two."

"Any idea where he might be?"

"I'm not his keeper." He turned to a hefty angel seated nearby. "Get you a refill, love?"

I grabbed the burly barkeep by his hairy arm. "Please."

The angel spun around angrily. "Get off of him."

The barkeep smiled. "I'd listen if I were you. I'm a bit of a universal treasure, don't ya know?"

I held up my arms, and the barkeep pulled away. "I don't want to fight. Please, the as—Charlie nearly killed me tonight. Anything you can do to help me would be appreciated."

The barkeep thought for a moment. "There's a girl. Cherub girl. He used to take up with her a bit if I recall." The barkeep looked at the angel as he finished a beer, teetering to one side and then the other. "You remember her? Pudgy girl. Stocky build. Beautiful hair."

"Yeah, I know her." The angel belched. "Clarice."

"Can you tell me where she is?" I asked.

"That depends," the angel said, slurring his words. "Is this next round on you?"

I nodded. "You got it."

"Then, yes. Pull up a chair, and let's get sloshed."

***

I walked out of the bar bleary-eyed the next morning. The angels and demons there sure knew how to throw a party. By the end of it, I was stumbling over my own feet, trying to find my way through the forcefield. When I tried to rush toward it, I tripped over my feet and fell in the grass. I was lying there, splayed out in the grass when a large shadow moved in front of the sun and blocked my view.

"This is unbecoming of you," the voice growled. When I pushed myself up, I saw Aziolith, the dragon who Julia begged to look after me before her untimely death. I recognized him even in his more palatable human form. He had a hefty supply of morphing syrup which he used to mingle among the mortals. In his true form, he was a 30-foot-tall red dragon with impressive scales and potent fire breath. As a human, he chewed a lot of mint gum.

"Come on, Kimberly," he said, wrapping his arm around my shoulder. "Let's get some food in you."

***

You would think that baked beans didn't go with breakfast, but you would be wrong. They were delicious alongside my bacon, eggs, sausage, and tomatoes. I enjoyed going full English whenever I was in the UK. I turned down the haggis, though, pushing it over to Aziolith. He who would eat anything that ever had a pulse.

"Feel better?" Aziolith asked as he munched on a chewy piece of a sheep's lung. "Hrm...I prefer raw."

"No. I feel way worse," I said, chomping down a spoonful of baked beans. "I'm less drunk now, but I have a splitting headache."

Aziolith pulled out a bottle of aspirin from his jacket and placed it on the table. I took it without saying a word and swallowed four pills. Aziolith wasn't really a friend. He was more like the father I never had, down to the withering stare he gave me whenever he disapproved of my life choices, which was often.

"What are you doing here anyway?" I said.

Aziolith leaned forward. "When you didn't come home last night, your roommate called your mother, who called me."

"Oof," I replied. "She must be worried. She hates you."

Aziolith smiled. "The feeling's mutual, but I told her I would find you, and I have."

"You would think after years she would get a grip on the idea that I'm not a child."

"Give her some credit. She just wants you to be safe. She knows you're doing something dangerous, taking risks."

I shoveled a forkful of eggs into my mouth and barely chewed before swallowing them. "The world isn't safe. My risks are mine to take."

"That is what your mentor said too, and look what happened to her."

"Low blow."

"I suppose this is about her, then?" Aziolith sighed. "What am I talking about? It's always about her."

"Not always," I replied, indignant. "But yes, this was about her and nearly getting my ass blown up last night."

"Hrm," Aziolith said. His right eyebrow lifted. "And you really think that your mother has no reason to be worried?"

I growled. "Fine. Maybe she does. Can you just please help me find the asshole who nearly killed me so I can figure out why?"

"Of course," Aziolith said. "Why else would I be here?"

***

If you enjoyed this preview, make sure to pick up *Darkness* today!

ALSO BY RUSSELL NOHELTY

NOVELS
My Father Didn't Kill Himself
Sorry for Existing
Gumshoes: The Case of Madison's Father
Invasion
The Vessel
The Void Calls Us Home
Worst Thing in the Universe
The Marked Ones
The Dragon Scourge
The Dragon Champion
The Dragon Goddess
The Sleeping Beauty
The Wicked Witch
The Fairy Queen
The Red Rider

COMICS and OTHER ILLUSTRATED WORK
The Little Bird and the Little Worm
Ichabod Jones: Monster Hunter
Gherkin Boy
How NOT to Invade Earth

www.russellnohelty.com

1000 BC – BETRAYED (HELL PT 1) /PIXIE DUST

500 BC – FALLEN (HELL PT 2)

200 BC – HELLFIRE (HELL PT 3)

1974 AD – MYSTERY SPOT (RUIN PT 1)

1976 AD – INTO HELL (RUIN PT 2)

1984 AD – LAST STAND (RUIN PT 3)

1985 AD – CHANGE

1985 AD – MAGIC/BLACK MARKET HEROINE

1989 AD – DEATH'S KISS (DARKNESS PT 1)

1985 AD – EVIL

2000 AD – TIME

2015 AD – HEAVEN

2018 AD – DEATH'S RETURN (DARKNESS PT 2)

2020 AD – KATRINA HATES THE DEAD (DEATH PT 1)

2176 AD – CONQUEST

2177 AD – DEATH'S KISS (DARKNESS PT 3)

12,018 AD – KATRINA HATES THE GODS (DEATH PT 2)

12,028 AD – KATRINA HATES THE UNIVERSE (DEATH PT 3)

12,046 AD – EVERY PLANET HAS A GODSCHURCH (DOOM PT 1)

12,047 AD – THERE'S EVERY REASON TO FEAR (DOOM PT. 2)

12,049 AD – THE END TASTES LIKE PANCAKES (DOOM PT 3)

12,176 AD – CHAOS

Milton Keynes UK
Ingram Content Group UK Ltd.
UKHW030909141024
449705UK00013B/662